Let There Be Bluebirds

by Ann Johnson

Printed in Victoria, Canada

Canadian Cataloguing in Publication Data

Johnson, Ann
    Let there be bluebirds

  ISBN 1-55212-471-1

    I. Title.
PR6060.O356L47 2000   823'.92   C00-911139-5

TRAFFORD

This book was published *on-demand* in cooperation with Trafford Publishing.
On-demand publishing is a unique process and service of making a book available for retail sale to the public taking advantage of on-demand manufacturing and Internet marketing. **On-demand publishing** includes promotions, retail sales, manufacturing, order fulfilment, accounting and collecting royalties on behalf of the author.

Suite 6E, 2333 Government St., Victoria, B.C. V8T 4P4, CANADA

Phone	250-383-6864	Toll-free	1-888-232-4444 (Canada & US)
Fax	250-383-6804	E-mail	sales@trafford.com
Web site	www.trafford.com	TRAFFORD PUBLISHING IS A DIVISION OF TRAFFORD HOLDINGS LTD.
Trafford Catalogue #00-0136		www.trafford.com/robots/00-0136.html

10   9   8   7   6   5   4   3

The shepherd will tend his sheep
The valley will bloom again
But Jenny will never sleep
In her own little room again

PROLOGUE

The thickening fog wrapped itself around the small, lone figure like an intangible blanket, enclosing her in a world of silence. Trudging along, arms aching, shoulders feeling as if they were about to slip their sockets at any moment from the weight of the heavy shopping bags, Jenny found it all but impossible to see ahead at all now and the only way to make any progress was by pushing out her right foot on every other step and scraping it along the bank at the side of the road, thus ensuring that she didn't drift to the centre. She had encountered fog like this on other occasions in her young life and was well aware how disoriented one could quickly become once all solid contact was lost.

This is how it must feel to be blind and deaf, she thought. How awful to be so totally lost for ever, having to grope your way around all through life. Although the inability to see was tiring and frustrating, it was the suffocating silence that frightened her so much. The sound of her own breathing, magnified in the utter stillness, appeared to come not from herself but from somewhere behind her. Her skin crawled as she imagined someone silently stalking her from behind.

She halted once again, holding her breath and listening intently for any sound, especially that of approaching vehicles. The thought that one of the frequent convoys of army vehicles might at any moment come lumbering through the fog brought small whimpers of fear to her lips. Even in broad daylight the heavy tanks, armoured cars and lorries rumbling by on the English narrow country roads terrified her. On other occasions when she had been carrying her loaded shopping bags back to the village, the sound of the convoys and the sight of their huge wheels passing so close seemed somehow to pull at her, drawing her inexorably towards them. It was as if they were taunting her, daring her to run in front of them and feel their might crushing her to pulp. To combat the fearful magnetic attraction she had to keep her eyes turned from them, drop her bags in panic and throw herself onto the grassy bank, scrabbling to grip tightly to clumps of grass, twigs, briars - anything to help hold her down. When finally the seemingly endless convoy did pass, Jenny would find herself trembling from head to foot and sobbing in sheer terror.

Now, hearing nothing, she moved slowly on through the gloom.

Suddenly the bank seemed to disappear. Probing with first one foot and then the other elicited only space. Panic seized her. She must have drifted to the centre of the road after all. She took a step to the right, then another and another, banging herself against a hard object. Dropping her bags and feeling the object in front of her, she found she had come up against a field gate set back from the road. Sighing aloud with relief, she sank down on the wet ground, leaned her head back between the bars of the gate, closed her eyes and rested. As her heart began to ease its pounding her thoughts turned to her father. Squeezing her eyes against the stinging threat of tears, Jenny said a silent prayer. "Please God" she prayed, "if you are there, please keep my Dad safe and send him back soon. I miss him so much, and Jimmy misses him, and if he knew what was happening to us he would be so angry. He would come and take us away from here and he would find our Mum and find out really why she had to leave us. She didn't leave us on purpose like they say she did God. Somebody made her do it. Then we could all go home and be together like a real family again. Are you really there God? If you are, why don't you help Jimmy and me?".

A feeling of guilt came over her as the last words echoed in her head. She knew it was wrong to doubt God and that he would know she doubted Him. Nevertheless, how could one believe in a God who loved little children when he had so obviously abandoned Jimmy and her? Hot tears forced their way through her closed eyelids as she sank further into her reverie.

Suddenly startled awake by a prickling and pulling at the top of her head, Jenny leapt to her feet. Turning toward the gate she could just discern the shape of a cow's head poking through the bars. It must have been chewing on her hair. "Stupid cow, you scared me," she shouted, her voice seeming to hang in the thick foggy air above her head. The cow lazily extended its tongue, curled it up one nostril and withdrew it again, not moving from the gate. Jenny flipped its wet liver nose with her hand and the cow jerked, banging its nose on the bar. Gathering her bags, she moved on into the blankness.

Dumb, stupid things, cows, she thought. Aunt Edith is always calling me a stupid cow. I wish I was a cow. All they have to do is stand around waiting to be milked and fed. They don't have to walk eight miles in the damp fog carrying heavy shopping, nor have to do all the housework and get beaten around for not doing things properly. I wish I was a cow.

She stumbled on, her thin, nine-year-old frame shaking now with cold. Her dress was so damp that it clung to her legs, chafing as she walked. Wet clumps of her hair flapped against her cheeks and across her eyes. There must be at least four more miles to go. At this rate it would be hours before she got home. She wished now that she had caught the bus, even if it would have meant leaving town without finishing the shopping. She would have been beaten for doing that of course, but at least she would be home and dry by now. She would be beaten anyhow for being late back so it would have made more sense to catch the bus.

The fog had lifted to mere wisps by the time she reached the outskirts of her village. One more mile and then there would be Aunt Edith. Her stomach began to churn. She was going to be beaten again and it was so unfair. Aunt Edith expected her to get so much shopping done in time to catch the bus back and Jenny truly did try. Sometimes she got lost and had to ask her way and there were queues in every shop. When Jenny's turn came to be served some shopkeepers ignored her and started serving the woman behind her, probably thinking she belonged to that woman and was just waiting with her. In one shop, when Jenny had protested the shopkeeper had told her not to 'push in' and to wait her turn. Then she had been made to wait while four more people were served. It did no good to try to explain these things to Aunt Edith because she would just say it proved how dumb and stupid Jenny was to let anyone push in front of her.

To be true, Jenny thought, she was a dreamer and did sometimes stand around lost in daydreams. She remembered her dad calling her "Dolly Daydream" sometimes and laughing at her. Aunt Edith didn't laugh. She got mad if she came across Jenny "standing around looking gormless and wasting time" as she put it, usually bringing her back to earth with a resounding whack across the ear. Her teacher didn't laugh either. Many a time a ruler had stung her knuckles, jerking her back to reality. Jenny didn't know why she daydreamed so much, but she knew that most of her dreams these days were of escaping from Aunt Edith and wondering why she had to be here anyway. The only answers she ever got to that question was that it was "because of the war", "it was wartime and not safe to be at home any more". She knew it was wartime. All anybody ever talked about these days was the war. That didn't explain what the war had to do with her and why she had to leave her home and lose everything she had ever known. *She* hadn't wanted the war, and still didn't understand what it was all about. So why? Why had no-one told her what was to happen to her that very first day? Three years ago - so long! Yet she could recall everything about that day as if it had only just happened. She even remembered the date - September 1, 1939 ...

ONE

September, 1939

"Jenny, will you hurry up and get down here before I lose all patience. Jimmy is almost ready and you are still dawdling around not half ready. What *are* you doing?"

Jenny dropped the little doll into her doll's house and dashed down the stairs. As she flew through the kitchen door, shoe laces trailing, hair a tangled mass, her mother looked at her in exasperation.

"Why do we have to go through this performance every morning, Jenny? It would be so nice if just once you could be ready and waiting for Jimmy instead of always being last. Come here and let me comb that hair."

Her mother raked angrily through her hair, tugging at the knots until tears stung her eyes. She jumped away from the pain, covering her head with her arms.

"I'm always last because you comb Jimmy's hair first. And you don't pull his hair like you do mine. I want my hair cut off like Jimmy's so it won't get in so many knots."

"Now you are being silly," her mother said. "If you were here to have your hair and shoes done first, you would have them done first. But you never do, do you?"

"Yes I do, but you still do Jimmy first. You don't like me, and Jimmy doesn't like me, but Daddy does, I know he does."

"Of course Daddy likes you. He loves you and so do I, but you always make me so cross because you are obstinate and stubborn. I don't blame Jimmy for getting fed up with you when you keep him waiting every morning. You cry if he leaves without you but you won't get a move on to be ready when he is."

Her brother Jimmy was standing impatiently by the back door while this was going on. Jenny looked across at him as he shifted from one foot to the other.

"You don't like me do you, Jimmy," she said, more as a statement than a question.

"Not when you get in your silly moods I don't," he answered. "And I don't like you when you make me late for school. If you don't get a move on, I'm going without you."

"See," she said to her mother. "I told you so."

She tore past her mother and out the back door. Jimmy ran after her and they raced each other down the garden path to the stile their father had built so that they could take the short cut across the field. Their house was one of two that stood at the end of a cul-de-sac, the other house belonging to an older couple by the name of Loader. Beyond these two houses were tree lined fields carrying on up to the main road. Solent Road was the main road leading out of Portsmouth to the suburbs where they lived. Cutting across the field in this way shortened the journey to school considerably. They usually returned home by the longer route down the lane past a long grove of trees and then turning into the far end of the cul-de-sac. This was because Jimmy liked to walk home with his friends and Jenny, as usual, tagged along behind.

In fact Jimmy, Jenny's elder by 16 months, was supposed to look after his young sister by accompanying her to school and back. There were times, however, when he either forgot her or purposely left school in the afternoon with his friends without bothering to look for her. It was on one of these occasions that Jenny, spotting him on the opposite side of Solent Road, raced across to catch up with him, neglecting to look both ways as she had been taught. The big furniture lorry that hit her sent her spinning. She crashed onto the road a few yards in front of the lorry as, with squealing brakes and screeching tyres, it hit her again. That sound and the sight of those huge wheels bearing down on her was something that would stay with her forever.

One of her teachers, witnessing the accident, had raced down the centre of the road, arms outstretched, as if he could hold back the skidding vehicle all by himself. The lorry driver had said later that had the road been wet, he would not have been able to stop and she would have been mincemeat. Crowds of people had gathered round the shivering Jenny until a policeman had appeared to take her hand and guide her home. She was more shaken than hurt, but what had hurt more was her mother's reaction. Instead of comforting Jenny, she had scolded her and sent her to bed for being so careless. The policeman told their mother quite sharply that a 5-year old child should not be left to cross such a busy road alone. At least Jimmy had crept up to see her and say he was sorry.

"Shall we go and see the haunted house before we go to school, Jimmy?" Jenny asked as they scurried across the field.

"No we won't. We are already going to be late if we don't run. Anyway, the house isn't haunted, it just looks like it is when the sun gets behind the trees. It's the wind blowing the branches that makes the light go up and down on the windows, not ghosts."

"Oh, you are a meany," Jenny said. "You told me it was ghosts making those lights, and I thought it was true."

"I know you did. You will believe anything, that's why you are so stupid. Well now I've told you the truth and it doesn't matter any more anyway."

"I'm not stupid," Jenny exploded. "You just tell me lies so you can laugh at me and call me stupid. Why don't you like me, Jimmy? I like you."

Jimmy stopped, grabbing her by the arm and pulling her to a halt.

"Look," he said, "I don't always not like you. You're alright sometimes, but when you make a lot of fuss I don't like you. Boys don't like their kid sisters following them around all the time either. You should play with your own friends and not keep tagging on to me when I want to play with mine. Now come on!"

Jogging beside him, Jenny thought how grown up her seven-year old brother was. Jimmy knew so much more than she and never flew into rages like herself. She so badly wanted to be like him and for him to like her. She had promised more than once not to follow him around, but when he went out with his friends they seemed to have so much fun that she wanted to join in too.

"Jimmy, what did you mean when you said it didn't matter any more about the haunted house?"

"Oh nothing. Just ... nothing," he said mysteriously.

They were scrambling through the last barbed wire fence onto the verge of Solent Road, before making their way up the hill to school. Jenny noticed that Jimmy's face had suddenly gone very pale.

"What's the matter?" she enquired. "Do you feel sick?"

"No, I'm alright," he answered. His voice sounded chokey and he turned his head away. Jenny was immediately perturbed. Something was wrong with Jimmy. He had been pretty grumpy this morning and now he looked odd. Perhaps he was afraid of going to school for some reason, but that wasn't likely - Jimmy loved school. It was she who never wanted to go.

They walked the rest of the way in silence. As they turned into the school yard, Jenny got her first shock of that interminable day - a day that was to change her life for ever.

TWO

The sight that met their eyes astonished Jenny. An array of double decker buses filed the big yard and playground. People were milling about everywhere, and for a moment she thought they had inadvertently come to the wrong place. But no, that was the school building. What could be going on?

"What are all these buses and people doing here?" she asked Jimmy.

Before he could answer, Miss Towner, one of their teachers came out of the crowd toward them. "Here are the Hardings," she called back over her shoulder. "Come along you two, you are cutting it rather fine aren't you?"

Jimmy gave Jenny a look that seemed to say "I told you so" as Miss Towner prodded them forward into a line behind several other children. Many children were already boarding the buses and soon it was their turn. Once inside they were ushered into a downstairs seat, Jenny being seated inside next to the window.

"Where are we going?" Jenny asked as soon as they were seated. "Did you know we were going on a bus today?"

"It's supposed to be a surprise," Jimmy said. "We are going on a trip somewhere, but I don't know where."

When everyone was settled, Miss Towner got on the bus and rang the bell. Soon the bus began to move slowly forward. Jenny turned to look out of the window at the people and unaccountably spotted her mother among the crowd. "Oh look," she cried. There's Mummy. She is coming too. Tell the teacher to stop the bus."

Jimmy was looking straight ahead and didn't turn his head to look where she was pointing. "No it isn't Mum," he said. "She is still at home. You know she was there when we left."

Jenny looked out the window once more. All at once a great sense of confusion overtook her. Her mother was no longer in sight.

Of course she had been at home when they left, but that *was* Mummy's face she had seen, she was certain of it. If she had come to see them off on their trip, why was she so far back and had not even waved to them? Looking back at Jimmy she noticed once again how pale he was. He wasn't very happy about this trip and suddenly neither was she. Something was not right and she wanted immediately to get off the bus.

They were already out onto Solent Road and picking up speed. More buses were in front and behind them and the further they went, the more worried Jenny became. It seemed no use to ply Jimmy with questions. If he knew much more than she he was obviously not telling. After about an hour of fretting and fidgeting she could contain herself no longer and burst into tears. Miss Towner came bustling down the bus demanding to know what all the fuss was about.

"I don't know where we are going - its too far. I want us to go back home," Jenny cried.

"Oh dear," Miss Towner sighed. "We can't go back just yet, but in a short time we will be stopping to get out and stretch our legs. You mustn't cry like that or you will upset the other children and then we could have pandemonium here. We don't want that do we?"

Miss Towner stood looking at the two children, momentarily deep in thought. "Jimmy," she said, "I want you to come to the back of the bus with me for a moment." "I won't keep him long," she reassured Jenny.

Jenny watched as Jimmy followed Miss Towner to the back where she talked to a master and then both adults seemed to be questioning Jimmy. More than ever now, Jenny felt something was very wrong.

"What were they saying to you?" she demanded once Jimmy was back in his seat.

"Not much," Jimmy replied. "They just wanted to know why you were bawling and said I had to tell you to stop because there is nothing to cry for."

This did nothing to lessen Jenny's mounting hysteria. She was certain now that this was no ordinary trip. She had always been told about outings days before they happened but had been completely taken by surprise at this one. The other children on the bus didn't seem as excited as they normally were on outings. In fact they were all very quiet. Too, other outings they went on had only ever involved the junior part of the school, but from the number of buses it seemed the whole school was going today. All very strange. Panic again gripped her. I want to go home, she thought. They are stealing us and taking us away and I don't know the way home. She felt like screaming.

Leaning over and stretching up to reach Jimmy's ear, she whispered to him. "Jimmy, I think they are going to steal us. They aren't going to let us go back home. I'm scared, Jimmy, I want to go home."

Pushing her away with his arm, Jimmy gave a big sigh. Then looking her right in the eye he said, "No they aren't stealing us. That's soppy! If you don't shut up, I'm going to ask to sit somewhere else."

Slightly reassured, and subdued at the threat that her brother might abandon her, Jenny subsided into silence. Jimmy had said they were not being stolen and he always knew more than her. Just the same, she had noticed that his pale face had flushed pink when he had said they weren't being stolen.

At long last the bus stopped in a strange town. They were told to alight in an orderly manner and stand in line. Other buses stopped there too and once everyone was arranged in tidy lines they were crocodile marched down the road and into a big shop. There they were walked around the shop in single file while someone handed them packets of biscuits, tins of meats and fruits, other groceries and the biggest bar of Cadbury's chocolate Jenny had ever seen. These things were packed into a carrier bag for each child, whereupon they were ordered to take the bags back to the bus.

"You will be told what to do with the items you have just been given once we reach our destination," Miss Towner announced when they were all seated. "Now you may take out your sandwiches and we will eat here on the bus before continuing our journey."

"What sandwiches?" Jenny asked her brother. "They didn't give me any sandwiches. Did you get any?"

There was no answer. Jimmy was already standing on the seat pulling down a cloth bag from the overhead shelf. It was a bag in which they sometimes carried items to school. Putting it down on the seat,

Jimmy proceeded to remove a couple of packages, dumping one on her lap.

"There are your sandwiches," he said. "And if you are going to ask me how they got here, Mum and me brought them up the school early this morning and gave them to Miss Towner."

Jenny was astounded. "You're lying! You couldn't have brought them or I would have seen you go."

"We did it before you were awake," he said. "Mum wanted us to get all the stuff to school so you wouldn't know."

"All what stuff? And why wasn't I allowed to know we were going on an outing if you knew? It's not fair!" Once again she was close to tears at the strangeness of this day and the unfairness of it all. "What stuff did you bring?" she asked again, her voice quivering.

"Oh, just ... the sandwiches and that," Jimmy said, sounding somewhat flustered. "Don't you go starting again," he said, recovering slightly. "Mum didn't want you to know because it was a surprise."

He unwrapped his package and began to eat, cutting off all further conversation. Jenny did the same although she was not feeling at all hungry. The food didn't seem to want to be chewed and stayed in dry lumps in her mouth. When finally she swallowed a mouthful it stuck partway down her chest. She ate no more, sitting silently whilst everyone else ate and chattered. Once again they were instructed to alight from the bus, marched in lines to a nearby cafe where they were provided with orange drinks and took turns going to the lavatory. Settled back on the bus once more, the entourage moved on.

"Are we going home now?" she asked Jimmy. He gave her a thoughtful look. "I dunno," he said. "Probably."

"Oh good'" she said, settling back to wait for the time to pass until they got home. Glancing idly out the window, it dawned on her that there were now only two buses going in their direction. Where had the others gone? As she watched, the last bus turned off and headed in a different direction. Now she knew they were not going home after all.

"Look, Jimmy," she shrieked. "The other buses have all gone and left us. They aren't taking us home - where are we going?"

"Keep your voice down," Jimmy admonished her sternly. "All the buses are not going to the same place and we haven't got to our place yet. If you don't pipe down we're going to get into trouble." He turned and looked back down the bus towards Miss Towner and Jenny was terrified that he was going to ask to sit somewhere else. She couldn't bear for him to leave her all alone. She determined to be good and try not to cry any more.

It was late afternoon when they eventually reached their destination and were again instructed to leave the bus. This was no town. There were no streets or shops. Just a road with no pavements to walk on, fields and trees as far as one could see, about half a dozen houses a short way down the road, and a dark and forbidding looking building opposite the place they were standing. This building stood some way back from the road, a paved area in front of it sloping down to a fence bordering the road. The grey stone edifice appeared high and narrow, its windows tall and arched at the top, resembling church windows. Huge trees stretched in two straggly lines a few feet from the building down to the fence. The whole area had an ominous look to it and the children, realizing that this was where they were to go, became subdued and apprehensive.

"Here we are at last children," Miss Towner was saying cheerfully. "Form into your lines again and we will march tidily into this school where we will find some very nice people waiting to meet us."

Now Jenny was speechless with fear. Held in its vice-like grip she moved like an automaton behind her brother.

They were led into a small dingy room, the lower half of its walls painted dark green and the upper portions murky brown. The ceiling was so high and pointed the top was barely discernable. Rows of chairs were set in a semicircle around the room on hard wooden floors. They were told to find a seat and sit down.

As soon as they were all seated, a door opposite the one they had entered opened and a stream of adults walked into the room, immediately proceeding to parade around the children, looking them over as though they were some strange animals escaped from a zoo. Jenny stared back at these people who stood in front of her, looking her up and down before passing on to the next child. She began to bristle at this imposition. Some of the people were asking questions such as "Is

13

this one on his own or does he go with the girl?" And terrifying statements like "I'll take this one if he don't mind dogs."

Then they were taking the children away!

She cast a quick sideways look at Jimmy. He was sitting as if turned to stone, his face whiter than ever. Too terrified to speak for fear of attracting anyone's attention, she pulled herself into a tight ball on her chair, hoping to make herself invisible. Two elderly ladies appeared in front of her. One asked "Are these two together or may we just take the boy?"

"These are brother and sister and must go together," Miss Towner said.

The old lady who had spoken before said something that sounded like "Pity, the boy looks a pleasant enough lad, but if they are together I suppose we must take the two."

"All right you two, please look at me when I speak to you."

Jenny looked, and what she saw caused her to shake even more. The lady was very old, dressed in a tweed skirt and thick grey jumper under a loosely worn brown coat. A brown hat with narrow floppy brim covered most of her grey hair. Her voice was deep and had a distinct sharpness to it.

"I am Miss George," she informed them. "And this is my companion, Miss Old. I have a pretty little cottage in the village and you are going to stay with us for the duration. If you behave yourselves and have good manners we shall all get along swimmingly. Come along now!"

No, no, no, please no. I want to go home, Jenny screamed inside herself. She grabbed her brother's arm and looked frantically around for a means of escape.

Jimmy got off his chair and leaned over her. "We will have to go," he said, sounding close to tears himself. "Don't start bawling now or you will make me start too."

Other children were crying now too. Some were being forcibly pulled from the room by adults, others walking behind sniffling. Jimmy began to follow the old ladies as they walked to the door. Miss Towner came up to inform Miss George that the children's luggage could be found on the ground behind the bus and that it would be labelled 'Harding'. So that was the 'stuff' that Jimmy had meant. He *did* know all along that they were being taken away!

They found the luggage behind the bus, two large suitcases and a small one. The bus driver was standing at the roadside guarding all the belongings.

"Good heavens my man," said Miss George. "Surely they don't expect my companion and I to carry these cases all the way to the cottage, and these children are hardly going to manage such a load either. Just wait here with Miss Old, children."

With that she strode across the road and up to the school again. She was not gone long, however, soon striding back to inform them that arrangements were being made for someone to deliver the cases later.

As they started away once more, Jenny was shaking uncontrollably and feeling that her legs were going to fold under her at any moment. Where on earth were they going - and why? She pulled at Jimmy's coat until he stopped for her. "What's a Duration, Jimmy? I don't want to go for a Duration. Please tell them we want to go home."

"I don't know. I never heard of it before," he answered. "Perhaps its something to do with the war - and we can't go home yet so shut up."

She had never known Jimmy so grumpy. He didn't even want to talk to her. She felt so utterly alone, frightened and vulnerable, and now she felt stupid too. Jimmy said a Duration might be something to do with the War - but she didn't know what a War was either.

THREE

Miss George led the way through fields and along lanes, striding at a fast pace with the two frightened and apprehensive children half running, half walking behind her, both still clinging to their carrier bags of groceries. Miss Old brought up the rear.

The cottage, when they reached it, was lovely. Neither of the children had ever seen a country cottage. This one had a straw roof, small windows and roses climbing all over the front. Miss George produced a very large key and unlocked the front door. Before entering, she turned and spoke to both children.

"Now this is where you are going to live for a little while with Miss Old and myself. We don't want to enter the house as strangers do we, and since all I know is that your name is Harding, why don't you both tell us your names?"

Live here? What did she mean? We haven't got to live here with two strange old ladies, we haven't. We are going home soon, I know we are! Jenny wanted to scream again.

Both children stood dumbly staring at Miss George, neither one uttering a sound.

"Come now, cat got your tongues? You boy, what is your name?"

"My name is Jimmy Harding and she's Jenny." Jimmy's voice sounded truculent. "She's my sister," he added as an afterthought.

"That's much better," Miss George said. "Let's go inside now so you can see your new home.

Stepping into the cottage, Jenny was sure now that she was in a nightmare and would thankfully soon wake up. Pretty though the place was on the outside, inside it was dark and gloomy. The ceilings were low, windows small and curtained, letting in little light, the air so still it was scarcely breathable. It was so quiet!

"All right, sit yourselves down there on the settee and we will have a little talk while Miss Old makes us a cup of tea. What do you have in your bags, Jimmy?" Miss George asked.

Jimmy handed over his carrier bag, pulling Jenny's from her hand and handing that over too. Despite the promise that they would be told what to do with these things once they reached their destination, this had not been done. Jenny tried to hold onto her bag in the faint hope that, since they had not been told what to do with them, this really wasn't their destination after all.

"Oh very nice," Miss George said, looking into the bags. Miss Old can put these things away while she is making our tea. She handed the bags to the waiting Miss Old, who to this point had not uttered a word. Miss Old took a quick peek into the bags, smiled at the children and disappeared through a door at the back of the room.

"Now, just to give you a little background," said Miss George. "I have no children of my own, but, I am a retired school Head Mistress, so I know all about children. So long as you behave yourselves and do as you are told we shall get along splendidly. Miss Old has never had much to do with children and you may find her a little quiet, so if there is anything you wish to know please come to me and don't bother Miss Old."

A smile crossed her lips, clamping them into a thin line and failing to reach her eyes.

"Well, now you know a little about us, how about yourselves. How old are you both?"

"I'm seven and a half and she's six," Jimmy said.

"That's about what I thought. But I don't think you should refer to your sister as 'she'. It's Jenny isn't it? Yes, well tell me about your family - what does your father do?"

"My Dad's in the navy," Jimmy volunteered. "He goes away a lot on his ship. He's a Chief Petty Officer and a 'lectrical arfister" he added proudly.

"Oh really! I take you to mean he is an Electrical Artificer. Quite a respectable occupation. Now I do realize that you are both going to feel a little strange and lost at first. We will show you around the village over the next few days and you will soon find friends and settle down. There were obviously quite a number of evacuees like yourselves at the school. Were any of them personal friends of yours?"

She seemed to be waiting for an answer. Jenny, pressed against Jimmy for support, had not the slightest idea what she was talking about. Neither of them spoke so Miss George tried again.

"Do you know any of the other children on your bus?" she asked, looking directly at Jimmy.

"Oh, no, I didn't see anybody I knew," Jimmy stammered. "Did you?" he asked, looking at Jenny.

For answer she gripped more tightly to his arm and tried to move even closer. As far as she could remember she had kept her eyes either out of the bus window or on Jimmy. She had seen no-one she recognized other than Miss Towner, but then she hadn't really looked at anyone else.

There was a knock on the front door, saving the need for an answer. Miss George opened the door and a man entered carrying the cases they had left at the roadside. Jenny's heart began to pound. This had to be their clothing - the 'stuff' Jimmy and their mother had taken to the school so early in the morning. They really were going to have to stay here all alone with these horrible old ladies. If this was her mother's idea of a surprise, it was a hateful surprise. They had been so long on the bus - how far away from home were they and why had their mother let this happen to them? Too afraid to cry, she sat huddled against Jimmy like a coiled spring. She had not said one word since leaving the school.

"Now that your cases have arrived, I'll show you where your bedrooms are. Follow me please," Miss George commanded.

"The bedrooms are somewhat inconvenient," Miss George was saying as they mounted the stairs. "This is my room," she said, indicating a door on the left. "The other three, as you will see, lead into each other. Because you will both be going to bed before Miss Old, we have given you the two end rooms. Jimmy, you will be at the far end, Jenny next to you, and this first one is Miss Old's room. Once you are in bed, you are to stay there until morning and not come walking back through Miss Old's room for anything. Is that understood?"

The three rooms were very small with low ceilings and even smaller windows than the downstairs rooms. After showing them where they were to put their clothes, Miss George left, saying that they need only unpack what they needed for the night and then come down for tea. They would need to get to bed early after their long day, she said, so they could unpack the remainder tomorrow. As soon as she had gone, Jenny made straight for Jimmy's room.

"I don't like it here, Jimmy," she sobbed. "Why do we have to be here? Why did you and Mummy bring our cases to school this morning and nobody told me? What did she say we were 'vacuees for? What is 'vacuees? I don't like those old ladies. Jimmy, let's go home."

She was hanging onto her brother's jacket, rocking to and fro as the tears streamed down her face. Jimmy yanked his jacket from her hands and pushed her onto the bed.

"Do you think I want to be here?" he said crossly. "How can anyone tell you anything when you keep crying. All I know is that we have to stay here in the country for a while because there is going to be a war and it is safer here. We have to stay until the war ends and we can go home. I don't know what evacuees are and I didn't know where we were going except to the country. Just don't keep crying, Jenny, I don't like it."

Jenny wiped her eyes on her sleeve and made a great effort to stop crying. "What is a war?" she asked. "When is it going to start and how long will it take?"

"War is people fighting. I don't know when it will start or how long it will take. Please, Jenny, go and unpack your things and stop asking questions."

She crept back to her room, more bewildered than ever. Why would they be safer here because people were going to fight? If staying at home wasn't safe, what was going to happen to Mummy? Shouldn't she have come with them? It made no sense at all. She hoped fervently that whoever was going to fight would get on with it and let them go home. She just wanted to go home.

She was utterly exhausted and sick with fear as she crawled into bed that night. Curling herself into a tight ball, she cried herself to sleep.

FOUR

Jenny simply could not adjust to the new circumstances. The shock of being so suddenly wrenched from the security of home and family disoriented her. She thought of nothing but the desire to go home. Each morning she awoke confused as to where she was. When realization dawned she would go to the window, looking across the fields to see if there was anyone out there fighting yet. There never was and she wondered when this was going to happen.

Jimmy was miserable too. He disliked the old ladies and although he had been in part prepared for leaving home, he was every bit as lost and lonely as Jenny. Because he was the eldest, he was expected to be responsible for Jenny and she had always been a pest at the best of times. Miss George had laid out their duties to them the day after they arrived. Jimmy was to clean all the shoes first thing in the morning and wash the dishes after tea in the afternoon. Jenny was to dry them and put them away. The dishes were only done once a day. At tea time, if the children wanted to put jam on their bread, they could not have cake to follow. If they wanted cake, they must eat their bread plain.

Miss Old did the cooking and most of the cleaning. Miss George appeared to do very little except rule everyone with an iron rod. Her clothing was always plain and serviceable and Jenny wondered if she slept at nights with her hair pulled back into that always tidy bun. The lines on her face were deeply etched.

Miss Old, on the other hand, was a gentle lady. Despite all her anxiety, Jenny began to feel more comfortable with Miss Old. True she spoke very little, but when she did her voice was soft and she smiled a lot. Her silver hair was cut in a short bob and she wore flowing skirts. She is probably as afraid of bossy Miss George as we are, Jenny thought.

They had been shown around the village the day after their arrival. It was a long rambling place. Groups of houses scattered here and there, narrow roads and little lanes with no pavements to walk on anywhere. Grassy banks at the sides of roads, fields, hills and trees as far as you could see. Roughly four miles in length, by the time Jimmy and Jenny had trotted behind the two elderly ladies on their bicycles, up and down lanes and roads, around and about, those four miles had grown to nearer seven. Both children were spent and hungry when they thankfully returned to the cottage.

The village was called Bishopstone, they were informed. It lay in what was known as the Chalk Valley, with the nearest town, Salisbury, seven or eight miles distant.

Little more than a week after their arrival, the children started back to school, this time in a makeshift room at the village hall especially set up for the evacuees. Although many of the children who had accompanied Jimmy and Jenny on the bus had been taken further up the valley to other villages, two more buses had arrived a day or so later, this time from London. The occupants were all boys of rough and ready nature whom no-one had apparently wanted to take in. They were therefore situated in a large house which lay back from the main road and which came to be known as the "Home". These children were almost instantly disliked by everyone. They swore, threw stones, fought among themselves, broke fences and trees, stole fruit and caused general disruption everywhere they went. Both Jimmy and Jenny soon learned to give the Home kids a wide berth whenever possible. At school this was not possible as they were all crowded together in the one room at temporary desks. On Friday afternoons the desks had to be dragged into a room at the back in order to leave the large room free for other village functions.

The ages of the children ranged from six to ten years, Jenny being the youngest. All were taught together and concentration was minimal. The lessons, such as they were, always seemed to be above Jenny's head and she comprehended little. Had they been at her level she still would not have concentrated; her mind had shut itself to everything but the desire to go home.

More than two weeks had passed with no sign of anyone showing the slightest inclination to start fighting. It was Saturday and Jenny had been allowed to play in the back garden. Jimmy had gone with Miss Old to the village shop. In future, he had been told, it would be another of his jobs to run to the shop when anything was needed. This time Miss Old had gone with him to refresh his memory of the location and show him the short cuts.

There really wasn't much to do in the back garden. It wasn't very big - just a lawn that ran the width of the house, bordered on its two sides with tall thick hedges. The lawn sloped down from the house for about twenty feet, culminating at the edge of a small stream roughly ten feet across. An oval plot containing shrubs and flowers was set into the lawn on one side and a willow tree overhung the stream at the edge of the lawn on the other side. Once a week an occasional gardener came to mow the lawn, keep the hedges in order and tend to the vegetable patch behind the hedge on the opposite side of the road to the cottage.

Today the little stream shimmered and danced in the autumn sunlight. Sitting at the lawn's edge, Jenny slipped off her shoes and socks to dangle her feet in its playful waters. The sudden cold shock took her breath away for a moment, but soon growing accustomed to the cold, she revelled in the tingling sensation of the water rippling against her feet. It was so quiet here, the only sounds being the rustle and splash of the burbling water. Little stones and bits of weed at the bottom were clearly visible, sometimes disappearing and sometimes changing shape as the ripples played over them. Small minnows darted by in groups, skillfully avoiding capture as she attempted to scoop some up in her hand.

"Jenny, come here child!"

Miss George's imperious voice shattered the peaceful quiet of the day, startling Jenny into action. I'm probably in trouble for taking off my shoes, she thought as she hastily rubbed her feet in the grass and pushed them into her shoes. Running into the living room to receive the expected lecture, she was stunned at the scene that met her eyes. Standing in the centre of the room with one arm around Jimmy's shoulders was her mother!

22

Squealing with delight, Jenny launched herself at her mother in an explosion of joy and relief. Mummy had come to get them and they were going home. The two old ladies vanished from her mind as if they had never been. All was normal and right again. Even Jimmy laughed as she all but bowled her mother over in her exuberance.

Laughing and crying at the same time, words spilled out of her in a jumbled torrent. "Mummy, Mummy. They took us away but you found us. I thought we'd lost you. They said there was going to be a war and people fighting but they didn't fight. I looked every day but nobody was fighting. I hate it here, I hate it. I didn't like being taken away. How did Jimmy find you, were you at the shop? He went to the shop with Miss Old. Shall we get our things now? I can get mine. Come on Jimmy, let's go pack our cases."

Nobody moved. All at once the room was so hushed it was a though everyone had suddenly turned to stone. Jenny looked at her mother enquiringly.

"Come here, Jenny love, and sit on my lap," her mother said, pulling her toward the sofa. "I want you to listen to me without interrupting while I explain things to you. You have obviously got everything all mixed up as usual, so this time try hard to understand what I am saying and please show us all what a brave girl you can be by not crying or making a fuss."

Jenny's heart, a few seconds ago so light and happy, shot right down to her feet. What was this? What was her mother going to say? It wasn't going to be very nice and she didn't want to hear.

"Jenny love, I have not come to take you home this time," her mother was saying. "I have just come to see that you are settling down and to tell you that I love you and miss you and am thinking about you both all the time. Yes dear, there is a war and it has already started, but you won't see anybody fighting around here. That is why you have been sent to the country - because it is safe here. I will come to see you as often as I can and I'll write to you. Then, as soon as it is safe again, you can come home. But you *must* stay in the country and be a good girl until then."

Jenny couldn't believe that her mother meant to go away and leave them again. Not now that she had found them. She couldn't!

"No Mummy, no! You can't leave us here. It's horrid and I'm frightened. I want to see Daddy, I want to go home. Please Mummy, I'll be good. I'll be really, really, really good I promise. If people are fighting I won't get in the way. They won't hurt us if we don't get in the way. Please take us home."

Her mother smiled a little at this outburst. Jenny didn't think it funny. She was pleading for a return to sanity and home and family, and it was no smiling matter.

Her mother hugged her and planted a kiss on the top of her head. "You are funny sometimes, Jenny, although I know you are not meaning to be. I'm afraid you don't understand what war really is. It isn't just a matter of a few men fighting each other in a field, but guns and noise and airplanes that drop bombs on houses and blow them to pieces. We are English, and England is fighting a country called Germany. Because Portsmouth is a dock area where we keep some of our big ships, Germany will drop bombs on it to try to stop our ships from sailing to the war. You can't keep out of the way of bombs, but down here in the country there won't be any bombs so that is why you must stay until it is over. Daddy and I don't want you or Jimmy to be hurt and I don't have to worry so much if I know you are safe. Now do you understand?"

She didn't. She didn't understand at all. Why did people have to go fighting and hurting each other? And if Portsmouth was going to be blown to pieces what was going to happen to Mummy? She would be killed and then they wouldn't have her any more at all. If this Germany was going to bomb the ships then Daddy would be killed too. There would be nobody left and she and Jimmy would be here for ever.

She sobbed tears of dreadful despair. Jimmy, leaning against his mother's legs, joined his own tears with hers. All this talk of violence, killing and destruction was beyond the understanding of both young minds.

"Oh come on," said their mother. "This is enough talk of gloomy things for one day. Let's go out for a walk and you can show me around."

"That's a very good idea," put in Miss George. "And I must say that is the most I have ever heard this young lady say at one time. It has been like trying to squeeze blood from a stone to get Jenny to say more than two words at once."

"Don't be too sorry about that," said mother. "Once she truly settles down you will find she talks the hind leg off a donkey. Normally the most difficult thing is to get her to keep still and stop talking long enough to eat or sleep. I'll take them both out of your way for an hour or so."

The walk was not a great success. Although Jimmy tried to be cheerful, pointing out to his mother where they went to school and telling her the names of roads that he had learned, his face had taken on a pallor and he was obviously still distressed. Jenny voiced her concerns that Mummy herself would be hurt or killed if she went back to Portsmouth, pleading yet again that her mother either come to live with them or take them back with her.

"Jenny," her mother said. "I know it is all so hard for you to understand, but you just have to try. I cannot come here to live because I have to stay and look after our home for us. It is not possible to sell it right now and I don't have enough money to come here and buy another house. You don't have to worry that I will be hurt. They are starting to build shelters for people to go to if there are going to be any bombs. I can get to a shelter quickly if I don't have you two to worry about as well. This arrangement is the best for all of us at the moment. This way we can all stay safe until we can be together again."

"But I don't want to stay here without you. I don't like Miss George - she's old and she's nasty. Miss Old is old too." A bubble of laughter escaped Jenny's lips as she realized what she had just said. "Miss Old is old," she repeated, giggling. Leaving go of her mother's hand, she skipped and danced along in front, clapping her hands above her head then slapping them against her legs. "Miss Old is old, Miss Old is old," she sang, the giggles rising in pitch; stopping as suddenly as they began. "I really don't like those old ladies, Mummy, truly. Miss Old is alright sometimes but Miss George makes us do things. Jimmy has to clean all the shoes for them *and* wash the plates, and I have to dry them and put them away."

"I don't suppose doing a few little jobs is going to hurt either of you," mother said. "Just the same, I do agree that such old women are not the best people to take charge of two children. I can't promise anything but I will see if there is any possibility of moving you before long."

That was all their mother would promise. When it was time for her to go Jimmy shed a few tears while Jenny grabbed her hand, refusing to let go while she cried and pleaded for them to be taken home. Finally her mother became cross, saying she would not come and see them again if Jenny was going to carry on like this. They still had each other, and this war would probably not go on for very long anyway.

She was gone. Jenny had a lump in her chest and couldn't eat her tea. Miss George gave her a stern lecture about how thankful she should be that her mother had sent her and Jimmy to a place of safety and that there were people kind enough to look after them. Her father would be helping to defend their country so that it would once more be safe for them all and she should not make things difficult for everyone by crying and complaining.

That night, curled up into a tight ball, Jenny cried herself to sleep again. No-one seemed to understand how frightened she was that both her mother and her father could be killed. Nobody cared how lost she felt and how she hoped every night that she would wake up in the morning and find it was all a bad dream. Emotionally drained, she fell into a disturbed sleep which brought with it a terrifying nightmare.

From somewhere out of the darkness a hand holding a small ball moved slowly toward her face. There was no body, just an arm and the hand holding the ball. Moving closer, the hand pushed the ball into her mouth where it slowly began to roll backwards, growing larger and larger as it turned. Her jaws opened as far as they could to accommodate the ball as it continued to grow and revolve. Flattening her tongue and pressing hard against her throat, it stretched her jaws to breaking point, preventing her from screaming as it choked the breath from her body. Just as she was sure she would die, she woke - gagging, retching and gasping for air. Trying to call out, her voice wouldn't raise itself above a hoarse whisper. Trembling with fear, she pulled the bedclothes over her head, screwed into an even tighter ball and waited for daylight, too afraid to sleep any more.

FIVE

One month after their arrival, Miss George told them that she and Miss Old had decided they were too old to cope with two young children. Another home had been arranged for them and they were to pack their belongings as quickly and neatly as possible. Miss Old would be taking them to their new home that afternoon.

Both were delighted at the news that they were leaving. "Aren't you glad we don't have to stay here any more?" Jenny enquired of her brother as they packed their cases.

"Yes! I don't like it here any more than you do. But I don't believe that they wanted us to go. Mum said she would try to get us out of here and I bet she did. She must have told somebody to move us. I wonder where we are going to go now."

In the excitement of leaving, she had given no thought to where they might be going. Now, struggling along with the smaller of the cases, Jimmy manfully trying to handle one of the big ones and Miss Old pushing the other balanced between the seat and the handle bars of her bicycle, Jenny began to feel a little apprehensive at the thought that they were headed for the home of strangers again.

It was a long walk, though in fact less than a mile. Both children had to set their cases down and rest frequently. Miss Old did not chastise them for the delay, instead waiting patiently until they felt their strength return enough to struggle a few more steps. Jimmy began to stagger from the weight of the big case so Miss Old suggested that between them she and Jimmy might be able to hoist it on top of the one on her bicycle. This they managed to do, then Jimmy took Jenny's smaller case and they made better progress. They came to a tall green gate set into a high stone wall where Miss Old stopped her bicycle. "Here we are at last." she said, turning towards them. As she spoke the top case slid to the ground, pulling the underneath one down with it. It bounced hard on one corner and burst open, spilling its' contents.

Miss Old let go of the handlebars and her bicycle crashed over onto the road.

"Oh dear dear. I do hope the cases aren't damaged," Miss Old said, looking very distressed. She looked at the children only to see them both doubled over with laughter. For a moment Jenny truly thought Miss Old was going to cry, she looked so upset. They pulled themselves together, stuffing the wayward garments back into the case and re-closed it. Miss Old picked up her bicycle and leaned it against the wall, opened the large green gate and ushered the children through.

Walking up a path between tall hedges, they came to the largest house either child had ever seen. The path led to the side of the house. Looking to the right they saw a very large lawn, flower gardens, trees, and, most astonishing of all, at the far end of the lawn an enormous round tower. The grey stone edifice stood as tall as the house, culminating in a pointed roof with a metal cross atop holding the letters N, S, E, W on each point.

Turning to the left, they walked around the house, past a large sand pit to the back door. The back of the house was shaped like the letter L. A roof, supported by pillars, ran from the back door along the wall forming the L. Away from the house and to the left was a thatched grey stone building the size of a garage. A thin iron bar with a ring on the end hung from the roof over the green back door. Miss Old gave a couple of tugs at the bar and the door was opened by a middle aged lady in a white cap and apron.

"So these are our two new additions then," the lady said, leading them into a large kitchen. Jenny was awestruck at the size of the enormous scrubbed wooden table in the centre of the room. How many people live in this house to need such a big table? she wondered.

"Put your cases down and wait while I see Miss Old to the door," White Apron said.

Miss Old placed a hand on each child's head. "Goodbye dears," she said. "I'm sure you will be happier here than with two old ladies. Mr. and Mrs. Williamson have two children of similar ages to yourselves."

Oddly enough, Jenny felt a wave of sadness as Miss Old left. She was really quite a nice lady, and now they were in this big house, not knowing anyone or what was to happen to them next.

"I'm Mrs. Rundle," White Apron said. "I am cook-housekeeper here and you can call me 'Cook' like everyone else does. I shall be looking after you for the most part and you will eat your meals here in the kitchen. This is a big house and there will be some places you will not be allowed to enter, but you will soon find all that out. Miss Old tells me your names are Jimmy and Jenny. How old are you?"

"I'm seven and a half," Jimmy said, pulling himself up to his full height.

"I see, and how about you Miss?"

"I'm six and a bit," Jenny whispered.

"Oh, six and a bit are you?" Cook smiled. "Two little blue eyed blondies. You are both as thin as little birds, don't you eat at all?"

The children looked at each other, not knowing quite what to say to this.

"Never mind," Cook comforted. "You'll eat plenty of my cooking I'll be bound. Come with me and I'll show you where to put your things." She picked up the two large cases, puffing her way up a wide winding staircase. I could lay on these stairs with my hands over my head and not touch the sides, Jenny thought as she pushed her hands into the deep pile of the blue stair carpet. Half way up they stopped on a landing. The stairs narrowed here, turning back on themselves to continue upward. However, Cook turned away from the next flight of stairs and led them along the landing to the left.

"This is where your bedrooms are," she said, panting from the strain of the cases. Those other stairs go up to Mr. and Mrs. Williamsons' room and to those of Howard and Fredda, who you will meet later. You are not to go up those stairs for any reason - the upper floor is out of bounds to you. Do you understand that?"

Both children nodded. They were to discover later that a great deal of the house was out of bounds to them unless they were specifically invited. In fact they were to live in what was known as the servants' quarters consisting of the kitchen, a living room, their own bedrooms and a play room. Once they settled in and found their way around, neither child really wanted to enter the portions of the house where the Williamsons lived. Not that Mr. and Mrs. Williamson were hostile, rather they were aloof and kept to themselves most of the time.

Having unpacked their belongings into the drawers and wardrobes indicated by Cook, they walked down the wide stairs feeling small and lost. Finding their way back to the kitchen, they discovered a thin, elderly man and an apple cheeked young woman seated at the table, upon which had been set cups of tea and buttered scones.

"Come on in and have a bite," Cook called to them. "This here gentleman is Peters the butler. You probably won't have a lot to do with him but you'll see him around. And this is Mary. She's the housemaid and is going to be looking after you two along with me. Now sit yourselves down and tuck in."

The man Peters gave them a cursory nod, while Mary beamed at them, her smile lighting up her shining brown eyes. An odd looking white lacy headpiece covered most of her forehead, encircling her dark wavy hair. "'Ello. Your names are Jimmy and Jenny aren't they. Cook told me you was 'ere. I bet you feel a bit funny comin into an 'ouse of strangers don't ya? I know 'ow you feel. I come 'ere meself a couple of years ago from London and I felt pretty 'omesick then. You'll soon settle down though - kids do."

Jenny felt immediately that she would like Mary. Before long Mary would become their chief ally and friend. Cook prepared their meals, watched their manners, checked them over before they left for school and told them what they could and could not do. It was Mary who saw them to bed, woke them in the mornings, played with them in the playroom in the evenings where they could paint or draw or paste their scrapbooks, and it was to Mary they turned in times of need.

Mrs. Williamson did come to check on them from time to time. She looked at their scrap books, asked them questions about their schooling in her soft, gentle voice, and seemed mildly interested in their progress. Jenny was never quite sure what to make of Mrs. Williamson as she watched her go about in her tweedy clothes. She wore such long laces in her walking shoes that they crossed up and over her legs almost to the knees. She was friendly enough but not really approachable.

Mr. Williamson was a different matter. Jenny knew exactly how she felt about him from the moment she met him. She was afraid of him. He seemed to be of the opinion that everyone was deaf and his booming voice could be heard all over the house. Ruddy faced and overweight, he always smelled of liquor. He was a gentleman farmer, the children were told. Jimmy said he reckoned that meant he was a farmer who never did anything. He didn't appear to do much in the way of work himself, mostly giving loud orders to others and riding around on his great big horse. That horse was the sole occupant of a group of stables on the opposite side of the road to the big house which belonged to the Williamsons. They owned other smaller houses in the vicinity which were occupied by people who worked on their farm.

The Williamson's two children, Howard and Fredda, were away at boarding schools when Jimmy and Jenny arrived. They both came home the following weekend. Howard was a little over a year older than Jimmy, whilst Fredda was Jenny's senior by two months. They both spoke with posh accents like their mother and behaved in a very friendly manner toward the two evacuees. At least, Howard and Jimmy got along right from the word go. Jenny felt a little in awe of Howard. Half a head taller than Jimmy, when he turned his steely blue eyes on her she felt he was telling her she was too young and too silly to bother with. With Fredda, however, she felt comfortable and at ease once she got used to the way Fredda spoke. There was one thing about Fredda that Jenny could never quite stop wondering at. Her hair and eyes were exactly the same as her mother's. It was almost like seeing double when she looked from Mrs. Williamson's large, kindly hazel eyes to those of Fredda - they were identical in colouring and expression. Both had the same dark wavy hair, although Fredda's was softer looking than her mother's. Whenever Howard and Fredda came home Jimmy and Jenny were pleased to see them.

The round stone and flint tower in the garden was a source of great interest to Jimmy. Howard had taken him into it when he was home from school, both boys revelling in its dank, dark interior. When Jimmy had asked Cook abut the tower, she told him that the house had once been considered almost a castle and had been surrounded by high walls and a moat, with a drawbridge that could be lifted and lowered to keep people out. There had been two towers, one at each end of the high south wall, but one had long since been demolished, as had the high walls, moat and drawbridge. These days a small portion of the one remaining tower was used as a garden shed while most of it was now a dove cote. All round the inside were rows of square holes dug into the cement lining to make homes for doves. Jenny didn't like it at all - it was dark and spooky and, worst of all, a home for bats. The bats could be seen flying from the window slits at night. Fredda told Jenny that bats could get tangled into your hair so they couldn't get away. Jimmy called Jenny a baby because she was afraid of the place.

SIX

Living in the big house was preferable to life with two ancient ladies, but Jenny still pined for home and asked almost daily if the war was finished yet. Mother wrote them a letter which Jimmy read to her as she was unable to read all the words. In it Mother said she would be coming to see them again as soon as possible and in the meantime would be sending them a few of their toys. Within a few days of receiving the letter, the toys arrived by carrier. They weren't just a *few* toys, they were all the toys the children owned. There was Jenny's big doll's pram, her doll's house and all her dolls, her cooking stove and dresser complete with pots and pans, tea set, books, puzzles. Jimmy had his toy soldier collection, farmyard with all the animals, his garage and cars, all his Jaffa comics that he had saved, and so much more. Their mother had even sent their bicycles.

Delighted as she was to see her beloved toys again, Jenny was disturbed and puzzled by their arrival.

"Why did Mummy send all our toys?" she asked Jimmy. "Aren't we ever going home again?"

"Of course we are, one day. I read you the letter where Mum said she was sending some toys so we could have them here to play with. We can take them back home again when we go. I'm glad to have my things here even if you aren't."

"Oh I am glad too, Jimmy, really I am." And she was.

Jenny's Raleigh bicycle impressed Mrs. Williamson so much that she said she would like to get one like it for Fredda. Jenny was pleased with her new feeling of importance as Mrs. Williamson watched her ride it around the big lawn and asked permission for Fredda to try it out. She was very proud of her ability to ride without wobbling or, worse, falling off. It had taken her a long time to achieve this status. An older girl by the name of Pat and who lived in their street in Portsmouth had been given the task of teaching Jenny to ride. All was well so long as Pat held onto the saddle and ran up and down the road behind Jenny, but whenever she suggested letting go for a moment Jenny would panic, wobble and fall off. As Jenny later discovered, Pat did in fact often let go of the saddle, continuing to run behind so Jenny wouldn't know. One day Pat stopped running and Jenny, realizing Pat was no longer with her, crashed headlong into the bank at the end of the road. In a furious temper she screamed at Pat that she would never, ever let her teach her again, mounted the bike and rode home by herself. As it dawned on her what she had just done, she ran down the road to hug Pat, all anger evaporated in the joy of knowing that she could now truly ride by herself.

Now Mrs. Williamson was admiring her bike and watching as she showed off her ability to get off and on and turn corners without falling off.

"That is a very nice bicycle," she said. "When your mother comes to visit you I shall ask where she got it and try to get one for Fredda."

It was four weeks before their mother came for her next visit. Mary had told them in the morning that she was coming and they were to try to keep clean and tidy. In their excitement Jimmy and Jenny several times raced one another to the gate to see if she was coming yet. When they did see her walking down the road she was not alone. Walking beside her, looking so smart and handsome in his naval uniform, was their father.

"Daddy!" they both screamed at once, yanking open the gate and racing to meet their parents.

This time it was Jimmy who burst into tears. Both children dearly loved their father and Jimmy was especially close. He spent more time with their dad than Jenny did, helping him in the garden and in the wooden shed that he had built himself and where he made so many things for them. Seeing him so unexpectedly was too much for Jimmy, and tears streaked his face as they both rushed to embrace their parents. Jenny's biggest emotion was relief that her dad had not gone to war on his ship after all.

"Is the war over now and are we going home, Daddy?" was the first inevitable question after the kisses and hugs had subsided. Before he could answer her, Jimmy was asking "Why is your cap navy blue, Dad? Where is the one with the white top you always wear?"

By this time they were at the house where Cook introduced herself and produced tea, after which she showed them into the living room and left them to enjoy their privacy.

Jimmy, wearing his father's cap, repeated his question as to why its colour had changed.

"That is because it's war time," his dad said. "We have to wear dark hats so the Germans can't see us so easily."

"I thought the war was finished," Jenny cried. "You have come to take us home now haven't you, Daddy?"

"No, my love, the war isn't finished yet and you can't come home with us this time. I have to go back to my ship tomorrow and Mummy has to go to work. Ladies are going to help by doing some of the jobs that the men who have gone to be soldiers can't do any more. So you see that you are in the best place here in the country in this nice house until it really is all over."

"But if you go on your ship the Germans will drop bombs on it and one might hit you and I don't want you to go. I don't like the Germans. Why doesn't somebody tell them to go away?"

Her dad laughed gently at her. "Don't worry yourself about me," he said. "I shall only be away a little while and I'll be quite safe. The Germans won't see me in my dark clothes," he added in a conspiratorial whisper. "And I have my gas mask to keep me safe. Here look, I brought it with me to show you."

He pulled out the gas mask from a shoulder case he had been carrying and fitted it over his face. It was black with a little window across the eyes and a very long nose like an elephant's trunk protruding from the centre. Jenny thought it ugly and scary and couldn't understand how it could possibly keep her father safe, unless he wore it to frighten the Germans away. Jimmy was quite fascinated by it and wanted to know how it worked.

"I don't like that thing, it makes me frightened," Jenny told her father. "I don't want you to go on your ship, Daddy, please don't go."

"Look, I'll tell you what," her father said, seeing that she was becoming distressed. "If you are very good and stay here without any fuss, after the war is all over and we are home again I will give you both a special treat. Now you both think very hard what you would like most of all and tell me."

They thought hard.

"I know what I would like," Jimmy said. "I would like to fly in an airplane."

"All right then, that's what it shall be. After the war you can both go for a ride in a real airplane."

"No!" Jenny screamed. Airplanes crash, I don't want to go in an airplane. Jimmy, don't go, you'll be killed."

Everyone laughed, including Jimmy. "You dopey thing," he said. "Airplanes don't crash and I want to go up in the air and fly all through the sky." As he spoke he ran around the room making flying motions with his hand, up and down and round and round. But nothing he or her parents could say could dissuade Jenny that the only way an airplane came down was to fall out of the sky.

"Okay then," her father said. "If you don't want to fly, what would you like instead?"

"I want you to make me a great big doll's house that I can walk in myself. And I want lights to turn on."

She knew he could do this because he had built their garden shed and put electric lights in it. He was clever and had made lots of things, including her doll's cot and the small doll's house that she now had. He promised that he would make her the house and Jimmy could have his flight so long as they would also promise to be very good and behave themselves until then. Jenny started to imagine herself in her big doll's house, turning the lights on and off, and promised to try to be very good. She was still disturbed at the thought of Jimmy flying, but perhaps by the time the war finished he would have forgotten about it or changed his mind. She earnestly hoped so.

Mrs. Williamson came later to meet their parents and discuss Jenny's bicycle. They had tea together and Jenny, true to her promise to be good, held back her tears when it was time to say goodbye. Both children accompanied their parents to the bus stop and waved to them as the bus pulled away, neither one knowing when or if they would see their father again.

SEVEN

"Wot's all this cryin' an noise about then? You're all upset 'cos your mum and dad's gone 'ome ain't you. Was you 'avin a bad dream or summit?"

Jenny grabbed Mary, pulling her down onto her bed. Shuddering and sobbing, she felt Mary's arms fold around her. "There, there, you're okay now. Was it an ol' nightmare you 'ad?"

Sobbing, Jenny nodded. The nightmare of the ball rolling down her throat had invaded her dreams again and she had wakened in panic just as she was about to suffocate. Sitting bolt upright in her bed her eyes were drawn to the wardrobe across the corner of the room. It loomed ominously in the moonlight that streamed through her curtained window. As she watched, horrified, she saw a shadow slide silently behind the wardrobe. Letting out a scream of terror, she threw herself beneath the covers, screaming and choking until Mary came running in.

"There's a man," she gabbled. "He's behind the wardrobe and he was choking me."

"Ah luvvie, that's just a bad dream. There's nobody be'ind that thing. 'Ed 'ave to be pretty skinny to get in there, now wouldn't 'e. There's only a couple of inches between the wardrobe and the wall. Look, I'll show you there's nobody there."

Mary walked over to the wardrobe, demonstrating that she could not get more than just her hand behind it. She heaved the wardrobe away from the wall until she could get behind it.

"There's nobody 'ere 'cept me," she reported. Poking her head out she called Jenny. "C'mon, do you want to look for yourself?"

Jenny didn't. If there was nobody there, he was probably under the bed by now and waiting to grab her ankles. She didn't want to say this to Mary so she just shook her head mutely.

Mary put the wardrobe back in place then lay on the bed with Jenny, stroking her hair and soothing her. As Jenny's trembling subsided, Mary said she must go back to her room. She told Jenny to go back to sleep and have happy dreams this time. When she was gone Jenny screwed herself into a tight ball under the bedclothes. Mary might not have seen the man but Jenny knew he was still there waiting for her to sleep so he could push the ball down her throat again.

Jimmy and Jenny lived in the least populated part of the village. Consequently they met few villagers and made no friends amongst the local children. They did occasionally pass some of these children on the way to and from school, but none made any friendly gestures toward them. They simply stared at the two newcomers, poking each other and sniggering about "they vacees".

Jenny normally sought out Jimmy at the end of the school day and walked home with him. One day, however, she was unable to find him so had no alternative but to make her own way. Being content to just follow Jimmy without taking any note of their surroundings, on this particular day she took a wrong turn and soon became lost. Trying to retrace her steps only brought her to more unfamiliar territory. Before long she was wandering around in tears when an old man came by. Seeing her distress, he walked over to her.

"Where bist gwan to, maid? Bist lost 'en?" he enquired.

Jenny looked at him dumbfounded. She hadn't understood a word he said.

"Casn't thee tell I where bist gwan then?" the old man tried again.

Suddenly galvanized into action, she turned and fled away from the man as fast as her legs could carry her. In blind panic she continued running until she found herself on the familiar road home. Bursting in the door to relate to Cook her dreadful experience in meeting a strange man who "talked so funny I didn't know what he was saying to me," Cook told her he was probably just a villager and she would have to get used to the local dialect if she was ever going to get along here. Confused at the thought that she and Jimmy weren't only living among strangers, but among people who spoke a wholly different language, she was even more certain that she didn't want to be here at all.

Cook started to send Jimmy to school ten minutes before Jenny in the mornings. This came about because Jenny was playing around on the way to school one morning, jumping up onto the top of the bank outside the shoemaker's house. The high bank ran the length of the house, separated from it by a wet muddy ditch and children often liked to balance along the top of the bank.

"I bet you can't walk along the top of this bank without falling in the ditch," Jenny teased her brother.

Jimmy looked at her, unimpressed. "You're just stupid'" he retorted.

"You're afraid to walk up here in case you fall in the ditch. Look at me, I can do it," she goaded.

With that Jimmy ran at her. Jenny thought he was going to jump on the bank in front of her and run to the end just to show her. Instead he gave her a shove that sent her tumbling face down into the ditch. By the time she had picked herself up and clambered out, Jimmy was nowhere in sight. Gobs of sticky mud dripped from her skirt onto her shoes as she stood in the road wondering what to do. There was no way she could go to school in that mess and would have to go home to change. Cook was so angry when she saw the state Jenny was in that she slapped her. Then she marched her to the bathroom, scrubbed the mud off and washed her hair.

Dressed in clean clothing, Jenny set out for school once again. Arriving half way through morning lessons, she was caned across her hand for being late, in front of the whole school. Seething with the unfairness of having been punished twice for what Jimmy had done to her, she wanted to kick her brother. The outcome of the escapade was that Cook decided they could not walk to school together any more, an arrangement that upset Jenny but suited Jimmy nicely.

Christmas that year wasn't the best that Jimmy and Jenny had ever spent. Both were dreadfully homesick although Cook, Mary and the Williamsons did their best to make it a happy time. They were permitted into the Williamson's sitting room to open their presents from home and to watch Howard and Fredda open theirs. Among

Fredda's gifts was a Raleigh bicycle from her parents. Similar to Jenny's but not quite the same, Fredda's bike had black handlebars and wheel rims where Jenny's were chrome.

"I'm afraid that because it is wartime, bicycles cannot be made with chrome accessories any more. We have to make do without trimmings until things are back to normal," Mrs. Williamson said in explanation.

"I don't mind about that," Fredda said. "It's a lovely bike and now I can ride around with Jenny instead of taking turns with hers."

It was cold outside, but wrapped in coats, scarves and gloves, Fredda and Jenny rode their bicycles around the village so that Fredda could try out her new toy. Later they all had dinner in the Williamson's posh dining room, served by Mary and Peters. Jimmy and Jenny felt favoured by being allowed to eat with the Williamsons, but both secretly wished they could be in their own home with their own parents. Looking round the table at people she now knew yet could not feel truly close to, a tear trickled down Jenny's cheek. It dawned on her then that it was useless to keep badgering her mother to take them home. Mummy was always going to say 'no' and she and Jimmy were stuck here for always.

EIGHT

1940

A fine rain was falling this early April morning. Jenny, later than usual, was running to school. Head down, her waterproof sou' wester pulled over her eyes, she rounded a corner and ran pell mell into Jimmy walking in the opposite direction.

"Where are you going?" she demanded. "We're going to be late for school and you are going the wrong way."

"I know that," Jimmy replied. "I've already been to school and now I'm going home for something. You had better get on because you *are* late."

Standing in front of her, one hand in his raincoat pocket and the other tucked into the front of his coat as if he were keeping something from the rain, Jimmy looked peculiar to Jenny. His face was pale and he seemed uncomfortable - almost as if he didn't want to talk to her at all.

"I have to go," he said, starting to walk away from her.

Jenny turned after him, pulling at his arm. "Why are you going home when its time to go to school? And what's that?"

As she jerked on his arm, his hand had come out from the front of his coat revealing a folded paper.

Jimmy pushed the paper back under his lapel again. "I can't tell you what it is. I've got to take it home to Mrs. Williamson."

"Why can't you tell me? What is it, Jimmy - please tell me, please." She was still holding on to him, walking back the way she had just come. Perhaps he had done something really bad at school and had to take a note home to tell Mrs. Williamson how bad he had been, she thought.

"I can't tell you because you will cry, that's why."

Why would she cry? If he was in trouble at school she wouldn't cry would she? No, it had to be worse than that. Her heart felt suddenly heavy with dread and she had to know.

"No I won't cry, why would I cry? Please tell me what that paper says."

"You'll cry because you always do," he said angrily. "That's why Mum didn't tell you we were coming to the country, because you would howl - you're always howling like a baby."

Stunned by the sudden attack, her first reaction was to retaliate. She thought better of it at once. If she shouted back Jimmy would run away and not tell her the secret.

"I won't cry, I promise I won't. I'm bigger now - I won't cry, honest. Go on Jimmy, please tell me," she wheedled.

Jimmy pushed her away, squeezing his eyes at her as if trying to make up his mind. He walked a few steps, stopped, rubbed one foot to and fro on the road, turned and came back.

"All right then, you promised. Well its about Dad. His ship sunk and he drowned. Dad's dead!"

Utterly stunned, she watched her brother's retreating back with unseeing eyes. Daddy gone. It wasn't true - it couldn't be. In her mind she saw him again, showing them the ugly gasmask that would keep him safe from the Germans. She had known the silly thing wouldn't work, she should have told him it was no good. But it wasn't true, somebody had made a mistake. Where had Jimmy gone? She wanted to ask him again, to look at the paper and ask what it said. Who wrote that paper anyway, and how would they know where her Daddy was? No, it was a mistake and Daddy would be coming to see them again soon.

Her stomach was churning and her head felt as if it had disappeared somewhere in the sky. How long she stood in the road in the misty rain she had no idea. Without thinking where she was going, she began to wander in the direction of the village hall. A screech of brakes brought her shockingly to earth. Looking around in sudden panic, she found herself on the main road, having walked right past the hall where her school was in progress. Retracing her steps in confusion, she walked into class, made her way to her desk and sat down, still wearing her wet outer clothes.

"Jenny Harding, come out here!"

"What do you mean by wandering in here half way through the morning? Where have you been and why are you so late?" Miss Towner demanded.

Jenny looked up at her school mistress's angry face. "I don't know," she said for want of something better to say.

"You don't know! You don't know where you've been? Put your hands out."

She heard the whistle of the cane as it snaked through the air and watched as it cut across first one palm and then the other. She thought how odd it was that she didn't feel a thing. Numbly she walked back to her desk and sat down again. The remainder of the school day passed in a haze. Not until going home time did she realize that Jimmy hadn't returned to school.

Keeping her promise to Jimmy was the most important thing in her mind now. She had promised not to cry and she hadn't. Strangely enough she hadn't felt like crying, but now that she was going home and would see Jimmy again she wondered if the promise would be too hard to keep. As it was, no-one said anything to her about her father when she got home and Jimmy was nowhere to be seen. Asking where he was, Cook said that he wasn't feeling well and she was going to take his tea on a tray to him. Cook was unusually busy that evening with little time to talk to Jenny at all. Only Mary looked at her with sympathetic eyes, which told Jenny they all knew but were saying nothing.

At bedtime when Mary came to tuck her in, Jenny could hold back no longer. "Jimmy said Daddy was dead but its not true is it. Somebody made a mistake and he is coming to see us again soon isn't he?"

"Aw luv, let me hold you," Mary said, wrapping Jenny against her stomach. "I understand as 'ow you don't want to believe it. It's too much for a little 'un like you to take. It's all right to cry if you wants to luvvie."

"I can't. I promised Jimmy I wouldn't cry so I can't." Jenny felt a traitorous stinging behind her eyes threatening to destroy her promise.

"Oh, 'ow can you make a promise like that. Why, Jimmy 'isself 'as bin cryin' most the day."

That was too much for Jenny. Tears held in all day now came flooding out. Sobbing as though her heart would break she cried for her father, who she could not believe was dead, for her brother who she knew loved his dad more than life itself, and for herself and Jimmy in their loneliness and misery at being so far from home.

"Did you see the paper Jimmy had, Mary?" she asked through her tears. "What did it say?"

"Yes luv I did. It said your daddy's ship 'ad been sunk by a German torpedo while it was stopped to pick up a man wot fell overboard. It said most of the men on board was drowned and that just a few was picked up by the German ship and taken prisoner."

A ray of hope flickered in Jenny's breast. "Did it say my daddy was picked up then?"

"No luvvie. They don't know who got picked up. It was only a very small number and they will now be prisoners of war."

"What are prisoners of war? What do they do to them?"

"I don't really know," Mary said. "I s'pose they keep them in prison somewhere in Germany and don't let them out till the war's over."

Well that's it then, Jenny resolved. My daddy isn't dead, he's a prisoner of war and we won't be able to see him until the war is finished. Then he will come home and make my big doll's house and take Jimmy for a ride in an airplane if he still wants to go. These thoughts were a secret, she decided. She wouldn't tell anyone that her daddy was a prisoner, then they couldn't argue with her and say he was dead.

When Mary had tucked her down and left, Jenny cried again for her father who was shut away in prison and couldn't come to see them any more until the end of the war. She would think about him every day and hope he could somehow know she still loved him and that she knew he was alive.

At the end of that week their mother came to visit. She wore a black coat and hat which depressed Jenny. Mummy spoke more quietly than usual, telling them they had to be especially good now that Daddy was dead because she had to manage everything by herself. Jenny wanted to tell her that daddy wasn't dead, but kept quiet for fear of being contradicted. She could tell that Jimmy believed Daddy was dead because he was so miserable nowadays, shutting himself away a lot and hardly talking at all.

For some reason not explained to either of them, the Williamsons didn't want to keep Jimmy and Jenny any longer. Mummy said they were going to have to move again soon and would be staying with a family who had one daughter of Jenny's age. They had been with the Williamsons for eight months, thinking this is where they would be until they were taken home again. Now they were to move again into the home of yet more strangers.

NINE

Nellie and Frank Matthews were ordinary working class people. Frank worked on a farm while Nellie did a few hours domestic work and supplemented their income by sewing. They lived in a fairly roomy three-bedroomed cottage which boasted electric light in the downstairs rooms only, an ancient iron hand pump in the back washhouse which pumped freezing cold water, and a bucket type lavatory at the end of the garden path. Despite a lack of luxuries, Nellie kept the home bright and shining. The feeling on entering the house was one of welcome.

"You two look as if you don't know whether you are coming or going," Nellie said to Jimmy and Jenny as they stood in her living room looking very unsure of themselves. They had just walked more than a mile from the Williamsons, accompanied by Cook and Peters who had carried the heavier cases. Their toys were to follow them in a few days.

"How about it if I show you around first so you can get your bearings and know where things are?" Nellie suggested. She had a pleasant voice, smiling a lot as she talked. Jenny thought she might like her, but since she was unsure decided not to say too much yet.

Nellie took them on a tour of the house, starting first with the front room and living room. These two rooms were side by side, the front door and small entrance hall nestled between them. The front room was small, longer than it was wide and felt chilly. It contained, among other furnishings, a single bed. The living room was larger, square and was heated by a large black leaded stove and oven set back into one wall. A polished table occupied the centre of the room with dining chairs pushed in close to the table. Comfortable armchairs were set on each side of the black stove, and a sofa stood against the opposite wall. A treadle sewing machine was placed in front of the cheerfully curtained windows.

A latched door beside the sofa led to a kitchen and large pantry. Against the far wall of the kitchen, separated by a wooden partition, were stairs leading to the upper floor. Running along behind the living room and front room, reachable through yet another latched living room door, was a back passage which became progressively cooler as they walked, culminating in the washroom and back door to the garden.

Above the back passage another passage or landing ran the length of the upstairs. The first medium sized bedroom on the left was to be Jimmy's room. The bedroom next to that, the largest, was that of Mr. and Mrs Matthews', and the long room at the end of the passage was to be shared by Jenny and the Matthews' daughter Verna.

The children had already seen the front of the stone and flint cottage with its slate roof and slab topped garden wall. Now Nellie took them out the back door to show them the back garden and lavatory. The garden was sizable, some lawn, shrubs and flowers, parts of it wild, the majority given over to vegetable growing. Various fruit trees grew back and front of the house which was surrounded on the left and back sides by a field. On the right was a tall hedge separating it from the chapel grounds next door. Jenny was delighted to see three hutches containing rabbits which hopped to the wire fronts to twitch their noses at her. Jimmy wanted to take one out but Nellie told him to wait until he was in his play clothes and then he could. The rabbits belonged to Verna she told them.

Another row of cages caught Jenny's eye and she ran to see if there were more rabbits. The inhabitants were not rabbits, they were long yellow creatures with red beady eyes. The stench coming from their cages was acrid and caught in her throat. She gave a questioning look to Nellie, who laughed.

"Don't know what they are do you?" she said.

Jenny shook her head. She didn't really like the look of these strange creatures.

"They're ferrets. And don't go sticking your fingers through the wire or you'll lose them. They bite real nasty."

"What do you keep them for then?" Jimmy asked.

"We don't keep them for pets, that's for sure," Nellie told him. "They belong to Mr. Matthews and he takes them out rabbiting. They chase the rabbits out of their holes and he catches them as they come out."

Jenny made a silent resolve to keep away from the nasty smelly ferrets. They were scary.

A path ran from the back door to the nether regions of the garden. Following Nellie down this path, beneath a hugh damson tree whose spreading branches hung low enough to touch the top of their heads, they came to a small shed. "This is the lavvie," Nellie said, pushing open the low door. Both children stood and stared.

Across the back of the shed was a wooden seat with a hole in the middle. A dirt floor, cobwebs hanging from corners and torn up pieces of paper hanging from a string on one side.

"Is this really the lavatory?" Jenny asked incredulously, finding her voice at last. "How do you pull the chain? "Where's the light switch?" she asked, searching with her eyes. "I can't see the light bulb."

"This is really it," Nellie said, laughing at Jenny's naivety. "There's no chain to pull and no light. You have to bring a torch after dark and sing as loud as you can. There is nothing we can do about the smell. Mr. Matthews empties it when it gets full. You haven't seen a palace like this before have you? This one's called Bucketam Palace."

"I don't like this place, it stinks," Jenny exclaimed with her usual lack of tact.

"Shut up, Jenny. You're not supposed to say things like that," Jimmy admonished her.

"That's all right. She's right anyway," Nellie said. "And I'll tell you something else you won't like, Lady Jane," she went on, looking at Jenny. "We don't have running water here so you will have to pump up what you need. It comes from a well and its cold enough to freeze the pimples on your nose when you wash in it. How about that?"

"I don't have pimples on my nose," Jenny retorted, feeling her nose with her hand just to be sure.

"Well you will have pimples on your nose and everywhere else when you wash in cold water," Nellie laughed.

The Matthews' daughter Verna had come in from play by the time they returned to the living room. Nellie introduced the children to each other. Of larger build than Jenny, Verna was her senior by nine months. Round of face, she wore her straight light brown hair bobbed below her ears with a fringe across her forehead. She gave a wide smile as they were told each other's names, all three standing around shyly, not quite sure what to say. As Verna looked up to her mother for direction, Jenny noticed what strange eyes she had. One was brown and the other half brown and half green. When Jenny looked into her eyes she had the weird feeling that she wasn't sure if Verna was looking directly at her.

"Say hello to Jimmy and Jenny then," Nellie told her. "You've been in and out all day to see if they've arrived yet. Now they are here you can show them some of your things and help make them feel at home."

Verna giggled and ran from the room.

"Pay no mind to her," Nellie said, picking up one of their cases. "Sometimes I swear she's not all there. She will be alright once she gets used to you. Let's go and get you unpacked and into some play clothes."

Jenny studied Nellie as she went about showing them where to put things and helping them unpack. She liked Nellie's twinkly blue eyes behind their brown rimmed glasses. She was of medium height, her permed brown hair streaked with grey. A floral overall covered her clothes, overlapping at the front and tied at the back.

"What do we have to call you?" Jimmy asked her.

"Oh you can just call me Nellie and you can call Mr. Matthews Frank if you like. It sounds more friendly than Mr. Matthews and Mrs. Matthews don't you think?"

Jenny had never called grown ups by their first name before and wasn't quite sure if she could do that. It sounded rude to her, but she would have to try.

TEN

It did not take long for the two evacuees to settle in and feel at home with the Matthews. Nellie made them welcome and gave them a sense of belonging that had been sorely absent since leaving Portsmouth. It became a home away from home for them in all respects but one - the exception being Frank Matthews. Right from the start both children feared him. They saw him as a total contrast to Nellie, as cruel, selfish and hard as she was kind, loving and gentle. His curly black hair and thick black eyebrows above deep set dark brown eyes gave him a forbidding countenance. He let them know at once that it was not his idea to have them in his home, but if they had to be there they should keep out of his way and not aggravate him. They did their best to avoid him as much as possible, and to both of them Nellie more than made up for his meanness with her sunny and cheerful disposition.

Up at the crack of dawn every day, never without a clean pretty apron, Nellie worked like a beaver, always singing as she worked. She polished the black lead grate until it shone, sewed bright cushion covers and curtains for the home, cleaned, polished, washed and ironed, gardened and cooked. Her cooking was the best either child had ever tasted - even better than Cook's. Apart from her own work, three days a week she cleaned house for the farmer's wife and took in sewing from the neighbourhood. They had three cats and two dogs - an Old English Bobtail named Ruffles and a Springer Spaniel named Uncle. Ruffles never came indoors because it was too hot for him with his dense coat.

The cats had names too, but Jenny was never quite sure what they were since they constantly changed. Nellie made up songs about the animals as she went about her daily chores and the cats ended up with different names each time she made up a song for them.

Frank's brother Alf lived with the Matthews. Smaller, light haired, very quiet and shy, he was a complete contrast to his older brother. He was so unassuming it was almost as if he wasn't there most of the time. Jenny liked Alf, though she found it hard to believe he was Frank's real brother. Not only were they different in their ways, they were also completely unalike in looks. It was Alf who slept in the single bed in the front room.

Jenny was pleased to have Verna in the same room with her at night. The man behind the wardrobe waiting to harm her had been a constant fear at the Williamsons. Here there was no wardrobe and there was company in the room, although Verna made changeable company. At times she appeared very friendly and wanted to talk, but at other times she wouldn't answer Jenny when she spoke to her, turning over in her bed to face the opposite wall with her back to Jenny.

"Why don't you like me?" Jenny asked her after one such rebuff. "Don't you like me in your bedroom? Do you want me to ask your mum if I can sleep somewhere else?"

"Who said I didn't like you? I don't care where you sleep. I don't want to talk that's all."

Jenny could get no more out of her and was puzzled as to what she could do to make friends with this funny girl. She didn't really like her much, preferring Fredda to Verna. But Fredda was gone and Jenny was going to have to live with Verna so she wanted to be friends. Even after school and at weekends it was difficult to know whether she would be willing to play with them, or whether she would say she would play with Jenny and not Jimmy, or if she would simply go off to find other friends and leave Jenny alone. They didn't go to school together since Verna went to the local school while Jimmy and Jenny were still being taught in the village hall. Being in separate schools didn't help them to get to know one another. One thing Jenny did soon learn about Verna, however, was that she had a bad temper and could get into terrible rages.

"You get up off that floor and put your coat on this minute you little sod. You're going to school if I have to drag you all the way myself."

"No! No! No! I won't! I won't."

Upstairs finishing dressing after breakfast, Jenny heard the commotion going on downstairs. Dashing out of the bedroom she collided with Jimmy and together they rushed downstairs. Out in the washroom Verna was on her back on the floor, screaming and lashing out at Nellie's legs with her feet.

"You little bugger - I'll get you off that floor."

Although not often given to swearing, when badly provoked Nellie could cuss as well as anyone. She disappeared out the back door, returning almost immediately carrying the outside besom - what the children referred to as the witch's broom. Bending over Verna, she yanked her to her feet, spun her around and gave her a push. As Verna staggered down the passage, Nellie whacked her across the backside with the besom.

"Now get your damn coat on and go!"

Verna snatched her coat off the peg on the wall and started struggling into it, still screaming "I'm not going, I'm not going, so there!"

Nellie ran at her brandishing the besom. Coat half on, Verna dashed through the door into the living room, round the table, out the other door, out the front door down the path, through the gate and up the road. Nellie raced in hot pursuit, brandishing the besom and thwacking at Verna as she ran. Jimmy and Jenny had watched the whole performance in astonished silence. They had never seen Nellie so angry and now Jenny was afraid. Perhaps she was going to come back and whack her too.

She needn't have worried. Nellie returned in a few minutes laughing. "Little bugger," she said to them. "I'll teach her whether she goes to school or not."

"What was the matter with Verna?" Jenny asked.

"Oh I don't know. She just decided she didn't want to go to school, but she won't get the better of me. Don't look so worried, I'm not really angry. Put your coats on now and get off to school."

That was how Nellie was, they discovered. It took a great deal of provocation to anger her and even then she was never cross for long. Verna was the one who caused her most aggravation but with Frank it was the opposite way round. Verna got away with a lot but Jimmy and Jenny could never do anything right - especially Jimmy.

Jimmy got on the wrong side of Frank quite early in their stay. Frank went rabbiting on Saturdays, setting out in the early morning with the dogs, a sack containing squirming ferrets slung over one shoulder. Returning in late afternoon he carried the sack of ferrets in his hand, while over his shoulder he held a long stick from which hung three or more dead rabbits, their hind legs crossed over the stick. Gaping holes evidenced where their stomachs and intestines had once been. Baked rabbit soon became the favourite meal of all three children.

Although both evacuees often helped Verna feed and clean out her rabbits and even collected food from the hedgerows for them, somehow neither of them related these rabbits to the ones Frank brought home. Verna had a white and a grey angora in one hutch. Their long soft hair had to be brushed and combed at least twice a week. In another hutch was a blue bevran and the third hutch contained two shaggy black and white rabbits. Verna was quite willing for Jimmy and Jenny to play with her rabbits and help her look after them. The rabbits had names and were pets. The wild ones Frank brought home on a stick were always brown and short haired. With their long limp bodies and lifeless black eyes, to the children they didn't resemble real rabbits at all.

"Thee's want to come rabbitin' wi' I the morrow?" Frank asked Jimmy one Friday evening.

"What did you say?" Jimmy asked.

Frank sighed. "I said DOS'T THEE WANNA COME RABBITIN' ALONG A ME THE MORRER? The boy's half daft," he added to no-one in particular.

Both children were still having difficulty with the strange Wiltshire accent and the peculiar words the villagers used. Most women, they found, didn't speak as broadly as the men and were more understandable. Nellie, and even Verna, did help them to understand when they asked. Verna giggling at their silliness in not understanding what was, to her, plain English. Verna giggled a great deal. They learned 'dos't' meant 'do you' and 'dosn't' meant 'do you not', 'cans't' meant 'can you' whilst 'casn't' meant 'can you not'. 'Bis't' meant 'are you' and 'bisn't' 'are you not'. 'Gwan' was 'going', and they seldom used the word 'with', instead saying either 'a' or 'wi'. They also used 'I' instead of 'me' and 'thee' for 'you'. It was very confusing to Jimmy and Jenny who constantly found themselves saying "pardon" or "what did you say?"

Struggling to interpret what Frank had asked him and stung by being referred to as daft, Jimmy reddened. "Oh, yes, I'd like to come rabbiting with you tomorrow," he said; not really sure that he did want to go but not wanting to make Frank any crosser either.

"Be up at six then or I'll go wi'out 'ee," Frank told him.

Jimmy was up and ready to go in plenty of time. Nellie packed lunches for them and Frank, Alf, Jimmy and the dogs set off for the hills. They returned in late afternoon while Nellie and the two girls worked in the garden.

"Here they come," called Jenny, spotting them as they rounded the corner. Running to the gate to greet them, she was shocked at Jimmy's appearance. Apart from being grubby, he had obviously been crying and was in some distress.

"What's the matter, Jimmy. Did you hurt yourself?" she asked.

Jimmy didn't answer, He pushed by her and ran into the house.

"What's up with the lad?" Nellie asked Frank.

"Ha!" Frank snorted. "What's up wi' 'im is right." Saying no more he walked into the woodshed attached to the side of the house. Alf swiftly disappeared round the back of the house looking embarrassed.

Jenny felt very uncomfortable. Jimmy seemed pretty upset but she thought it better not to follow him and ask any more questions. Nothing more was said until they were all sitting around the table for tea. Jimmy had cleaned himself up but was pale and quiet.

"Well boy, bis't gwan to tell thee sister about thy day out?" Frank asked Jimmy.

Jimmy hung his head and said nothing.

"Noo?" Frank goaded. "Then p'raps I better tell 'em for thee."

Jimmy got up and ran through the kitchen towards the stairs.

"GET BACK IN HERE BOY!" Frank roared at him. "Don't thee get up from this table until thee bis't told or I'll tan thy bloody hide," he raged as Jimmy crept back to his place.

"Our brave young feller 'ere comes rabbitin this mornin'." he announced to everyone. "'Afore us went ferretin' we went to check the traps. First one we comes to 'as a rabbit caught by the foot. 'Oh,' says our 'ero 'ere. 'Poor little thing.' I took the trap off its foot. 'I'll wring its neck and it soon won't be no poor little thing, it'll be somebody's dinner,' I told 'e. Next thing 'e throws 'isself at I, pullin' at the bloody rabbit - 'Don't hurt the baby bunny' 'e says, howlin' like a bleedin' girl. 'Don't hurt the baby bunny'."

"Ain't that right boy - speak up! Don't hurt the baby bunny," he repeated in a girlish voice.

"I wrung its neck, slit its belly and gutted it. Big boy 'ere turns green and throws up all over the place. A right day we 'ad after that. Bloody kid's no use to man nor beast."

There was an embarrassed silence as he finished his tale. Jenny felt sick to her stomach at the ugly story. She would have cried too if she had been there to see the rabbits hurt, she knew. Those dead things on the stick had suddenly become real to her as they must have done to Jimmy. Sympathy for her brother in his humiliation mingled with growing anger at Frank for being so cruel. She glowered at him, dropping her eyes immediately to her plate. She would like to shout at him but didn't dare. She was mortally afraid of him. He was so strong and wiry and when he turned his wrath on you his eyes seemed to turn black with hatred. He startled everyone by throwing his head back and emitting a loud laugh. "Baby bunny, my ass," he roared. "Ha, ha, ha." That was just like Frank, he didn't laugh at funny things. If someone was hurt or distressed, especially if he was the cause, he laughed a loud mirthless laugh. Never otherwise.

In the evenings Frank slumped himself down in his chair on top of the fire, legs stretched out so that no-one else could feel its heat. Reading the paper or listening to the wireless he smoked one Woodbine after another as the fire burned lower and lower.

"Nell! This bloody fire's goin' out," he would shout.

Nellie would drop what she was doing to clamber over Frank's legs and reach for the full coal scuttle by his elbow. Lifting the ring from the top of the stove she shovelled the coal in. Then she would go out to the washhouse to wash her hands and get back to her sewing or whatever she had been doing.

"Why dos't let the damn fire get so low?" Frank would grumble. "Now it will be bloody ages before it warms up again."

"I'm not sitting there watching it am I?" was as much answering back as Nellie would venture.

Jenny found herself seething at such times. I'd let the fire go out or tell him to make it up himself if he was my husband, she thought. She wondered why someone as nice as Nellie had married such a nasty man.

In the evening after the 'bunny' incident, she heard Jimmy crying in his room. She crept along the landing to him but he wouldn't talk to her.

"I hate Frank too'" she told Jimmy. "I wish I could hit him for you but he would kill me."

Jimmy threw himself onto his face and buried his head in his pillow. "Get out and leave me alone," was all she got for her proffered sympathy.

ELEVEN

On Jenny's seventh birthday in May, her mother sent her a book, some hair ribbons and a letter. She could read some of the letter but still needed help from Jimmy or Nellie. Jenny had been hoping her mother would come to see her on her birthday because she hadn't been for over six weeks. However, Mummy said she could not visit for a while yet. She had sold the house, she said, and was now working in a hotel in Cornwall and it was difficult to get up to see them. Jenny was horrified at the news that their house was sold. How could they go home now? And how would Daddy know where to find them if the house was gone?

"Why did Mummy sell the house? Now we can't ever go home can we," she said sadly to Jimmy. She didn't want to mention their dad because only she knew he was really alive.

"I don't know," he said. "I suppose we will get another house after the war. How do I know why Mum sold our house." He didn't look any too happy about it she noticed. Perhaps he was worried that they might not go home too. Even though she was beginning to love Nellie, Jenny couldn't bear to think they would never go home and be all together again. Nellie tried to make her birthday a happy one, baking her a special cake and singing a silly song she made up for her, but nothing could lift the heavy feeling in her heart after reading the letter.

Other events soon pushed the loss of their house to the back of the children's minds. The 'home kids' were moved from the house on the main road and dispersed. Some returned to their homes and others were moved further up the valley. The villagers had been disgruntled at the use of their hall for a school. They needed it for other things such as ARP and Home Guard meetings, Women's Institute meetings, socials, dances, etc. With the 'home kids' gone there was no longer a need to use the hall for schooling so the remainder of the evacuees were to be integrated into the village school system.

Arriving on the first morning with Verna, Jenny's heart sank as she saw again the tall dark building where they had been picked over like animals. The noise of the other children shrieking as they ran around the playground and between the trees did little to dispel her sense of foreboding. A lady, who she later learned was the head teacher, Mrs. Mergrin, clanged a loud hand bell and immediately all the children stopped playing and lined up in four rows. They filed up the stone steps to an open door, pointed at the top like a church door. The room they entered this time was a great deal larger than the one they had sat around in a semicircle, the ceiling even higher. This one was known as the 'big room' and the other as the 'little room'. Infants aged five and six were taught in the 'little room' and juniors, seven to ten years, occupied the 'big room'. A large pot bellied stove surrounded by an iron guard rail stood just inside the door to the left. Beyond that was the big teacher's desk in front of which, starting from the far left wall down to about 20 feet from the right wall, were rows and rows of desks facing two blackboards on the wall behind the teacher's position. Another blackboard on an easel stood to the right of the door.

Once the local children were all settled at their desks, Mrs. Mergrin spoke to the nine evacuees standing huddled by the door.

"My name is Mrs. Mergrin and I will be your teacher from now on," she told them. "I want each of you to come to my table in turn, give me your name, address and birthday, then I will tell you where to sit. Memorize your place once it has been given to you. I don't want anyone coming to me saying he or she has forgotten where they sit."

"My name is Jenny Harding and I'm seven. I live with Verna Matthews and Jimmy but I don't know what the address is called," Jenny said when it was her turn.

"I see," Mrs. Mergrin said, looking at her over her half glasses. "As it happens I do know the Matthews' address. Perhaps you had better find it out for yourself and remember. You also need to learn some grammar it seems."

Mrs. Mergrin was very strict, they soon learned. She carried a heavy ruler with her at all times which she didn't fail to bring down on unsuspecting knuckles when she spotted a mistake or caught anyone not paying attention. From the start Jenny didn't like her, nor did she like many of the village children they were now forced to associate with. They were still hostile to the evacuees for the most part, calling them names, pulling their hair and ostracizing them from their games. Even Verna wouldn't talk to her at school although they were getting on better at home now. A large part of the reason for Verna's hostility was her cousin Daisy.

The road to the Matthews' house began at a crossroads. The road directly opposite housed the post office and general store on the left corner and ended at the farm where Frank worked. Of the two other roads that formed the crossroads, one turned left and wound around until it met the main road, and the other, known locally as the Drove, narrowed to become an unpaved lane which continued up hill and down dale until it met the main Blandford Road four miles away. Nellie's sister Doris had come from London to a house off the Blandford Road at the outset of war. Her daughter, Daisy, had to make the long trek all the way down the muddy, rutted Drove every schoolday morning shod in her wellington boots. She left her shoes at Nellie's house and called in every morning to change into her shoes, changing back to her 'wellies' in the afternoon to walk the four miles home. Daisy was ten years old and a bully.

Nellie gave Daisy a cup of tea and toast each morning, then she and Verna usually walked to school together. When Jimmy and Jenny first started going to the village school they all went together and all was well for a few days. Then Jimmy made friends with a couple of evacuee boys and went with them instead. From then on Daisy began to bully Jenny. She found the slightest excuses to slap Jenny around, push her into bushes, knock her down and always swore at her and called her names. She forbade Verna to speak to Jenny at all, either at school or at home. The fact that she wasn't at home in the evenings to see whether Verna spoke to Jenny or not didn't seem to matter to Verna. Daisy said she would know if Verna disobeyed her and would 'clout' her the next day if she found out. Daisy was strong, standing head and shoulders taller than Jenny and it was obvious that Verna was afraid of her and wanted to stay in her good books.

Jenny's life was being made miserable by Daisy and by the fact that Verna refused to speak to her. She asked Jimmy to start coming to school with them again and he did for a couple of days, then got fed up and wanted to re-join his new friends. They had teased Jimmy about going back to walk with his sister and he didn't like that. Jenny's stomach started turning each morning as Daisy arrived, especially after those afternoons on the way home when she had promised Jenny she would get 'a bloody good clouting' the next morning.

"I don't like Daisy, she keeps on hitting me on the way to school and back." she told Nellie.

"Oh, does she?" Nellie said. "Well I don't suppose there is anything I can do about it. If I talk to her she will probably only punish you more. Try not to show her you care and just stick it out. She will be leaving this school when it breaks up the last week in July and going on to the elementary school up the valley. That's only another couple of months so try to do your best to ignore her."

That was all very well for Nellie to say. To Jenny two whole months of being pinched and punched and pushed around was a long, long time. She started to sleep badly, and although she had not had the ball nightmare for some time, another recurrent one came to take its place.

She would be walking with Daisy and Verna along Sandy Lane, a narrow lane covered in small stones and orange coloured gravel which was their usual route to school. Then Daisy and Verna would be gone and she would be walking alone. Behind her she would hear panting noises and running feet. Turning, there would be a man, so black his eyeballs shone white in the moonlight. He had a knife in his raised hand and was running after her to stab it into her back. Attempting to run from him her legs moved so slowly that the strain of forcing one leg painfully in front of the other made the veins swell in her neck and her heart pump madly. Trying to scream in terror, her voice wouldn't obey her, nothing but a small squeak escaping her lips. Just as the man was about to grab her she would wake, sweating with fear and frustration, scarcely able to breathe. Deafened by the pounding in her ears, she would lie still until she could hear Verna's even breathing, muttering a little prayer of thanks that she was not alone.

"Ration Books! What next are they going to think up to complicate our lives," Nellie muttered, looking at the little buff booklets she held in her hand.

"What are ration books? What do you have to do with them?" Jenny asked her. She was helping Nellie today, peeling potatoes in a bowl on the kitchen table, the only sink in the house being the one in the washhouse.

"Food has gone on ration now," Nellie explained to her. We are only allowed tiny amounts of butter and sugar and meat and just about everything. We have to register with a shop and that will be the only place we can get groceries. These silly little books are full of coupons that have to be stamped or cut out when we have got our rations. There isn't going to be so much food about so we will have to pull in our belts."

"Why isn't there so much food about? Is it because of the war?"

"That's right. The ships that bring food to us can't get through without being bombed and sunk, so now we have to give coupons for everything".

Jenny thought about that for a moment. "Well, that will be good won't it? If we have to give coupons for food instead of money, you can save up lots and be rich."

"Oh," Nellie laughed, "yes, that would be good. It doesn't work like that I'm afraid - we have to give coupons *and* money, and far from being rich, everything is going up so we will be poorer."

"That's not fair. They shouldn't make us give coupons then, if we still have to pay."

"Yes it is fair. It's a nuisance but it's fair because it makes sure everybody gets a share. If they didn't do that the rich people would buy up all the best food and us plain folks would go hungry."

TWELVE

The war hadn't really touched them in the country. Apart from the search lights that had recently come to the Drove and the sound of planes droning overhead, there was little reminder of the war. There was blackout of course. At dusk everyone had to pull black blinds down over their windows and switch off lights if they opened outside doors. On moonless nights it was completely black outdoors at night. Going to the lavatory was done in pairs where possible, one standing 'cavey' outside while the other used the lav and vice versa. It was too scary to go alone, running into cobwebs across the path, the damson branches clutching your hair, and the ever present fear of bats and bogey men.

The search lights were about a half mile up the Drove. Manned by soldiers housed in specially built Nissen huts they sent their great beams skywards in the night, crossing and recrossing each other to trap enemy aircraft. Then the guns would go off, shooting at planes caught in the beams. If they brought any down, which was not very often, people would go over the hills on a search the following day, bringing home pieces of shrapnel as souvenirs.

Church bells were not allowed to ring on Sundays any more. Instead they were used as warnings of possible air raids in the country where there were no sirens. If the bells rang out in the night, everyone was supposed to get out of bed and take shelter - 'shelter' being under the kitchen table or under the stairs or any other stout piece of furniture or portion of the house considered suitable. The first time this happened Nellie had great difficulty waking Jenny. Once asleep, Jenny was a very heavy sleeper. It was exciting all being huddled under the kitchen table when you were supposed to be asleep in bed. (All except Frank that was, who refused to be routed from his bed). They sang songs and Nellie told stories until someone banged on the door shouting 'All Clear!' The second time, Nellie could not waken Jenny at all and the first Jenny knew of the excitement was in the morning when it was all over. She felt quite put out to think that Nellie would leave her in bed to be blown up.

"Don't you love me any more," she asked her. "I could have been killed in my bed all by myself last night."

"No such thing," Nellie told her. "You looked so peaceful I didn't want to disturb you. Its all a farce anyway, no-one is going to drop any bombs on us here. We won't be getting up any more - to heck with it."

Another aggravation of the war was the gasmask. Everyone had been issued a gasmask early in the war. The children had been constantly told they would soon have gasmask drill, but never had until shortly after Jimmy and Jenny started attending the village school. Jenny would ever remember it as one of the most traumatic experiences of her young life. She had looked at the gasmask once, decided she didn't like it at all and never taken it from its box again. The day of the drill the children stood in lines in the empty space on the right of the Big Room and were ordered to take the masks from their boxes and hold them out in front of their faces. Mrs. Mergrin demonstrated how to put the strap over the head while holding onto the short snout with the other hand. She lifted her chin, inserting it into the mask, pulled back on the strap at the same time wiggling the snout to settle it on her face. Then she gave a little flip to the black rubber sides so the mask fit flush to her face. Turning her head from side to side, looking at the children through the little perspex window across the eyes brought a rash of giggling from the assembled class. She looked so foolish standing there in a black rubber mask, its protruding metal snout punctured with small round holes.

"Silence!" she said, holding up her hand, her voice muffled and indistinct.

Lifting the mask by the snout, she pulled it back over her head and stared sternly at the children. "Now that was not at all difficult. Everyone please do as I did and fit your masks on."

Jenny struggled to get into hers, but easy as it had looked when Mrs. Mergrin did it, she couldn't get it on.

"What are you doing? Weren't you paying attention to my demonstration?" An angry Mrs. Mergrin was standing in front of her.

She pulled the mask from Jenny's hand, pushed the strap over her head, pulling on the front so hard that Jenny staggered. Then she pushed it over her chin and flicked the sides.

Immediate panic assailed Jenny. An overpowering stench of rubber and an inability to breathe overtook her at once and she tore the mask from her face. Mrs. Mergrin raged.

"Don't you dare do that," she snapped. "Put it on yourself this time." Jenny stood rooted to the spot, not moving.

"You stupid child. Come here." Mrs. Mergrin yanked her forward by the hair and once again forced the mask on her face. In blind panic, Jenny tore it off, this time hurtling it across the floor.

"I can't, I can't," she cried. "I can't breathe."

"Pick that gasmask up and go and stand outside in the porch," Mrs. Mergrin commanded. "I can't have anyone disrupting this drill. Stand in the porch and I'll deal with you later."

Jenny picked up the mask and went to stand in the porch. The suffocating smell of rubber had reminded her of two occasions when she had smelled a similar smell, both of them fraught with fear. The first had been when she had been taken to the dentist at the age of four. Jimmy had been to the dentist a short while previously and had been so good the dentist had given him a tooth brush. Jenny wanted a tooth brush too and determined to be as good as Jimmy. She had needed some fillings but as soon as she had felt metal instruments banging against her teeth she had panicked, kicking at the dentist and screaming so that he had refused to treat her. Her mother had then obtained another dentist who came to the house, laid her on a table in the spare bedroom, fitted a mask over her face that smelled of rubber and proceeded to pour some evil smelling liquid on the mask. She had tried to fight but had soon become unconscious. She awoke in her own bed minus five teeth, sick, bleeding and sore.

The second occasion was a few months later when she had been taken to hospital to have her tonsils and adenoids removed. This time she had been laid on what appeared to her to be an enamel stove. Once again the mask was applied to her face but this time she knew what they were going to do. She fought like a banshee and it had taken five nurses to hold down her flailing arms and legs before she gave in to unconsciousness. After the operation they had brought her a kidney shaped bowl to be sick in. She had not been sick. That is, not until her mother came to fetch her. Then she had been sick in the taxi - all over her mother's fur coat, for which sin she had been severely chastised. There was no way she was ever going to have a mask over her face again, choking off her breath and suffocating her.

When the others had completed the drill, Mrs. Mergrin called her back into class. "The purpose of the exercise is to teach you how to wear the mask so that if we are subjected to a gas attack you will survive. If you don't wear a gasmask, the gas will kill you. Do you want to die?"

To Jenny, the choice of whether to wear the mask or die was no choice at all. She didn't want to do either.

In front of the whole class, Mrs. Mergrin attempted to fit the mask on Jenny's face yet again, and yet again the rubbery stench nauseated her and blind panic won the day. Mrs. Mergrin was no match for Jenny in such a terrified state, the mask ending up on the floor for the second time.

"All right," Mrs. Mergrin said. "If you want to die, so be it. Put that mask back in the box and take your place."

For Jenny the choice was made. To die or wear the mask? She would have to die.

Although she never again took the mask from its box, she, like everyone, still had to carry it everywhere she went. The square buff coloured box hanging from the shoulder on a piece of string was uniform, causing countless accidents from being swung into people or tripped over. Whenever gasmask drill was held, Jenny was excused while Mrs. Mergrin announced to everyone that Jenny Harding preferred to die.

Jenny didn't really care that she had been shown up in class, her biggest regret of that day being that Jimmy was ashamed of her performance and refused to speak to her all that evening.

At six each evening Frank turned on the wireless to listen to the news and whilst he listened everyone had to creep around like mice. News meant little to the children. They heard names such as Churchill, Montgomery, Hitler, Mussolini, and knew that Churchill was boss of the war for England and Hitler was the horrible German who started the war. Nellie said that the ordinary German people didn't want to fight any more than the English people did. To Jenny's mind, if all these people didn't want to fight it would make more sense for someone to shoot Hitler and let them all go home. It was such a simple thing to do, she thought, wondering why grown-up's made everything so difficult.

Frank refused to join the Home Guard like many of the men in the village. "Bloody daft," was his opinion. "What the hell they think they'm gonna do if the war get to 'ere beats me. They think they'm gonna fight all them bombs an' fancy guns that 'itler's got wi' a couple of pitch forks. They'm all bloody daft. Catch me runnin' round the fields wi' a damn pitch fork, fallin' down rabbit 'oles an' kissin the ground. If I see any bloody parachuters I'll just shoot the buggers."

Jenny believed he would do just that. He often took his gun out with him to shoot hares, foxes and sometimes rabbits. He didn't like to shoot rabbits because the pellets that got stuck in them could break your teeth when you ate them. But she had seen him shoot foxes when they came to try to steal the chickens that ran free range in the field behind the house. At night the chickens were shut in their wooden houses but the foxes sometimes managed to get in and take some for their suppers. If Frank saw any around they didn't live long.

One thing they were never short of despite food rationing was eggs. Nellie said that people in towns who didn't keep chickens were rationed to one egg a week, but they always had plenty. When the hens weren't laying well enough they ate them too and bought more laying hens to replace them.

THIRTEEN

Daisy was still the bane of her life and for Jenny the school holidays couldn't come soon enough. She tried to remember Nellie's advice and not cry, because the more she cried the more Daisy teased her; but it wasn't easy and she did often end up in tears. Eventually the weeks passed and school broke up bringing welcome relief.

Verna quickly woke up to the fact that her protector had now left her and she became much more friendly. Together the three of them played in the sun, took sandwiches for picnics, climbed trees and explored. Holidays were good times to get shoes repaired. Verna and Jenny were given the task of taking their school shoes to Potter, the local shoe maker. Jenny had reason to remember where he lived since that was where Jimmy had pushed her into the muddy ditch. They sat on a bench in Potter's little shed to watch and wait for their shoes to be mended. They were fascinated by the iron contraption he used, like a cross with four different sized feet on each arm. Wheezing as he worked, Potter astounded Jenny by suddenly lifting one leg to lay it across a bench in front of him and proceed to tap nails straight into his leg.

"Ahhh," she cried in horror.

"What's up, maid," he asked, his wrinkled face breaking into a grin. "Casn't stick nails into thy leg 'en?"

"No I can't," Jenny said, feeling her eyes widen in disbelief.

Potter threw back his head. His tangled grey mane shaking and his large paunch wobbling up and down as he laughed. "Lookie here then," he said, rolling up one trouser leg to reveal a wooden peg leg. "If thee's had one of they, thee could stick nails in 'un too."

"Oh! What happened to your real leg,"

Potter then proceeded to tell them how he had been a pirate and had his leg shot off by cannon balls when he was raiding a ship. He said he had been caught and put in jail for ten years where he had nothing to live on but bread and water. Full of the romantic tale, they relayed it to Nellie when they got home.

"Ho!" she exclaimed. "Don't you go believing any of that rubbish. Potter's never been out of this village to start with. He lost his leg falling downstairs when he was a little boy. He tells all sorts of tales about his peg leg but its only in fun."

Only mildly disappointed that the wonderful tale was not true, the children soon forgot about it in the excitement of the harvest. Frank actually allowed them to help with the harvest and it was the greatest fun yet in Jenny's life. A damper was put on things for the first two days because Jimmy wasn't allowed to go. He was being punished. It all came about because of some cheese.

Frank had his own enamel plate and his own fork with a black bone handle. No-one else could use these items. No matter what Nellie prepared for supper, as soon as Frank got home from work he always wanted a plate of melted cheese. Half an hour before he was due home, Nellie placed sliced cheese on his plate, setting it on the range to melt. Not until Frank had eaten his cheese was supper permitted to be taken. When cheese went on ration Frank had eaten his allowance in two days, even though Nellie sliced it thinner than before. Life was not worth living if Frank didn't have his cheese so everyone agreed to forego cheese to placate Frank - all except Alf. Nellie refused to use Alf's ration saying he needed cheese to take in his sandwiches. Frank's melted cheese always smelled so good and one evening Jimmy ventured to ask Frank if it tasted good.

"Why? Want some do 'ee, lad?" Frank asked.

Unable to believe his ears, Jimmy said yes, he would like some.

"Open up then", Frank said, dipping his fork into the centre of the plate, winding off some gooey cheese and shoving it into Jimmy's mouth.

Jimmy screamed as the hot cheese seared his tongue. Tearing at his mouth, he rushed for the washhouse to pump cold water over his tongue. Tears streaming down his face, he returned to the living room. "You bloody asshole!" he yelled at Frank who was roaring with laughter.

Chair clattering to the floor, Frank was up and around the table in a flash, unbuckling his thick leather belt as he went.

"Don't you swear at me, you little shit," he roared, lashing at Jimmy with the belt. Jimmy tore up the stairs, slamming the bedroom door behind him. Frank ran after him and gave him several swipes across the backside, confining him to his bedroom, except for mealtimes, for a whole week.

Jenny hated Frank when he was so cruel. He had burned Jimmy on purpose and then punished him for answering back. She wished she was big enough to punch Frank and black his eyes. When he said they could help with the harvest, however, she half forgave him for the cheese incident.

Harvesting the corn was a mixture of hard work and carefree frolicking. As the tractors worked in a circular motion from the outside of the field toward the centre, cutting down the standing corn which the men tied into bales, rabbits, hares, foxes, mice and other animals dashed out, zig-zagging across the fields with the dogs in hot pursuit. The dogs caught a few mice but little else, enjoying themselves immensely in the effort. The men and children walked behind the tractor lifting the bales and stooking them into hiles to lean against one another for the sun to dry. A few days later the heavy horses trundled round the field drawing carts, into which the bales were tossed. The horses pulled the full carts to a corner of the field where the bales were then stacked into ricks to await threshing.

At midday the children sat against the tractors and carts with the men to eat thick slabs of bread, pieces of ham and chicken or cold rabbit, all washed down with water and cider, which made the children a little giddy. Their skin browned and both Jenny and Jimmy's hair turned almost white. Verna's hair took on a golden glow. They were scratched, torn and bleeding from the rough stubble and coarse corn stalks but they loved every moment.

It was during the summer holidays that Jenny fell in love. The unlikely object of her undying affection was the big black cart horse named Boxer. The thought of falling in love with a horse had never occurred to her because in reality she was afraid of the creatures. Her only close contact with a horse had been when she was three. Running down her street one day towards home she had to pass the vegetable man's horse and cart that was stopped outside a house. She passed the cart and was about to pass the horse when it turned its blinkered head to look at her. Frozen to the spot with fear she was certain it meant to bite her. Her screams brought the vegetable man running to her aid. "Lordy, lordy, what's all the carry on? Did you hurt yourself love?" he had asked.

"That horse is going to eat me," she had screamed. "Look, he's looking at me again."

"No, he's not going to eat you. He's a friendly old fella. He eats oats, not people," he had told her, laughing.

The man took her hand and guided her past the horse who, seeing his master walk away began to follow them. That was enough for Jenny. Sure now the horse meant to bite her she snatched her hand from the man and raced home yelling in fear, slamming the door hard behind her. From then on she had kept well away from horses.

One of Alf's jobs was to look after the cart horses. He gave the children a ride home on the cart after the day's work, suggesting they stay and watch the horses have their collars and tackle removed and eat their suppers. Neither Jimmy nor Verna wanted to stay but Jenny hesitantly did because she liked Alf and thought he wanted someone to walk home with. There were two horses, Boxer and Kitty. Boxer was hugh and black, Kitty smaller and brown. Both had long manes and fluffy fringes on the backs of their feet. At first Jenny stayed well out of the way as they stamped and chomped while being undressed. When they stood at their mangers, snorting and crunching their oats, Alf suggested she come over and touch them.

"No," she said. "I'm afraid of horses."

"'Fraid 'o 'orses?" Alf sounded shocked. "You come 'ere 'an touch old Boxer. A kinder, nicer old fella you won't find. "E's soft as a bebby. Kitty's a different kettle 'o fish an you 'ave to watch 'er feet, but old Boxer 'ere wouldn't 'urt a flea."

Reluctantly she had touched Boxer's front shoulder. Alf told her to touch his nose and feel how soft it was. She did, and jumped as Boxer snorted, blowing oat husks all over her.

"That's all right," Alf said. "E's just sayin 'ello. Why don't you sit on 'is back? 'Ere, I'll give you a bunk."

Before she had time to refuse, Alf had hoisted her onto Boxer's expansive back. Horsy smelling steamy heat rose around her and his big body moved beneath her as he swayed and stamped his feet. She liked the smell of him. In fact the smell of sweaty horses and horse manure soon became her favourite perfume. Horse manure smelled vastly different from the stinky cow pats they often trod in when crossing the fields. These, when dried, they called pancakes and kicked them around, but when wet they smelled foul and stained your shoes - and clothes if you fell in them! Horse manure was nothing like that.

Once deciding that she liked Boxer and the smell of horses, she stayed every evening waiting for the horses to finish supper. Then Alf would hoist her onto Boxer's back, open the yard gates and turn both horses loose. Together they would trot down the road, Boxer leading with Jenny aboard and Kitty trotting behind. Turning left they continued along the road, turned right, trotting down another road and through the open gate to the field beside Nellie's house. There Boxer waited for Jenny to clamber off onto the gate before moving down the field to roll in the grass. Soon Jenny was in love with the loveliest horse in the world. Nellie didn't share her enthusiasm about the smell of horses, pinching her nose and saying "Pooh!" when Jenny came in stinking of horse sweat.

Becoming quite emboldened, Jenny wanted to try riding Kitty one evening. Kitty was full of tricks. First she cut the corner very sharply so that Jenny had to draw her leg up quickly to avoid getting it crushed against the wall, then, when they got to the field she didn't stop. Instead, she carried on down the field and ran beneath a tree with low branches trying to brush Jenny from her back. Jenny had flattened herself so that the branches scraped her back but didn't unseat her. The field slanted downwards and Kitty kept running straight into the small stream at the bottom where she stopped so suddenly that Jenny shot over her head and into the stream. After that Jenny decided only to ride Boxer home. On days when he wasn't working and Jenny was at home, she sometimes sat on the field gate and called to Boxer. He always came to nuzzle against her chest and be stroked. If he jerked his head too hard and knocked her off the gate at times, she forgave him knowing he hadn't meant to do it.

Although the holidays, helping with the harvest and her new love for Boxer filled Jenny's life with happiness, there were moments when she felt disturbed. Their mother had come to see them twice in the early days of their stay with the Matthews, but since then she had not come and for some time now she had not even written. The second time she had visited she had spent most of the time talking with Nellie while Jimmy and Jenny played outside. When it was time for their mother to leave, Nellie had walked with her to the gate. It had struck Jenny then how tall her mother was. Still in her black coat and shoes, her dark hair close to her face in deep permed waves, she had looked very elegant. Nellie had appeared tiny beside mother.

If Jenny spoke of her concern to Jimmy he appeared not to be unduly bothered. "You know Mum has to work now and she doesn't get much time. She will be here before long." Nevertheless Jenny had a suspicion that he was more bothered than he let on. Many more planes were flying over at night and both children heard tales of bad bombings in places like London and Portsmouth. Their mother was not in Portsmouth now, and Nellie had said that Cornwall was a pretty safe place, but Jenny still worried and wanted to know for sure that her mother was safe.

The halcyon days of holidays and harvest came to an end for Jenny one week before they were to return to school. The reasons were twofold, one being an injury and the other an event that was to shatter the lives of herself and Jimmy still further.

The horses hadn't worked on Saturday. Jimmy and Verna had got a lift home sitting on the mudguards of the tractor. There had been no room for Jenny so she was walking the two miles down the rutted track. Most of the men had bicycles and had ridden off. Alf also had a bike but he was pushing it so he could walk with Jenny. After she had twice tripped over the hard ruts and fallen down, Alf suggested she sit on the bar of his bike and he would ride her home. Feeling weary after the long day in the fields, she readily agreed.

"All comfy now?" Alf asked as he settled her sideways on his bar. Not exactly 'comfy', she nodded her head. "Yes thanks."

As Alf leaned over her to grab the handle bars she had to bend forward. They got up speed down the Drove, bumping over the uneven ground. The bicycle bar bit into her leg and when she could stand it no longer she wriggled in an attempt to ease the pain. The bike wobbled off course and Jenny's left leg shot forward, her foot catching in the wheel spokes. Alf and Jenny somersaulted through the air as the bike turned over. Somehow Alf managed to grab her and roll himself over her before they thudded to earth. Winded, bruised, nose and mouth bleeding, Alf struggled to his feet. He spat a mixture of blood and teeth as he helped Jenny up. An excruciating pain shot through her foot as she attempted to stand but she was otherwise unhurt, Alf taking the brunt of the fall.

"Oh Alf, I'm sorry," she cried when she saw the state he was in. "I didn't mean to stick my foot in the wheel, are you hurt awful bad?"

"Don't worry, maid, you couldn't help it. T'was a daft thing to do anyways. Christ! Look at me poor bike."

The front wheel was all out of shape, the spokes bent and twisted. The handlebars had been turned sideways. A couple of men who had seen the accident came back to help, one carrying Jenny piggyback fashion and another lifting Alf's bike onto his shoulder to carry it while pushing his own. Frank laughed and refused to help, calling Alf a bloody fool for putting Jenny on the bar and Jenny an even bigger fool for sticking her foot in the wheel. Jenny's foot was badly swollen by the time they reached home and the next day it was black. She couldn't walk on it so Nellie made a bed for her on the sofa, putting pillows under her foot to keep it up.

That afternoon Nellie helped her hop into the kitchen and lifted her onto the table to replace the cold compress on her foot. As the sun streamed through the window behind her, Jenny noticed fine silvery hairs on Nellie's face. She hadn't realized Nellie had hair on her face, as far as she knew ladies never had hair on their faces. She reached out and gently stroked Nellie's face to see if she could feel them. She could, they were soft and downy. Touching her own face to feel if she had soft down too she felt only smooth skin. Puzzled, she touched Nellie again. Without warning a flood of love filled her whole being. The soft down made Nellie special, and she *was* special.

"What *are* you doing? Have I got soot on my face or something?" Nellie asked.

"No. I love you, Nellie." She threw her arms about Nellie as far as she could reach and leaned her head against her.

"What's all this? You are a funny little thing sometimes."

"Do you think I'm funny because I love you? I just do that's all."

"No of course I don't," Nellie said hugging her. "You're all right. You're a nice little girl really." "It's such a shame," she added.

Jenny thought that a strange thing to say. Why was it such a shame to be a nice little girl? "Why is it a shame?" she asked.

"Oh ... nothing," Nellie said, sounding odd. Jenny looked up at her and detected a glittering behind the glasses. Were those tears? Goose pimples replaced the glow of a few moments ago. She was about to ask what the matter was when Nellie suddenly changed the mood. "Well, I don't think you will die from your war wounds after all. Lets get you back on the sofa and you can read your books." She helped Jenny hop back then went back to cooking the supper, singing silly songs as usual.

Jenny couldn't forget the tears she had seen and wondered what had upset Nellie. The time for questions had passed but it bothered her.

The following day she was going to find out exactly what the trouble was.

FOURTEEN

The following morning Nellie told Jimmy he couldn't go harvesting because she needed him to do something for her. Disappointed, Jimmy asked what she wanted but she said she would tell him later. After the men had gone he asked again what he had to do and again Nellie said to wait. She told him he could go out to play for a while but not to go far away. All morning he was in and out, sometimes talking to Jenny, and both were mystified as to why Nellie said she needed him but gave him nothing to do.

Shortly before lunchtime Jenny heard the gate latch click and watched as a lady walked up the path to the front door. Nellie stayed outside talking to the lady for a while, then brought her into the living room at the same time calling for Jimmy to come in. As soon as he was inside, Nellie introduced the lady to them.

"This is Miss Gray, and she's come especially to talk to you two," she said. "I'll just pop and make a cup of tea as I'm sure Miss Gray must be thirsty."

As Nellie disappeared into the kitchen, Miss Gray sat down at the table and surprised the children by speaking their names.

"You are Jimmy and Jenny aren't you? You are surprised that I know your names I know, but we will get to that later. Tell me, what have you done to your poor foot?" she asked Jenny.

Jenny told her and they chatted about the holidays and the nice weather, while both children wondered why this person had come to talk to them. She seemed nice enough. Smartly dressed and wearing glasses, her fair hair short and straight, neither of them recognized her as anyone they should know. Nellie returned with the tea, suggesting that she should now go out in the garden and leave them to talk.

"I would rather you didn't if you don't mind. This might be a little easier if you were to stay."

Nellie looked concerned. "Oh ... well if you really want me to ..."

Miss Gray said she would prefer Nellie to stay, so Nellie sat herself at the opposite side of the table. Jenny looked at her brother to see if he looked as disturbed as she felt after hearing those words. He glanced at her and she noticed how large the blacks of his eyes had grown.

"Please sit on the sofa by your sister, Jimmy, because I have something to tell you," Miss Gray said. Jimmy did as he was bid and Miss Gray smiled at them both.

"As you know, my name is Miss Gray," she began. "I am what is known as a welfare worker. I have come from Bristol where I work for the Ministry of Pensions. The Ministry has many functions and my particular job is helping look after widows and orphans in that I recommend allocating funds and make visits to see that the cases on my list are managing and well cared for."

Jenny glanced at Jimmy again, wondering if he understood any better than she what Miss Gray was talking about. He was looking down at the floor and refused to meet her eye.

"Now you are probably wondering what all this has to do with you. Unfortunately it is my unpleasant duty to tell you that we have been unable to locate your mother for some considerable time. We were in contact with her after your father's death in order to arrange a pension for herself and for you two. For some time now she has not been making any contribution to the Matthews for your keep and try as we may we cannot find her."

"My mum works in a hotel in Cornwall. We know where she is don't we Jimmy! She has been busy and hasn't been able to come and see us," Jenny said. A feeling of hostility had risen up inside her at this person who seemed to be saying that her mother had run away. "Jimmy, tell Miss Gray where Mummy is." Looking across at Nellie she carried on. "Nellie knows too don't you. You can tell her where Mummy is."

"No dear, your mother is no longer in Cornwall to the best of our knowledge," Miss Gray told her. "We were aware that she did work in an hotel there but she left without telling the proprietor where she was going. The point is, although we are pretty certain she is still alive, for all intents and purposes you are both now considered orphans and we, the Ministry, will be taking responsibility for you."

"We are not orphans!" Jenny protested. She knew what orphans were because her mother had once told her that Daddy was an orphan and that it meant he didn't have a mother or father when he was little.

"Orphans are children with no parents and no-one to take care of them." Miss Gray went on to explain. Your mother's pension has now been stopped and the money will be used on your behalf. Poor Mr. and Mrs. Matthews have been struggling to keep you on their own income and that is not fair. From now on we shall see that they receive proper payment for you.

Jenny felt even more hostile. Jimmy was saying nothing to defend their mother and Jenny couldn't understand him.

"If orphans are children without parents and don't have anybody to take care of them, we aren't orphans," she repeated. "We have got parents and Nellie takes care of us so we aren't orphans," she said defiantly.

Looking over at Nellie Jenny discerned tears in her eyes for the second time in two days. Why didn't anyone say anything to help her? She didn't want to be called an orphan. First they had been called evacuees and now there was another label being stuck on them - and they were *not* orphans anyway. She tried to stand and run to Nellie, forgetting her foot until the pain reminded her and she fell down.

Nellie picked her up and sat her on her lap, putting her arm around her and squeezing her.

"Obviously this is hard for you to understand, and you are right - you are not orphans in the strict sense of the word since it is quite possible that your mother is still alive. Just the same you will be treated as such from now on. And yes, Mrs. Matthews has said she will continue to take care of you so you are luckier than many. In my job I have to tell many children that they have lost their parents and lots of them are in dreadful circumstances. It is an awful job and I dislike this part of it intensely, but someone has to do it. You appear to be two lovely children and it is beyond my comprehension why anyone should want to desert you. But you are fortunate that you have a good home here with Mr. and Mrs. Matthews."

"They *are* good kiddies and it's a damn shame," Nellie said with feeling. "Come over here, Jimmy lad," she called. Jimmy came to stand beside her and she put her other arm around him, kissing him on top of his head. "Don't you worry, we'll look after the pair of you," she said.

Jimmy hadn't spoken at all. Neither of them said goodbye to Miss Gray when she left. She told them Nellie had her address and they could write to her any time they wished. She said she would be coming to see them as often as work and travel time permitted and hoped they would forgive her for being the bearer of such bad news.

Jenny didn't know what to think. As Nellie walked to the gate with Miss Gray, she asked Jimmy why he hadn't said anything and if he thought it was true their mother had gone away. To her consternation Jimmy burst into tears and ran upstairs. Jimmy seldom cried and when he did Jenny always felt her heart rend in two. He was her big brother and if he cried she wanted to cry also. Now she didn't know what to think or do. Her mother wouldn't leave them for always unless something awful had happened to her, of that she was sure. Or at least she was sure Mummy wouldn't leave Jimmy. He was always the good one; it was she, Jenny who had been bad. Jimmy never had tantrums like she did, nor did he argue. No, Mummy wouldn't just leave them, something terrible had happened to her. Perhaps she was a prisoner too like Daddy. Perhaps Miss Gray knew that and wasn't going to tell them.

Verna wanted to know what had been going on when she came home. Nellie told her never mind, she would tell her later on. Jenny expected to be questioned in bed that night but Verna fell asleep almost immediately. Jenny lay on her back in the dark, trying to imagine what could have happened to her mother. Maybe she *had* run away because Jenny had been such a nuisance. She had after all once told Jenny she was the bane of her life. Jenny wasn't sure what 'bane' meant but thought it was something quite bad. Granny hadn't liked her either. She often told Jenny she was a bad girl.

Granny! Why hadn't she thought of that before! They weren't orphans anyway because they still had a Granny and Grandad! Leaping out of bed she rushed down to the living room. "Nellie, me and Jimmy aren't orphans because we still have my Gran and Grandad."

"What the 'ell dos't think thee's doin' down 'ere. Get on back to thy bed," Frank growled at her.

"Oh leave her be for once," Nellie chided. "Come here Jenny. What's all this about your Gran and Grandad? You have never mentioned them before."

"I just thought about it," she answered. "They live in Portsmouth but not near us. My Gran doesn't like me but she likes Jimmy. She used to bring him a Jaffa comic every week but she didn't bring me anything. My Grandad likes me though. He used to tickle my back because I liked it. If I stood by his chair he would tickle my back for ages. My Mum used to tell him off and say he shouldn't spoil me, but he didn't mind. They grow big black grapes outside their house and they've got two lots of stairs because their house is tall and has two lots of bedrooms. I gave my Grandad a skipping rope because he said he was getting too fat and wished he could skip like me. He wouldn't let me see him skip but he said he did it every morning."

"And do you know your Gran's address so we could write to her? Is she your mum's mother or your dad's mother do you know?" Nellie asked when she could get a word in.

"No. I can't remember the name of her road, but p'raps Jimmy does. My Gran is my mum's mum because my dad was an orphan. But we're not orphans. My Gran might know where Mummy is."

"Send that bloody kid up to bed Nell 'an let's 'ave some peace and quiet 'ere," Frank ordered.

"Off you go now," Nellie said. "We'll talk about it some more tomorrow. Enough's enough for one day."

FIFTEEN

Jimmy couldn't remember the name of their grandparents' street either when he was asked the following morning. In his opinion it wouldn't be much good trying to find them in any case. They wouldn't take them back to Portsmouth because it was still dangerous, and even if it wasn't he didn't think their Gran would want to look after them. "I don't want to live with Gran anyway," was his final comment.

That surprised Jenny because if their Gran had liked anyone, it was Jimmy. Jenny's own memories of her Gran were not good. She could well remember being heaved out of bed on more than one occasion of Gran's visits, being pushed into Jimmy's room and shown how neatly his clothes were folded on his chair while hers were strewn around her bedroom floor. Gran constantly upbraided Jenny for not being more like her brother. Her mother too dreaded Gran's visits because she was always criticizing and telling Mummy off. If Mummy had any new clothes she would hide them if Gran was coming because Gran shouted at her for wasting money. Jenny remembered one particular long shiny dance dress her mother made for herself. Jenny thought it lovely. When Mummy knew Gran was coming to visit she took the dress to the neighbour's house and told Jimmy and Jenny not to tell Gran about it. Jenny's memory of Gran was that she looked like a bird, a thin lady with sharp nose and piercing blue eyes.

Mummy had told them that she was an only child and that when she was little she wasn't allowed to play with the neighbours' children. Gran used to dress her in pretty dresses that she wasn't allowed to get dirty and she had to keep her hair tidy. Gran made her wear her hair in long ringlets. Mummy said that she used to watch the other children and wish she could play with them but Gran said she had to grow up to be a young lady.

Thinking it over in the cold light of day, Jenny decided that Jimmy was right as usual and she didn't want to live with her Gran either. If someone wrote to Gran she just might come and take them away and that wasn't such a good idea.

She told Nellie as much, saying that she really didn't like her Gran and perhaps they had better not look for her. Nellie said she understood, but on the other hand it might be wise to try to find out where her grandparents were so that they had at least *somebody* to contact. Otherwise it looked as if they had no relatives in the world at all. She said she would write to the Ministry and see what they thought.

"Jimmy, do you know what that Ministry of Pensions is that Miss Gray said was going to look after us?" Jenny asked her brother when she felt she could venture to talk to him about it. She didn't dare bring up the subject of their mother again, having done so the day after Miss Gray's visit. "She wouldn't just leave us, she's dead!" had been his only comment. The look he gave her then told her he wasn't going to discuss it any more. Now she wanted to know what this Ministry was.

"There's lots of Ministries," he said. "Ministry of Labour, Ministry of Food, Ministry of Pensions; you hear about them all the time on the wireless. They are just a lot of men who sit in offices at big desks scribbling on bits of paper. Pensions means money. That's all they care about - money. They aren't going to care about us."

"Oh, don't you think so? Who told you about Ministries then?"

"Nobody told me. I listen to the news sometimes and I know what they are."

Jimmy was so clever. He always knew so much and was getting on at school lots better than she was. "I wish I was clever like you," she said. "Why can't I know things like you do?"

"Because you never listen."

Thinking that one over, she had to agree he was right again. She really didn't listen properly to much that was said. She got bored and started daydreaming at school, couldn't be bothered to listen to the news, preferring to go out to play, and constantly forgot what she was told. If she listened properly from now on and didn't cry any more perhaps Jimmy would be proud of her. Sometimes she said she didn't care if her brother didn't like her, but really she did. She wanted his approval more than anything else in the world.

School started the following week. Jenny's foot had improved enough for her to walk on it and Alf's cuts and bruises were healing. He had lost two teeth in the mishap and had to go to the dentist to get false ones. Jenny was mortified that she had caused him such harm but he told her not to worry about it, being more concerned that her foot recovered than about a couple of teeth.

Playing outside together one evening about three weeks later, Jimmy, Jenny and Verna were chasing one another along the slab topped garden wall at the front of the house. None of them noticed Frank emerging from the woodshed and striding across the garden until too late. He caught Jimmy a blow behind the legs that sent him crashing off the wall to the ground.

"Get up you little sod! I'll wring thee bloody neck for 'ee!" Petrified, the girls stopped in their tracks as Jimmy struggled to his feet and Frank grabbed him by the hair. What on earth had they done and why was Frank so mad at Jimmy? Was it because they were making so much noise?

Frank held onto Jimmy's hair and marched him, yelling in pain, into the woodshed. Jenny and Verna looked at each other in consternation, clambered off the wall and crept behind to see if they could find out what was going on.

Inside the shed to the right, built against the front and side walls, was a second lavatory. It had a wooden seat with a hole in the centre and an earth floor just like the one at the bottom of the garden. They never used this lavatory because after he had built it Frank decided that it would make too much stink in the shed where he often worked. The only thing it was used for was to house a couple of guinea pig cages on the floor. The guinea pigs were Nellie's and she looked after them.

Frank pushed Jimmy into the lavatory and forced his head over the hole in the seat. "Did you do that?" he bellowed.

"What! What! What did I do?" Jimmy shouted in fear.

"Just look in there. Use thee bloody eyes - just look!"

Jenny and Verna couldn't see what Frank was so angry about but they began to smell something burning.

"There's a bloody fire in there an' you're the one what did it. Don't lie to me boy, I know you did it. You could 'ave burned the whole place down, 'ouse an' all. Get on indoors this minute an' I'll deal with thee presently."

He pushed Jimmy violently and the girls shrank back as Jimmy dashed for the front door yelling "I didn't do it! I didn't know there was a fire in there. I didn't do it!"

Frank snatched the bowls of water from the guinea pigs' cages and tipped it into the hole, then poked around with a stick for a few moments. Satisfied that the fire was out, he stormed past the girls and into the house after Jimmy. As soon as he had gone, the girls crept in to look down the hole. It was dark down there but by sticking their heads down the hole they could see small scattered bits of wet black paper. Verna and Jenny looked at each other in disbelief.

"It wasn't a very big fire," Jenny said. "Jimmy didn't do it because he was playing with us all the time. He couldn't have gone and lit a fire without us seeing him."

"I know," Verna said. "Jimmy never done that. I don't know who done it."

Both afraid to go indoors, they hung around outside hearing sounds of thwacks from Franks' belt mingled with Jimmy's screams of pain. Jimmy protesting through his screams that he hadn't done it and Frank roaring that he was a 'bloody little liar'. When eventually Nellie called them in to supper the atmosphere was charged with unspoken hostility, all of it directed toward Frank. Well aware of this, Frank's blazing eyes forbade anyone to say one word. Jimmy had been sent to bed with no supper and Jenny didn't feel like eating at all. Nellie had made faggots, Jenny's second favourite after baked rabbit but she didn't want to eat. Thinking of Jimmy upstairs hurting and hungry, she thought of slipping a faggot into the pocket of her pinafore dress to take to him later, but it was covered in gravy and would make a mess.

"Eat thee supper!" Frank commanded her. "We ain't 'aving food wasted in this 'ouse an' you ain't leavin' this table till thee eat it. Get on wi' it!"

Choking the food down, she puzzled over the matter of the fire. Could Jimmy have snuck away while they were playing and lit it? She couldn't recall any time when he hadn't been with them, and neither had Verna left. She herself hadn't done it, Nellie hadn't come outside at all and Alf wasn't even home from work by then, so who could have lit the fire? They had a piece of sponge cake each for afters and while Nellie was cutting the cake Frank left the table to fetch a mug of water. Jenny slid her cake into her pocket, looking up to see that Nellie had caught her. Another piece of cake arrived on her plate immediately and Nellie's right eye flicked a wink.

At bed time Jenny sneaked along the landing to Jimmy's room and crept in. Jimmy had lit his oil lamp and was lying face down on his bed, still fully dressed. Jenny was horrified at the angry red welts across his legs, all the way from his ankles to the edge of his short pants. She pulled the somewhat squashed piece of cake from her pocket and offered it to him. "I saved this for you, Jimmy," she whispered. "I know you didn't light that fire."

Jimmy sat up, wincing as he did so, his face all blotchy. "Thanks," he said taking the cake. "No, I didn't do it. I didn't even go in the shed. You'd better go on back before we get into more trouble."

Continuing to puzzle about the fire as she lay in bed, Jenny wanted to tell Nellie that Jimmy hadn't done it and that Frank was wrong. Plucking up courage she got out of bed and started creeping downstairs. She would say that she had tummy ache and see if she could get Nellie to come upstairs. Nearing the bottom she heard Frank's voice. "E's got to go and that's that," he was saying. "The bloody kid's never been any good and damned if I'm goin' to 'ave 'im burnin' the place down. That shed's joined on to this 'ouse an' if it 'ad caught fire the lot would've gone. You get down that Post Office in the mornin' an' ring that Gray woman an' tell 'er she's got to get 'im somewhere else."

"Oh Frank," Nellie's voice said. "I don't believe he did set that fire, and if he did that's the only bad thing he's ever done. You have to give him another chance."

"Do as I say, woman, an' don't bloody argue!"

Silence! Jenny turned and crept back upstairs shaking with horror. Frank was going to send Jimmy away!! But Nellie had promised only a few weeks ago that she would look after them. Surely she wouldn't let Frank do this? And what would Jenny do without Jimmy? And where would Jimmy go? Tossing and turning for hours,

she heard Nellie and Frank go to bed and still stayed awake. Confusing
fact with fantasy she hoped that she had been asleep and dreamt it all.
In the morning it would turn out not to be true. All because Frank said
Jimmy had lit a fire that he hadn't lit. Suddenly she felt as if a hammer
had hit her in the head. She shot up in bed with a start. Oh no!

Frank had lit the fire himself!

Nothing was said in the morning about what Jenny had
overheard. All day she went about with a heavy heart, hoping against
hope that Nellie had talked Frank out of his decision and that Jimmy
would stay. She said nothing to anyone. If Nellie did save Jimmy then
he need never know that Frank wanted him gone and that he had been
the one who lit the fire. Jenny was convinced of it now.

That afternoon all hope was lost when Nellie had the dreadful
job of telling Jimmy that he had to leave. She didn't know where he
was to go but had spoken to Miss Gray who was going to arrange
something and come to fetch him. Jenny lost her resolve, crying
buckets of tears and pleading with Nellie not to send her brother away.
Jimmy stood as if turned to stone, listening to his sister's pleas which
were all to no avail. She couldn't argue with Frank any more, Nellie
said, and sorry as she was, Jimmy would have to go.

The next few days were total misery for them all. Jenny even
tried begging Frank to let Jimmy stay but all he said was "If thee's goin'
to keep on like that, thees'll be the next one to go an' pretty damn
quick." Fearing he would do just that she left him alone, turning
pleading doe eyes on Nellie every chance she got.

"It's no good you looking at me like that, Jenny," Nellie said
when they were alone one day. "I know you don't want Jimmy to go
and nor do I. With all you two have had to put up with I could cry
myself that this has happened. But I can't do anything about it so
please don't make it any harder."

"I know something," Jenny said to Jimmy later. "Frank lit that
fire himself. You could tell Miss Gray that and she might make them
keep you."

"Don't be daft," Jimmy said. "I know Frank lit the fire, it
doesn't take much brains to work that out. He was the only one in the

shed. He did it because he wants to get rid of me, and he has hasn't he. Nellie isn't going to do anything to help me and telling Miss Gray won't make any difference. You just best forget it or he'll get rid of you too."

It was two weeks before it was decided where Jimmy should go. He was to live with a family called Foster who lived at the bottom of the Drove, just a quarter mile from the Matthews. Both children were aware of the family but knew little about them other than the fact that Mr. Foster was old, small and grey haired and had a hump on his back. Mrs. Foster was considerably younger, probably middle aged, and they had a seventeen-year-old daughter named Barbara who worked in a factory somewhere. They also knew that the Fosters had a small holding on which they grew vegetables for market and kept a few goats, pigs, chickens and three cows, and that Mrs. Foster took in washing.

"Why are they sending Jimmy to the Fosters'?" Jenny asked Nellie. "Mr. Foster is so old and he has a hump. Jimmy won't want to live with him!"

"There's nothing wrong with Mr. Foster just because he has a hump," Nellie said. "In fact he's a nice man. He's quiet and doesn't talk to people much, but once you do get him talking he's alright." She told them that Mrs. Foster was Mr. Foster's second wife and that he was twenty-five years or so older than her. His first wife had died after having a large family. In fact the father of the other family named Foster who lived just down the road from the Post Office was old Henry Foster's son. Both children knew the second Foster family, also a large family of nine girls and one boy.

Jimmy was more resigned to leaving than Jenny was to see him go. When Miss Gray came and she, Alf and Jimmy set off with Jimmy's cases, Jenny felt desolate. She wanted to go with them but Jimmy said no. It hurt horribly to see her brother walk away even if he was only going a short way and she could visit him and would see him every day at school. Her fear of Frank turned to a deeper feeling of hatred for what he had done to her only brother, but such feelings had to be kept deep inside or he would do the same thing to her. Nellie was all she had left now and if she were to be sent away from Nellie she was sure her life would end.

SIXTEEN

Jenny missed her brother sorely. She saw him at school but he made little comment about whether he was getting on with the Fosters or not. He had been with them about three weeks when Jenny finally asked him if he liked it there.

"Not really," he said. "Mrs. Foster is okay. She doesn't hit me or anything but I think they only wanted me so I could help with the work. She doesn't care about me at all."

He sounded so resigned to that fact that Jenny was shocked. She thought he might be just saying it to make her feel bad because she was still with Nellie. She determined to visit him at the weekend.

When she arrived Mrs. Foster was hanging washing on the line. Jenny walked over to her and told her she missed her brother and wanted to see him if she was allowed. Mrs. Foster said she was just about to go back in the house and of course Jenny could come and see Jimmy. It was a shame they had to be parted, she said, and Jenny could come and see him anytime. She seemed about the same height as Nellie, Jenny thought, but was wider round the middle. Her hair was mousy colour and cut very short. As they walked into her back door they entered the washhouse, a large cold room with concrete floor. Jimmy was busy cranking the handle of the washing machine and looked none too pleased to see Jenny. "What do you want up here?" he asked her.

"That's no greeting for your sister when she's come to see you," Mrs. Foster told him. "Do you want to show her your bedroom?"

"No, I'm too busy. What would she want to see my bedroom for anyway?"

"I just came to see you, Jimmy. I don't want to see your bedroom if you don't want me to. I just wanted to know if you were alright."

"Of course I'm alright, I told you that the other day at school. Now buzz off and leave me alone." Jimmy was obviously not at all pleased to see Jenny and she felt crushed.

"Jimmy, take Jenny and show her the animals. At least you can do that and not be so unkind," Mrs. Foster said.

"Oh all right. Come on then," he said to Jenny.

"Jimmy, please don't be so grumpy at me," Jenny said as they walked over to the small holding behind the garden fence. "I only came because I thought you might want somebody to talk to, and I miss you. Do they really make you do a lot of work?"

"Yes they do if you want to know. I have to fetch and take back washing, crank the washing machine handle though she says I don't do it fast enough, chop up wood, help feed and clean out the animals and in the spring I will have to do a lot of the gardening. If you keep coming up here it only makes me have to work later and I don't need anyone to talk to. There's the animals if you really want to see them."

Jenny looked at the goats and cows without much interest. She didn't want Jimmy to have to work all the time and he didn't want to talk to her. She felt miserable. They walked back to the house where Mrs. Foster said she had made a cup of tea for them. Jimmy refused, saying he had the wood to chop and didn't want to be doing it in the dark. Jenny thought she had better stay and have some tea as it had been made for them so she followed Mrs. Foster down a narrow passage with stairs on the right. Mrs. Foster turned left through a doorway into a roomy living room which contained a table with a cloth on it in the centre, a fireplace in the middle of the far wall, some ancient arm chairs and a few hard backed chairs. Despite the fire in the grate, the place seemed dingy, not at all warm and cheerful like Nellie's living room.

The tea was too hot to drink and while she waited for it to cool Jenny told Mrs. Foster she had never seen a washing machine like hers before. "Haven't you really," Mrs. Foster said. "Well come and have a look if you like."

It was a strange contraption; a big iron belly that had to be filled with buckets of water pumped by a hand pump over the sink in the corner and heated from a gas ring underneath. A heavy lid with a protruding handle on top and a long paddle underneath was fitted on so that when the handle was cranked to and fro the paddle swished the washing about. Mrs. Foster's washing was mostly sheets and pillow cases and tablecloths that villagers brought to her, but now she had lots more to do because the searchlight soldiers brought their washing to her as well. When the washing had been swished enough in the machine she lifted it out with a heavy wooden stick and put it in a big boiler in the corner that was built in with bricks and heated from a fire underneath. Then she lifted it out from there and rinsed it all in three different rinse waters in big galvanized baths on the floor, the last rinse having a brick of blue powder crushed into it to make the sheets whiter. When she had wrung the sheets by hand she folded them lengthwise, put them through the hand turned mangle and hung them on the line.

"That must take such a long time to do," Jenny said as Mrs. Foster explained it all to her. "You must be washing all day."

"Well not quite," Mrs. Foster said. "I'm always up at half past three in the morning and the washing is done by ten, and so is most of the housework, and all the animals fed."

Jenny thought Nellie was always busy, but to have to get up at half past three in the morning was awful.

"Do you like Jimmy?" she asked when they were back to the cups of tea.

"Why yes of course. He is a nice polite lad, although he didn't speak to you very nicely did he. I expect he is still feeling a bit strange and he is bound to miss you and the Matthews girl because there is no-one here his age. Still, we keep him busy and I think he will be a big help."

Jenny wanted to say that Jimmy shouldn't have to be busy and do the work, but she thought she had better not. Mrs. Foster was alright but it wasn't a nice place like Nellie's and she wished Jimmy didn't have to be here. Mr. Foster came in while they were having tea. He nodded to Jenny when Mrs. Foster told him who she was, took a cup of tea and went to sit by the fire. He was smaller than Mrs. Foster and whistled down his nose when he breathed. That noise and the hump on his back gave Jenny the shudders. As soon as she had drunk her tea she left, running to find Jimmy chopping wood.

"Oh Jimmy, I don't want you to stay here. You shouldn't have to all this work. Do you want me to ask Nellie to tell Miss Gray so that she will move you?"

"No I don't," he said. "Why don't you get it into your head that they don't care? Please go home, Jenny, and don't keep coming to see me."

There was nothing to do but walk away. Jimmy just wasn't Jimmy any more. He thought nobody cared about him and it didn't matter if she tried to be good and remember things or not cry, he didn't care about her any more either. In the chapel Sunday school they said that Jesus loved children. If she said special prayers at night for Jimmy, Jesus might help him. Somebody had to help Jimmy.

SEVENTEEN

Autumn turned to winter and the little bottles of milk left outside the school each morning sported tiny cardboard hats atop their long necks of frozen cream. The Government decreed that all school children should drink one third of a pint of milk each day whether they liked it or not, and most of them didn't. Miss Mergrin had the children bring the crates in and stand them around the pot-bellied stove to thaw. By break time when they had to drink the milk, it was luke warm, smelled sickly and nauseated the children. They would much prefer it left frozen so they could bite off the cream and crunch the bits of ice. Even in summer the milk caused problems with the cardboard tops. There was a perforated hole in the centre they were supposed to push in with a thumb and insert a straw, but it didn't work too well. More often than not the whole lid caved in shooting milk all over their clothes and they stank for the rest of the day.

Prayers were said every morning before lessons. That was okay, but having to say catechism after prayers annoyed Jenny considerably. It was the silliest thing grown-ups expected of children yet, she decided. They all had to stand while Mrs. Mergrin read from a book, asking set questions which they had to answer. "What is your name?" Mrs. Mergrin would ask. "N or M," they would chorus. "Who gave you that name?" "My godfathers and my godmothers at my baptism." they would have to reply. Jenny had never heard anything so silly. Her name was Jenny Harding, not N or M. In any case, she had never been christened N or M or anything else. Her mother had told her that she had never got around to having Jenny christened although she had meant to. Jimmy was christened, but he hadn't been christened N or M either. It was silly and annoyed her to have to say something so daft.

Hostility toward the evacuees eased off considerably. They were permitted to join in games at play time and made friends with one another. Jenny found a friend named Kathy with whom she played at school but not at other times because Kathy lived at the far opposite end of the village - even further away than Miss George's cottage she discovered. Jenny asked her if she knew the two old ladies and Kathy said she knew of them but hardly ever saw them. Jenny had never seen either of them since she and Jimmy had left the cottage, nor did she particularly want to. She had once seen Mrs. Williamson in the Post Office who had said hello to her and asked how she was getting on. Jenny thought she was just being polite and didn't really want to know. She didn't feel anything at seeing Mrs. Williamson. It was funny, she thought; just like they had never lived in her house at all. She found she didn't particularly want to see any of the Williamsons again either.

Verna and Jenny seldom walked home together any more, each finding other friends to walk and play with on the way home. A boy named Tom Roper took a liking to Jenny, deciding to walk home with her sometimes. They usually took the main road route which took them past a farm. A high clay wall topped with rounded bricks bounded the yard on the road side. At the bottom of the wall a low grassy bank sloped to the road. Jenny had scrambled up the bank once to look over at the yard. She could see across the yard to a field with bushes and hedges at the bottom, broken here and there by bare places bounded by barbed wire strands. Through the strands she could see the orange sandy lane they sometimes walked and which featured in her bad dreams. In those dreams Verna and Daisy no longer appeared - just herself and the black man who ran after her while her legs refused to move. She was gazing over the field trying to pick out the tree stump which was also always in her dream and wondering if the black man really did hide there in the bushes when her attention was drawn to a very pretty lady and a little girl walking into the yard. The lady had long black straight hair and the little girl's hair was long and blond. As she watched, the lady looked up at her and smiled. It was the saddest smile in the world Jenny thought. For days she kept thinking about the lady, wondering why she had smiled and looked so sad at the same time.

"Do you know whose farm this is," she asked Tom as they were passing the wall.

"Everybody knows whose farm this is," he said. "It's Mr. Planter's farm an' 'ee's cracked."

"What do you mean, he's cracked? What does he do?"

"E's proper crackers that's wot 'e is. Don't you dare go walkin' across 'is fields or 'e'll shoot 'ee in the back."

"You're kidding me," Jenny said in disbelief. "Nobody is allowed to go round shooting people."

"Oh no? Don't 'ee believe it. Old man Planter 'as shot at lot's of folks - and 'e's killed dogs that 'as dared to walk in 'is fields too. That's true, I'm tellin 'ee. 'E goes bonkers when there's a full moon."

Jenny was sure now he was pulling her leg. "What's the moon got to do with it? Why should he go bonkers when there's a full moon?"

"Cos some people do that's why. Don't believe I if thee don't want to, but if thee walks across 'is fields, thees'll find out. 'E's got a wife an' a girl an' they'm never seed out because 'e won't allow 'em to go out. 'E says 'e'll shoot 'em if they leaves the farm, so they don't go nowheres."

The lady had looked very sad, Jenny thought, so perhaps it was true after all. Tom changed the subject before she could say any more. "Wot's thee wanna be when thee grows up?" he asked her.

"I don't know, I never thought about it," she said. "I s'pose I will be a mummy and have a boy and a girl."

"Yeah," Tom agreed. "I'm gonna 'ave two kids an' all. I wants a girl to look pretty and a boy to emt' the lavvy buckets."

Jenny burst out laughing at this revelation. It was a funny reason to have a boy - just to empty lavatory buckets.

"You wanna come an' see my sister?" Tom asked. Jenny was taken aback by this question. She knew Tom had an older brother Joe who was in the top class at school but didn't know about any sister. "Is she still a baby then, your sister?"

"No. Margie's older 'n me. She's nearly eight now. Our Joey's ten and I'm seven last week."

"Why isn't Margie at school then? I thought everybody had to go to school."

"Margie don't go 'cos she can't walk proper. She went in the river to play when she were four an' got polio. Now she 'as to 'ave callipers on 'er legs an' walk wi' crutches. My mum 'as a lady come to learn Margie at 'ome, an' she can read better 'n our Joey and write and do sums. Wanna come an' see 'er or not?"

"Yes," Jenny said, trying to take in all this news at once. "What's polio, Tommy?"

"I dunno. Summat wot stops thee legs growin'. Our Margie's legs are all skinny 'n small. She 'as to sleep on a plaster of paris bed wot's made into a shape like 'er body. It's bloody 'ard. I wouldn't wanna sleep on it but Margie don't mind."

The Ropers were landlords of one of the two village pubs. Tom took her to the back door, which was the entrance to their living quarters, shouting as he got inside, "Mum! Jenny wanted to see our Margie so I bought 'er 'ome. She's 'ere." Jenny felt her face flush at this bending of the truth but Mrs. Roper came smiling to the door and told Jenny to come in. Margie liked people to come and visit she said.

Jenny stepped into the kitchen and saw a girl who was obviously Margie, sitting on the kitchen table having her legs rubbed with oils by a thin, dark haired lady. Margie smiled at Jenny. "Hello, have you come to play with me?" she asked.

"Well, I better not stop too long or I'll be late home'" Jenny said. "But I'll come and play with you on Saturday if you like." She studied Margie's legs as they were being rubbed. As soon as the lady put one leg down it hung pale, thin and lifeless from the table edge. She felt queasy inside looking at them, but Margie was chatting away happily saying she would like Jenny to come on Saturday.

"This is my Aunty Joan," she told Jenny. She comes every day to massage my legs but she's nearly finished now haven't you, Aunty Joan?"

"Just about," Aunty Joan said. She picked up what must be the callipers Tommy talked about. They looked like metal poles with pieces of leather joined to them. She strapped these around Margie's legs, lifted her from the table and handed her a pair of crutches. Margie walked over to Jenny by leaning on the crutches, letting first one leg swing forward, then the other. "I've got lots of games and puzzles we can do. Do you want to come up and see my toys?"

Jenny followed her through the living room and was astonished to see that Margie could walk up the stairs by herself. She dropped one crutch at the bottom, put the other one on the first stair and by using that and the stair rail, heaved herself up both legs together. Placing her crutch on the next stair she did the same thing, all the way up the stairs. In her bedroom was a white object the shape of a body with the legs apart. "Is that your bed?" Jenny asked. "How can you sleep on something so hard?"

"It's okay," Margie said laughing. "I have to have my legs strapped in and stay on my back but its not too bad. Tommy thinks its awful, but I don't mind."

On the way home Jenny wondered if she would be as happy as Margie if she couldn't walk properly. She didn't think so. Margie was a pretty girl with dark curly hair and green eyes. She had thrown her crutch downstairs and slid down on her bottom, holding the rail and using her other hand for balance. Jenny liked Margie, she decided, and would go to play with her on Saturday.

Jenny and Margie soon became firm friends. Margie could manage outdoors as well as in, although Jenny's heart stopped every time she watched her negotiate the steep concrete slope from her back door to the road. It seemed to Jenny that Margie never stopped smiling. She said "Hello," to everyone they passed when they were out and everyone seemed to know her. In fact all Margie's family were happy people. Her mother never minded children running in and out of her house and gave them tea and small cakes that she baked. Her father worked on his brother's farm during the day and helped in the pub at night. If he came home while Jenny was still there he always chatted to her.

One day Margie wanted Jenny to walk with her to her Aunty's house a half mile away, just round the corner from the Fosters where Jimmy now lived. Margie's father, her Uncle Ted and Aunt Joan were brothers and sister. Aunt Joan and Uncle Ted lived together on the farm as neither of them had married. Jenny knew where the farm was but had never been into the yard. Ted Roper was known to be the sloppiest farmer in the village, always milking his cows by lantern light when other farms had long since turned their cows back into the fields and churned all the milk. His few crops were always sown late and harvested late, but somehow he muddled along.

Uncle Ted was in the yard when they got there, trying to fix something on his battered old tractor. The yard was a smelly mess of sloppy cow muck and mud which the girls skirted around on the driest ground they could find. One quarter of the yard was taken up by a mountain of old straw and cow manure which Margie said her uncle used for fertilizer when he got round to it. It didn't look as if he had got round to it for years.

"'Ello Margie," Uncle Tom called. "Don't see thee over 'ere too much. Go on into the 'ouse luv, thy Aunty's in there." A short plump man with a round red face and flat grubby cap perched atop his head, he waved towards the house at the side of the yard. They picked their way carefully round the yard and through an open gate in the hedge. The garden was a tangled mess of overgrown grass and scattered pieces of rusting iron, blackened wood and other unidentifiable garbage. Aunty was surprised to see that Margie had walked so far, immediately putting the kettle on to make tea.

"Sit yourselves down," she told them. "Your arms must be tired out pulling yourself all this way on those crutches."

"Only a bit," Margie said as she heaved herself into a wooden chair by the kitchen table, her legs sticking straight out in front of her. Jenny seated herself in the only other available chair on the opposite side of the table, all other chairs in the room being hidden under piles of old clothes. A jumble of shoes and smelly Wellington boots lay on the floor by the back door. Aunty made tea and offered them biscuits but Jenny had difficulty finding a space on the table to put her cup and saucer down. Packets of breakfast cereal, papers, dirty crockery, opened tins with mouldering contents, the whole lot covered in crumbs took up almost all available space. From where she sat Jenny could see partially into the living room, noticing patches of torn wall paper hanging limply from the walls. She wondered how anyone could live in such a mess all the time and still manage to do ordinary things like cooking. There was no working space anywhere.

By the time they got back to the pub, Margie was tired so Jenny left. The pub stood by itself, sideways onto the road. Roughly a house length away from the pub was a tiny white house like a doll's house in which lived the two Mr. Browns. Brothers, the two elderly men never went anywhere and the only time they were to be seen was when they walked across the road to their garden to use the lavatory or to throw dirty water in the river; or when one or other of them shuffled over the bridge to the spring for fresh water. Margie had told her that there was only one room downstairs and one room upstairs in the little house. At the side of the little house was a paved yard, open at the front and with a high wall at the back, by which it was linked to the next door house; a red brick building belonging to a family named Stafford.

Turning left at the Stafford's house, Jenny intended to walk over a white bridge and make her way home. Several children were playing on the bridge, so she decided to join them. A favourite pastime of local children was to swing and do 'turnovers' on the rails of this bridge. About thirty feet long and four feet wide, the bridge was bounded by three-foot high iron posts with a round iron rail on top of the posts, running the length of the bridge on both sides. A great attraction to children who loved to push themselves up until their groins were at rail level, then to drop their upper bodies over the rail and swing over and over, or to drop down until the rail was behind their knees and then hang upside down over the river. Often they missed the bridge when dropping back to their feet and ended up in the river. Since it measured no more than two feet deep at its deepest point this caused nothing more than lots of giggling and finger pointing. Although there were many other bridges in the village there were none like this one, most others being just humps where the road lifted over the river with four foot high brick walls at each side.

Jenny joined in the fun on the bridge, with much laughter, shrieking and pushing one another off the bridge, when Mrs. Stafford came out of her house.

"Will you damn kids clear off," she shouted, waving her arms angrily at them. "You've no right to be making all this racket outside my house and I won't have it. Clear off, the lot of you."

Scrabbling up discarded coats and shoes, grumbling among themselves, the children ran off the opposite side of the bridge. As soon as Mrs. Stafford disappeared into her house they began to catcall after her. "Staff-Staff, riff-raff," they chanted. None of them liked Mrs. Stuck-up Stafford, or her spoiled five year-old daughter. Mrs. Stafford reappeared glowering and the children scattered. Jenny ran on home where she told Nellie what she had been doing, including the catcalls at Mr. Stafford.

"Well that isn't going to please her any, calling her riff raff," Nellie said. "She thinks she is better than most in the village and considers those beneath her as riff-raff. She isn't any better than anyone else; her father is a farm worker in a village over the hill. She only married Reg Stafford because he owned his own house and that makes her feel she's better than the rest of us that live in tied cottages." It appeared that nobody liked Mrs. Stafford too well - neither her nor her spoiled brat of a daughter, five year-old Celia.

EIGHTEEN

"Thee two go over Feathers 'an get I ten Woodbines," Frank ordered Jenny and Verna one evening, handing them some money.

"We can't go in the pub, we're not allowed," Jenny protested.

"Thee's don't 'ave to go in the bar, thee can go round the back. Thee's go over there enough playin' wi' thick girl o' their'n don't 'ee?"

The girls took the money and walked over to the Plume of Feathers, going to the back door to ask for the cigarettes. They stopped for a while to chat to Margie and as they left they noticed four men standing in the road beside the pub. All the men had very dark hair and all wore brown outfits.

"Here. Come to here," one of the men called, beckoning with his arm. Both girls stood where they were as the men walked over to them. One of them held out a ten shilling note saying in a heavy foreign accent, "You go buy ginger beer?" Verna and Jenny looked at each other, not sure what to do.

"I think they want us to buy them ginger beer from the pub," Jenny said. "Do you think we should?"

"I dunno," Verna said. "Why can't they get their own beer?"

Jenny pointed to the other side of the building. "You can go up there and get ginger beer yourself," she said to the man holding out the money.

"No. No can go in pub. Pub not serve. You get ginger beer. Four. Four bottle," he said, holding up four fingers and pushing the note into Jenny's hand.

Feeling a little nervous and uncertain, the two girls returned to the back door to do as they were asked. They liked ginger beer themselves, which was not beer at all but a slightly fizzy ginger ade. As they handed the bottles and change to the spokesman he said, "Good. Very good. You good nice girls." The other three smiled, voicing their thanks by saying "Yes," "Yes," "Hah," and laughing. The girls walked away, looking back to see the four men sitting on a low wall beside the pub, drinking from the small brown bottles. On returning home they found Frank in a bad temper, wanting to know what took them so long when he was waiting for his fags. Most of the wasted time had been whilst talking to Margie, but not wanting to admit that, they told him about the four men.

"Thee's got ginger beer for they Eyetyes? They bloody Eyetye prisoners? I 'as to wait for my fags while thee gets ginger beer for a bunch o' bloody foreign prisoners! If thee gets caught talkin' to they, thees'll end up in gaol. Thee's better not get talkin' to they any more or thees'll get my belt."

"I never talked to them, it was Jenny," Verna whined. "She got their ginger beer, I never."

"Huh. What else do 'ee expect? Bloody kid. I'll belt thee hide if I catches you talkin' to they agin," he threatened Jenny.

Jenny went into the kitchen to find Nellie. "What's Eyetyes, Nellie? Frank says they're prisoners and we mustn't talk to them. Why?"

"Well we're not supposed to talk to them. They're Italian prisoners of war and they're not allowed to drink or go into the pubs for anything."

"Why aren't they in prison if they are prisoners? Are prisoners of war allowed to go where they like?"

"The Italians have to work on the farms and after work they are allowed to walk around. They have to wear brown uniforms all the time and aren't allowed on buses or in pubs. They can't run away very far. Even if they got to the coast they couldn't get any further. Don't you know that England is an island with sea all round? I don't suppose they want to run away anyway, they get looked after too well," she laughed.

"Well why can't we talk to them then, if they work on our farms?"

"Oh, because they are our enemies I suppose. Don't ask me Jenny. None of this war makes a lot of sense. We aren't supposed to talk to them, that's all I know."

If prisoners of war were allowed to walk around, then perhaps Daddy was not locked in a cage after all. Perhaps he worked on a German farm and walked about with his friends. Jenny didn't feel half so bad to think that her dear Daddy wasn't starving and locked in a German prison after all. If she saw the Italians again she would talk to them and not tell Frank. She wanted to think somebody would talk to her father if he wanted to drink ginger beer in Germany.

Trying not to get on the wrong side of Frank was difficult for Jenny these days. Since Jimmy had left Frank had turned to blaming her for most things that went wrong, a number of times confining her to the bedroom without supper. Sometimes when this happened Nellie would sneak food up to her, showing Jenny that she thought her punishment unfair. On one occasion she felt the lash of Frank's belt as Jimmy had done.

The girls were always in bed by half past seven since Frank wanted peace and quiet in the evenings. Nellie allowed them to sit in bed for an hour to read or sew by lantern light. Nellie had taught them to sew and often gave them left over bits of material with which to make dolls' clothes. Jenny had moved over to Verna's bed one evening when they were sewing, and Jenny's thread had twisted itself into a knot. Grumbling to herself, she was attempting to unpick the knot when Verna picked up the scissors and sliced the thread.

"Oh! I didn't want to cut it, I wanted to undo the knot," Jenny protested, thumping Verna on the back. Verna began to choke and splutter. "I had a pin in my mouth," she wailed. "Now you've made me swallow it." "Muuum! Muuum!" she yelled.

Nellie came rushing up the stairs closely followed by Mrs. North. Frank worked for farmer North on one of the wealthiest farms in the village. They were not only farmers, but builders and undertakers also. Farmer North and his wife were elderly. Their only son lived with his wife and nine year old son in a large house opposite Nellie and Frank. Nellie worked for the younger Mrs. North, cleaning, sewing, ironing and whatever else Mrs. North Junior desired. She was a very demanding person, expecting Nellie to drop everything else she was doing whenever 'Lady North' as she was nicknamed, needed something done. Since Frank worked for the Norths also and the cottage belonged to them, Nellie had little choice. This particular evening she had come over to arrange for some sewing to be done and was in the house when Verna started to panic.

"Jenny made me swallow a pin. She hit me and made me swallow a pin," Verna bawled. "I got a pin inside me and it'll stick in my insides and I'll die."

"Whatever did you do, you stupid child," Mrs. North said, looking daggers at Jenny. "We shall have to get Verna to hospital at once," she said to Nellie.

"Oh I don't think so. I doubt she even swallowed a pin. It's probably in the bed somewhere," Nellie said, trying to soothe things down. "I'll take her downstairs and make her some bread and milk. That should wrap it up and help it down if it's in there at all."

"I didn't do it on purpose, it was an accident," Jenny protested. "I didn't know she had a pin in her mouth, honestly."

Mrs. North gave her another withering look. "I still think we should get her to hospital just in case. I told you before Nellie that you had enough to do without taking in evacuees. You don't need this kind of bother."

They all went downstairs, leaving Jenny shivering in her bed. Nellie held out against taking Verna into hospital or calling the doctor and Mrs. North left in a huff. When she was gone Frank rushed up the stairs and laced Jenny three times with his belt across the buttocks. It burned so badly that she screamed, leaping out of bed and dancing around holding her rear end. It seemed an eternity until the burning eased enough for her to get back into bed.

The next day Nellie said that Frank probably wouldn't have hit her so hard had Mrs. North not been in the house when the trouble started. He didn't like his employer's family to find any fault with him or his household and felt that Mrs. North had been critical of them last night. He was mad with Jenny for causing the trouble. As it was, Nellie didn't think that Verna had really swallowed a pin at all, and neither did Jenny. If she had it did no harm because she was right as rain the next day. It was Jenny who was in pain.

NINETEEN

Winter turned to spring and early summer. Jenny passed her eighth birthday in May with no word from her mother, just as there had been none at Christmas nor on Jimmy's ninth birthday in January. Jenny constantly worried and wondered where their mother could be and why she had to leave, but no answer ever came. She had gone to the Fosters' on Jimmy's birthday to give him a pencil case she had sewn for him from pieces of felt, on which she had stitched his name. He had been pleased to see her that time and liked the pencil case. She still saw him at school of course, sometimes walking back with him in the afternoon. He usually asked her how she was getting on, saying he was 'alright' when she made the same query, but otherwise having little to say to her. A constant lump of sadness dwelt in her chest whenever she tried to talk to Jimmy. He was her big brother but he just wasn't the same any more.

Miss Grey came to see them every few weeks. She went to see Jimmy first, then came to visit Jenny. She just asked how Jenny was getting along, telling her that she was pleased to see Jimmy settling in so well and was glad that Jenny was happy. When Jenny asked if Miss Grey had found their mother, she said no, there was no point looking any more. Jimmy was right, Jenny thought, neither Miss Grey nor the Ministry really cared about them.

Whenever she felt miserable or sad Jenny went to talk to her dear friend Boxer. She still rode him from the stables to the field at times. Other times she would call him to the gate and by dint of pushing and shoving at his huge rear end she had got him to understand that she wanted him to stand with his side to the gate so she could clamber on his back. Boxer now whickered in answer to her call, stood for her to climb aboard and wandered around contentedly chewing grass while she lay on his back talking to him. If she gave a little kick to his sides he would obediently lift his head and trot around the field as she held onto his mane. She loved him dearly, believing that he understood everything she said to him.

In early June, Verna and Jenny joined a group of other children in a field through which the river ran. At one particular spot the river fell into a hole about six feet deep at the centre. The river was about twelve feet across at this point and the hole roughly fifteen feet in length, becoming shallower at the edges. Village children often wore their swimming costumes to play in or near the hole, the bolder ones venturing to the centre and those unable to swim well enough playing and splashing around in the less deep water. Verna and Jenny had been told to be home in time to clean up for supper and although neither they nor any of the children they played with carried watches, they usually gauged time pretty well by the position of the sun and the state of their stomachs. On this day they stayed later than they should, running home like rabbits when they realized how late it had become.

When they got home, Nellie, Frank and Alf were just finishing supper and Frank was angry.

"About time you got here," Nellie said as they dashed panting into the living room. "Get your clothes and go change out of those wet costumes in the washhouse. Your suppers are drying up in the oven, so be quick."

"They don't get no supper!" Frank said angrily. "They casn't git 'ome in time fer grub, they don't git any! Git on out an' change thee togs," he shouted at the girls. "An' make sure thee rinse that stinkin' river water outa they costumes an' 'ang 'em on the line."

Nervously the girls rushed to change their clothes, rinsing the costumes under the pump. "We're not getting any supper now and it's all your fault," Verna grumbled at Jenny.

"Why is it my fault? I don't know the time any more than you do. I'm starving. If we say sorry perhaps your dad will let us have supper."

"Some hopes," Verna said as she ran down the garden, leaping up to fling her costume over the line. Jenny followed suit but as she flung her costume at the line it twisted round and round, knocking Verna's costume to the ground. "Now look what you've done," Verna cried, picking up her costume to throw it back, this time knocking Jenny's down.

"You did that on purpose!" Jenny shouted, deliberately knocking Verna's costume off the line once more. Verna charged at her, sending her sprawling into the shrubbery behind her. "I'm gonna tell Dad on you 'an he'll belt you. He don't like you anyway," Verna yelled.

"Well, I don't like him either, he's always on at me and you're his pet. I hate your dad!" Jenny screamed back, scrabbling to her feet and launching herself at Verna. An all out battle ensued, hair pulling, biting and scratching at each other as they rolled on the ground. Jenny was on top when the belt came whistling across her legs with stinging fury.

"Git up the pair of 'ee!" Frank roared. "I'll teach 'ee to do as thee's bloody told."

"It was her fault Dad, she knocked my cossie off the line on purpose. Don't hit me!" Verna wailed.

"I saw an' I 'eard." Frank was furious, lashing out at Jenny's legs as the two girls ran for the house. "Git on up those bloody stairs an' don't let I 'ear another word outa either of 'ee."

Big red welts appeared on Jenny's legs as they raced to the bedroom. "You're a pig an' I hate you. I wish my Dad would get rid of you," Verna whispered as loudly as she dared.

"Oh shut up," Jenny countered. "You never even got hit. I'm not talking to you any more." She flung herself face down on her bed, refusing to even look at Verna. She was hurting and she was afraid. Frank was so angry she was sure they had more punishment to come.

They did. Or at least Jenny did. Three days after the incident, Nellie told Jenny that she was going to have to leave. There was nothing she could do, she said. She had argued black and blue with Frank but he was determined.

Shock and disbelief drained the blood from Jenny's body, leaving her cold and shaking. "You won't let me go Nellie. You promised! Please, please don't let Frank send me away!"

"I have to Jenny. If I say I won't let you go he'll throw me out as well - and then what? You've done it to yourself, you silly girl. He heard you say you hated him and he has been looking for any excuse to get rid of you. You should have been more careful after what he did to Jimmy. I thought you knew that."

Jenny did know that. Ever since Jimmy went she had been afraid he would do the same to her, but never really believed it. Why had she said she hated him? She wished like anything they could go back to that day and not be late home from the river. She was afraid and desperately unhappy. Where would they send her? She didn't want to go, didn't want to leave Nellie. Oh please God save me. I'm sorry, I won't do it again, she cried inside.

She walked around in the grip of fear as the days passed. Nellie began to pack her belongings into her case, telling her that Miss Grey would be coming to take her to her new home. "Nellie, please," Jenny begged, tears streaming down her face. "If I say sorry to Frank do you think he will let me stay ?"

"Oh dear, I don't know," Nellie said. "You don't know what a job I had stopping him from sending you away over that silly pin business. But you can try."

Standing by Frank's chair that evening, Jenny's heart was pounding. "Frank," she whispered. "I didn't mean what I said. Please let me stay and I'll be good. I'm really sorry Frank. Please don't make me go."

"Hah!" Frank said. "You'm goin maid, that's all there is to it. Sorry bist? Well you'm gonna be a lot sorrier I can tell 'ee. Now clear off."

It was no use. She had no idea what Frank meant by saying she would be sorrier. "Where are they going to send me?" she asked Nellie miserably.

"It's been a bit of a job finding anywhere," Nellie said. She hesitated, looking at Jenny, then away. "I believe you are going to the Staffords," she said.

"The Staffords!" Jenny shrieked in horror. "No! I'm not going there. Nellie, don't send me to the Staffords. I don't like Mrs. Stafford - she's bossy and horrible. Oh please don't make me go there." She couldn't believe they were going to do this to her. Nobody liked Mrs. Stafford and Jenny had catcalled 'riff-raff' to her along with the other children when she ordered them off the bridge. How could they send her there?

Stunned and with mounting apprehension she waited out the few remaining days hardly knowing day from night. Lonely and deserted, she wanted her father, she wanted her mother, but there was no-one. Even Nellie had deserted her. She sought comfort from her dearest friend Boxer, laying on his back soaking him with her tears. She was sitting on the gate letting him nuzzle her chest when Miss Grey arrived.

Traipsing beside Miss Grey as they walked to the Staffords, Jenny only half listened to her cheerful assertions that she had seen the Staffords, they had a nice home and a little girl, and Jenny was sure to be happy there. It was half-term holiday from school so she would have a whole week to settle in. Jenny didn't want to hear any of it, her heart was in her shoes.

It had reason to be, for Jenny's life was about to take a very different road.

TWENTY

1941 - 1943

Miss Grey and Jenny made their way over the white bridge and into the unfenced yard between the old Mr. Browns' little house and the Staffords, turned into a green wooden porch sheltering the back door and knocked. Mrs. Stafford opened the door almost immediately and smilingly ushered them in. Tea and sandwiches were laid out on a white clothed table in front of the fireplace opposite the back door.

"Hello again, Miss Grey. Do come in and have a cup of tea." Mrs. Stafford said in an affected voice. "Well Jenny, this is nice. So you are coming to live with us now. I'm sure you will soon settle down and feel at home, and Celia will be happy to have someone to play with. Sit yourselves down and let me pour us a cup of tea. Come on, Celie love, you can have tea too."

Celia, who had been hovering by the table, ran to sit beside her mother where she stared at Jenny. Jenny ignored her, looking around at the unfamiliar surroundings. To the left of the back door was a sink with a single tap. Beside the sink a wooden dresser reached to the ceiling, its shelves housing plates of various sizes standing against the wall, saucers, jugs and bowls set in front of the plates, and cups hanging from little hooks screwed into the front of the shelves. The dresser took up the rest of the wall on that side of the back door. The left wall contained a window, through which Jenny could see the white bridge.

The fireplace wall was recessed on both sides, the window side containing a wooden, waist high cupboard with shelves set into the wall above it; the other recess having a narrow closed door at the back and another wider latched door at the corner of the right hand wall. Here the wall jutted into the room, running up to another door before joining the back wall. From the way the wall jutted out, Jenny guessed the stairs were behind that wall.

Linoleum covered what felt to be a stone floor, with a red bordered rug spread before the fireplace and green bordered rug in front of the sofa under the window. One easy chair stood beside the fireplace, over which ran a high mantlepiece containing a clock and other ornaments, and another arm chair rested against the stair wall.

"You seem more interested in looking around than eating dear," Mrs. Stafford said. "Would you like to see the rest of the house while Miss Grey is still here?"

"That's a nice idea," Miss Grey answered for Jenny. "Let's have a look round so you can at least start to get your bearings."

Mrs. Stafford took them first through the wide latched door. "This is the scullery where all the work is done," she laughed. "There is no water in here, we carry it from the living room sink. We intended to have the sink moved in here but that will have to wait until after the war now - whenever that might be." A scrubbed table stood against the far wall under a very high window. The ground outside the house reached up to the bottom of this window, much higher than the road in front of the house. "That ground belongs to the pub. It runs behind the Browns' house and ours. Our own garden is across the road," Mrs. Stafford explained. The scullery, or washhouse, contained a gas stove, another old table, a pantry, small meat safe and a gas boiler. The floor was cold grey stone.

Opening the other door in the recess, Mrs. Stafford took them down a narrow dark passageway. Halfway down she opened a door to the left to show them a small square carpeted room with a fireplace across the inner corner, a window looking onto the road, furnished with smart looking easy chairs, matching sofa, and a standard lamp. "This is the best room," she explained. "We just use this when we have visitors."

A door at the end of the passageway opened into a large airy room, also containing a fireplace but otherwise bare of furnishings. "We don't use this end of the house at all," Mrs. Stafford said. "One day we will, but furniture is hard to come by these days so that's something else that has to wait." They continued through the room, peeking into a smaller bare room on the right, then out a door opposite the one they had entered to find themselves in a small passageway with the front door on the left and a flight of stairs on the right. Upstairs to the right was a very large bare bedroom through which they passed into a small dark, doored passage. Opening the far door they stepped into a fair sized room furnished with double bed, chest, wardrobe and chair.

"This is our room," Mrs. Stafford explained. "And next is the room where you will sleep with Celia, Jenny."

A door on the far left of the bedroom opened to a small dark landing above a flight of stairs. "Be careful," Mrs. Stafford warned them. "It's so dark here you could fall down the stairs." A step up to the right took them to the bedroom Jenny and Celia were to share. In the centre was a double bed, a small bed occupying a space in the corner under the window, its headboard against the opposite wall. A wardrobe stood against the wall at the foot of the double, three feet or so from the side of the small bed. A chest of drawers occupied a space on the remaining wall. "This is where you will sleep Jenny. The small bed is for you. We will get your things unpacked after Miss Grey leaves."

Groping their way down the dark stairs, Mrs. Stafford opened the stair door and light flooded in. "Here we are, back where we started," she said. "It's really just a long straight house, and as I said, we don't use the far end nor the front door. Well, do you think you will soon feel at home?" she asked Jenny.

Jenny shrugged. She didn't think she would ever feel at home here. She was fighting an almost overpowering urge to dash for the door and run back to Nellie's. That was her home, she was supposed to be there. What was she doing here anyway?

As Miss Grey left, after saying she was certain that by the time she came for her next visit Jenny would be happily feeling at home, Jenny began to shiver. With Miss Grey gone she was alone. Standing in the centre of the floor beside her cases, the world seemed unreal. She felt she belonged nowhere.

"First thing, let's get these cases upstairs," Mrs. Stafford said, coming back after seeing Miss Grey to the door. Putting the cases at the foot of the small bed, she told Jenny she could put her hanging things in the wardrobe and the bottom two drawers of the chest were for her other clothes. "Just find your night things for now," she said. "Perhaps it will be better to unpack the rest tomorrow morning."

Jenny was glad about that. She didn't want to unpack anything. If everything stayed in the cases she could take them all back to Nellie's. I'm not going to stay here, she thought. Please God don't make me stay here.

Finding her nightgown and throwing it on the bed, she followed Mrs. Stafford downstairs. "I must set about cooking the evening meal," Mrs. Stafford told her. "First we have to clear this table and wash dishes. Perhaps you would like to do that while I get on with the vegetables? Just collect the dishes and bring them to the scullery and I'll put the kettle on for hot water."

Feeling she had little choice, Jenny began to stack plates and saucers while Celia leaned against the table, her brown eyes watching every move. Jenny looked at the round face framed by straight dark hair, cut just below the ears. Celia stuck out her tongue and ran to the scullery after her mother.

"When the kettle boils, tip it into that bowl on the table. You can get water in this enamel jug to cool it down. Here is the washing powder and dishcloth, and you can drain the dishes on this," she said, pulling a tray from under the table.

Still shivering, Jenny washed the dishes as she had been shown, draining them on the tray. Mrs. Stafford busied herself in and out of the room fetching water, peeling potatoes and shelling peas while Celia lounged against the door, eyes fixed on Jenny. "I've done them," Jenny said, uttering her first words since leaving Nellie's.

"My, you are slow. It's probably because you are new and nervous yet, but you will get faster in time," Mrs. Stafford said as she examined the dishes. "Look, there is still lipstick on this cup, do that one again."

Re-washing the offending cup, Jenny took sideways glances at Mrs. Stafford. She was taller and thinner than Nellie, her dark hair curling to her shoulders. Jenny wasn't used to people wearing bright red lipstick, it looked like a slash of blood on the long thin face and seemed to make the brown eyes glitter. She had been talking in a posh 'put-on' voice all afternoon. Jenny knew she didn't really talk that way, having heard her bawling at the children on the bridge enough times.

"I'm going out on the bridge for a little while," Jenny said, walking to the door.

"Good heavens!" Mrs. Stafford sounded astonished. "You can't leave those dishes going cold and smeary. Get the tea towel from that rail there and dry them as quick as you can. Then you will have to empty the bowl and rinse it out."

"Where do I empty the bowl?" Jenny asked, feeling annoyed. Celia can dry the dishes while I do that."

"Celie can't do dishes yet, she's only six. She will learn to do things when she is your age. Please get on with it or you will have to wash them all again to get the smears off."

Jenny dried the dishes, emptied the bowl into a bucket, rinsed the bowl in the living room sink, then took the crockery to the dresser and arranged them as she was shown.

"There now, that wasn't too bad was it?" Mrs. Stafford said. "Now take the tablecloth off carefully and shake the crumbs outside, then put it on the table again and lay up for the evening meal. The cutlery is in the dresser drawer and the every day plates are in the cupboard underneath."

Jenny was becoming exasperated, particularly as Celia was following her about everywhere, simply staring and saying nothing. "I want to go out on the bridge," she said. "I want to be by myself."

"Oh I'm sure you do. I'm sure we would all like to play all day, but there are things to be done. If we are good enough to give you a home when nobody wanted you, you will have to do your part and help with the extra work you cause." Mrs. Stafford's voice had lost its posh touch, sending a tinge of fear into Jenny. Feeling completely out of place and more lost than ever at being told nobody wanted her, she set about her new task. Mr. Stafford returned home from work as she was laying the table, stopping in the porch to remove his work boots and carrying them inside.

"Hello! You're our new evacuee then. Jenny isn't it?" he said cheerily. "See you're making yourself useful already."

Jenny nodded. She had seen Mr. Stafford before but had never spoken to him. Mousy hair sparsely covered his round head, his chubby cheeked smile reflected in pale blue eyes. Slightly taller than his wife,

Mr. Stafford had the beginnings of a paunch. Working as a carpenter for the Norths, he was thought of in the village as a pleasant, quiet nonentity. "You think you're going to like it here with us?" he asked Jenny, seating himself in a chair by the table.

"Dad, I played with my dollies this morning," Celia said, climbing onto his lap. "Do you want to see what dress my dolly has on?" she asked, putting her hands to his face and pulling it round to make him look at her.

"Reg, will you please get your hands washed and leave Jenny to lay up the table," Mrs. Stafford said, coming out of the scullery. "She is trying to learn where things are and doesn't want you bothering her."

"All right dear," he said, putting Celia down and going to the sink to wash his hands.

Seated round the table for supper, Jenny picked at her meal of bacon, peas and boiled potatoes. She still wasn't hungry, her stomach was filled with a sick feeling of dread.

"If you're not going to eat your supper properly, I won't be able to give you any pudding," Mrs. Stafford said. "Don't you like what I have cooked for you?"

"Yes. I'm just not hungry that's all," Jenny answered.

"Yes what? Where are your manners? You say 'Yes thank you', if you please."

"Yes thank you, Mrs. Stafford," Jenny said tonelessly.

"That's better. We can't have you calling us Mrs. Stafford and Mr. Stafford all the time, can we? You can call us Aunt Edith and Uncle Reg if you like."

Jenny didn't like. Mrs. Stafford wasn't her aunty, she wasn't her anything. I don't like her and I don't want to be here, she thought. I'm not going to call her Aunt Edith. Longingly she thought of Nellie, wondering what they were eating for supper. In danger of crying, she brought her attention back to her plate.

Supper over, Mrs. Stafford announced that she would wash the dishes this evening and Jenny could dry them. She would just do them this once though, in future it would be Jenny's job to do all the dishes. Even more, Jenny decided, she didn't like this place. When Miss Grey came to see her she was going to tell her to take her away from here. If she couldn't go back to Nellie, she would ask if she could live with Margie.

At last it was bed time. Celia ran upstairs and came back carrying her nightgown. "You go on up and get to bed. Celia will be up in a minute," Mrs. Stafford told Jenny.

Fumbling her way up the dark stairs, Jenny went to her narrow bed and began to undress. This house, like Nellie's had electricity downstairs but not up. It was still daylight outside however, and the sound of children's voices drifted in the window. Slipping on her nightgown she knelt on her bed to watch a couple of children trying to catch minnows in a jam jar at the edge of the river. She heard Celia come into the room, bouncing onto her bed. The springs creaked as Celia jumped up and down. "This is my bed," she teased. "You've only got a little one. Mine's bigger than yours." Jenny looked at her and said nothing, pulling back the covers to crawl into bed.

"I don't like you so there," Celia called. "You can't play with any of my dollies 'cos I won't let you."

"I don't care. I don't like you either," Jenny said, flinging the clothes over her head and screwing into a tight ball. Shivering and lonely, the events of the day finally overtook her and she slept.

TWENTY-ONE

First confusion, then a sinking despondency overtook Jenny when she awoke the following morning. Realizing it was not all a bad dream, that she was truly here in the Stafford's home rushed in on her in a wave. Mrs. Stafford was calling them down to breakfast. Celia sleepily rubbed her eyes, slid from the bed and padded out of the room without a word. Jenny sat on her bed not wanting to move and face the day, but there was nothing else to do so she followed Celia down.

"What are you doing down here in your night clothes? Go back and get dressed at once."

Taken aback, Jenny looked from Mrs. Stafford to Celia, still in her nightdress.

"I kept my nightie on because Celia did. I thought we were supposed to," Jenny said, bewildered.

"What Celia does is no business of yours. You are a big girl and old enough to dress yourself in the morning. I don't want you coming down in night clothes again."

Flushed with embarrassment, Jenny went back to the bedroom and dressed. Celia ate breakfast in her nightdress. When she had finished, Mrs. Stafford dressed her while Jenny watched in astonishment. Celia was six and couldn't even dress herself! Jenny had to unpack her belongings after breakfast and was making her way upstairs when Mrs. Stafford called out to her. "Make your bed while you are up there. And make Celia's as well."

What a cheek! Why should I have to make Celia's bed? I didn't sleep in it. I didn't even have to make my own bed at Nellie's, she thought. Fuming inside, she unpacked her cases, made her bed, flung the top covers over Celia's bed and went downstairs to find that she was alone in the house. Deciding to investigate the garden, she wandered past the end of the house to a gate on the other side of the road. The long garden, bordered on both sides by hedges, sported a lawn and flower beds to the left, the remainder given over mostly to vegetable growing. The road ran the length on one side, the river streaming past on the other. Walking down the path by the roadside hedge, she came to a big garden shed. There were the usual piles of wood and coal, benches and tools, and in the corner a lavatory with wooden seat similar to the Matthews'. Part of the shed was partitioned off and could only be reached through a pair of rickety doors. The doors were locked but by shading her eyes and peering through the cracks, Jenny saw a small shiny black car. "Crumbs!" she said to herself. "I didn't know the Staffords had a car. They must be pretty rich if they own their own house and have a car as well!" Other than the farmers, the Williamsons and Miss George, hardly anyone in the village owned a car.

Past the shed the garden narrowed to a point, ending in a grove of trees that continued up the hill on that side of the road. Trees, scrub and hedges bordered the other side of that road, simply known as the Lane. The Stafford's was the last house until the road turned left at the top. Then there were a few scattered houses on both sides of what was known as Woodside Road, which further on bent to the right with a farm and farm buildings on its left and row of farm houses on the right where it joined the main road.

"Jenny where are you? Come here now, I want you." Mrs. Stafford called. "What have you been doing out there?" she asked as Jenny ran indoors. "Did you finally finish unpacking?"

"Yes I did, and I was just looking at the garden and finding where the lavatory was."

"Well now that you've found it please wash your hands and help me make sandwiches for lunch."

Jenny quite enjoyed helping make sandwiches. Spreading meat paste on the bread, she said to Mrs. Stafford: "You've got a car down in the shed. Does it go"

"Oh, so you've found that out already have you, Miss Nosy Parker. Yes we do. It's an Austin Seven and it does go, but petrol's on ration, when you can get it at all, so we hardly ever use it now. Just high days and holidays - if then."

When they had eaten, Celia jumped down from the table and said she was going out to play. "I suppose I have to wash the dishes,"

Jenny said, looking at Mrs. Stafford. To her surprise, Mrs. Stafford said she didn't. It was not worth boiling the kettle for those few plates, they could be left and done with the supper things. She could go out to play for a while so long as she didn't go very far. "I shall want you back here later on, so stay within calling distance," she was told.

Jenny contented herself by swinging on the bridge for a while but somehow it wasn't much fun today. There were only two boys in the river, looking for knockheads under the stones. Catching minnows was easy but knockheads, big headed fish slightly larger than minnows, were much harder to find and catch. Most of the children must be out in the fields or over the water hole, Jenny thought. Even Celia had disappeared. She stood watching the river, trying to trace its journey through the village in her mind.

Entering the village through the far eastern end near the church, it flowed through meadows, past Miss George's cottage into fields, tumbled past a still occupied mill house no longer used as a mill, continuing on through more meadow land and running quite rapidly along the borders of the Williamsons' grounds. From there it passed under a road bridge and out into fields before coming into the more populated western part of the village. Here it was dammed and had been divided to make a loop, the man-made loop passing under a hump-backed road bridge to flow gently past the bottom of the old Mr. Browns' garden, under the white bridge where Jenny stood, past the Stafford's garden and on to rejoin the main river.

The main arm carried on from the dam past watercress beds, under a further hump-backed bridge, winding its way along the bottom of Boxer's field, out over the fields where the children swam in the deep hole, and on to a second mill. This mill was still in operation grinding corn into flour and making animal foods, its hugh wooden wheel churning and splashing the river into a roaring waterfall. From there the river raced out of Bishopstone and across fields to villages further along the valley. This was the River Ebble, one of five rivers that ran through Salisbury, there meeting to run thirty odd miles to the sea.

Coming out of her reverie, Jenny felt very lonely. Deciding to go and visit Margie, she started to walk off the bridge.

"Come in here this minute, I have something to say to you!" Mrs. Stafford sounded angry and Jenny blanched, running in to find out what the trouble was.

"I thought I told you this morning to make Celia's bed while you were upstairs," she said, shoving Jenny roughly through the back door. "Get up those stairs."

Jenny scrambled up the stairs in front of Mrs. Stafford, recalling how she had thrown the cover over Celia's unmade bed. Feeling herself gripped fiercely by the back of her neck, she was propelled through the bedroom door. "You call that made? You think you can just defy me and get away with it? You have something to learn, I can see. Pull those covers back and make that bed properly. And I'm going to stand here and see that you do it."

Shaking with fright and anger, Jenny turned back the covers and began to pull them up straight. They were violently jerked from her hands as Mrs. Stafford flung them back again. "You haven't straightened the bottom sheet yet. Don't you know how to do anything right, you stupid child?"

Close to tears of frustration, Jenny walked from one side of the bed to the other, straightening it up, tucking it in and pulling the covers back. Mrs. Stafford stood with arms folded watching her every move. "That's better," she said when it was done. "Don't you ever try to defy me again or you will be very sorry! You can get in the scullery and peel potatoes now."

Seething with outrage at having had to make Celia's bed, Jenny stomped into the scullery. "Where's the potatoes?" she asked sullenly.

"In that sack under the table. But before you do that, take Celia's nightdress off the chair in the living room and put it under her pillow."

Jenny exploded. Making Celia's bed was imposition enough. She wasn't going to carry her nightdress up for her if she was too lazy to do it herself. "I'm not taking her damn nightie up for her, she can do it herself."

Searing light flashed up before her eyes and pain shot through her skull as it hit the stone floor. Groggily struggling to her feet she became aware that her right cheek and ear were burning where Mrs.

Stafford's stinging blow had caught her. She felt herself grabbed by the clothing on her left shoulder, pushed into the living room and forced onto a dining chair.

"Let's get one thing straight from the start here," Mrs. Stafford was saying. "I have agreed to have you here out of the goodness of my heart because your own mother has walked off and left other people to look after you and your brother. Don't think for one moment that I have you here for the money the Ministry pays for your keep. If you had to live on that you would soon starve I can tell you. If I am to keep you, then you will at least make yourself useful around here and earn that keep."

Rising from her chair, Jenny made to leave the room. She wanted to hear no more of this tirade. Mrs. Stafford grabbed her by the arm, forcing into the seat once more.

"You sit there until I tell you to leave," she said, angrily. "Now, it will depend on you how well and how efficiently you do your chores as to whether you get out to play or not. When I tell you to do something, you do it and you do it properly or you do it again and again until it is right. I'll put up with no answering back or cheek from you so don't ever speak to me like that again. Do we understand one another now?"

Jenny felt her eyes burn with defiant anger as she listened to these words. Who did Mrs. Stafford think she was to say her mother had walked off and left her and Jimmy? It wasn't true. Nobody knew where her mother was or what had happened to her, and Mrs. Riff-raff Stafford didn't even know her mother.

"My mother didn't just leave us. You don't know anything about my Mum," she blurted, unable to control her tongue. "If you're going to make me do all your work and hit me about, I'm telling Miss Grey and she will take me away from here. I don't want to live with you. I'm going to run away!"

Mrs. Stafford put both her hands on Jenny's shoulders, digging her finger nails in and holding her in a vice-like grip. "Oh is that so, my fine young madam? And who do you think Miss Grey is going to believe when I tell her you are just a little liar, hey? And as for running away, go ahead. I don't know where you think you will go, because anyone finding you will only send you back. If you are picked up by the police they will put you in a home for bad girls and if you think it is so bad here, wait and see what they will do to you. If that's what you want, go on and run away."

"I'll go back to Nellie's. She doesn't make me do all her work because she doesn't get enough money. You don't make Celia do anything and that's not fair."

Another stinging blow to her already burning ear sent Jenny crashing against the table. "You cheeky little sod! That just show's you what she is, letting a kid of your age call her Nellie. And what do you think you are doing here, aye? You are here because your precious Matthews threw you out. You are here because nobody else wants you and I am the only one kind enough to take you in. As far as Celia is concerned, I have told you once already that what she does and what I do with Celia is no concern of yours. She is my daughter, you are not. You are just an evacuee and I'll teach you to do as you're told if I have to knock the life out of you doing it. Now take that nightdress upstairs, then get on with the potatoes."

Her head ringing from the double blows, Jenny snatched up the nightdress, taking it upstairs and stuffing it under Celia's pillow. I am going to tell Miss Grey, I am, she told herself. As soon as the thought of telling Miss Grey entered her head, doubt followed close on its heels. What if Mrs. Stafford did say she was a liar, who would Miss Grey believe? If she believed Mrs. Stafford then she wouldn't take her away and Mrs. Stafford would hit her even harder when Miss Grey was gone. And she couldn't run back to Nellie. She knew without Mrs. Stafford telling her, that the Matthews had thrown her out and didn't want her any more. Would the police really put her in a home for bad girls if she ran away? She couldn't run away because there was nowhere to go. Peeling the potatoes, sick with misery, she felt like a trapped animal.

"Oh my God, what are you doing? Don't you know there's a war on and food is hard to come by. Don't peel those potatoes so thick, you are wasting good food. I'm fast losing all patience with you and just about ready to hammer you into the ground. This is going to be one long uphill struggle but we are going to get there." Once again she was doing things wrongly and getting a blasting. Mrs. Stafford demonstrated how to peel thinly, filling her hand with dirty water and flinging it in Jenny's face as she threw the knife back in the bowl.

By the time Mr. Stafford came home that evening the meal was ready and the table laid. Smiling as usual, with Celia clinging to his legs, he asked how Jenny's first day with her new family had been. Before she could reply Mrs. Stafford answered for her. "Oh we've been getting to know each other fairly well today. Jenny is settling in and getting to know the ropes. Aren't you dear?" Jenny glowered at her, taking this as some form of sarcasm.

As to be expected, the supper dishes were all hers to do, both washing and drying. She was told off for not doing them in the right order "First the glass, then the silver (by which was meant the cutlery), then the china, starting with the cleanest, and lastly the saucepans. That way we keep the water cleaner longer." When the dishes were finally finished she was told off again for taking so long. Jenny was heartily fed up. Washing up on the table made her arms ache because it was so high. She couldn't do them any faster with aching arms; not if they were to be done properly.

Bedtime was a blessing. She had never wanted to go to bed early before, but tonight she wished time would pass more quickly so she could get away from Mrs. Stafford. Wishing she had a bedroom of her own and didn't have to sleep in the same room as rotten Celia, she climbed the stairs and crawled into bed.

TWENTY-TWO

As the week wore on more and more jobs were added to Jenny's list. She had to empty the chamber pots into a pail, rinse the pots, carry the pail down the road to the lavatory to empty it, then rinse the pail in the river. The two old Mr. Browns threw their slops into the river but Mrs. Stafford didn't approve of that. Sweeping the floors and dusting furniture were now her jobs as well as washing up, making her own and Celia's beds, peeling potatoes, fetching vegetables from the garden, laying and clearing tables and whatever else Mrs. Stafford chose to give her. Everything took her much longer than it should because Mrs. Stafford was never satisfied, making her do things over and over again until she could scream in frustration. She was sure this was done on purpose to stop her having any time to go out to play.

Celia joined in Jenny's torment, sticking out her tongue, calling her names and telling her to fetch and carry for her. The first time she did this Jenny told her go do it herself. Celia pouted and demanded more loudly that she do it for her. When Jenny said no, Celia swung her doll at Jenny's head, catching her across the nose. Jenny slapped Celia's face in retaliation and Celia ran bawling to her mother. For that misdemeanour she was beaten across the back with a broom handle and told never to lay a finger on Celia again. From then on she had the added humiliation of having a six-year-old bossing her about with threats of "I'll tell Mummy of you," if she refused Celia's demands. For the first time in her life, Jenny was looking forward to going back to school to avoid everlasting housework and Mrs. Stafford.

Jenny soon learned she had made a big mistake in thinking that life would be easier on returning to school. As soon as Mr. Stafford left for work at seven o'clock on Monday morning, she heard Mrs. Stafford calling from her bedroom: "Jenny! Jenny! Get downstairs and put the kettle on. Then lay the table for breakfast and be quick about it." Tumbling from her bed, she threw on her old clothes from the day before and hurried downstairs. When all was done and tea made, Mrs. Stafford came down in her housecoat, followed shortly by Celia. Mrs. Stafford supervised breakfast and when it had been eaten she ordered Jenny to put the kettle on again to heat water for Celia's wash, after which she must clear the table and go upstairs to empty the slops, making her own and Celia's beds while she was up there.

Simmering with resentment, considering herself as being used as a free housemaid, Jenny completed her tasks, including rinsing the bucket in the river after emptying it. Mrs. Stafford was combing Celia's hair after washing and dressing her. Jenny lifted the kettle to find very little water in it. "Shall I fill the kettle again, Mrs. Stafford?" she asked.

"Whatever for? I told you the dishes can all be done in the evenings after supper."

"I need some water to wash myself. I've got to go to school and I'm going to be late if you make me do any more jobs." Jenny said, letting her voice show her resentment.

"Then you had better get on and wash hadn't you. You won't have time to wait for the kettle and you don't need warm water at your age anyway. AND I thought I told you to refer to Mr. Stafford and I as Uncle Reg and Aunt Edith. Please remember what you are told because I don't like to have to repeat myself."

"You said I could call you that if I like, you never said I had to and I don't want to. You're older than me and you wash in warm water so why am I too old?"

Mrs. Stafford was across the room in an instant. Grabbing Jenny by the shoulders she propelled her backwards into the wall, banging her head against the hard surface three times, then slapping her a stinging blow across the face. "What have I told you about answering back! I will not have it. Don't think you can ever beat me you miserable little toad. It will take a damn sight more than you to get the better of me." She bent to put her face about an inch from Jenny's. "Now say 'I'm sorry Aunt Edith, I will never be cheeky again.'"

Dazed and afraid, Jenny's spirit was not yet crushed and an urge to spit in the hateful face boiled up in her. Gritting her teeth to hold back the desperate urge, she said nothing.

Wham! The blow this time sent her crashing sideways into the stone sink and she grabbed frantically at its rim to stop herself falling. Mrs. Stafford grabbed at her again and lifted her hand.

"No, no. Don't hit me again. I'm sorry. I won't be cheeky any more."

"You're damn right you won't. Not if you want to live. What did I tell you to say? If you don't want to feel my hand again, say what I told you to say."

"I'm sorry Aunt Edith, I won't be cheeky again," Jenny said as meekly as she could, feeling a burning hatred against this ugly woman. Celia sat on a chair with her hands to her face giggling. Mrs Stafford turned to her. "You had better get off to school Celie love. Just because this one's going to be late there is no need for you to be late too. Off you go now and be a good girl."

Jenny washed herself in cold water with Mrs. Stafford watching over her. Attempting to use the towel, she found it snatched from her hands and the cold wet flannel slopped around her neck. "You don't dry until you are clean. Wash that neck again properly, it's still filthy."

At last ready and permitted to leave, Jenny ran all the way to school, arriving in the middle of prayers. Mrs. Mergrin was extremely cross at her lateness, making her stand by herself until prayers were over, then smacking her hard across the left palm with the flat of her ruler.

During the day she sought out Jimmy to tell him how much she hated being at the Staffords. "She's horrible Jimmy," she told her brother. "She just wants me there to be a slave. She makes me work all the time and won't let me out to play. And stinky Celia tells on me all the time and orders me about, and I'm not allowed to hit her but she can hit me. Do you think if I tell Miss Grey what they do to me she will take me away?"

"You can do what you like," he said. "I don't know how many times I have to tell you they don't care, but you can find out for yourself if you like."

"But Mrs. Stafford keeps on hitting me Jimmy. She says I've got to call her Aunt Edith and she says I don't do anything properly so she hits me about with the brush handle, and before school today she banged my head on the wall and knocked me over. She keeps on hitting me and I'm scared of her."

Jimmy did look concerned that Mrs. Stafford was hitting her around. "She didn't ought to be knocking you about, but I don't know what you can do about it." He shrugged. "What d'you expect me to do? I can't do anything. I don't like it at the Fosters either. She makes me work all the time too, but she doesn't hit me around. I don't know what you think I can do about it," he repeated.

"I don't s'pose you can do anything. I just wanted to tell you that I'm frightened of her, that's all." Jenny felt her voice begin to waver and tears were not far away. That would make Jimmy cross she knew, so she turned and ran through the trees, dashing in and out as fast as she could to blow away any tears that tried to squeeze through.

At the end of the school day she didn't want to go home. Celia was in the infant class who went home half an hour earlier than the juniors, so she wouldn't have to walk with her. She walked with Tommy and a couple of other children and when they got to the Feathers she decided to go in with Tommy and talk to Margie. She could see the Stafford's house as she walked up the concrete slope to Margie's back door and the sight of it filled her with dread. She wondered if Margie's mum would let her live with them if she asked her. It would be nice there, everybody was always smiling and laughing. Yes, she would ask Mrs. Roper if she could live with her.

"Oh hello Jenny," Mrs. Roper greeted her. "We haven't seen you for a while. I hear you're living almost next door now so I suppose you've been settling in. It'll be nice for you and Margie to be closer now won't it."

How badly Jenny wanted to tell her that she hated living almost next door. Listening to Mrs. Roper chattering on, and Margie joining in as they walked into the living room, somehow she just couldn't say anything. They all seemed so happy for her to be nearer now and thought she was happy too; so she said yes, she was happy to be closer and was settling in. She stayed for fifteen minutes or so, then thought she had better go in case Mrs. Stafford got mad with her for being late home.

A blow to the back of the head sent her careening into the table. "And where have you been all this time might I ask? Celia has been home for almost an hour. Would you mind explaining just what took you so long?" Mrs. Stafford had been waiting behind door as she walked in, and now her eyes were blazing.

"Just talking to Margie for a minute. I haven't done anything wrong. What did you hit me for?" Jenny said, feeling herself shake.

"Just talking to Margie for a minute," Mrs. Stafford mimicked. "Well, while you are 'just talking to Margie' there are things waiting here to be done. Did I or did I not tell you to come straight home?"

"I don't remember. I wasn't long. What do you want me to do?" Jenny jerked her arm up to her face to fend off any further blows.

"I want you to change your clothes then get in there and peel the potatoes to start with. And when I tell you to come straight home, I mean straight home. Do you hear me?"

That evening Jenny was made to sit at table without any food. This was to help her remember to be obedient in future. Mr. Stafford looked uncomfortable eating his meal while Jenny had an empty space in front of her. "Don't you think she should have just a little bit dear?" he asked.

"She shall eat when she has learned to do as she's told. You're not here to see the defiance and downright cheek I have to put up with from that one. Don't you go sticking up for her or there is going to be another war; this time right in this house."

Jenny was hungry. "I promise to come straight home every day," she said. "Please can I have something to eat?"

It was no use pleading. She was allowed nothing. In bed after doing the dishes, her head hurt from the morning's battering and she couldn't sleep for the hunger pangs in her stomach. Praying to God to tell her mother what was happening to her and to Jimmy, she pleaded with Him to send her back to fetch them. "I don't care if bombs come down so long as we can be together again." she prayed.

TWENTY-THREE

The pattern of Jenny's new life was now set. Up early each morning to get her allotted chores done before school. More often than not being late for school to earn the anger of Mrs. Mergrin. Straight back home to more chores which were never done well enough to satisfy Mrs. Stafford, thereby earning more wrath and beatings. Friday nights were bath nights. The smaller of the two tin baths, which hung outside on the wall beside the porch, was brought in and placed in front of the fireplace. Buckets of water had to be heated on the gas stove, tipped into the bath, cooled, then Celia would be undressed and bathed. Celia liked bath times, never wanting to get out until the water got chilly. When she did get out, the bath was dragged into the scullery for Jenny to bathe in Celia's dirty, now almost cold, water. Jenny had objected to this at first, asking if she could put on the kettle to warm the water. She had received a slap in the face for her cheek and never made such request again. Another, non-repeated, mistake she made on the first bath night was to call to Aunt Edith, as she now grudgingly called her, and ask if she would please wash her back. Aunt Edith had looked at her askance. Then she had smiled and said, "Oh of course I'll scrub your back for you," and she had. Literally. She had fetched a nail brush, rubbed soap on it and almost scrubbed the skin from Jenny's back. Jenny had screamed in agony and her back felt as if it was on fire for several days. If she rolled onto her back at night, the heat was so fierce it woke her.

On Saturdays, Mrs. Stafford went shopping in Salisbury market and was away from 10:00 a.m. until 4:00 p.m., always ensuring Jenny had enough work to do to prevent her from going out to play. Her Saturday chores had now increased to taking the floor rugs outside to sweep off with a small stiff bristled brush, sweeping and washing the living room floor, polishing the linoleum, scrubbing the scullery floor and dusting all the furniture; as well as all her previous jobs. Sunday was the only time Jenny had any respite from constant work. She and Celia attended Sunday School at the Chapel beside the Matthews' house in the mornings and neither of them were allowed out to play on Sundays, having to stay in and either read or play indoor games. The only work Jenny had to do on this day was dish washing, bed making and potato peeling.

Summer holidays rolled round again and Jenny remembered what fun it had been last year helping with the harvest. She plucked up enough courage to ask Aunt Edith's permission to join in the harvest again this year, knowing in her heart she would be refused. "I can't think why you would even want to go where any of the Matthews were, seeing how they threw you out. In any case you can't go because there's too much to do here." Aunt Edith never missed an opportunity to remind Jenny that the Matthews had thrown her out and that nobody wanted her. She hadn't really thought she would be allowed to go harvesting anyway.

Early in the holidays, Miss Grey came to visit, having called to see Jimmy first. Aunt Edith had told Jenny the day before that Miss Grey was coming, and all that night she had tossed in her bed trying to decide how best to tell Miss Grey how miserable she was at the Staffords. The opportunity did not arise, however, because Aunt Edith never left them alone for a second. She had made sure Jenny was dressed in clean clothes, had even combed her hair for her, and had spoken to Miss Grey in her false posh, sweet sounding voice, calling Jenny 'Jenny dear' and telling Miss Grey how well Jenny was doing and how they all got along so nicely. Miss Grey smiled at Jenny. "I'm so glad you are settling so well. Are you happy here Jenny?"

Feeling as if Aunt Edith's eyes were burning a hole in her back, Jenny felt totally trapped. "Yes, thank you," was all she could think of to say, and as she did so the hopelessness of her situation hit home. Panic gripped as the thought flickered through her mind that her only hope of escape was about to close. But no, she could say she wanted to walk with Miss Grey to the bus stop and then she could tell her everything. The pounding in her heart almost deafened her as Miss Grey said it was time to leave.

"Can I come to the bus stop with you?" she asked.

"Why Jenny, of course, if you wish. But do you really want to? The way the buses are these days we may be just right to catch it or we may have to stand around for another half hour before it gets here."

"Don't be silly, Jenny dear. Miss Grey doesn't want you going to the bus with her, you will just be a hindrance. Say goodbye to her now and let her go, there's a good girl." Aunt Edith's eyes glinted unmistakable messages to Jenny as she spoke.

Despite the fear shooting through her as she read those eyes, Jenny felt she had already cost herself a hiding at the very least and had little to lose by persisting. "I just want to walk with you, that's all. Please can't I?" she asked Miss Grey as innocently as she could.

"Oh dear, of course you can if it means that much. Come along then, but we shall have to hurry now," Miss Grey said, holding out her hand to Jenny. Jenny took the proffered hand without daring to look back at Aunt Edith and they left. Walking at a fast pace, not speaking at all during the walk, Jenny searched her mind for a way to open her appeal to Miss Grey. There was no sign of the bus when they reached the stop and Miss Grey voiced her hope that they hadn't already missed it.

"That was nice of you to accompany me, Jenny," she said. "I am so pleased you are happy with the Staffords. They do seem such nice people and they like you too." Smiling, she put her hand on Jenny's head. "You don't need to wait with me dear, I'm sure the bus won't be much longer. Why don't you pop on home now?"

Jenny's new found resolution left her. How could she tell Miss Grey what Aunt Edith was really like? She would never believe her and she might even tell Aunt Edith what Jenny had said and then Aunt Edith would surely kill her. With leaden heart she said goodbye to Miss Grey, walking back to what she knew without doubt awaited her. This time it was not the handle of the long brush but the head that caught her squarely between the shoulders, knocking the breath from her body so that she gasped for air as Aunt Edith vent her towering rage. "And what did you tell your precious Miss Grey," she bellowed. "You defiant little bitch, if you've tried telling tales there is no way they'll believe you because I'll tell them what a bloody little liar you are." Grabbing Jenny by the hair and yanking her from the floor, she shook her to and fro viciously. "Still think you can defy me don't you! Well I'll teach you if its the last thing I do." The veins on her neck were standing out, her face all twisted and ugly. She let go so suddenly that Jenny, off balance, crashed to the floor again. The fall seemed at last to loosen Jenny's breath and she screamed.

Aunt Edith kicked her in the side. "Shut up and get up or I'll give you something to scream about. Get up those stairs and change, and get back down here double quick." Scrambling to get to her feet, Jenny found she couldn't straighten up, a pain like stitch shot through her side where Aunt Edith had kicked her. Doubled over, her elbow crooked into her side, she half walked, half crawled upstairs to change. Perched on the edge of her bed, she tried to stifle the sobs rising unbidden from the depths, each involuntary jerk of her chest sending shooting pains through her chest. Why had she ever thought she could tell Miss Grey and get away with it? How stupid she had been. There was no way to beat Aunt Edith and she was going to be here for ever; or at least until Aunt Edith killed her. Suffused in misery, she began painfully to change her clothes.

TWENTY-FOUR

Returning from the Post Office & General Store where she had been sent to make some purchases, Jenny was surprised when Aunt Edith picked up a piece of paper that was lying on the table and handed it to her. "This came for you while you were out," she said.

"For me? What is it and who brought it?"

"Read it and you'll see. It's a telegram in case you've never seen one before."

A telegram? Who would be sending her a telegram? She hadn't ever seen one before and looked at it in wonderment. The words were on little strips of paper stuck on to the larger piece, and read: 'Granddad passed away this morning. Writing. Granny.' Jenny read the words two or three times in puzzlement. "What does it mean? Who sent this to me?" she asked Aunt Edith.

"Your grandmother sent it of course. It means just what it says I suppose. Your grandfather died this morning and your grandmother will be writing to you."

Granny? However did Granny know where she was? She thought nobody knew where she was and now here was a telegram from Granny. Did it mean Mummy was back or that Granny knew where her mother was? Granny was going to write. Then she would have an address and could write back to her. Jenny hadn't wanted to live with Gran but now it seemed like heaven compared to living with Aunt Edith. But Granddad was dead. The reason for the telegram sank into her mind and she was saddened. Granddad had always been nice to her and tickled her back. She didn't believe he really had skipped with her rope but he pretended he had and she had loved him. Somehow Granny and Granddad seemed from another world, belonging to someone she had known but never really was. Trying to think back to family times, it was all so unreal, like a dream she had watched but wasn't really part of. Now she was awake and all the dream people were dead. Daddy, Mummy, Granny, Granddad, Jimmy. Jimmy!

"Are you going to stand there gaping all day? I don't know why you're looking so stunned, you've never mentioned any grandparents since you came here so they can't mean that much to you. In any case, old people die you know. Nobody lives for ever and you won't live a lot longer if you don't get moving."

"No. Aunt Edith, I have to tell Jimmy. Please let me go and tell Jimmy about Granddad."

"I should imagine that if you got a telegram, he got one as well. He probably knows already so there is no need to rush up and tell him."

"But p'raps he didn't. P'raps Granny doesn't know where he is and thinks I'll tell him. Please let me go. I won't be long I promise. Please."

Aunt Edith sighed. "Well, all right then. But don't be more than an hour or it will be the last favour I ever grant you. One hour only mind."

Ecstatic to be free, if only for an hour, Jenny raced over the bridge and up the road to the Fosters. Jimmy was in the garden thinning out carrots when she arrived. "Hello Jimmy," she called over the wall. "Come here, I've got something to show you."

"Yes I know," he said, walking across the garden. "You had a telegram from Gran I suppose. I had one too. Granddad's dead. It's a shame we can't see him any more."

"Mrs. Stafford said you probably had a telegram too. I never had a telegram before did you? Jimmy, how did Gran know where we live so she could send us telegrams?"

"I should think the Ministry must have told her where we are don't you? They're the only ones who could have."

"Well now she knows where we are she's going to write to us. It says so on the telegram. When she does shall we ask her to come and take us away to live with her? I know she isn't very nice but she's better than Mrs. Stafford, and you'd like her better than Mrs. Foster wouldn't you?"

"Jenny, you always go off half cocked at everything," her nine-year old brother said. "If you thought what you were saying sometimes,

I wouldn't get so fed up with you. To start with, Gran is an old lady and won't want a couple of kids with her. Granddad's dead and she won't want us two to look after by herself. And in case you've forgotten, the reason we're here is because there's a war on and Portsmouth is dangerous. Besides, what makes you think she cares about us anyway? She hasn't even bothered to come and see us or even write a letter in two years. You do what you like, but even if she would take us, I wouldn't go."

Dejectedly, Jenny retraced her footsteps. Why did she always end up making Jimmy fed up with her? Was it so silly to prefer Gran to Mrs. Stafford? And if Gran could live in Portsmouth without bothering about bombs, why couldn't they? He was probably right that Gran wouldn't want them anyway, but when her letter came she still thought she might ask.

TWENTY-FIVE

Mrs. Stafford got herself a morning job serving in the International Stores in Salisbury. She left on the eight o'clock bus in the morning, catching the two o'clock bus back in the afternoon and arriving home shortly after half past two. Jenny had allotted chores to do every day, being forbidden to go out to play until after Aunt Edith returned. Then, if things were done properly and there was time, Aunt Edith said, she would see about letting her out. Nothing was ever right so Jenny never got to play outside. After two weeks of constantly being kept in other than running errands, Jenny's frustration was growing intense. She decided that if she was never going to be allowed out, she would go without permission while Aunt Edith was at work. No matter how much time she spent trying to do each job well, there was always something wrong, so why keep trying. She could go out to play for an hour or longer, then come back and race round the chores before Aunt Edith got back.

One thing she had to do every day was prepare sandwiches for Celia at lunch time. Celia went out to play every day. Her best friend lived on Woodside Road at the top of the hill and round the corner. If Celia went up there to play, she was away all morning, but if her friend came down instead to play in Celia's garden, Jenny was unable to slip out for fear of Celia seeing her. Celia constantly told tales to get Jenny into trouble. Jenny tried being very nice to Celia, suggesting that she make her sandwiches early so she could take them with her and picnic in her friend's garden at lunch time. Celia liked that idea, taking her little package with her to her friend's house. With Celia gone, Jenny could nip out to swing on the bridge, visit Margie or play in the river with other children, catching fish in a jam jar. Sometimes she went up the Lane part way to play hide and seek in the bushes. She became adept at cutting corners with the chores, flinging the slops in the river instead of taking them all the way down the garden to the lavatory, sometimes sweeping the dirt under the mat, flicking the bits off the rugs with dustpan and brush instead of taking them outside. She learned how to pull the top covers up neatly on her own and Celia's beds without bothering to strip them back and straighten the undersheet. Of course, she got into trouble for sloppy work and took many beatings, but she got that whether she tried her best or didn't bother. It made no difference.

She got away with this for over two weeks until Celia came crying home one day, having fallen down and grazed her knee. She found Jenny in the river fishing, demanding that she come and bathe her knee. Celia made no mention of having seen Jenny at the river until they were seated at the evening meal. Then she announced, "Jenny was playing in the river when I hurt my knee. She's not s'posed to play out is she." Jenny flushed scarlet. "No I wasn't you liar," she said. "I was rinsing out the slop bucket, I wasn't playing." The blow to the face caught her across the nose, blood immediately dripping onto the tablecloth.

"Don't you dare call Celie a liar. Get over to the sink at once and don't bleed on the cloth, the stains won't come out." Aunt Edith jumped from her chair to tip Jenny onto the floor before she could get out of the seat. Yanking her up, she shoved Jenny to the sink, pushed her head under the tap and turned the cold water over her neck. Sending Celia for a flannel, she soaked it under the tap, pulled Jenny's head up by the hair and slapped the sopping flannel in her face. "Clean that nose up, then sit down and we'll get to the bottom of this. Now just what were you doing at the river?"

"She had a jam jar with string on it. She didn't have the bucket, I saw her." Celia said.

"I see. Are you going to call her a liar again?" Aunt Edith asked Jenny. "I wouldn't if I were you because I can tell who is lying and who is not." Jenny sat mutely, trying to stop the shaking in her stomach with the realization that she had been caught. "Very well, you get no supper tonight, and tomorrow we shall have to make arrangements to see that you don't have so much time that you can go out when you have been expressly told not to."

Next day she was given the pantry to turn out, wash all the shelves and restack everything tidily. She also had to clean all the brass ornaments in the house, including the brass rail of the fender around the fireplace. These on top of the everyday chores. From that day on Celia was told to play only in the garden and around the house so she could keep an eye on Jenny. The brief hours of stolen freedom were over.

Saturday nights were dance nights for Aunt Edith. Her nineteen year old niece, Rita, came to their house from her village over the hill and together she and Aunt Edith went to the village hall to dance. Uncle Reg stayed home to watch the girls, allowing them to stay up later than usual on those nights. Sometimes he read them stories, Celia sitting on his lap and Jenny on the floor beside his chair. Occasionally Jenny sat on his lap for a while, but Celia usually got nasty and kicked her off, saying Jenny squashed her. Uncle Reg was a terrible reader but Jenny didn't mind. Just to hear someone talking to her in a normal voice gave her a small feeling of warmth. It was hard to talk to Uncle Reg. He smiled and gave short answers if he was spoken to, but never made conversation or wasted words. He didn't seem to mind Aunt Edith going dancing without him. His night out was Friday, bath night. Then he would go to the Feathers for a couple of pints of beer, coming home at half past ten, closing time.

One Saturday afternoon towards the end of the summer holidays, Aunt Edith busied herself in the scullery baking cakes and pies, making jellies and a large trifle. She set Jenny to polishing the living room floor and all the furniture, then to peeling a second batch of potatoes. "What are you making all this food for? Is there somebody coming to tea?" Jenny asked.

"Yes, Miss Nosey Parker, there is. We are having some people to tea tomorrow and I want everything looking nice. And you mind your manners when the visitors are here, or you will be sent to your bedroom with no tea."

The following afternoon Jenny helped set the table. There was more food than she had seen in a long time, almost as if there was no rationing any more. Sliced ham and corned beef, potato salad, pickled onions, bread spread with real butter, and the cakes, pies jellies and trifle prepared the previous day. When the visitors arrived they turned out to be four soldiers from the searchlight up the Drove. Sometimes people in the village invited one or two of the soldiers to share a meal with them, and Aunt Edith had sent a message to invite four soldiers to tea. As soon as they arrived Aunt Edith started to talk in her posh voice, gushing at the men and laughing with them. If she spoke to Jenny she called her 'Jenny dear', acting as if she was the kindest person in the world.

Rita came and they all sat down to eat. Everyone was in a good mood and there was lots of laughter. Uncle Reg beamed at the guests, joining in the conversation here and there, but mostly just smiling. During tea Jenny made the most of her opportunity to eat as much as she wanted. Normally only allowed margarine on her bread because Celia was given her butter ration, she ate three slices of buttered bread with the ham and potato Aunt Edith had put on her plate. She also ate a slice of cake and a piece of pie after eating the trifle and jelly she was given. She avoided Aunt Edith's eyes which would probably flash a warning at her if she were to look, instead chatting to the soldier next to her.

The soldier was nice. He asked her name and told her he had a little girl at home who was just two years old. Jenny asked him if he was scared when he turned the big lights on the airplanes and shot guns at them. He told her he didn't really do any of those things, he just kept them in good order and fixed anything that went wrong. While they were all eating the wireless was playing softly and Vera Lynn came on singing 'White Cliffs of Dover'. "I like that song don't you?" Jenny asked the soldier.

"Yes, I do," he said. "I only wish it was true today."

"Why? What does it mean then?" Jenny liked the song for its pretty tune, but had never really thought about the words, or what they meant.

"Well, it's what they call symbolic I suppose. Bluebirds mean happiness and the song means that when the war is over and peace comes, bluebirds will fly in over Dover instead of the grey birds of destruction that fly there now."

"Where is Dover. I don't know that place."

"Its on the east coast of England," he told her. "That's where most of the German planes come in to bomb our towns."

"So why did you say you wish it was true today? Don't you believe about the bluebirds?"

"Jenny dear, stop asking so many silly questions and let George eat his tea, there's a good girl," Aunt Edith said in her sickly sweet-posh voice.

"Oh, I don't mind," said soldier George. "Its good for kids to ask questions. And yes Jenny, I believe about the bluebirds, but it won't be tomorrow. Not for a hell of a lot of tomorrows the way things are going. But when it is over," he said, smiling and tucking a finger under her chin, "then Jenny will go to sleep in her own little room again."

Jenny hadn't missed the warning glance that Aunt Edith shot across the table at her so she asked no more questions, instead thinking about what George had said. When the war was over, would she really go home again? Mummy had sold the house and nobody knew where she was. What would happen to them when the war ended? Mummy would come back, that's what would happen. And Daddy would come out of prison and they would get another house and be a family again. Wanting so much to believe what the soldier said, she sent up a little prayer. 'Please God let the bluebirds fly soon. Let there be bluebirds for me and Jimmy.'

After tea everyone left for the dance except Uncle Reg and the girls. This was the beginning of many such Saturdays, with different soldiers coming to tea and all going on to the dance afterwards. They often brought food with them, tins of meat, sugar, butter, tea and other things that were rationed or difficult to get. Jenny made the most of her chance to eat well at these parties even though Aunt Edith warned her not to make a pig of herself. Jenny had learned that although Aunt Edith would look daggers at her, she would not punish her in front of the guests, and by Sunday she was normally in a happy mood after having danced the night before, forgetting Jenny's defiance of her instructions.

As winter approached Jenny found herself with yet another job, one which she came to hate above all others and caused her more beatings for incompetence. As soon as Uncle Reg left for work Aunt

Edith would yell at her to get up as usual, but now she ordered her to get the fire going so it would be warm for her and Celia to dress in front of when they got up. She had been shown how to crumple newspaper, lay sticks crossways on top and place coal carefully on the sticks, but the paper burned and fire constantly went out so that she had to start over. Tears of frustration fell as Aunt Edith bellowed from upstairs that she had better have the fire lit, table laid and tea made by the time she came down or there would be hell to pay. She had seen Aunt Edith hold a double page of newspaper across the front of the fire to make it draw, but when she tried that the draught sucked the paper in over the fire and set it alight. The whole sheet flamed and roared up the chimney, frightening Jenny to death lest she set the house on fire. The paper burned and fell back in black sooty pieces all over the fire and hearth, and the fire went out again. When finally it was going she had to clean up the hearth, polish it with black lead polish, and fill the coal bucket.

Shivering with cold as she shovelled coal, the full bucket became too heavy to lift. It was no use taking it back half empty so with two hands she lugged it a couple of steps and put it down. All the way along the garden path, across the road, down past the house and in the back door, she heaved the heavy bucket. Arms and shoulders aching unbearably, she was filthy from head to toe by the time all this was done. Washing in cold water, she could never manage to get the grime from her hands. Constantly late for school now, she was forever being caned with the ruler. Then she would get another whack for having such dirty hands. If she managed to wake early, she sometimes crept downstairs before Uncle Reg left and asked him in a whisper if he would please light the fire. Sometimes he did, putting his finger to his lips as he left to indicate it was their secret.

Christmas held little anticipation for Jenny that year. She had long ago stopped believing in Father Christmas and expected no gifts from Aunt Edith. There was no-one else to give her presents and Christmas would probably mean even more work for her to do. Although she had waited daily for a letter after receiving the telegram from Gran, no letter ever arrived. Jimmy had received none either, but he had not expected that Gran would bother to write, and neither child thought Gran likely to send them any gifts. In school they made

Christmas cards and decorations from coloured paper and paste. Jenny enjoyed doing this, catching some of the excitement from the other children for whom Christmas meant so much, but as the day approached she became despondent.

Christmas, in fact, was not as bleak as she expected.

TWENTY-SIX

Jenny woke to Celia's excited shouts that Father Christmas had come. Opening her eyes she saw Celia bouncing on her bed tipping parcels from a pillowcase, pouncing on a gift to tear the paper from it. She turned her back to Celia, pulling the clothes over her head to block out the sight and sounds, and as she did so something heavy rolled over her legs and thumped to the floor. Sitting up to see what had fallen, she saw a blue sock stuffed into an odd shape. Picking it up she was delighted to find it contained two apples, a bag of chocolate pennies, two coloured hair slides, a rolled book of Aesop's Fables and, of all things, an orange. Oranges were almost impossible to get and she couldn't remember the last time she had eaten one. Aunt Edith must have put these things on her bed. All of a sudden, Jenny wanted to cry in gratitude that Aunt Edith had cared enough to buy something for her. She wanted to go and give her a hug and a kiss, but Celia had already rushed into her parents' room to show them what Father Christmas had brought for her. She was making a lot of noise and Jenny could hear Aunt Edith exclaiming over the things Celia was showing her.

She looked at her chocolate pennies, all wrapped in gold coloured foil. Sweets were rationed and although Aunt Edith did buy some, using Jenny's coupons as well as everyone else's, she seldom gave Jenny any. Now she had a whole bag of chocolates to herself. Putting the slides into her hair, she walked to the door of the Stafford's bedroom. "Thank you for my presents," she said when Aunt Edith noticed her there. "I didn't think you would give me anything. Would you like a chocolate penny?" she asked, walking further into the room.

"Did you really think I would leave you out? Well, that shows what you think of me doesn't it," Aunt Edith said, taking a penny and putting it on the table by her bed. Jenny felt her face flush at Aunt Edith's words as she offered the bag to Uncle Reg.

"No thanks," he said. "I don't think I could eat chocolate before breakfast, but thanks anyway." Feeling obliged, she gave a penny to Celia who unwrapped and ate it right away. "I just meant I didn't think I deserved any presents," she said to Aunt Edith by way of explanation. "Thank you." She bent towards Aunt Edith and planted a quick kiss on her cheek and ran from the room.

"Huh! Whatever was that all about?" she heard Aunt Edith say. "Jenny, get dressed now and put the kettle on. Uncle Reg will light the fire this morning. He'll be down in a minute."

After breakfast, Aunt Edith wanted the dishes washed and put out of the way to give her more room to prepare Christmas dinner. Jenny did this, then peeled potatoes, prepared the brussels sprouts that Uncle Reg brought in from the garden, scraped carrots and peeled a swede. Dinner preparations done, Aunt Edith made a cup of tea and told Jenny and Celia to sit down. Disappearing down the passage to the front room, she returned carrying a big box which she gave to Celia, and a smaller, brown paper wrapped parcel which she dropped in Jenny's lap. "I did buy a present for you as you had no-one to give you anything," she said to Jenny. "But since somebody has sent something for you after all, I shall not give you my present."

Jenny stared at her parcel in astonishment. "Who sent me a parcel?" she asked. "Is it from my Gran?"

"How do I know? I can't even read the postmark because its all smudged. Best you can do is open it and then you'll know."

Jenny removed the brown wrapper and a small card fluttered to the floor. Picking it up Jenny read: 'Happy Christmas Jenny. This is just a little present for you. I hope you are being a good girl. I cannot come to see you just now but will come as soon as I can. Love you dear, Mum.'

"It's from my Mum!" Jenny squealed. "My Mum knows where I am and she's going to come and see me as soon as she can. Look, it says so on this card."

"What's in your parcel. Why don't you open it and see what's in it?" Celia said, walking over to Jenny with her new doll. Aunt Edith had said nothing to Jenny's excited outburst, merely sniffing in a disapproving way. Celia poked a finger at the coloured paper around

Jenny's gift, itching to know what was in it. "Don't," Jenny said, pushing her away. "I don't want to open it yet, I'm going to save it for later." She read and re-read the little card, turning it over to look for an address, but there was none. There was nothing on the brown paper to show where it had come from either. How was it, she wondered, that her Gran and her mother both knew where she was but the Ministry said they couldn't find anybody. When Miss Grey had come last, Jenny had told her about Gran's telegram and asked if she knew Gran's address. Miss Grey said had no idea where her Gran lived and doubted the Ministry could have told her where Jimmy and Jenny were. They truly did not know where her Gran lived nor where her mother was. It was all so mysterious. Jimmy said the Ministry must have told Gran and Miss Grey said they hadn't. Jenny wasn't sure she believed Miss Grey.

"Well if you're not going to open your parcel, you may as well get up and make the beds. I have to get on with the dinner," Aunt Edith said.

Jenny took her parcel upstairs with her. When the beds were done, she sat on hers and opened the parcel. It was a white fluffy swan with folded wings, about fourteen inches long, with a slim arched neck. It was beautiful and graceful, but Jenny felt a tinge of disappointment that her mother should send her a fluffy toy when she was eight and a half years old. Idly stroking the swan first one way then the other, she jumped when its back suddenly flew up to reveal a hollow inside filled with little wrapped parcels. How clever of her mother to find such a lovely present. Excitedly she opened the small parcels to find a necklace of pretty coloured glass beads, a bracelet to match the necklace, a brooch in the shape of a teddy bear, and a pink angora pixie hat. Her mother must have knitted the hat especially for her. She put it on and tied it beneath her chin. So soft; it would keep her ears lovely and warm in the cold winter. Decking herself in beads, bracelet and brooch, she picked up the swan to show Aunt Edith. Something made her close the back of the swan and decide not to tell anyone that it was hollow. Celia had a way of poking into anything belonging to Jenny and it might be a good hiding place from her prying fingers.

"Well aren't you the lucky one," Aunt Edith said as Jenny walked proudly into the living room to show off her presents. "Its very nice for some people to send the odd gift to their children and forget their responsibilities for the rest of the year, I must say."

Tears of humiliation stung the back of Jenny's eyes at this remark. She turned away so that Aunt Edith couldn't see how much her words had hurt. Her mother didn't forget her responsibilities, she was just not able to come for some reason - it said so on the card. Aunt Edith was being horrid on purpose and Jenny hoped fervently that her mum would come very, very soon so that she could tell her how miserable she was in this place.

One thing Aunt Edith couldn't take away from her. Somewhere her mother remembered and loved her and had made this Christmas special. Jenny wondered if she had sent Jimmy a present too and felt sure that she had. One day soon she would come back and take her and Jimmy away.

TWENTY-SEVEN

Uncle Reg had to go to see his mother who lived in a village several miles away. She had become ill and someone had brought a message from her asking for Uncle Reg. He decided to go on Saturday and return sometime on Sunday. It was the first time Jenny had seen the car brought out of the shed. Uncle Reg pushed it out backwards, then spent considerable time and effort swinging the starting handle while the car popped and spluttered, eventually roaring into life. Red faced, sweat shining on his moon face, Uncle Reg stowed the handle in the boot, climbed into the driver's seat and started away. Phut-phutting its way slowly down the road, the car rounded the corner and out of view.

Because he was away on Saturday night and Aunt Edith didn't want to give up her dance night, she decided to take Celia and Jenny with her to the dance. "You can look on it as a special treat for just this once, but don't go expecting it every week because it won't happen," she told them. Jenny wasn't sure that going to watch grown-ups dance was any sort of treat, but as they had no choice there was not much they could do. Jenny, who had very little in the way of clothes by now, dressed in her blue school skirt and pale blue jumper. Celia was dressed in her best winter dress, it being March and still chilly.

The dance, as Jenny had feared, proved to be anything but a treat for the girls. The first thing they noticed on entering the hall was that the whole expanse of wooden floor was covered with white powder. Attempting to walk across the floor, both girls lost their footing and fell down.

"That's French chalk," Aunt Edith laughed. "You have to be very careful how you walk on it because its extremely slippery so that people can dance on it." Picking themselves up, the girls skidded the rest of the way to the other side. Hard backed chairs were set side by side around three walls, the top of the room being taken up by the stage. A fire burned in the grate at the far end, protected by a metal guard. Aunt Edith told them to sit in two chairs fairly close to the stage so they could watch the band, got them a glass of lemonade each and left them to themselves. They had come early and as people drifted in, Celia skidded up and down, bumping into people and showing off as usual for a while. Eventually she got fed up and came back to sit by Jenny.

Soon the hall was packed with people, a great many of them soldiers in uniform. These were not only the searchlight soldiers, but a number of Americans, or Yanks as they were called by the locals, who had recently been based four miles away, near the Blandford Road. They were to be seen a lot around the village these days, roaring around in their noisy jeeps, shouting at the tops of their voices. Aunt Edith didn't much like the Yanks, preferring the searchlight soldiers who still came to tea on Saturdays, but the village girls who had previously dated the soldiers were now dating Americans. They always had lots of money, their uniforms were smarter and they gave the girls things like nylon stockings, which they couldn't buy in England.

As the night wore on and the room grew smoky, dusty, noisy and hot, the two children became sleepy, their eyes were sore and smarting, and both longed to go outside to breath fresh air. The chairs were hard and uncomfortable, making both of them fidgety. Jenny thought the noise the band made was awful, nothing at all like the music she heard on the wireless. The pianist was the local carrier who also played the organ at church. He thumped out tunes on the out-of-tune-piano at least half a beat behind the rest of the band, a yellowing cigarette stub stuck to his upper lip. A farm worker fiddled on a squeaky violin, and an old man Jenny didn't know strummed a double bass. The fourth member of the band was the milkman who tried valiantly to keep a beat going on the drums, occasionally clashing out a dreadful noise on the cymbals attached to the big drum. The resulting din was anything but musical and Jenny wondered why anybody bothered to come at all, let alone manage to dance to such a racket. From what little she knew of dancing, she did know that you had to move to the beat of the music, which was just about impossible here. Despite the band, everybody seemed happy and having a good time.

Aunt Edith remembered them from time to time, coming over to see if they were alright. By the time it was over, both girls were almost too tired to walk, and Celia grizzled all the way home. Jenny hoped they would not be given another 'treat' like that for a long time, if at all.

Soon after this, Aunt Edith took on a Saturday morning job cleaning the village hall and preparing it for the dance. Taking Jenny with her to help, they had to sweep the large floor, set out the chairs and dust them, lay in the fire, put out the cups in the kitchen and fill the tea urn, lastly sprinkling the floor with French chalk. It was a dirty job, the floor sweeping created clouds of dust, and Jenny was always glad to get out of the hall into fresh air after choking in all that dust. It seemed a waste of time to clean the chairs because by the time the dust all settled they would be covered again, but Aunt Edith always insisted it be done.

One Saturday in April, Aunt Edith wanted to go to Salisbury for the market, telling Jenny she was to do the hall by herself. She gave her the hall key, telling her to make sure it was all done properly. When Jenny finished the cleaning and left the hall she was surprised to see several army lorries parked in the road outside. At first she thought it was the Americans, but then she noticed that these soldiers wore very different hats. As she passed by the lorries a soldier jumped from the back of one and called to her. "Hey, come here little sweetheart, I want to ask you something." Jenny stopped and smiled. Nobody ever called her 'little sweetheart', and the soldier had a funny accent. Seeing her smile, the soldier smiled back. "Hey, look at those dimples," he said. "Come over here, Dimples, and tell me where I can find a shop around this place." Jenny tried to explain where the Post Office was, but the soldier took her hand saying that if she would take him to the shop he would buy her some sweets for taking him.

"I can't do that," she said. "I have to go home. Anyway, you can't buy sweets because they are on ration."

"Aw c'mon. You don't know what I can do, you wait and see. It won't take long and you can go straight home after, I promise. How about it, Dimples?" He seemed nice and friendly so Jenny allowed him to hold her hand and walked with him to the Post Office. On the way, he told her that they were Australians just passing through. He asked Jenny her name, saying he had a little girl at home in Australia. At the Post Office he made his purchases, sweet talking Mrs. Monday, the owner, into letting him buy a few toffees. "There, what did I tell you. We Aussies can talk our way into anything," he said as he handed Jenny the toffees. On the way back, Jenny pointed out her house and said she must go now, but he kept hold of her hand, insisting she come back to the lorry with him.

"Now," he said when they were back outside the hall. "Just hang on there a minute, Dimples, and I'm going to give you something else for being such a nice kid." He disappeared inside the back of the lorry, coming out holding a long canvass bag. Pulling open the tie strings, he dug around inside and brought out a tiny grey toy bear. "That's a koala bear. He's my mascot and I want you to have him because you're a good kid and I love those dimples. You keep that just for me eh?" Jenny thanked him and promised that she would always keep the bear. Running away, she heard him call again and turned around. "You make sure to look after my bear and he'll be lucky for you," he shouted. Jenny waved and ran home, dashing upstairs to stow the toffees and bear into her swan.

There were few toys left of those her mother had sent when she and Jimmy were at the Williamson's. Aunt Edith had made her give her stove, dresser and dishes to Celia, saying she was too old to play with such things. Some things had been broken and her lovely Raleigh bicycle had disappeared from the shed. Aunt Edith said it must have been stolen but she had never done anything to try and find out who had taken it. The only large toy she had left was her doll's pram which was kept in the shed under a sheet. She had one black doll with little braids of hair sticking out all over her head. Her father had brought this doll back from abroad for her when she was small and she treasured it. This doll and a few other small toys she kept in a cardboard box beside her bed, on top of which she kept her swan. Although Celia had picked up her swan at times, she had never discovered it had a hinged back.

Putting the little bear in the swan, she stroked its back, telling him that he now had a friend to keep him company. "You look after him and he will be lucky for us," she told the swan.

Her mother had never written again after sending her the swan. Jenny hadn't lost hope, saying silent prayers for her every night. As long as she had the swan by her bed, she felt sure her mother would come to fetch them one day. Now the little koala would help bring her too.

No soldiers were coming to tea that day. Aunt Edith prepared supper and they were all seated at table when Celia looked up at her mother. "Mummy, I saw Jenny holding a soldier's hand today and they were walking over Crossroads together," she said. Jenny froze!

"What's all this? What have you been up to as soon as my back is turned. My God!" Aunt Edith exploded, "can't you be trusted out of my sight for five minutes. You had better have a good explanation my lady, or else!"

"H-he w-was an Australian soldier," Jenny stammered. "H-he asked me the way to the shop when I came out of the hall. I-I just showed him where the shop was, that's all."

Aunt Edith smacked her hard across the mouth. "You damn little liar. There are no Australians anywhere near here. How dare you sit there telling bare faced lies and expect me to swallow them. We'll get to the bottom of this, never fear."

Pulling Jenny from the chair by her hair, she threw her into the scullery, slamming the door behind her. "Now," she said, picking up the broom, "see if you can't do better and tell the truth for once." Terrified, Jenny couldn't think of a suitable lie that would satisfy Aunt Edith. Weeping, she repeated the story she told at the table, swearing it was the truth. The broom head came down with such force on her shoulder it knocked her to the floor. She screamed as searing pain tore through her shoulder. Aunt Edith kicked at her. "Get up and let's have it again. The truth this time," she yelled lifting the broom for another blow. The door opened and Uncle Reg grabbed the broom away. "Control yourself, you're killing the child," he said. This was the first time he had seen Aunt Edith beat Jenny, although he had heard her shouting and seen her slapping Jenny numerous times.

Aunt Edith rounded on him. "I'll kill her. I'll kill her alright," she screamed at him. "She's just a dirty little bitch. Not nine years old and already sneaking out with men as soon as my back's turned. No doubt he bought her sweets from the shop. What else did he do I wonder? Now you can see for yourself what a sly, scheming little bitch she is. I told you before but you always make excuses for her. Now what have you got to you say?"

Uncle Reg put down the broom and walked away. As always, he had nothing to say.

Yanked up from the floor by the arm, shocking pain seized her shoulder and Jenny screamed again. "We're going to get to the bottom of this if I have to beat you black and blue," Aunt Edith raged. Shaking uncontrollably, Jenny thought of the koala upstairs, terrified now that it would be found and destroyed. "You can just stay here and think about your lies. I *will* find out the truth and woe betide you when I do." Aunt Edith went back into the living room, slamming the door behind her. Left to herself in the cold scullery, Jenny shivered and sobbed, holding her shoulder and wondering why showing somebody the way to a shop should cause so much agony. The soldier had been nice. What was he supposed to have done to make Aunt Edith say all those horrid things. She was glad he wasn't here to see her punishment for doing nothing.

The door opened and Aunt Edith ordered her to get to the table and clear it off. Lifting her arm to collect the plates, the pain in her shoulder was so severe that an involuntary shout left her lips. Aunt Edith smacked the back of her head. "Don't pile on the agony, just get on with those dishes." By the time the dishes were done Aunt Edith had left for the dance and Jenny was bathed in sweat although she was far from warm. Uncle Reg suggested she go straight to bed as her face was ghostly pale.

Sitting on the edge of the bed, she tried to undress but couldn't lift her left arm above her head. Giving up the struggle, she rolled into bed with her clothes on, hoping Aunt Edith wouldn't look in and pull her out again.

In the morning the shoulder was badly swollen and bruising began to show all down her upper arm. Aunt Edith said it was her own fault, and although on Sundays she hadn't so many chores, each thing she attempted brought agony. The pain lasted for weeks, during which time Aunt Edith had found out that Australian soldiers did in fact come through the village on the day in question. She never acknowledged that Jenny hadn't been lying, still saying she was a sly little bitch and would grow up no better than her mother. Disturbed by this remark, Jenny asked what she meant. No-one could speak about her mother in that way, particularly Aunt Edith who had never seen her mother. "What do I mean?" Aunt Edith said. "What do you think I mean. Your mother's no better than she should be and she certainly doesn't bother about her kids, leaving other people to bring them up while she flits around having a good time."

Jenny said she had to go to the lavatory, running out of the door to get away from Aunt Edith's stinging words. She was so distraught that had she stayed she would have picked up a knife and stuck it right into Aunt Edith.

TWENTY-EIGHT

If Jenny hoped that her mother would write again for her birthday, she was sadly disappointed. Her ninth birthday passed without a word from anyone. Walking to school that day, she met Jimmy coming over the humped bridge. It was warm and there had been no fire to light, so she was on time for once. "It's my birthday today," she told Jimmy as they walked together.

"I know," he said. "I haven't been able to get you a present, but here." Digging in his pocket he brought out four pennies which he handed to her. "Its all I've got," he said. Jenny looked at the pennies lying in her hand and her heart swelled. Jimmy had given her all he had; a horse of her very own wouldn't have meant so much to her at that moment.

"Oh thank you Jimmy," she said, throwing her arms around her brother.

"Hey, steady on," he said. "Its only fourpence, don't make a big thing of it." But she did. She guarded her pennies all day and in the evening put them into her swan. They were the only gift she received that birthday and they were from her brother. He did care for her after all. Jimmy was ten now, so grown up. He was taking his eleven plus exam this term and would be leaving the school at the start of summer holidays.

Her swan contained a growing number of treasures. She had slowly eaten the toffees from the Australian until there was one left. That one she would never eat, nor would she spend a single penny that Jimmy had given her. The little koala was safe in the swan along with the beads and brooch her mother had sent her. She had little possessions and less clothing. When she had first been evacuated her clothing had caused comment in the village. Even Mrs. Williamson had been impressed with the quality and amount of both her own and Jimmy clothes. Jenny had thought little of it then, but now, with what little she had being of poor quality and almost all too small, she realized how well their mother had dressed them. Aunt Edith complained to Miss Grey that there wasn't enough money to buy clothes for Jenny and Miss Grey agreed to send a cheque. When the cheque came Aunt Edith bought her a new pair of shoes, a second hand coat, skirt and two jumpers that were all too big. It was to give her room to grow into them she was told. Shortly afterwards, Celia got a brand new coat and dress. Jenny wondered if some of the money Miss Grey sent had gone to Celia.

Jenny was not doing well at school. She often found it hard to concentrate, giving in to daydreaming, gazing through the high windows to watch the clouds drift by and thereby earning knuckle raps from the ruler. At times she even fell asleep on her desk, earning even more severe reprimands. Always hungry and tired, the only 'good times' she looked forward to were when the soldiers came to tea and she could make a pig of herself.

One particular soldier was a Welshman known as Taffy. A strange man, given to moody sulks and fits of bad temper, he was not well liked by his mates. Whenever he came to tea Jenny felt nervous of him, although he seemed always to like Aunt Edith and wanted to sit near her. He had been the butt of a practical joke played on him by a group of soldiers and villagers, since which time he had been even less approachable than before. He had become smitten with a local girl, one of the ten Foster children - eighteen year old Pearl. He tried to date her many times without success until Taffy and his dating attempts were becoming a joke. One day he received a note signed 'Pearl', asking him to meet her outside the village hall at half past eight on a certain evening. The note had been written by another soldier who, with the help of some villagers and his friends, dressed himself in women's clothes, high heels and all, made up his face and put a on a blonde wig. The village was pitch dark by the time 'Pearl' stationed himself outside the hall.

Not only was 'Pearl' waiting for Taffy, but so were a number of soldiers and local people who were hiding behind hedges in and around the hall, straining their ears to hear what was going on. Taffy turned up at the appointed time, seeming completely fooled by his soldier mate speaking in a high pitched voice. They talked for a few minutes, then decided to go for a walk - trailed by folk creeping behind the hedges, smothering titters. They hadn't gone far before the soldier decided he couldn't hobble any further in the high heels, nor keep up the pretence, and burst out laughing. So did everybody else, while Taffy screamed in humiliation. Not many weeks after the incident, Taffy went away for two weeks leave, failing to return on time and was listed as Absent Without Leave.

May had started out warm but had turned chilly, so Jenny was back to fire lighting. Aunt Edith bellowed for her to get out of bed, continuing her harassment for Jenny to hurry up and get a move on or she would feel her hand upside her ear, while Jenny scrabbled into her clothes in the dark. She never got used to this constant shouting, wondering how Celia managed to sleep through it all every morning.

She made her way downstairs in the dark, opened the stair door and was surprised to find the living room in darkness. Uncle Reg must have turned off the light before leaving. She slid her hand up the wall to find the light switch and as she flicked it a hand suddenly clamped itself across her mouth and another gripped the back of her neck. Almost dead from fright she tried to scream but only managed a small muffled squeak as the hand on her mouth pressed tighter. Rolling her eyes around, she recognized Taffy as he dragged her into the room making shushing noises at her.

"I'll let you go, but be quiet and don't shout," he whispered to her, gradually releasing his hold. Jenny gasped for air and stood looking at him with hammering heart. He sat down, putting his finger to his lips to indicate silence, then turned his head away. Jenny didn't know what to do. He must have slipped in after Uncle Reg left for work and turned off the light. She knew the police were looking for him and wondered where he had been all night. There were no buses early in the morning so he must have been in the village somewhere.

"What's going on down there? I can't hear any work being done. If that fire isn't going in ten minutes I'll come down and set light to you, you lazy little bitch."

Jenny looked at Taffy and he shrugged, putting out his hands as if to say she could go. She set about cleaning out the fire and resetting it, and going about her morning chores. After she got over her fright, she began to enjoy the fact that Taffy was there to hear Aunt Edith ranting and cursing and letting herself down in front of one of her soldier friends. Now perhaps someone who thought she was so wonderful and kind to the little orphan evacuee could see what she was really like.

When all was done, she called up the stairs that the tea was ready and Aunt Edith came down in her dressing gown, hair all askew and wearing the ugly expression she reserved for Jenny. She saw Taffy immediately, and Jenny wanted to laugh at the shocked look on her face. "What on earth are you doing here?" she said. "Don't you know the police are looking for you?"

"Yes I do," he said. He hung his head, looking so unhappy, Jenny thought he was going to cry. "I could have killed Spider for that rotten trick he played on me. When I realized that the weird noises I heard were half the bloody village watching the 'show', I got so damn mad I didn't want to stay here any more. I didn't go home to Wales on my leave, I decided to clear off and not come back. It was dumb. I should have asked for a transfer or something. Now I'm AWOL and hunted and you're the only friend I've got, Edie. What am I going to do? I don't know what to bloody do."

"Pour Taffy a cup of tea," Aunt Edith ordered Jenny, disappearing upstairs, to return a little later dressed, hair combed and wearing lipstick. Preparing breakfast, she gave Jenny cereal and toast instead of her normal one slice of bread and margarine. Jenny even managed to leave for school without filling the coal bucket, knowing that Aunt Edith wouldn't want Taffy to see her struggling with it. He was gone when she got home from school. Jenny later heard Aunt Edith telling Uncle Reg about it, saying he had better lock the door behind him in future and drop the key back through the letter box. She said she had managed to persuade Taffy to go back to the searchlight and take his punishment. Jenny wished he would tell everyone else how Aunt Edith treated her so that someone would come and save her, but she doubted he would. He was in enough trouble himself.

TWENTY-NINE

Aunt Edith ran the Infirmary League for the village. People paid sixpence a week to belong, for which they received free doctor's visits and hospital treatment when needed. The money was paid monthly to Aunt Edith, who entered it all in a special book against each person's name and marked the cards they brought with them. She showed Jenny how it was done and left her to receive the money one Saturday when she went to the market. Jenny managed the job with the aid of some of the people, who helped find their names and told her where to put the figures. At the end of the day, Jenny was pleased with herself when Aunt Edith said it all added up right.

"What did you do this for?" Aunt Edith asked as she studied the book.

"Do what?" Jenny asked, looking to where Aunt Edith was pointing. At the top of each page was printed 19__, leaving space for the year to be written in. Several pages had figures written in ink - 42, 43, 44, 45 and so on. "I didn't do that," Jenny said, not having noticed it before.

"Don't lie," Aunt Edith said, becoming mad. "That is your handwriting Jenny Harding, just look at it!" She banged Jenny's head down on the book so hard it made her nose bleed. "Oh that's right," she said angrily. "Now go bleeding all over the book why don't you. You realize you've put all these figures in the wrong place and messed up the book don't you."

"It can't be my writing because I didn't do it," Jenny protested, holding her hands under her nose to stop the blood dripping onto the table. Aunt Edith sucked in her breath, eyes blazing. Snatching up the short handled brush from the hearth she brought it with such force across the left side of Jenny's face that the skin on her cheekbone tore and ran blood. Jenny staggered sideways, blazing with sudden fury. She would *not* scream or cry this time. Sick and tired of being beaten and accused of things she didn't do, she summoned up the full force of her will against this woman who tormented her so. Charging back at her, she knocked Aunt Edith off her feet so that she collapsed into the arm chair behind her. "Stop hitting me, I didn't do it. I never wrote those numbers, I didn't even see them. Just stop hitting me," she screamed.

Aunt Edith jumped to her feet. "You damn little sod. You think you can fight me? Well let's see." Grabbing Jenny by the hair, she ran her full tilt into the wall, bashing her forehead against it three or four times. Still holding her hair, she yanked Jenny back against the table and began to slap her viciously on each side of the face, left, right, left, right, left, right, until all Jenny could hear were rushing and popping sounds. Thrown to the floor, Jenny curled herself into a ball to protect her stomach against the kicks. "Tell me when you've had enough," Aunt Edith was shouting. "Because I can keep this up as long as you can."

"Yes, yes. Stop, please stop. I'm sorry," Jenny cried. She could take no more and her will, so iron strong a few moments before, burst like a pricked balloon under the assault. Aunt Edith commanded her to get up. "Now," she said. "Let's have the truth. Did you write in that book?" "Yes," Jenny said sadly. "I'm sorry, I didn't mean to."

"Didn't mean to? How can you write something if you didn't mean to, you stupid cow? All you had to do was admit it in the first place. I would have boxed your ears but you would have saved yourself a lot of misery. I can't stand liars. You know I can't stand your lying and will always get to the truth, so why do you try me so with your damn lies?"

Jenny had no answer. She hadn't written the figures and didn't know how they got there. She had got Celia to sit by the money when she went to the lavatory so perhaps she had done it. Jenny didn't know and cared less. From that day her attitude underwent a change. No longer did she look for anyone to save her, nor did she hope any more for her mother to come back. In place of the resentment and hatred she felt for Aunt Edith came a desire to please and be liked by her. True, there were times when the old hatred would flare and she would long to see Aunt Edith hurt or dead, but it seldom lasted.

On the night following the dreadful beating, Jenny had her strangest dream yet, one that was to be repeated with growing frequency. She found herself standing on the top of the stairs. Putting out a foot as if to step down, she felt herself lifted to the bottom without touching the stairs. Floating through the closed door, she rose horizontally into the air and drifted through the window. On and up towards the clouds she sailed, feeling a gentle breeze caress her as she watched the village and fields below. When she was so high she could barely see the village, she became frightened. Heights had always scared her and now she began to panic. By dropping her feet, she discovered she could bring herself down to float softly into a field. Running across the field without touching the ground, she could jump over trees as if an invisible rope was lifting her up and setting her softly down the other side. She woke before Aunt Edith started calling, remembering the feeling of freedom and peace the dream had brought.

Standing at the head of the stairs that morning, the memory of her dream was so vivid that she truly believed she had floated down the stairs and could do it again right now. All she had to do was put out a foot and she would be lifted to the bottom. She held out her foot but doubt stopped her. Maybe she would try it one day, but not today. The dream would not leave her, the clarity of it staying with her for days each time it recurred. In her heart, Jenny knew that she really did go sailing in the clouds on those nights, but nothing would make her admit this to anyone. It was her only means of escape and she felt that God had given her that special power.

THIRTY

Shopping became a new item on Jenny's growing list of jobs. Aunt Edith inexplicably gave up her job in the International Stores, but since she was registered there it meant going all the way to town for the rations. She took Jenny with her on three separate occasions, telling her after the third trip that she was now to do the shopping herself on Saturdays. Horrified, Jenny didn't think she could possibly manage that alone. Everywhere they had gone people jostled and pushed and there were queues at all the shops. Saturday was market day, meaning more crowds than ever and there was only a certain amount of time between buses to get everything done.

"I can't do that by myself, I'll get lost. I don't know where all the shops are and I can't remember the way to the bus station."

"Then you should have paid more attention, shouldn't you," Aunt Edith said. "If you get lost you have a tongue in your head and can ask. See if you can't do a simple job like shopping and get it right."

The following Saturday Jenny was given the ration books, money, a list with everything she had to get beside the names of the shops, and the price that everything should cost. Told not to come back without completing the list and with the right change, she took the shopping bags and caught the bus to town. She was lost as soon as she got to Salisbury bus station and had to keep asking her way around. Not sure if shop assistants were cutting and marking the right coupons, she found herself pushed to the back of queues or ignored by assistants who thought she was waiting for an adult. Never having owned a watch, she pestered people for the time every few minutes, the bags growing heavier with each purchase. Asking her way yet again, she staggered back to the bus station. Exhausted, Jenny concluded she would much prefer to stay home and scrub floors than go shopping, but the choice was not hers to make.

Almost as soon as she got home from shopping on the second Saturday, Aunt Edith sent her into the unused far end of the house with buckets, brooms and cloths, telling her to clean it all thoroughly, upstairs and down, not forgetting to brush the stair carpet with the stiff brush and dustpan. "Why have I got to do that, are we going to start using that end now?" she asked.

"You just mind your own business and do as you're told. You'll find out soon enough," was all the answer she got.

There wasn't enough time to do much because soldiers were coming to tea and Aunt Edith didn't want them to see Jenny working, so even though Sunday was not normally a working day, Jenny was sent back to cleaning, scrubbing and polishing that Sunday. It took up most of the day before Aunt Edith was satisfied. After supper Jenny had her dishes to do and by bedtime she was tired out. The whole weekend had been taken up with shopping, scrubbing, cleaning and polishing. Still tired in the morning, she had more than usual difficulty in concentrating at school. At one point she knocked her pencils off her desk and on bending down to pick them up she caught sight of Jimmy's knees beneath his desk in the next row. For some odd reason the sight captured her attention and she thought what lovely knees her brother had. Still leaning out of her chair, she studied her own bony, knobbly knees and looked back at Jimmy's. So smooth and round, she wished she had knees like his. She wished she were more like him in lots of ways. It came over her that she was going to miss him greatly when he left school this summer, despite the fact that they didn't play with each other or even talk that much.

Whack! The ruler caught her knuckles and she snatched her hand from the desk, toppling her chair and falling onto the floor. She had still been leaning gazing at Jimmy's knees and not heard Miss Mergrin coming. Shame-faced she got up, put her chair back and sat down. "Are you ready now to continue lessons with the rest of us?" Miss Mergrin asked sarcastically. Jenny thought she had better try harder to concentrate.

A double bed, dresser, wardrobe, table, chairs and a stove, all second hand and well worn, were delivered by carrier and arranged in the end rooms, and at the weekend Jenny got her answer as to why all the sudden activity. Two Czech ladies, who had been living in rooms with another village family, arrived to take over the unused end of the Stafford's house. They were mother and daughter, the mother very elderly, the daughter middle-aged. They had apparently lived in various rooming houses in the past two years or so and had been told to leave their present rooms and had nowhere to go. Aunt Edith thought it a good idea to let off the end of the house, bringing in money and providing a place for the Czechs. Miss Frieberg worked as an orderly in Salisbury Infirmary, her mother too old to work and too stubborn to learn to speak English.

Certainly it was sensible to let off unused rooms and make money from them, but it soon was apparent that the Frieberg's idea of cooking was nothing like English cooking. Before long the house reeked from the strong spices and whatever else they used in their meals and Aunt Edith wondered if she had made a mistake. Apart from the stink, the two women were no trouble, keeping to themselves and paying regularly. Miss Frieberg told Aunt Edith that she had a brother in a concentration camp somewhere in Germany, but other than that she said nothing about her family or why they were in England.

THIRTY-ONE

Summer holidays started again and proved to be a repeat of the previous year. Aunt Edith returned to her job at the International saying that the reason she left previously was because she had fallen out with a woman who worked there. Now the offending woman had left and the store asked Aunt Edith to return. That meant the brunt of the work fell on Jenny again and she could never play in the sunshine. At least, she thought to herself, now Aunt Edith is in town every day I won't have to do the wretched shopping. But once more she was wrong. Aunt Edith did bring home some purchases, but when each month's new coupons were validated, Jenny was sent to shop for the bulk of the groceries.

Jimmy had taken his eleven plus exam and left school when they broke up. During the holidays he heard that he had passed the exam and would be going to a branch of the Portsmouth Grammar School for Boys which had located in Salisbury for the war years. Jenny didn't hear the news until the holidays were over and Jimmy had started his new school, then she asked Aunt Edith if she could be late home from school just for once because she wanted to wait for Jimmy to come off the bus. To her amazement, Aunt Edith said she could not be late home, but that she could wait out on the bridge until he passed by and speak to him then. When she saw him walking down the road her heart swelled with pride. Jimmy was wearing long trousers! The trousers were grey and he wore a jacket to match. Jenny had never seen her brother look so smart.

"Hello you," he said when he saw her waiting. "What's on then?"

"Oh, nothing, Jimmy. I just wanted to see you because I've only just heard you passed the eleven plus. You do look lovely in long trousers and that jacket. Did Mrs. Foster buy them for you?"

Jimmy had the grace to blush at her compliment. "No, of course she didn't, dopey. Can you see Mrs. Foster taking me to town for clothes? Miss Grey came and took me into town. This is uniform, everybody wears the same thing in that school."

"Well I bet they don't all look as smart as you. What's the school like anyway, do you like it?"

Jimmy said the school was okay. A lot different from the village school with its rows of different standards all in one room. He hadn't been there long enough to know if he would like it or not, but now he had to go and get changed to chop wood and do his work.

Jenny had been surprised that Miss Grey had taken Jimmy to town for his new clothes because she hadn't come to see Jenny. When she thought about it, she supposed there wouldn't have been time if she had to go shopping with Jimmy, but it was a shame in a way since Jenny wanted to ask for new shoes. She had asked Aunt Edith, but she had simply asked Jenny in return if she thought money grew on trees. The Ministry didn't send enough for clothes unless specially asked, and Aunt Edith thought her shoes perfectly good for a while yet. The shoes were too small and cramped Jenny's toes painfully, so she took to removing them when she was out of sight of the house and walking barefoot. She did this for some time until a lady named Mrs. Ernie saw her. She told Jenny to put her shoes on or she would get diseased feet, but when Jenny protested that her shoes hurt, Mrs. Ernie took pity on her. "I've got a pair of our Jean's sandals at home that she hardly wore. If you like you can have them."

After school Jenny called on Mrs. Ernie and was given the sandals. She tried them on, finding they were over a size too big, but took them anyway and thanked Mrs. Ernie. When Aunt Edith came home Jenny showed her the sandals, thinking she would be pleased not to have to buy new shoes for her.

"You mean to tell me you have been begging round the village for shoes?" she ranted. "That's very nice isn't it, going round telling people I won't buy you any shoes. Is that what you want? Hand-outs? They look miles too big to me."

"I didn't beg anywhere. Mrs. Ernie just asked me if I would like Jean's sandals because they are too small for her and she didn't wear them much."

"Oh, I'm sure, Miss Sweet Innocent. I've always said you're as sly as a cartload of monkeys and you are. Well if you want to go slopping around in sandals miles too big, you do that." She made Jenny fetch her school shoes and dump them in the dustbin. "Now you haven't anything else but your wonderful new sandals have you," Aunt Edith said. From then on Jenny wore the sandals, flopping around on her feet whatever the weather. She was wearing them the day she went shopping in Salisbury and missed the bus again. Caught in the fog on the way home, she was dreadfully late, expecting yet another beating on getting home. In that respect she was lucky. She was so late that soldiers were due to come to tea at any moment when she finally reached the house. Aunt Edith was mad but didn't dare beat her then, instead sending her to her room without food. Wet, cold, tired and hungry, she waited on her bed until they all left for the dance. Then she went downstairs to clear away and wash the dishes, going straight up to bed as soon as they were done.

As the winter wore on, Jenny's strength ebbed and she became pale and thin. It seemed that everything she did took twice as long, earning her either further beatings for laziness, or being deprived of food. She couldn't remember the last time she had tasted either sweets or chocolate, but one day her luck changed - or she thought it had.

She removed everything from the high mantlepiece above the fireplace and ran the duster along it. Something slid off the end as she pushed the duster along. Picking it up, she looked at the small package wrapped in silver foil in a pale blue sleeve. She sniffed at it. Chocolate! The package had been opened so she slid it out. Tiny chocolate squares, smaller than any she had seen before, with two squares missing. Temptation made her mouth water. If she bit off a little bit, it would notice. Aunt Edith never missed anything - or almost never. Perhaps if she took a whole square no-one would miss it. Giving in to temptation she snapped one square off, re-wrapped the package and replaced it on the shelf. She bit off half the tiny square and savoured it. It was definitely chocolate but had a strange after-taste. Deciding to save the other half for tomorrow, she took it upstairs and popped it into her swan.

In bed that night, she was semi-awakened by severe cramping pains in her stomach. She rolled into a ball, pressing her arms against her stomach and groaned. The pain almost took her breath away, but finally it ebbed and she drifted back to sleep. In her dreams the pain returned, and with it the realization that she needed to get to the lavatory quickly. She saw herself streaking across the road and down the path to blessed relief. In the morning another realization hit her with a hammer blow. It had been only a dream and she hadn't moved from her bed, but she had relieved herself. There was no way out of this. Terrified, she began to cry. Aunt Edith came to see what the trouble was and was furious. She got the small bath from the wall, commanding Jenny to fill it with cold water and sit in it. Never so cold in her life, Jenny scrubbed herself as swiftly as possible and ran upstairs to dress. Meanwhile Aunt Edith heated a bucket of water and after she and Jenny had struggled to the river to empty the bath, she tipped the hot water into the bath while Jenny added cold.

"Get hold of the other end of the bath," she ordered Jenny. "We're carrying this out to the road and you can wash those disgusting sheets out there."

Jenny was horrified. "It's freezing cold out there, and everybody will see me."

"Exactly! Everyone will see what a dirty little bitch you are and that will be a lesson you won't forget." They carried the bath outside and set it against the house. Shamed and humiliated, Jenny knelt and scrubbed at the sheets till her knuckles could take no more. The stains wouldn't come out and she was near despair. Aunt Edith said that would do, the stains would probably fade out as they froze on the line. She helped Jenny carry the bath to the river where they tipped it out, sheets and all, and Jenny rinsed them in the freezing water. When she got back inside after hanging them on the line, she was chilled to the marrow. Aunt Edith had lit the fire and made tea, allowing Jenny a cup of tea but no breakfast. Jenny couldn't stop her teeth chattering and was still chilled when she got to school.

Off and on all day, stomach cramps bothered her and sent her running. At lunch time she ate her sandwiches and immediately more cramps gripped her. Aunt Edith was still mad at her in the evening, allowing her only one sandwich for supper while the rest of them ate their cooked meal. Jenny went to bed hungry again that night, the cramps having lessened to a dull ache. Sitting alone on her bed, Celia still undressing downstairs in front of the fire and coming up later, she thought of the piece of chocolate square in the swan. She removed and ate it before Celia could see her. That night the same thing happened and the dawn brought renewed terror. This time Aunt Edith insisted the bath be placed in the centre of the road so that people passing would have to walk around her and see what she was doing. Jenny's disgust at herself knew no bounds, the cramps had returned with greater vigour and she felt totally unable to help herself. She couldn't understand what was happening to her. Aunt Edith threatened that if she did this once more, she would be sleeping out in the yard in future.

Fear kept her awake the next night, and when the cramps started again she managed to crawl out of bed and make her way in the freezing, dark night to the shed. She stayed there, shivering and dozing for most of the night, but her bed was clean in the morning. Gradually the cramping faded and she began to sleep easier. About a week later, Aunt Edith called her from the scullery where she was washing the evening's dishes. Standing next to the mantlepiece, Aunt Edith had the small package of chocolate in her hand. "Did you steal a piece of this chocolate?" she demanded. Shocked, Jenny denied it.

"Come here to me," Aunt Edith said. "Now I'll ask you once more. Did you steal a piece of this chocolate?" Trying to decide whether it was best to own up or deny it, Jenny said no again. The expected whack on the ear knocked her sideways, but she didn't fall. "You are a liar. Do you want me to tell you how I know? This 'chocolate' is not chocolate - it's a laxative. See, it says on here EX-LAX. It helps you go to the lavatory if you're constipated, and that's why you messed the bed last week. You only need about a quarter square, any more will turn you inside out and could kill you. If you took a whole square I'm surprised you aren't dead. Do you want to deny stealing it again?"

The enormity of what she had done stunned Jenny to silence. In stealing the chocolate she had come close to killing herself. There was no way to deny it now. Shame-faced, she stood waiting for her punishment.

"See! See! See what I say," Aunt Edith said, looking at Uncle Reg. "She's nothing but a damn little thief and a liar. You can't trust her anywhere and she's as sly as they come. You're also too stupid to live," she said to Jenny. "Why the hell I go on putting up with a piece of rubbish like you is beyond my understanding. I must need my head read. Just get on out to the scullery and get out of my sight, I'm sick to death of you. And let this be a lesson to you," she shouted after Jenny's retreating back.

It was a lesson to Jenny. She was never going to do anything to please Aunt Edith, and Aunt Edith was right. She was a thief, and a liar, and she was worth nothing.

THIRTY-TWO

Christmas was coming again and this year they were to spend Christmas Eve, Christmas Day and Boxing Day at Rita's house. Rita's mother was Aunt Edith's sister. Aunt Edith had taken Celia to visit her a few times, but Jenny had never met her. Ordinarily Jenny would have been excited at the prospect of her first ride in the car, and at spending time in someone else's house where she would escape from drudgery, but she was not feeling at all well. The strength that had been sapped by the Ex-Lax incident had never fully returned and she was at a low ebb.

The car was pushed from the shed once more, and again Uncle Reg battled with the starting handle before it sputtered to life. It was slow going and when they reached a steep hill the car popped and stuttered, finally stalling altogether. No amount of swinging the handle would get it going again so there was nothing to do but all get out and push. Celia sat in the driving seat with instructions to release the brake when told, and to steer as the rest of them pushed. Slipping and sliding on the icy road, the three of them heaved, lost their footing, tried again and at last got the car to the top. They coasted down the other side until the engine caught once more, and continued their unsteady progress. Twice they had to go through this performance, while Aunt Edith nagged at Uncle Reg for being too stupid to put chains on the wheels. Uncle Reg said that you couldn't put chains on the wheels when there was no snow because it would tear the tyres to pieces, but Aunt Edith didn't want to hear this, insisting that chains would have got them over the hills without trouble. Jenny felt so ill that all she wanted to do was find a place to lie down and be left alone. Everyone was in a bad mood by the time they reached Rita's house - all that is except Celia, who thought it great fun to sit in the car and steer while everyone else pushed.

Rita rushed out to greet them and help carry their baggage into the house. Inside was warm and cheerful and tempers soon recovered. "So this is your evacuee," Aunt Mary said when first greetings were over. "Are you feeling alright, dear? You look awful peaky to me."

"Yes, thank you," Jenny said, feeling anything but alright. She hated being referred to as the 'evacuee' or the 'orphan'. It made her feel like an object, not a person at all.

"Well I don't know. She doesn't look at all well, Edie. I think we should put her to bed," Aunt Mary said.

"Oh rubbish, she's fine. She's probably sulking because we had to push the damn car. You just behave yourself," Aunt Edith said, scowling at Jenny.

Jenny liked Aunt Mary, despite the fact that she had called her 'your evacuee'. Apart from the same brown eyes, she looked nothing like Aunt Edith, her younger sister. Frizzy, mouse coloured hair and matronly of figure, she was kindly and caring. Jenny and Celia had to sleep together in a double bed in the sitting room, much to Jenny's annoyance. Celia fidgeted and bounced the bed in her excitement, making Jenny feel sick. Waking early on Christmas morning, Celia grabbed her stuffed pillowcase and ran to find her parents. Gratefully, Jenny snuggled deeper into the bed, wanting only to sleep in peace. She was wakened again later by Aunt Edith prodding her to get up. She noticed a sock, similar to last Christmas, on the bed, but felt too ill even to be bothered to look in it.

Sitting at the breakfast table, the sight of food nauseated her, and she couldn't eat. Aunt Mary looked closely at her. "That child is sick, Edie. Look at her. She should go right back to bed." "Do you want to go lie down again, dear," she asked Jenny. Gratefully, Jenny replied that she would.

"Oh Mary. Take no notice of her. You don't know her. She's a very good actress and just trying to get attention. You don't know what I have to put up with, with that one. Believe me." Aunt Edith glowered at Jenny. "I thought I told you to behave yourself. Buck up and eat your breakfast. I'm not allowing you to spoil our holiday."

Jenny tried to eat, but it wouldn't go down. She began to shiver while Aunt Edith tried to ignore her. "Edie, I don't want to cross you, but I do think you're wrong. Take a look at that child's eyes, they have a definite yellow tinge. I'm afraid she's coming down with yellow jaundice."

"Christ, that's all we need," Aunt Edith said angrily. "No she hasn't got yellow jaundice. She's probably eaten something that upset her - she's fond of doing that. Just don't pamper her or she'll lay it on as thick as butter. If she doesn't want to eat, let her go without."

Aunt Edith wouldn't allow Jenny to go back to bed. Instead, she sat about, half asleep and half awake while the festivities went on around her. By the evening not only her eyes, but her skin was yellow also. She ate nothing all day, and although Aunt Edith denied that she had yellow jaundice or anything other than slight food poisoning, she didn't allow her to sleep with Celia that night, but got Aunt Mary to make her up a bed on the floor. She was hot, sick and a dreadful colour when they returned home on Boxing Day afternoon, but still Aunt Edith would not allow her to rest in bed. The whole of Christmas, 1942, passed in a haze for Jenny.

By the time school re-started, only her eyes retained a trace of yellow. She was near skeleton thin and had not regained much appetite. The overlarge sandals she was still forced to wear had worn through, and walking with part of the foot exposed caused blisters on the balls of her feet. Stuffing cardboard into them seemed a good idea, but as soon as the wet soaked into the cardboard it disintegrated, making her feet more sore than ever. Aunt Edith refused to buy her any more shoes, saying she still had plenty of room in the sandals and had shown preference for hand outs over anything Aunt Edith could buy.

Close to the nail, the second finger of her right hand hurt. Studying it for a possible splinter, Jenny could discover nothing to cause the pain. When it became so bad she couldn't hold her pen, she tried pushing the pen further down between her fingers. Mrs. Mergrin noticed the odd way of holding the pen as she paraded up and down the rows, overlooking each pupil's work, and told Jenny to hold the pen properly. Jenny tried, but dropped her pen.

"What's the matter with you?" Mrs. Mergrin asked.

"Nothing Miss," Jenny answered. She didn't want Mrs. Mergrin looking at her hands. They were so filthy these days.

Handling coal and black lead polish left them ingrained with grime that no amount of scrubbing could remove. Mrs. Mergrin then pushed the pen into Jenny's fingers and squeezed them. Jenny let out an involuntary "Ouch", again dropping the pen. Mrs. Mergrin snatched up her hand and studied it. "Well no wonder you can't hold the pen, you have a whitlow under your nail." She heaved a sigh. "I'll go and put the kettle on. The rest of you get on with your work, and no talking." She came back carrying a basin of hot water, a bandage and a needle. Not knowing what a whitlow was, Jenny thought it some kind of splinter, and that Mrs. Mergrin was going to pick at her finger with the needle. Instead, she inserted the needle right into the side of her finger and under the nail, bringing beads of sweat to Jenny's face. Then she dunked the finger into the hot water, telling Jenny to hold it there for five minutes. "I don't know why I have to do such things in the middle of class when they should be done at home," she said crossly. She said nothing at all about the state of Jenny's hands.

Thick, blood-streaked matter oozed from the finger into the water and the pain rapidly abated. Mrs. Mergrin bound her finger, telling her that keeping it clean was most important. A whitlow was caused by germs she said, giving Jenny a stern look. Jenny felt ashamed and guilty about her grubby hands and wished she knew how to get them clean. That afternoon she fell asleep on her desk, and although Mrs. Mergrin woke her, she didn't cane her or send her outside to the porch.

In early February, Jenny was struggling across the road with the coal bucket. A man on a bicycle rounded the bend at breakneck speed, having just free-wheeled down the hill. Jenny neither saw nor heard him until he frantically rang his bell. By then it was too late. He cannoned into her, knocking her flat onto her back and riding straight over her stomach, before crashing to the ground. The noise of the crash, Jenny's squeals and the man's shouting brought Miss Frieberg to the window. She rushed out to help Jenny up, concern showing on her face. "You should look from where you are going," she said to the man, who was picking himself up from the road. "Come on mine Jenny, let me help you to go in."

"I'm sorry missus, I never saw 'er 'til I hit 'er. You okay love? Wouldn't 'a done that for the world. I 'ope you're gonna be alright."

Jenny was trying to stand. The back of her head was bleeding from hitting the road and her stomach hurt. Aunt Edith came out to see what the bother was, pretending concern at the mishap. "I never saw 'er, honest I never," the man explained again to Aunt Edith.

"Don't worry about it," Aunt Edith reassured him. "She'll be fine after a cup of tea. She probably wasn't looking where she was going so its her fault as much as yours."

"She did not see him because she was trying to carry the so heavy bucket," Miss Frieberg said. Aunt Edith ignored the remark, ushering Jenny into the house. The man, bloody grazes on his hands and face, carried the bucket into the house. He wouldn't stay to be cleaned up, saying he had to get off to work. Limping, he left to salvage his bicycle.

Aunt Edith gave Jenny a cup of tea, roughly washed the sore spot on the back of her head, telling her to get on with her work and not make a fuss. It hurt to bend down and get up again, it hurt to walk, making her late and behind with everything. Prayers were almost over by the time she got to school. She waited in the porch until they were done as no-one was permitted to walk in during prayers, then went in expecting the ruler. She got as far as Mrs. Mergrin's desk, hearing her teacher asking for an explanation as if her voice was coming from a paper bag. Mrs. Mergrin's face became all fuzzy, her voice faded, and Jenny collapsed.

The haze began to clear and she discovered that she was lying on a board in the schoolroom, covered with a blanket. Lessons were going on as if nothing had happened. Embarrassed, Jenny tried to get up, but fell down again. Mrs. Mergrin came over and asked if Mrs. Stafford would be in if someone took her home. Jenny told her that Aunt Edith wouldn't be back until the half past two bus, so she was made to lay down again and rest. In the afternoon she was pushed home in a wheel chair that was kept in the school in case of emergency. A senior boy was given the task of pushing her, which he didn't mind a bit since it meant escape from school. Mrs. Mergrin had sent a sealed note with him to give to Aunt Edith.

Not at all pleased to have Jenny brought home in this manner, Aunt Edith was even more displeased with the note. Mrs. Mergrin had apparently written that she was concerned with Jenny's condition of late and that she intended to call a doctor to Jenny if Mrs. Stafford did not do so herself. Feeling she had no choice, Aunt Edith put Jenny in Celia's bed and walked to the Post Office to call a doctor.

Jenny was beyond caring what happened to her. Tired beyond belief, all she wanted was to be allowed to sleep. The doctor, an elderly man who had been on the point of retirement at the start of the war but had been pressed back into service for lack of a younger replacement, was kindly and gentle. He examined Jenny, took blood from her arm, told her to rest, and said he would return the following day. Celia had a put-you-up bed made up for her in her parent's room and Jenny spent the most peaceful night she could remember. Next day the doctor returned bringing tablets and a large bottle of green medicine for Jenny. "This child is very anaemic and shows signs of rickets," he told Aunt Edith as they stood by the bed. "She has been allowed to get into a very poor condition, and I find traces of yellow jaundice. When did this occur?"

"She had jaundice over Christmas. We were at my sister's and she was seen by a doctor who treated her. Are you suggesting that I have not taken care of her?" Aunt Edith asked, very much on her high horse.

"I'm not suggesting anything," the doctor said. "But you can thank your lucky stars that she isn't dead. She is as close as I ever want to see, and she didn't get this way without severe neglect. I will call in every day and expect to see improvement."

"Well really!" Aunt Edith said angrily. "I don't like your attitude. You seem to be suggesting that it is I at fault. The truth is she hasn't been eating properly at all since Christmas, and its not because I haven't provided good food. She just won't eat."

"Well she will now. You take that medicine, my dear, and before you know it you will have the appetite of a horse. Rest now and I'll see you tomorrow," he said to Jenny.

After they left the room, Jenny heard him say: "If that child dies, there will be some very awkward questions asked, and I will personally see to it that they are. It is in your best interests to take great care of her and get some nourishment into her."

Wavering in and out of sleep, Jenny spent the next three weeks in bed. She couldn't stay awake for longer than it took to eat or get out of bed to have her bed made. Sometimes she thought of what the doctor had said - "if she dies" - and wondered if she would. She hadn't thought herself that ill, and strangely, the possibility of dying brought no fear at all. Sometimes she hoped that she would die. Nowhere could be worse than living with Aunt Edith and dying only meant going somewhere else. Somewhere pleasant where people loved you, and where they cared about how you felt. Besides, if she died Aunt Edith would be found out and get into trouble. Perhaps they would put her in prison and never let her out. It would be worth dying if that were to happen. In her sleeping times, Jenny frequently had her flying dreams. They continued when she was half awake too, and then she wondered if she was already dead.

She didn't die, however, but spent five weeks at home. She liked the green medicine the doctor gave her. It smelled of rusty nails but tasted lovely. There was a bold print of tyre marks across her stomach in the early days, but they gradually faded to yellow and were almost gone by the time she was ready to return to school. Aunt Edith had looked after her grudgingly, constantly grumbling about the inconvenience, but had made sure she was well fed. By the time she returned to school, Jenny felt better than she had in a very long time.

THIRTY-THREE

Things soon returned to normal once Jenny was better. She got all her chores back, was beaten as much as before, but now she was not deprived of food as often. Jenny found too, that with her renewed strength, her hostility to Aunt Edith had also recovered.

Miss Grey had not been to see her for some time, and Jenny wondered if she was not going to visit any more. In fact, she was not. The next time someone came from the Ministry it was another lady, Miss Hargreaves. The Ministry always sent word before a representative came, so Aunt Edith bought a new pair of shoes and a new dress for Jenny before Miss Hargreaves' first visit. The dress was green, not a colour that suited Jenny's wan complexion in the least, and the shoes were black laced boys shoes. Jenny was pleased with the dress and glad at last to have waterproof shoes, though she didn't like the fact that they were heavy and meant for boys. Miss Hargreaves was taller, softer spoken and more kindly than Miss Grey. She had curly brown hair and soft brown eyes. She asked the usual questions as to whether Jenny was happy and to which Jenny answered the usual 'yes, thank you', commented on Jenny's pretty dress, and said how pleased she was to see Jenny looking so well. Jenny felt Miss Hargreaves was more truly interested in her than Miss Grey had been, but was not prepared to trust her any more than she had Miss Grey.

The day after Miss Hargreaves' visit, Aunt Edith told Jenny to take her shoes to Potter on the way home from school and have him nail studs all over the bottoms. She was not going to have Jenny wearing out new shoes in five minutes, she said, and the studs would ensure longer wear. Jenny did as she was told and when all the studs were nailed in she could barely lift the shoes off the ground. Not only did she have boys shoes, but now they were full of studs that sent up sparks as she walked and made her sound like an elephant. She would rather have worn the old tattered sandals.

175

Miss Hargreaves had apparently told Aunt Edith that the Ministry was displeased with Jenny's progress at school, especially considering that her brother had done so well. She had suggested that Jenny be taken to a psychologist for assessment, for which the Ministry would pay. Jenny knew nothing of this until Aunt Edith told her one day that she would not be going to school because she had to get her head read. Aunt Edith had to take a morning off work to take her, she told Jenny, and she wasn't pleased to have to take her to some expert so that he could tell them she was daft. If the Ministry wanted to pay her the amount of a psychologist's fee, she could tell them right now that Jenny was a stupid dimwit who would never amount to a bag of rotten potatoes. However, this was their stupid idea so they had to go.

Jenny was quite horrified at having to have her head read. She knew she wasn't doing well at school, but she was not at the bottom of the class. She hovered somewhere between middle and bottom and, as far as she knew, no-one else had been sent to have an expert say they were stupid. Aunt Edith said that when brains had been given out in her family, Jimmy had got the lot and there was none left when Jenny came along. Jenny knew that was silly, but she also knew that Aunt Edith considered her stupid and dumb.

At the psychiatrist's office, Jenny was given a paper of questions to answer, then the psychiatrist asked her questions, and lastly she had to fit different shapes into holes. For most of the time she sat in the waiting room while Aunt Edith was in the office. Aunt Edith wouldn't tell her what had been said, but at the supper table that night she told Uncle Reg in front of Jenny and Celia that the psychiatrist had said Jenny was backward and had no hope whatsoever of passing the eleven plus the following year. In other words, as Aunt Edith had predicted, she was stupid.

In bed that night Celia made the most of what she had heard, calling Jenny 'dafty' and poking fun at her. Jenny grew angry but refused to answer back, knowing that if she did so, Celia would call her mother. Unable to provoke Jenny, Celia tried another attack.

"I know where your mum is and you don't, and I'm not going to tell you, so there."

That was enough. Jenny sat up in bed and shouted at her. "No you don't know where my mum is. You don't know anything, and if you don't shut up I'm going to smash you."

"I do so know," Celia taunted. "She's run away with a Dutchman and he's a captain on a ship. She's got another baby and she isn't never coming back for you. I know 'cos Miss Hargreaves told my mum, so there, see."

Red flashes tore across Jenny's eyes. In the dark, she leapt out of her bed and across to Celia's in an instant. Grabbing at her, Jenny felt for her hair, poking Celia in the eye in the process. With her hands entwined in Celia's hair, Jenny shook her. "You liar, you liar. You don't know where my mum is. You don't know anything. Its not true and you're a liar!" Jenny was shouting at the top of her voice while Celia screamed for her mother.

Aunt Edith burst into the room carrying a candle, shielding the flame with her cupped hand. "What the hell is going on here. What do you think you're doing," she shouted at Jenny, pulling her off Celia by the hair. "How dare you attack Celie. Haven't I told you a hundred times that if you dare to touch her you'll have me to reckon with?" By this time she had set the candle down and heaved Jenny from the bed. Still furious at Celia's taunting, Jenny yanked herself away. "She's telling lies about my mum. She said horrible things about my mum and they're not true, they're not!"

"Oh is that so. And what did she tell you about your precious mother that were such lies, eh? Tell me about these lies."

"No. She was just being horrible. She's a liar and you should smack her and wash her mouth out with soap."

Instead, it was Jenny who received a stinging slap in the mouth. "What have I told you about calling Celie a liar? There's only one liar in this house and I'm looking at her right now. And did Celie tell you that your so virtuous mother has another baby? Is that what she told you, eh? And did she tell you that dear Mummy has taken up with a Dutch sea captain and doesn't give a damn about her kids. She even had the new baby adopted? Did she tell you that? Well my fine lady, if that's what Celie told you, you can say sorry to her this minute because she told you the truth. Go on, say sorry to Celie right now!"

Stunned, Jenny's head was reeling. No! It couldn't be the truth. Aunt Edith was lying just like Celia. How would Miss Hargreaves know such things about her mother if the Ministry didn't know where she was? It was lies. Somebody was telling lies. Celia was sniggering on the bed, Aunt Edith standing, hands on hips, glowering at Jenny and waiting for her to apologize. Bile burned the back of Jenny's throat. She would rather die than apologize to Celia or Aunt Edith. "I'm not sorry. She's lying and so are you. You always say nasty things about my mum, and Miss Hargreaves didn't say that." Tears of rage and fright accompanied her words. Knowing very well she was about to be beaten, Jenny could not now, or at any time, say she was sorry for defending her mother. Aunt Edith attacked her with a fury. Slapping, punching, and banging her into the furniture, she beat her around the room. "You little sod. You don't want to believe the truth about that whore of a mother of yours because you are going to end up no better than her. You're too damn stupid to believe the truth when it stares you in the face. But you're going to apologize before I leave this room if I have to hammer you all night. Now say you're sorry," she roared, hands gripped tightly in Jenny's hair pushing her face into the corner of the room.

"I'm sorry. I'm sorry. Don't hurt me any more," she cried, suffused with shame at being such a traitor to her mother. 'I'm not sorry. I'm not sorry,' she repeated inside her head. Desperately fighting the urge to lash back and kick Aunt Edith, she didn't dare risk more pain. "That's better," aunt Edith said, releasing her hair. "Now say sorry to Celia for calling her a liar." Swallowing the rising bile, Jenny repeated the hated words to Celia, who giggled and stuck out her tongue. Curling up in her bed Jenny suffered agonies of pain, both physical and mental. No way would she ever believe what Aunt Edith had said. In her heart she cried to her mother to forgive her for apologizing, assuring her that she knew the truth, that her mother was being held somewhere and couldn't come back yet.

Aunt Edith's treachery rankled in Jenny's breast and wouldn't be abated. Renewed hatred burned constantly inside her and she physically shuddered any time she was close to her despised enemy. She sought in her mind for ways of getting back, frustrated to think she could never beat Aunt Edith. Opportunity presented itself, however, in an unexpected way.

THIRTY-FOUR

Young as she was, and having little understanding of the ways of adults with regard to marriage, courting and dating, Jenny nevertheless had long ago come to the conclusion that Aunt Edith and Uncle Reg were not happily married. Uncle Reg seemed content enough, but Aunt Edith was not. She ran Uncle Reg down to other people when he wasn't around, and quite often called him a fool to his face. He never seemed upset by the names she called him, always trying to please her, and saying 'yes dear'. Jenny had also heard her laugh about that to other people. To Jenny's mind, Uncle Reg *was* a bit dopey and not the sort of husband she herself would like, but Aunt Edith was married to him, and when you are married you aren't supposed to flirt. Jenny thought Aunt Edith did flirt with the soldiers. Almost ten years old now, Jenny knew enough to recognize that Aunt Edith flirted with other men.

Hanging the cups back on their little hooks on the dresser one evening, Jenny happened to glance up at the cups on the highest shelf. Noticing that one cup appeared to hang further out than the others, she dragged up a chair to stand on and lifted the cup. There on the hook hung a golden wedding band. It was Saturday evening and everyone had gone to the dance. Uncle Reg was down in the shed and Celia had followed him. Jenny lifted the ring down. It could only be Aunt Edith's ring. She had taken it off and hidden it so she could go to the dance pretending she was single. Jenny felt a rising excitement at this find, but what could she do about it? Replacing the ring and cup, she got off the chair, thinking hard.

What if she told Aunt Edith what she knew and threatened to tell Uncle Reg if Aunt Edith didn't stop beating her and making her do all the work? That way she would get out to play and not be a slave any more. No. Aunt Edith would simply beat her up and say she was a liar. She could put the ring back on and say Jenny had made it all up. Better to show Uncle Reg where it was and get Aunt Edith into trouble from him. But would he do anything about it? He was such a dozy halfpence he would likely say nothing at all. Deciding to leave it for later, she got on with her chores.

Bed time came, and Jenny hadn't made up her mind what to do. She lay in bed thinking. If she showed Uncle Reg the ring, she would have to make him promise to say he found it himself. He was dumb enough to say Jenny had shown him, and then she would be in dire trouble. She waited until Celia was asleep, then, with fluttering heart, crept downstairs.

Uncle Reg was sitting with his eyes closed, listening to the wireless. He looked up as Jenny stepped into the living room, asking what she wanted. "I wanted to tell you something," she said, heart pulsing in the back of her throat.

"Oh? What is it then? It must be important if you have to get out of bed 'specially to tell me," he said, smiling.

"Well before I tell you, I want you to promise me something on your honour. You have to promise honest-to-God, or I won't tell you."

Uncle Reg laughed. "Alright. What do I have to promise? If its to cut my leg off, I won't do it."

"No, silly," Jenny said. "You have to promise that you won't tell Aunt Edith I told you. If she knows I told you, she'll beat me up, so you have to promise. Promise 'so-help-me-God'."

Uncle Reg stopped smiling. "Okay," he said. "I promise I won't tell Aunt Edith that you told me. Now what is it?" "So help me God?" Jenny asked. "So help me God," he said.

Jenny took a deep breath. "Go and look under that cup that's sticking out on the top shelf," she said, pointing to the dresser. Uncle Reg got up and walked to the dresser, lifting the cup. He took down the ring and looked at it. "Who's ring is this?" he asked.

"Don't you know? You should know," Jenny said, unable to believe his stupidity. "You must've given it to her. Its Aunt Edith's wedding ring of course. She hid it up there so she could go dancing without it."

"Hmm," he said, studying the ring. Turning back, he hung it and the cup back on the hook. "You'd better go back to bed now. Thanks for showing me."

Jenny turned to go, stopping at the stair door. "If you're going to say anything to Aunt Edith, remember you promised not to tell her I showed you." Uncle Reg gave her a half smile. "Okay, I promised," he said. "Goodnight now."

Unable to sleep, Jenny tossed and turned in her bed, straining her ears to listen for Aunt Edith and Rita to come home. Frightened now, she wondered if she should have told Uncle Reg. She was not at all sure he would keep his promise if Aunt Edith bullied him to tell her how he knew. Normally, Uncle Reg went to bed before the dance finished, but tonight he waited up. Jenny was dozing when the sound of voices brought her back to wakefulness. Slipping out of bed, she crept to the top of the stairs and crouched there.

For a while there was just normal conversation until she heard Aunt Edith ask why Uncle Reg was still up. "Surely you weren't missing me," she said.

"No, not exactly," Jenny heard him say. "I just wanted to ask you about this."

Jenny imagined him lifting down the ring and showing it to Aunt Edith. "Well, what about it?" Aunt Edith said. "I hope you're not trying to imply that I left it on purpose. I always hang it up there when I wash my hands and I forgot to put it back on, that's all. Don't try to make anything of it. If I wanted to hoodwink you, I could do it without taking off my ring. How did you know it was there anyway?"

"Hmm. I just noticed it there when I was listening to the wireless. Why would you hang it all up there when you washed your hands. I've never notice you take it off to wash your hands."

"No you didn't notice it up there. You couldn't see it unless you took the cup off," Aunt Edith said, ignoring his question. "You didn't see it at all. Who told you it was there? I know you. You didn't find it for yourself. Who told you?"

"If you must know, Jenny told me," he said.

Oh God, no! Jenny turned to stone. She *shouldn't* have told him, he was such a fool. Now she was in for it, Aunt Edith would surely kill her now.

"Don't you go belting her," she heard Uncle Reg say. "She just told me because she thought you'd forgotten it and might think you'd lost it. There's no need to get mad at her."

Jenny crept tremblingly back to bed, not wanting to hear any more. Uncle Reg was only making it worse by suggesting that Aunt Edith might have reason to beat her. Pulling the covers over her head, she shook as she dreaded what the morning would bring.

Still shaking as she got up next morning, Jenny awaited the coming storm. Rita slept over on the settee on Saturday nights, having left to catch her bus home by the time Celia and Jenny returned from Sunday School. Nothing was said to her at all in the morning, nor when she returned home. Probably because Uncle Reg was still around, she thought. Later, when she was helping with the vegetables, Aunt Edith looked at her with slitted eyes. "Aren't you the smart-ass," she said in a hissing whisper. "Well you're not as smart as you think you are, and you'll get yours, never fear. Just you keep waiting." A shiver travelled the length of Jenny's spine as she fixed her eyes intently on the carrots she was scraping. What was Aunt Edith going to do to her?

Aunt Edith, in fact, did nothing. Except remind Jenny from time to time that she 'had it coming', keeping her in a state of tense anxiety. It was Celia who wrought what Jenny later considered retribution for her attempt to bring trouble between Aunt Edith and Uncle Reg. Although what happened had nothing at all to do with the ring incident, Jenny saw it as God punishing her for being so wicked. Then she believed she deserved it, wishing with all her heart that she had never tried to cause trouble.

Celia often stole the sugar, and always Jenny got beaten for it. Time after time she shovelled teaspoonsful of sugar into her mouth, crunching it in front of Jenny and daring her to do anything about it. Aunt Edith always missed the sugar. She hid the package so that Jenny couldn't refill the sugar basin, so she knew when sugar was missing. Jenny knew it was useless to say Celia had stolen it, she would be doubly beaten for accusing Celia and calling her a thief and a liar. Celia got so bold that she would announce to Jenny that she intended to steal sugar later in the day, and did so. It was fun to Celia, she got to eat the sweet sugar she loved so much, and got Jenny into trouble for stealing, which she also enjoyed. One day during the Easter holiday, Celia said again that she would steal some sugar later. Jenny didn't dare hit her, there was no way of locking the pantry door, and Jenny didn't know what to do other than hide the sugar, for which Celia would likely wallop her with a plank until she told her where it was, and she would be unable to fight back.

A clever thought suddenly occurred to Jenny. Aunt Edith hid the sugar packet, but she didn't hide the salt. Fetching a cup, Jenny tipped the sugar into it, hiding it upstairs under her bed. Then she tipped salt into the sugar basin up to where the sugar had been and put it back in the pantry. Celia came in later on and shovelled a spoonful into her mouth. Spitting and spluttering she screamed for Jenny. "You put salt in the sugar basin. You made me eat salt. Well I'm telling my mum of you and you'll get a good hiding."

"Oh yeah!" Jenny shouted back at her. "Well you go ahead and tell your mum. Then she'll know who's been stealing the sugar won't she. Don't bother telling her, I'll tell her myself if you like." Celia's face went red with anger, but she knew she was caught and could do nothing about it. "You just wait," she spluttered. "You wait. I hate you."

She ran outside and Jenny smiled to herself. At last she had got one over on Celia. She couldn't tell her mother without giving herself away and Jenny felt like singing. Remembering to throw out the salt and return the sugar before Aunt Edith returned, she intended to repeat the process if Celia ever tried stealing again.

The following day, Jenny heard Celia run upstairs during the morning and saw her come down and go outside with a bulky bag. She took little notice, thinking Celia was taking some toys out to play with in the garden as she often did. Needing to go to the lavatory some time later, Jenny noticed odd little bits of white fluff all over the road and in the garden. As she neared the shed, she saw on the ground what was unmistakably part of her swan's wing. Racing back to the house and tearing upstairs, she saw that the swan was gone. Back to the garden, she ran all over the place searching for the contents. Desolate at the loss of her swan and frantic to find the koala and other treasures, she combed the whole garden, including the undergrowth beyond the shed, finding no sign of them. What she did find in the tangled growth brought her sobbing to her knees. The smashed remains of the black doll her father had given her lay tossed in a careless heap. Jenny lay beside the doll, sobbing in dreadful distress. There was nothing left. No swan or koala to guide her mother back. Nothing to touch that her father had held, to bring his memory back. Every treasure she had loved was gone, and she was desolate. Was this God's punishment for her badness?

Dragging herself back along the path, she saw Celia's head bob over the hedge. Feeling nothing but contempt for the silly grinning face, Jenny ignored her. "I chopped up your swan with the scissors," Celia called after her. Jenny kept walking.

The loss of her small treasures was truly the end of all her possessions. Her pram had been given to the youngest daughter of the Cole family who lived in the mill house, after they had lost everything in a fire. The fire had been caused by their only son, then twelve years old, who was cleaning plugs with paraffin on the second storey wooden floor of the mill. By himself, he had attempted to burn off some of the grease on the plugs, immediately setting the whole place on fire. He had leapt from the building unhurt, but the mill had gone up like a tinder box, setting fire to the adjoining cottage where the family lived. Practically the whole village had turned out, passing buckets of water to try to keep the blaze down until the fire engine arrived, but it was useless. Mill and cottage burned to the ground. The homeless family, parents, three elder daughters, the son and five year old youngest daughter had been given shelter by various villagers. The son now lived with Jimmy at the Fosters.

The parents and small daughter were offered rooms in a house on Woodside Road. None of them managed to rescue any possessions and Aunt Edith suggested Jenny might like to donate her pram to the little girl. Since Jenny was too old for dolls in any case, she was happy to give her pram away. Mrs. Cole was delighted with the gift, thanking

Jenny for her kindness. Jenny often saw young Linda pushing it around the village.

Jenny had also discovered what happened to her Raleigh bicycle. Trudging back from town with the shopping one day, having missed the bus yet again, the village carrier stopped to offer her a lift. Gratefully she had climbed into his battered green van. She didn't care if they were only going slightly faster than she could walk, nor that the carrier talked to her with a yellowed cigarette stub stuck to his upper lip; she was more than grateful for the lift. While they were talking, he mentioned that he was surprised she let such a good bicycle go, particularly since she wasn't too big for it. Surprised, Jenny asked him what he meant. He said that Aunt Edith had told him to come and pick it up one day, saying that Jenny didn't want it any more and she was sending it to Salisbury Market. Jenny was astonished and angered at what the carrier told her. Aunt Edith said the bike was stolen, and she had sold it without asking Jenny. She learned then that she was *not* the only thief and liar in the house. Aunt Edith was too.

THIRTY-FIVE

Jenny's deep seated grief over the loss of her possessions continued to haunt her. Whenever she thought of Celia slicing through her beloved swan with scissors, she felt as if she had been deprived of the last slim threads connecting her to her lost family. In her desperate loneliness, her hatred for spoiled, rotten Celia festered anew. She could barely bring herself to look at the smug, stupid face without yearning to put her hands around that neck and squeeze the life out of it.

Saturday morning, two weeks or so after Celia had destroyed the swan, Jenny was working in the house while Aunt Edith was getting the hall ready for the dance. Celia had gone to play in the garden with a group of friends. Crossing the road to fill the coal bucket, Celia saw her coming. "Here comes smelly Jenny," she shouted. "Come on, don't let's let her in the garden." The children all rushed to the gate to push against it, one of them jamming a stick into the latch. Jenny tried to push the gate but their combined weight was too much. "Alright, I'll just climb over," she said to Celia, putting her foot on the first rung of the iron gate and swinging herself up. "Push her, push her," Celia cried, and a group of hands shoved her back into the road. Raging fury boiled up in Jenny with such velocity that it seemed to explode in her chest. With a strength she didn't know she possessed, she charged at the gate, tearing the latch from its post and sending the children staggering.

"Ohh!" Celia wailed as the gate caught her in the face. "I'm telli..." She got no further. Jenny whipped round the gate, catching Celia by the throat and shaking her like a rag doll. Dragging her out to the road, she flung her to the ground and knelt on her. She slapped Celia's face hard several times, then grabbed her by the hair, bashing her head up and down on the gravelled road. Celia struggled and screamed at the top of her voice, and Jenny was scarcely aware of Miss Frieberg's voice calling "Cecia, Cecia. Vat is, Cecia?" She felt Miss Frieberg's hand come round her face and smelt the pungent smell of her cooking.

Miss Frieberg bent her head backwards until she let go of Celia. "Jenny, Jenny. Vat for you do to Cecia?" she asked. "You vill surely kill her like zis."

"She wouldn't let me in the garden and I have to get the coal or I'll get into trouble," Jenny shouted, still raging. "She made all those kids hold the gate so I couldn't get in."

Miss Frieberg was helping wailing Celia to her feet. Blood dripped from the back of her head and she shook with fright. "Oh dear, dear, dear. You must bose of you please come inside and ve vill clean Cecia from blood."

"She hurt me, she hurt me, and I'm telling my mum," Celia sobbed. "My mum will kill you," she screamed at Jenny.

"No she won't and you won't tell her," Jenny shouted back.

"Now, now, now," Miss Frieberg admonished them. "Cecia, let me vash your head. You must not tell your musser from zis. You very bad girl to Jenny and I vill tell your musser zis if you tell ze tale from Jenny." She bathed Celia's head, sponging blood from her dress as Jenny watched. Jenny felt no regret for having beaten Celia, wishing she could have hurt her more. Somewhat surprised that Miss Frieberg was willing to stick up for her, she hoped it might save her from a beating, although she didn't really care at that point.

"Now Cecia, you must help Jenny for to carry ze coal bucket. Poor Jenny alvays vorks and you play. Go now and do zis."

"No I won't. I don't have to do anything. She's supposed to do the work, not me. If you make me I'm telling Mummy."

"I don't mind vat you tell your musser, because I vill tell her you are so bad girl from Jenny. I tell you now to help carry ze coal and you vill."

"Its not fair," Celia said, stamping down the path behind Jenny. "And I *am* going to tell Mum. She won't believe you or Miss Frieberg if I say its all lies. You're not allowed to hit me 'cos she said so. She'll bash you into next week and I'll laugh."

Jenny dropped the bucket and spun round so fast she made Celia jump. She grabbed Celia's throat again and began to squeeze. "Do you want me to do it again?" she asked. "This time I won't let you up 'til you're dead!" Celia's eyes widened with fright. "No, no, let go," she gurgled. Jenny let go. "If you go telling tales to your mum, tomorrow I *will* kill you, and I can do it."

Celia said nothing, staring wide eyed at Jenny. "When I first came here," Jenny said angrily, "your mother said you would have to do jobs when you were older. You're as old as I was when I came but you don't have to do anything. You can make your own damn bed now because I'm not doing it any more. You can carry that bucket too, and fill it up." Celia picked up the bucket and carried it without a word. She shovelled the coal into it and they carried it back between them.

Celia said nothing to her mother all afternoon. By supper time Jenny's rage had long gone and she was becoming apprehensive. "My head hurts, Mum," Celia said as they sat at table. Jenny's heart plummeted. "Why, what's the matter with your head, Celie?" Aunt Edith asked. "I fell down and bashed it on the road this morning. You feel," Celia said, getting down from the table to stand with her back against her mother.

"Good heavens," Aunt Edith said, as she parted Celia's hair. "How did you come to fall down on your back and get a crack like that?"

"I don't remember. Oh yes, I ran into the gate and bumped my face and fell backwards ... and the latch got broke," she added.

"Well go and eat your supper and I'll look at it afterwards. If your head still hurts when I've gone out, get Daddy to give you an aspirin. Do you hear that Reg?"

Jenny kept her eyes on her plate. She didn't dare look at Celia or she would have laughed out loud.

THIRTY-SIX

1943 - 1944

The battle brought a change of attitude between Jenny and Celia. Jenny found Celia easier to deal with although she still couldn't stand her. Celia no longer ordered her about or told tales. Jenny continued to make Celia's bed in the mornings before school, but on Saturdays and holidays Celia did it herself. Jenny was amazed that Celia was still apparently afraid of her because since her one outburst she doubted she could find the courage to attack Celia again. Careful not to let Celia know that she was really as nervous of her as Celia seemed to be of Jenny, the situation between them remained reasonably peaceful.

Summer holidays began once more, and with it a slight easing of Aunt Edith's sarcasm and anger. Jenny couldn't help noticing that her beatings were becoming less frequent. It wasn't that Aunt Edith was becoming more friendly, rather that she sometimes seemed not to notice Jenny at all. For some reason Jenny could not explain, she had a disastrous week starting a few days into the holiday. First she accidentally caught the tea towel on fire when attempting to lift the kettle from the lighted stove, using the towel as a heat pad. She threw it to the floor and stamped out the flames, but there was a huge hole in its centre. Curiously Aunt Edith told her off for carelessness, but didn't even box her ears. Next she dropped a cup and broke off the handle. She tried to glue it back on but it was a mess and she had to own up. Once again, there was no violence. Aunt Edith merely told her to throw it out.

The third mishap frightened Jenny and this time she was certain of a beating. Aunt Edith had a teapot of which she was very proud. She had told Jenny often enough that if she ever broke that teapot her life wouldn't be worth living. Just as Aunt Edith walked in the door one day, Jenny dropped the favourite teapot and it smashed to pieces. Cold with shock, there was nothing she could do - Aunt Edith had seen her.

"I'm sorry, I'm sorry, I didn't mean it. It fell out of my hand, I didn't do it on purpose," she said, frantically.

"Oh I know that," Aunt Edith said. "Don't stand there grovelling, I can't stand it. Get the dustpan and brush and sweep it up. Then get upstairs and start to pack your things."

Something lurched in Jenny's chest. What did Aunt Edith say? She looked at Aunt Edith blankly. "What?"

"Don't 'what' me. You heard. Sweep up that mess, then go and start packing."

"Packing? What do you want me to pack?" Jenny was afraid to believe what she thought. "I don't know what you mean."

"Well I always said you were stupid didn't I. Now what do you think I mean by pack? And what could you possibly pack would you say? I mean, fetch your suitcase and start packing your clothes. You can keep them in your case for the next little while because you are leaving. Is that clear enough for you?"

It was clear. It was clear but it wasn't. Still afraid to believe what she was hearing in case it was some trick, Jenny stood with her mouth open.

"For God's sake don't just stand there gaping. Can't you understand that you're leaving? If you don't clean up that mess right now I'll crack the brush over your head. Perhaps that'll knock some sense in."

Jenny jumped back to sanity. Dashing to get the dustpan and brush, she began to sweep the broken teapot into a pile. "Are you sending me away because I broke your teapot? Where are you going to send me?" It still didn't make sense. And she still wasn't sure that it wasn't a cruel joke.

"No. I'm not sending you away because you broke my best teapot. I have my own reasons and that's all you need to know. As to where you're going, I have no idea and nor do I care. Miss Hargreaves will be here at the beginning of next week and no doubt she will tell you. Don't try my patience any further, just go and do as you've been told."

Upstairs, Jenny's head was spinning. Was this really true? Was she really going to escape Aunt Edith at long last? She stood at the window and looked up to the sky. Where was God? Was He really up there somewhere? If it was He who punished her when she lost the swan, it must be He who was saving her now. Not always sure if she believed or not, most of the time she knew she did. I wonder where I'll go now, she thought. But it didn't matter that much just then - she was leaving, leaving, leaving. She began to pack her case. There wasn't much to put in it anyway.

Her excitement had been hard to contain for the four days of waiting. Jenny tried hard not to appear too happy at the prospect of leaving in case Aunt Edith got mad. In fact, Aunt Edith ignored her for the most part and seemed strangely different. Perhaps she was just as happy that Jenny was leaving as Jenny was herself. When on Tuesday morning Aunt Edith said that Miss Hargreaves would be arriving, Jenny tried not to grin. She went upstairs to put the last remaining items in her case and snap it shut. Looking at her case there on the bed, a bubble of excitement made her chest tremble inside. Feeling as daring as she knew how, she told herself that this morning she was not going to make her bed, nor Celia's, and neither would she wash any dishes, clean floors or anything at all. She was going to play outside until Miss Hargreaves came. Dying to jump up and down, she thought she had better not until Aunt Edith had gone.

"Come down here, Jenny. I want you." Aunt Edith was calling. Hurrying downstairs, she saw Aunt Edith standing by the door ready to leave. "I suppose I should say goodbye to you," Aunt Edith said. "I'd like to think you've learned some things in the two years you've been here, gratitude being one of them. To be honest, I don't see much sign of that at all. No-one *has* to give you a home or feed you, you know, and its about time you began to be thankful for the kindness of people who do bother to look after you. I have to be off now, and you'll be gone by the time I get home. Just make sure that wherever you go, you show a little gratitude. Don't go thinking that because someone takes you in you will be one of the family and have the same rights, because you won't. Well goodbye now, and remember what I've said."

Jenny felt her face flushing as Aunt Edith walked out the door. Wandering after her to watch her hurry down the road, a bevy of mixed emotions took hold of Jenny. She would never again have to look at that hated face with its blazing eyes and slit red mouth screaming hateful words at her. She was free. And yet what was this strange lump that has suddenly settled in the middle of her body? She was sure she would never miss Aunt Edith, but there was this feeling of something familiar ending and empty space taking its place. Aunt Edith's last words came back to her, bringing first resentment that she was supposed to be grateful for being given a home where she was beaten, starved and made to work all the time. Aunt Edith was telling her she was a nobody and could never expect anyone to treat her as they did their own children. That made her feel angry, resentful and sorry for herself all at once. Why couldn't somebody, somewhere see that she was the same as other children and treat her the same. But they never did, she was always different, and how she hated being different.

Sitting on the bridge watching the river, she thought again of those words of Aunt Edith. They had made her face flush and that was because she had felt a sense of shame. Aunt Edith was right really. Nobody did have to look after her and she would never be a real part of anyone else's family. Why couldn't her mother come back? Why couldn't *she* be the one coming today instead of Miss Hargreaves, so that Jenny could have someone to belong to and not have to be always grateful? The only other person who had allowed her to feel real was Nellie, but that was such a long time ago. Aunt Edith had said something about two years. Was that all the time she had been here? Yes, it was June when she came and now it was July. Two years and a month, it seemed a whole lifetime. I wonder where I'm going now, she thought. Please God don't let it be to anyone like Aunt Edith. She felt that odd lump of sadness again as she turned to go back indoors. She decided to make the beds and wash dishes after all.

Celia and Jenny had eaten their sandwiches by the time Miss Hargreaves arrived. "Hello Jenny. Hello Celia. Well, are you all ready to go and wearing your best smile?" she asked Jenny. "Its a lovely day to be starting a new life, dear," she said, taking hold of Jenny's hands. "I know you have been moved around quite a bit and its unsettling, but let's hope this is going to be the last move." She let go one of Jenny's hands touched her shoulder. "Say goodbye to Celia now, and let's get along." She picked up Jenny's case and moved to the door. "Goodbye Celia," Jenny said, giving her a quick glance. There were no regrets whatsoever in leaving Celia. "Bye," Celia answered, following them out.

Miss Hargreaves headed towards the white bridge with Jenny behind her. At the other side, Jenny moved up beside her. "What is it like where I'm going? Have they got any children my age?" she asked.

"Why do you ask that?" Miss Hargreaves said. "Don't you know where you're going? Didn't Mrs. Stafford tell you?"

"No. She said she didn't know and that you would tell me."

"Really? How strange. Well of course I'll tell you. You're going to the Matthews family. I understand you were there before and were happy. Isn't that right?"

Something like a hammer banged inside Jenny's head. She stood stock still. "The Matthews? Nellie? You're really taking me back to Nellie's? I didn't think she wanted me any more."

"Did you? Well I suppose that is understandable, seeing they let you go. But she does want you, Jenny. She wants you very much. Don't you want to go back there?"

What a question! Jenny's spirits rose up all the way from her feet to her head, and she let out a squeal. "Ohh! Yes I do want to go. I want to go more than anything in the world. Is it true that Nellie really wants me back?"

"That's what she said, and I saw no reason not to believe her. Yes, truly, she is looking forward to having you back, and obviously you are happy to be going back. I'm pleased for you, Jenny."

So was Jenny pleased for Jenny. She wanted to run all the way, but managed to stay at walking pace beside Miss Hargreaves, contenting herself with a skip and a jump now and again. As they opened the familiar gate and walked to the door, Jenny's heart was racing.

Nellie opened the door, smiling. "Come in, Miss Hargreaves, I've been waiting for you. Hello Jenny. Come along in, dear." Jenny wanted to hug her, but held back. It wasn't as if she had never seen Nellie since going to the Staffords, but any time she had, she had tried to avoid having to speak to her. It hurt too much to simply say 'Hello' as if Nellie was like any other acquaintance. For the same reason she had avoided walking by the Matthews' house. Now she was back and standing in the living room again. It appeared strangely smaller, and she didn't feel as immediately at home as she had expected on the way over. The two years away seemed much more, just as it seemed that she had been at the Stafford's for ever. She had been a month away from her seventh birthday the first time she had stood in this room, now she was ten. So long ago.

Feeling suddenly awkward, Jenny began to wonder if she really would be able to settle down here again. She wanted to be here, wanted to feel as she had before, that this was home. When she had felt like that though, they had suddenly sent her away. How did she know they would't do it again? She didn't know, and that was what was making her feel so strange. She wanted to hug Nellie, wanted to love her again, but she didn't know how.

Miss Hargreaves had been talking with Nellie, but Jenny hadn't been listening. Now Miss Hargreaves was saying she must go because she was to see Jimmy before getting her bus back to town, and then catching her train to Bristol. "Goodbye then, Jenny. I'll be back to see you again before too long. Hopefully by that time there will be some roses in those wan cheeks. Be happy, dear."

Nellie saw her to the gate, and when she returned Jenny was still standing by the sewing machine. "Have you forgotten where things are here while you've been away?" Nellie chided her. "You're standing there looking like a lost lamb. Does it feel strange to be back?"

"Yes, a bit," Jenny confessed. "I don't really feel as if I live here any more. And it seems smaller." She wanted to cry, not quite knowing what for.

"That's because you're bigger. The place isn't any smaller I promise you. You certainly have grown upwards, but not outwards very much have you. I think you're taller than Verna now, but there's more of her," she laughed. "Can you manage that case upstairs by yourself? You are in the end bedroom on your own this time. Your own bedroom - d'you think that's good?"

Jenny thought it would be lovely. She hadn't had a room to herself since she left the Williamsons. And then she hadn't liked being on her own; too afraid of the man behind the wardrobe. She carried her case up to her very own room and began to unpack.

Something had happened from this house since Jenny had left, something that had caused a bit of a stir in the village. Alf had married. It had been a nine-day wonder since no-one thought the thirty-four year old shy bachelor would ever marry. But he did. He married a widow lady who owned her own house and had a daughter of eight and a boy of six. She was quite an attractive lady, and Alf now lived with his new wife in her house situated near the hump backed bridge, on the road between the Post Office and the white bridge. Jenny's new bedroom had been Alf's after Jimmy left, and now it was her own.

Settling down at the Matthews' again did not come too easily, as Jenny had begun to suspect. For a while she woke in the mornings with a start, leaping out of bed with pounding heart because she thought she had overslept and Aunt Edith would beat her. Other times she would wake in the night feeling dizzy and disoriented, not sure where she was until full realization dawned on her. She was nervous at the food table, expecting Frank to start shouting at her for something, for in her mind she mixed up Frank and Aunt Edith. Frank had sometimes frightened her when she lived here before, and Aunt Edith had frightened her all the time. Now she felt jumpy around Frank, afraid she might accidentally annoy him. She was also cautious in her approach to Verna, remembering that it was a fight between them that had resulted in her being turned away. Her violent teaching at the hands of Aunt Edith that you didn't touch any child of the family had left its mark. It was silly of course. Nellie had never taken sides in any squabble between Verna and Jenny, and it wasn't the fight so much as what she had said that made Frank send her away. But caution was there.

As a matter of fact, Verna was not at all upset at Jenny's return. They had seen each other continually at school, and although not friends, neither were they enemies. Within a few days of her return, Verna gave Jenny her big blue buck rabbit to have as her own. Jenny was delighted to have an animal of her own. When Verna warned her that she would have to keep him cleaned out and pick a sack of food for him every few days, Jenny thought that was play compared to the things she had been doing. She loved 'Bucky' from the moment Verna gave him to her, though to be truthful, his character wasn't exactly lovable. He was given to biting, and scratching hard with his hind feet. But he was hers.

Frank had not had too much to say to her when he had come home the first evening. "So thee's back. Looks like thee's sprouted some. I hope thee's sprouted some sense to go wi' it," was all he had said.

THIRTY-SEVEN

"I hope you're soon going to stop being so nervous and jumpy," Nellie said after Jenny had been there one week. "You're making me jump just to look at you. Nobody's going to hurt you here you know. Not unless you do something bad enough to get Frank's dander up, and you should know by now how to keep out of his way. I really don't like to see you like this, it makes me feel so guilty."

"I'm sorry," Jenny said, surprised. "I'm not being jumpy on purpose. Why does it make you feel guilty? You never used to hit me."

"Oh, don't think I don't know something about what you went through at the Staffords'. I would never have let you go there if I'd known how you would be treated, and I've been sorry ever since. I tried to get you back about eighteen month's ago, but Mrs. Stafford was downright rude to me, and there was no way she intended to let you come back here. I wish I had got you back then. You wouldn't be in this state now if I had."

This news so astonished Jenny that she burst into tears. She had no idea Nellie had ever tried to get her back, or even that she wanted her at all. To think she had cared all the time brought floods of grateful tears. "I hated Aunt Edith, she was horrid to me, but I didn't know anybody knew. She pretended to be so nice to me in front of other people."

Nellie put her arms around Jenny. "You'd be surprised how many people knew how cruel she was to you, Jen, but nobody knew what to do about it. But if it will make you feel any better, I've got some news for you."

"What news?" Jenny asked, sniffling. She dragged her hankie down her sleeve and rubbed at her eyes. "What news are you going to tell me?"

"Are you ready for this?" Nellie said, laughing now. "The so wonderful Mrs. Stafford, who thought herself above the rest of us peasants, has cleared off and left her husband. She's taken Celia with her and run off with a sergeant from the searchlight. There now, what do you think of that?"

Dumbfounded was hardly the word. So that was why Aunt Edith had so suddenly decided to get rid of her, Jenny thought. Well fancy that! So not only was she out of that awful house, she would never have to see the hated faces of Aunt Edith and Celia again.

"Wow! Is that honest? Did she leave Uncle Reg all by himself? I wonder what he thinks about that. I knew she didn't really like him at all, and she used to flirt with the soldiers all the time. I knew that too. I wonder which one she ran off with. If the soldiers run away they get the police after them don't they? That one called Taffy had the police after him. How can they run away without getting caught?"

"Well I don't think he's run away. I think he's just gone with her up North somewhere, where he comes from. He's on leave, they say, and will have to come back, or perhaps he's arranged for a transfer, I don't know. He's married too, his name is Austin or something like that. I don't know the soldiers. But good riddance to her wouldn't you say. And poor sod him when he finds out what he's got."

"Austin? I remember him. Yes, he is married. I know that because he brought his wife down once to stay with us. She was a nice lady, and they both stayed for a weekend. They all went to the dance, those two and Rita and Aunt Edith. Doesn't she stink, to go and run off with somebody else's husband. I don't have to call her Aunt Edith any more, do I. And I don't have to see her ever again."

Jenny was elated. It was as if a heavy load had been lifted off her shoulders, and she was truly free. She was sorry for nice Mrs. Austin, and even a bit sorry for silly Uncle Reg - Mr. Stafford - he wasn't Uncle Reg any more. He'd probably be lonely all by himself, and feel pretty stupid with everyone knowing his wife had run away from him. Oh well, if he'd had more sense he wouldn't have married her in the first place. Jenny giggled at Nellie's remark about Mr. Austin being a poor sod. He'd probably live to be very sorry.

"That's better," Nellie said. "Let's see you laughing a lot more. Why don't you go and see your old friend next door. I bet he'll be glad to see you back."

Old friend? "Who?" Jenny struggled to think who Nellie was talking about. What old friend could she have forgotten?

"Who? You ask me who? He won't be too pleased about that. I mean Boxer of course. Who else?"

Boxer! How could she have forgotten him, how could she? She raced out of the house, round to the field gate and called. There he was. Lumbering up the field to her call, he whinnied. More tears flowed as she let him nuzzle her and kissed his big black face. She climbed on his back and hugged him. He hadn't forgotten her, hadn't even forgotten to stand with his side to the gate to let her get on. Laying along his neck, she told him she had only forgotten him for a little while, but had really missed him all the time. Staying with him all afternoon, sometimes crying, sometimes dreaming, the world seem to come back right. When she went indoors covered in black hairs and greasy dirt, Nellie smiled. "Pooh," she said, holding her nose. "Now I know you're back."

THIRTY-EIGHT

Harvest was in progress. Verna and Jenny went to the fields as they had two years before. This time Jenny was taught to drive the tractor and trailer to pick up the bales. Both horses and tractor were used for this purpose, and as Jenny drove, the men shouted 'wook off' and 'whoa there' to her, telling her to start and stop as though she were a horse. The pedals were stiff and sometimes she didn't manage to stop in the right place, but on the whole she didn't do badly and was proud of being allowed to drive. Alf seemed really happy to see her again. He still worked with the horses and swore that Boxer had moped when she first went away. By the time the holidays were over, Jenny was much more settled in her mind. She was still skinny but her skin had a golden tan and her hair had bleached almost white once more.

She had not had a very good report at the end of the school year. Mrs. Mergrin had written at the end of her remarks that Jenny would be entering the eleven plus year at the commencement of the new term. 'I do not see her passing this examination unless there is a complete change of attitude towards her school work. Even then it is doubtful. Jenny needs to concentrate a great deal more and daydream a great deal less,' she had written. Nellie had to sign the report for her to take back to school when term started. Verna had had a poor report too, Nellie said. Perhaps the both of them could help one another by giving each other words to spell and sums to do. Verna turned up her nose at that. She didn't care if she never passed the eleven plus, she said. Hardly anybody did from their school anyway.

"I won't pass the eleven plus either," Jenny said. "Mrs. Stafford had to take me to a psychologist man and he said I was daft. Mrs. Stafford said that when my mum had Jimmy, she had given him all the brains and there was none left for me when I was born. I know that's silly, but she kept on telling me how stupid I am."

201

"Good grief," Nellie said. "No psychologist or any other head doctor would ever dare say someone was daft. He couldn't have said anything of the sort. You just get that right out of your head. Mrs. Stafford never had much in the way of brains herself, so you don't have to go believing anything she told you. You just do your best, that's all anyone can do."

Jenny gave her report back to Mrs. Mergrin. "Not that good, was it Jenny?. I understand that you are now back with the Matthews. I'm happy to see you looking decidedly better than you were. You will now be in standard ten, which, as you know, is the eleven plus grade. If you are to ever come close to passing, there will be a lot of work to do and you simply *have* to pay more attention. You will be sitting in the front desk where I can make sure you are not daydreaming."

Not too pleased about being in the front, Jenny took her new position. At least she wasn't ashamed to be in the front where everyone could see her clothes, as she would have been had she been still wearing the scant few ill-fitting garments Mrs. Stafford made her wear. She had brand new shoes and a new coat. Nellie had thrown out her heavily studded boys shoes in disgust, and with the money the Ministry sent her for Jenny's clothes - and probably some of her own - she had bought the coat and shoes, underclothes, jumpers and socks. She had also bought material and made skirts and dresses for both girls. Jenny was especially proud of the pleated Scots plaid kilt Nellie had made her. Nellie said it wasn't very good material, but then nothing was these days with only utility rubbish everywhere.

Everyone grumbled about the utility stuff. There was utility clothing, utility furniture, the utility loaf, utility bedding, even utility lavatory paper. Jenny often thought the utility lavatory paper was made out of the same stuff as the utility loaf. It was the same grey colour with course bits in it, and was pretty useless. There were course, inedible husks in the bread and it was like trying to eat cardboard. The Matthews were unaffected by the lavatory paper because they still cut up squares of newspaper to hang on the string in the 'Palace'.

Verna hadn't liked Nellie's idea of testing each other with sums and spelling, but Mrs. Mergrin had other ideas in any case. All the children in standard ten were given extra work to take home on

Mondays, having to have it done and handed back by Friday morning. Jenny and Verna were allowed to stay up until eight o'clock now so long as they got on with their home projects and didn't argue or squabble over pencils, etc. If there was the slightest noise, Frank would order them to bed whether they had finished or not.

Jenny was sleeping much better. Since coming back to Nellie's she had not had any of the flying dreams. In a way she was disappointed because the feeling of flying had been so real and so lovely. When she thought about them, she felt she wouldn't dream them any more anyway because they had always started the same way, with her standing on top of the Stafford's stairs. They must be special dreams that she could only dream in that house and now that she had escaped, she wouldn't need them any more. In another way she was not sorry they had stopped. Whenever she had floated too high she had been terrified. She had been afraid of heights ever since she was four, and well remembered the fist time she discovered that fact.

Her mother had been deciding which school to send Jenny to, and had taken her to visit a few. Jenny couldn't remember anything much about the schools except seeing a lot of children, but she remembered that one had a playground on the roof. They had gone up to look at the playground, surrounded by high iron railings, and while her mother was talking, Jenny had run to look through the railings. The moment she looked down she had panicked. She felt herself sway, and the more she looked down the more she felt as if a magnet was trying to pull her through the railings and down to the road beneath. She had screamed and screamed. Her mother and the teacher who had taken them up there had both tried to pry her hands away from the railings which she was gripping in sheer terror. She felt like that whenever she was anywhere high - as if something was pulling at her and tempting her to throw herself down. It was the same sort of temptation and magnetic pull that the wheels of the heavy lorries had on her as they rumbled by on the road.

For a time, Jenny forgot about her fear of heights but was reminded about it forcefully. She had made friends with Jean Foster, the youngest of the ten Foster children. Her sister, Pearl, was the girl the soldier Taffy had got into such trouble over. Jean was a couple of months younger than Jenny, and a complete tomboy, unafraid of anything. Jenny thought Jean was clever, too, because although she did not do particularly well at school, she could sit at the piano and play any tune she heard on the wireless without music. She had never taken music lessons and couldn't read music, yet she only had to hear a tune once and she'd play it with both hands. Jean ran fast, climbed and jumped over anything, never worried if she fell and hurt herself, and if any boy hit her, she would hit him back just as hard. Jenny admired Jean, and Jean seemed to like her.

The day Jenny forgot about her fear of heights, she and Jean were out in the fields jumping up to catch the lower branches of trees, swinging themselves up and over, and dropping to the ground again. Jean decided to climb right up one tree and shinned up like a monkey. High up in the top, she began to sway the branches to and fro. "Come on up here," she shouted down to Jenny. "You can see for miles, its great. Come on and look." Jenny started up the tree. She was not as good a climber as Jean, but eventually reached the branch where Jean was sitting. "You can't come on this branch with me," Jean said. "You sit on that one underneath me and we can rock the tree." Jenny looked down at the branch she was to sit on and was nearly sick. Everything began to swim and she felt the pulling sensation trying to drag her from the tree. She grabbed hold of the trunk, shaking and unable to breath. She couldn't answer Jean when she asked what the matter was, just closed her eyes and held on tight, trembling like a aspen leaf. Jean climbed down to stand behind her.

"You're going to have to get down," she told Jenny. That was just the trouble, Jenny couldn't get down. She couldn't move at all. Jean did all she could to persuade her down, but it was not until Jean threatened to leave her there, that Jenny shakingly followed Jean's instructions, allowing Jean to hold on to her and guide her down. At last on firm ground, she lay on her back while the world spun. She was grateful to Jean for not mocking her or telling anyone else how scared she'd been. She was disgusted enough with herself for being such a coward.

Trying to make up for what she considered her cowardice, Jenny determined to become more daring in other ways. Several times she had asked Alf if she could put a halter on Boxer and ride him over the fields. He always refused, saying Boxer needed to rest after work because he wasn't as energetic as Kitty. He wouldn't be any good anyway, Alf said, because he was too slow and would only stop and eat. She could take Kitty if she liked. Jenny was nervous of Kitty's biting and kicking, but thought that would be a way to prove to herself that she could be brave like Jean. Thereafter she did take Kitty out on occasions on a rope halter. Kitty was skittish, walked and trotted much faster than Boxer, and sometimes took off, running under trees to try to brush Jenny off, but Jenny stuck with her, recovering some of her lost confidence. She followed Jean into various escapades, never as good in running, jumping or climbing, but always trying. She even challenged Jean to fights, where they dragged one another to the ground, rolling and scrapping to test their strength. They put all they had into the fights, pulling hair, biting and punching, but no matter who won, they remained friends.

THIRTY-NINE

On one of Miss Hargreaves visits, Nellie had told her how Jenny's bike had been stolen and sold. Miss Hargreaves was shocked, and a little while later a new bike arrived for Jenny. The new bike was nothing like her lovely Raleigh, but Jenny was only too happy to have any sort of bicycle again. This one was all black and appeared to have no brakes. What good was a bike with no brakes, Jenny wondered. It would mean she could only go slowly or she couldn't stop in time. Gingerly trying it out, she discovered that it did after all have brakes. They were in the pedals. As soon as she stopped pedalling and tried to freewheel, the bike stopped dead, Jenny and bike crashing to the ground. This was going to take a lot of getting used to. The bike was meant to stop as gentle pressure was applied backwards on the pedals, the trouble being that as soon as you ceased pedalling but kept your feet on the pedals, the bike stopped and over you'd go. Jenny called it her 'back-pedaller', eventually mastering it after numerous scrapes and bruises. If she wanted to freewheel, she lifted her feet from the pedals, allowing them to whiz round and round on their own, then letting the pedals whack her in the back of the leg a few times to slow it down. She took it up to show it to Jimmy when she first got it and he had a go, grinning sheepishly when it threw him to the ground.

Although she could pop up to see Jimmy more often now, he was always busy and never wanted to talk to her for very long. Jenny was sad that he still had to work so much and wished he could come back to Nellie's with her. She asked him if he would like her to try and persuade Nellie and Frank to ask him to tea, then perhaps Frank would feel sorry for what he'd done and let Jimmy come back too. To her dismay, he said he didn't want to go back there ever again. He still didn't like it at the Fosters but he wouldn't hear of going back to Nellie's, even though it was much nicer.

"They threw me out for nothing once. I'd never go back there again, I'm alright where I am," he told her.

"But Jimmy. You don't like it at the Fosters, you said so. Wouldn't you come back if Frank said sorry?"

"Hah. That's a laugh," he said. "Can you imagine Frank Matthews saying sorry to anyone, let alone me? Don't bother asking if I can come to tea, I don't want to go back there at all."

Jimmy liked his school and was doing well, which was what Jenny expected. He said it was hard to get his homework done because Mrs. Foster never seemed to understand that he had to do it. She thought he had homework because he hadn't got all his work done at school, telling him that he should do it there and not bring it home. He couldn't get it into her head that it was home work, not day work, and he had to do it, whether it made him later getting his chores done or not.

"She's not bad," he said to Jenny. "She just doesn't understand much about school work other than learning to read and write. She never asks me how I'm doing or gives me any praise for anything. I don't care any more. I don't want to move anywhere else, I'm alright here."

Jimmy and Jenny never spoke about their mother or father. Jenny had learned that Jimmy couldn't mention their dad without his eyes reddening, and he hated that. If she ever mentioned Mum, his eyes would blaze in a way that turned Jenny's stomach. "Don't talk to me about her. I don't know her," he had said once. Hurt, Jenny decided to avoid the subject for a while.

She did talk about her mother to Nellie, however. Distressed to find she could no longer recall the faces of either parent, she asked what her mother looked like. "Is she pretty? Do I look like her at all?" she wanted to know.

"Pretty is hardly the word to use for someone so tall," Nellie had told her. "She is a striking looking woman. Handsome, I'd say. Always very smart. I suppose you'd say she's the sort of person you'd look at twice. And no, I don't see you anything like her at all. Not you or Jimmy. Your mum had dark hair and big hazel eyes. You two are both blue eyed blondes."

Disappointed that she didn't resemble her mother, now that she had got Nellie talking about her, she brought up something else that worried her. "Nellie, Mrs. Stafford used to say horrible things about my mum. She said that Mum had run away with a Dutch captain of a ship and she had another baby. She said Mum could come back but didn't want us, and she had let the new baby be adopted. She said Miss Hargreaves told her. Its not true is it? Mrs. Stafford used to tell lies didn't she? She kept saying my mum was bad and that I'd grow up no better than her."

"She certainly did tell lies," Nellie said. "And she's a fine one to talk anyway, isn't she. Running off with a married man and all. To be honest, Jen, I've heard those rumours too, but I don't know what truth there is in any of it either. They say there's no smoke without fire, but I've seen a heck of a lot of smoke and no flame many times. What can you do by worrying yourself about it when none of us knows the truth? One day you'll find out I'm sure. Then you can make up your own mind about it."

That was true. Nevertheless she did worry about it quite a lot. She wouldn't believe her mother had had another baby. Their family was Dad, Mum, Jimmy and her, there wasn't room for any more. And the baby wouldn't belong to them anyway because Dad wouldn't be its dad. It was rubbish in any case because Mum had never had another baby. She was going to come back and say who had been keeping her, and then all these gossips would be very sorry. Dad would be mad too when he heard what people had been saying about Mum.

'Lady North' had been over to the house several times since Jenny returned, and was still snooty-nosed towards her. She made Jenny feel an intruder, pointedly speaking to Verna and ignoring Jenny. Although she didn't really care about Mrs. North, she was decidedly uncomfortable when 'her ladyship' was in the house. "Why is Mrs. North still mad at me? Verna never did swallow that pin did she? I don't know why she still doesn't like me," she said to Nellie.

"Oh take no notice of her," Nellie said. "Its nothing to do with the pin. She still thinks she owns me and says I have enough to do without taking on evacuees. It's only because she wants me to be free to run around after her. That's just too bad because its none of her business what I do. You're not missing anything not having her as a friend, Jen."

Jenny knew that was true. 'Lady North' was a royal pain, as Nellie put it. Her only son, Jack, was eleven years old now and caused her no end of trouble. At least, she said he did although really he didn't. Any trouble was her own doing and came about because she wanted him to be one thing, and he was determined to be another. She sent him to boarding school to learn to become a little gentleman. Jack had no intention of ever being a gentleman. Jack had farming in his blood, he was a happy outgoing boy who got along with everyone. When he came home he loved to get out with the other kids, whoever their parents were. Jack was round and jolly, always the one with the most outrageous ideas, including leading raids on his own parents' orchards and peach trees. There wasn't a child who didn't like Jack, and no-one Jack didn't like. He led the gang, and the gang included anyone who wanted to come along. He spoke with the same broad dialect as other kids, despite the expensive elocution lessons his mother insisted upon. He did his lessons dutifully, and ignored them. "What do I want elocution for?" he would laugh to the gang. "The farm's going to be mine one day, there's nobody else for it to go to. I don't need to talk la-di-da to muck out cow sheds or go to market." Jack was Jack, and if his snooty mother could understand that there would be no problem. Unfortunately she didn't, and each time Jack did the slightest thing against her wishes, she would take to her bed with an attack of the vapours. Nobody told her that vapours were out of date, and that going to bed with a wet towel on her head wouldn't change Jack. Whenever she took to her bed the local people just laughed at her. "Oh-ah," they'd say. "What's our bad Jack supposed to 'a done now?" Jack was popular with children and adults alike.

That year loads of snow fell during the Christmas holidays. When the large gang of children Jenny was playing with had enough of snow balling and tussling with each other in the snow, Jack had a great idea. "Hey, let's go sleddin'," he suggested. "Good idea," somebody said. "But we ain't got no sledges so p'raps its a bloody daft idea." "What do we want sleds for?" Jack said. "Granddad's got a whole pile of galvanize sheets down in one of the barns, we can pinch a few of them."

Jack led them to the barn where they pulled down about half a dozen of the sheets, found an iron spike and hammered two holes in the front of each one. All working together they managed to bend up the fronts, tie binder string through the holes, and there were their sleds. They dragged them up the Drove to the highest hill they could find and all had the time of their lives. Jenny disgraced herself by wetting her pants. At ten years old, she wet herself. It came about because on one ride she was sitting behind Jack. He turned round to shout something back to her and in doing so pulled harder on one side of the string. By the time he turned back it was too late. At breakneck speed they were headed for a tree. The sled whacked into the tree and both Jenny and Jack carried on down the hill without it. They both had bruises from hitting the tree, and the shock had caused Jenny's 'accident'. There was no getting away from it, the yellow stains in the snow told the tale. Jack was not going to let her forget that one.

FORTY

Jenny had not forgotten her friend Margie. When she moved to Nellie's for the second time she resumed visiting Margie, wondering at first if they would be less friendly to her as she had seen very little of Margie for the past two years. She needn't have worried, they were just as happy to see her as before. Mrs. Roper understood how Jenny had not been allowed to visit while she was with the Staffords, and was pleased that Jenny was looking so much better and more like a little girl again. "I don't think I'm a little girl any more," Jenny had said. "I'm gone ten now." Mrs. Roper laughed. "I know that," she said. "So's our Margie. But you're a long way from being grown up yet, you're still a little girl. Doesn't look like you're ever going to get any fat on you though, does it?"

Margie still had to use crutches, although she got around a lot faster these days. She was studying for the eleven plus too. She wouldn't be going to any grammar school if she did pass, but she wanted to see if she could get the Certificate. To sit the exam, she was going to have to be wheeled to the school in a wheel chair and write it with the other children. To her that was quite an adventure since she had never sat at a school desk. Now Margie's family was moving away from the Feathers because her dad, who had always preferred farming, had got the chance to buy a farm. The mad Farmer Planter, who truly did shoot at people who crossed his fields just as Tommy had said, had moved back to his former village to take over his father's farm when the old man died. Margie's dad bought the Planter farm, so they were moving. Margie would only be a few hundred yards away from the school now. Jenny knew she could call in on the way home from school sometimes. so she would still see Margie.

Getting along with Verna was still something of a problem. They were alright with one another indoors, though seldom playing together outside. Jenny still found her strange. At times flying off into temper tantrums, other times deciding she didn't like Jenny, then changing her mind and saying she did, that silly sounding giggle had remained with her. She pushed her tongue to the roof of her mouth when she giggled, so that the sound seemed to come down her nose. To Jenny's mind it made Verna sound pretty gormless. If she sometimes dismissed Verna in her mind, thinking it not worth the trouble of trying to understand her, a strange occurrence took place that made Jenny look at her differently.

It started at school during the morning break when all the children were outside. A black car stopped in the road at the bottom of the playground, staying there the whole time the children were out. There appeared to be a man and a woman in the front, and a girl of about twelve in the back seat. They sat in the car, scanning the children with their eyes, neither getting out of the car nor winding the window down to speak to anyone. A number of children stopped playing to stare back at them, asking among themselves 'wot the 'ell these people thought they were gawpin' at'. Few people owned cars in the village, and most of the cars passing through from other villages were known to the local people and the children. This car was a stranger. The children were called back to classes and the car drove away, but at lunch time it returned, the occupants sitting watching the children as before.

Shortly after they had settled down to afternoon lessons, there was a knock on the schoolroom door. Mrs. Mergrin opened the door and Jenny, sitting at the front of her row directly opposite the door, saw a dark haired woman standing in the porch. "Yes?" Mrs. Mergrin said. "Uh. I'm wondering if I could speak for a moment with Verna March," she said. Mrs. Mergrin snorted. "We are in the middle of class. What do you want with Verna that you would interrupt her in the middle of lessons?"

Jenny was puzzled. Who was Verna March? There was only one Verna in the whole school and that was Verna Matthews. Mrs. Mergrin must have misheard the lady and thought she said 'Matthews' because she hadn't said there was no-one of that name here.

"I'm her mother," the lady was saying. "I won't keep her a moment, but I would like to take her to the car to talk to her sister."

"In that case," Mrs. Mergrin said, "it would be better if you visited her at home after school. I can't let her see you now." This made even less sense to Jenny, they were obviously not talking about her Verna. But who could they be talking about? "I can't do that," the lady said. "We have to leave in a few minutes so I won't be here when school is over. Please let me talk to her for a minute."

"While the children are in school they are my responsibility, and none are permitted to leave the premises. If you want to talk to Verna, it must be here in the porch and she must not leave the building. That is all I can do." Mrs. Mergrin turned and called to Verna to come to the door. "This lady wishes to speak to you Verna," she said. "You may talk to her, but you are not to leave the porch. I absolutely forbid it. Is that understood?" Verna nodded, looking thoroughly confused, and Mrs. Mergrin pushed her gently through the door and closed it. Then she quickly sat and wrote a note which she gave to one of the biggest boys. "Go through the little room and run as fast as you can to the Matthews. Give this note to Mrs. Matthews," she told him.

This was becoming very mysterious. The lady had said she was Verna's mother, but that made no sense. Verna's name was Matthews and she was the daughter of Frank and Nellie. Why was she talking to the wrong Verna? Mrs. Mergrin kept looking at her watch and at the door, and after about ten minutes, she opened the door again. Jenny could see Verna, the lady, and the girl who had been in the car. Verna was crying. "I can't allow Verna out here any longer," Mrs. Mergrin said. "If there is anything more you wish to say to her you must make arrangements to visit her at her home. Come along now Verna, you have to get back to your lessons."

Verna walked back to her desk with tears streaming down her face. Mrs. Mergrin shut the door, saying no more to the two people in the porch. A little while later they heard the car start up and drive away. Within the hour, Nellie knocked on the door and Mrs. Mergrin talked to her in the porch, after which Nellie left. At the end of the day, Mrs. Mergrin herself walked Verna home. There had been no opportunity to ask any questions because Verna had been kept in at afternoon break. Jenny was almost bursting with curiosity by the time she got home, but it was not until Nellie had talked for some time to Verna in the bedroom that she got an answer.

Verna stayed in her bedroom after Nellie came down to get on with the evening meal. Jenny hung around, watching Nellie as she sliced Frank's cheese and set it on the grate, offering to lay table and help with the supper, all the while waiting for Nellie to say something about the strange happenings of the day. She said nothing, however, seeming troubled and thoughtful until Jenny could stand it no longer. "Am I allowed to know what's happening? That lady who came to school asked for Verna March, not our Verna, and she said she was her mother. What's it got to do with us?"

"Yes, you must be wondering," Nellie said. "And it's better I tell you than you hear rumours outside. That 'lady' you saw *is* Verna's real mother. She has only lived here since she was four.

"Honestly?" Jenny was flabbergasted. She had lived here for over a year the first time, and now had been here a further seven months, yet never had the slightest reason to doubt that Verna was Nellie and Frank's real daughter. "I never knew you weren't her mum. Did Verna know? Why is she so upset that her real mum wanted to see her, doesn't Verna like her?"

"There's no reason why you would have known I suppose, although it isn't a secret. Verna's called us 'Mum' and 'Dad' for so long she's probably forgotten her own parents. We never talk about them, but not because it's a secret. She's upset now because today they turned up out of the blue, after all this time, and tried to get her to go back with them."

"Oh no! She doesn't want to go back does she? If she hasn't seen her mother since she was four, that's six years. She isn't an evacuee is she, so why did her mother give her to you when she was four?"

"I'll tell you what happened and then you'll understand what its all about," Nellie said. "Verna's family lived near London. When Verna was four and her sister six, their father was out of work and they were in a lot of debt, so they decided to give their children away. They put an advert in the paper saying they were giving the girls up for adoption because they couldn't afford to keep them. When I saw children advertised in the paper like that, I thought it was terrible. We hadn't any children so Frank agreed we could have them. I wrote to the address in the paper and thought someone would write back to say they wanted to see us, or at least want to see where their children would be going. All I got was a short note back saying the older girl had been taken and the four year old would be on a train arriving in Salisbury on whatever date and time - I can't remember now.

"When the train came in, the guard got out holding the hand of this little waif with a note pinned to her coat. All it said was 'Verna March, Salisbury Station'. That was it. If I hadn't been able to get the bus to the station that day for any reason, nobody would have known where she was going or where she came from. There she was, just in the clothes she stood up in. Nothing else. We never heard another word from her mother. When we'd had her for about six months, I wrote to the address again and said we wanted to adopt her, but the letter came back. We've even tried to adopt her through the courts, but we couldn't because nobody could find her parents. Now here they are, out of nowhere, wanting her back again. And now you know it all."

It was an awful story. Poor Verna. Jenny suddenly thought of her own mother. Verna was just like herself in a way, she had a mother somewhere else and hadn't known where she was. If Mum ever came for me, I would go with her, she thought. But that was different. Verna had been here since she was four and thought of Nellie as her mother. Jenny didn't know what to think. "You don't want her to go back now do you, Nellie? They went back without her anyway, but I s'pose they might come back again."

"Oh yes," Nellie said. "They told Verna they would come back in a fortnight to see what she wanted to do. They've got the sister back and used her to try to persuade Verna. Of course we don't want her to go, but it has to be what she wants in the end."

It was a terrible two weeks. Verna cried a lot, especially in the night. When Jenny asked her what she wanted to do, Verna said she didn't know. She said she would like to be back with her sister, even though she didn't really remember her. She loved 'Mum' and 'Dad', but they weren't her real mum and dad and she wanted to have a real mum and dad like other children. Jenny knew exactly what she meant by that and didn't know what to say to help. Frank said if she wanted to go back to a mother who only wanted her because it wouldn't be long before she could go to work and bring in money, it was up to her. Jenny thought that was mean. "Verna won't be able to leave school for five years yet," she said to Nellie. "They can't just want her to work, like Frank said." To her surprise, Nellie agreed with Frank. "She can bring in money when she's twelve, working evenings, weekends and holidays. I don't know if that's the reason they want her back though."

Nellie walked with Verna and Jenny to school and fetched them in the afternoons in case Verna's mother tried to snatch her off the street. When she did come, she came again to the school, but Mrs. Mergrin insisted she wait until both Nellie and the village constable were sent for. When the constable came and had everything explained to him, he took everyone to his house to talk about it there. Verna was at home when Jenny got there in the afternoon, looking better than she had for two weeks. She told Jenny that there had been an awful row and that when her real mother started shouting at 'Mum', she decided she didn't want to go with her after all. Her sister had cried and that had upset Verna, but she wanted to stay with Mum and Dad for always now.

Jenny was glad Verna wanted to stay with Nellie. If it had been herself, she didn't know what she would do. She daydreamed that Nellie wanted her for always too. Would she want to stay here or go with her mother if the same thing happened? Now she was not quite so sure. Nellie said she was going to go to court to try again to adopt Verna. The constable had insisted on knowing the address of Verna's mother, so now she could give it to the court. She didn't say she wanted to adopt Jenny too, but Jenny consoled herself with the thought that nobody knew where her mother was, so perhaps that was why Nellie didn't say anything about adopting her as well.

Wondering what Jimmy would think about it all, she went to see him at the weekend. Since his twelfth birthday in January, Jimmy had been helping Ted Roper on his farm for part of the weekends, earning a little pocket money for himself. Everything about Ted Roper's yard was as sloppy and mucky as ever. Now that Margie's dad had his own farm and couldn't come to help his brother, Ted's farm had become even worse. She found Jimmy cleaning out the cowsheds which, by the state they were in, looked as if they only got cleaned out when Jimmy could get there to help. Telling him about Verna's parents coming out of the blue to get her back, she asked him what he would do if somebody wanted to adopt him and then Mum came back for them.

"That's the sort of dumb question you would ask," he said. "It isn't going to happen so why worry about it. Nobody's going to want to adopt me and Mum's not coming back. I wouldn't go anywhere with *her* if she did. Sounds like Verna found a bit of sense, though I don't know where from. She'd have been pretty stupid to go back to parents who didn't care if she was alive or dead for six years. Must have been quite a bit of excitement in the old school. Gives people something to talk about for a couple of weeks."

Why was Jimmy always so critical about everybody? He sounded as if he didn't care about anybody or anything, but Jenny was sure he did. It was as if he wanted people to think he was so tough, nothing could ever hurt him or matter to him. Steve Cole was still living at the Fosters and sharing Jimmy's bedroom. Jenny knew Jimmy didn't like sharing his room and that he didn't particularly like Steve, but that shouldn't make him so cool with her. Although in her heart she knew he was not as uncaring as he pretended to be and she shouldn't be upset or hurt at the things he said, she nevertheless was. He still saw her as a silly crybaby, even though she hardly ever cried any more. Someday she would do something so smart and clever, he would be proud of her. Then he would stop thinking of her as his pest of a sister.

FORTY-ONE

March and April of 1944 were fairly eventful months. The searchlight soldiers packed up and left, the dentist came to school, Jenny found a boyfriend, and Frank had an accident.

The war was by no means over, but raids on England were infrequent now, and there had been little work for the searchlight in their village for some time. The soldiers left behind their nissen huts which the children soon turned into wonderful playhouses. They played houses, schools, hospitals and all sorts of imaginative games in the various rooms of the huts. Jenny thought it was a good thing for Mrs. Stafford that she had run off when she did because she would have hated not to have the soldiers around to invite to tea and flirt with at the dances. Perhaps she had known they would soon move away and that's why she had gone. Who knew? Who cared? Some of the village girls would miss the soldiers as well, but they still had the Americans, who they preferred anyway.

The coming of the dentist was by no means an enjoyable event. The little room at school was cleared for him, the infants desks being brought into the big room for the few days he was there. Jenny had always feared dentists and this one was worse than any she had been to. It was said of him that he was an ex-army dentist and had suffered shell shock in the first world war. Whatever the truth, he had a permanently shaking head that wobbled from side to side as he stood at the back of the chair, leaning over his victims. All the children thought of themselves as victims and everyone was terrified of him. When it was Jenny's turn she shook as she leaned her head back over the school chair and looked into those cold eyes. She had reason to shake. Using no anaesthetic, he stuck a finger in her mouth and pulled back her lips. Then he picked up a silver tool, fitted it over one of her teeth and pressed down, twisting the tooth as he did so. A horrible crunching, grinding sound accompanied the pressure and pain. Jenny let out an 'urrgh' and the dentist's finger yanked at the side of her mouth. "Shut up and sit still," he said, pulling her tooth out with one jerk. His nurse squirted water into her mouth and watery blood flowed out of her mouth and down the front of her jumper. The nurse followed her back to the classroom and called out "Next!"

When it was the turn of Tony Ernie, one of the sons of the lady who had given her the sandals, his normally rosy face was white. He walked through the classroom door as if going to his execution. The nurse stood by the door a few moments to say something to Mrs. Mergrin, then followed Tony into the little room. There was no sign of him. He had gone. He didn't come back to school that day, nor the next day. The rest of them thought it hilarious that Tony had managed to disappear. When he finally returned to school, after the dentist had gone, he told them that when he got into the little room the dentist wasn't in there, so without waiting a second he bolted across the room and out the other door. "I ain't 'avin that butcher muckin' about wi' my teeth," he boasted. "I'd 'a told 'im that anyway." Of course, they all knew he wouldn't have done anything of the sort, but he was a hero in any case for managing to escape so swiftly.

Shortly after that, a note landed on Jenny's desk when Mrs. Mergrin's back was turned. She looked around to see who had flicked it at her, but everyone was busy with their work. Opening it she read: 'I love you if you love me. Meet me by the cress beds after school. Tony'. She giggled to herself. There was only one Tony - Tony Ernie, the escape hero. She had no idea that he liked her, let alone loved her. It was funny, but as well it was a nice feeling that somebody said he loved her. She looked across at his desk, but he was very intent on his writing and didn't look up. After school he raced out of the door and down the playground before she could speak to him. Well, she had to pass the watercress beds anyway, so she would drop down onto the path and see if he was at the other end.

He was there. Walking towards him, she wondered what you were supposed to say to someone who had said, 'I love you if you love me.' She didn't think she loved him. She'd never really thought about him at all. She said "Hello", which was all she could think of to say when she got to him. "Hello," he said to her. The next few moments of awkward silence while they looked at each other began to embarrass Jenny, and she wished she hadn't come. "What did you want me to meet you for?" she asked. "I dunno," he said. "I wondered ... I wann'ed to know if ... like, wot I said in the note. Do you? ... you know."

"Oh. You want to know if I love you? Well, I don't know, I never thought about it. If I say I do, what d'you want to do?"

"I dunno," he said again. "I s'pose we're s'posed to kiss or summat. D'you wanna do that?"

Jenny didn't think she did at all, but not wanting to lose a friend who said he loved her, she agreed. Bending their heads forward, they pressed firm hard lips together for a split second. Glad that was over and done with, she smiled at Tony. "What do we do now?" she asked. "We don't have to do that any more do we?" "Nah," he said. "You can be my girlfriend now if ya like, an' I'll be your boyfriend."

"Okay," she said. It sounded nice. She'd never had a boyfriend before, and now if anyone tried to bully her she could say, 'I'll tell my boyfriend of you'. It felt good. "I've got to go home now," she told him. "You can play with us on Saturday if you like. We play in the nissen huts, and if we play houses, you can be my husband if you want."

Tony inclined his head to one side and shrugged his shoulders. "Alright then," he said, and they went their separate ways.

From then on he played with her on Saturdays and in the playground, and walked home with her from school. Jenny decided she liked having a boyfriend and did love Tony after all. He was what she always wanted Jimmy to be, giving her the feeling that he would protect her like a big brother was meant to do. Not that she ever wanted to put that to the test, seeing what a coward he was with the dentist.

FORTY-TWO

Frank's accident caused quite a stir in the village, giving them something else to talk about concerning the Matthews. It brought the ambulance out from Salisbury, and that was a rare occurrence. Frank had been changing the huge tractor wheel, something he had done a number of times, but this time he made a mistake and the wheel fell on him, crushing his ribs. He was kept in hospital overnight, returning the next day with strapped ribs. Three were broken and he had suffered concussion. He looked sick when he got home so Nellie told him to go right to bed. That evening, worried about the ferrets which no-one had fed the night before, he sent for Jenny.

"Nel's makin' bread an' milk for the ferrets an' you git out there an' feed 'em. Nobody bothered to give 'em any grub last night when I weren't 'ere, so git an' see to it now."

"Why me?" Jenny asked, horrified. She hated those evil, smelly creatures. "I don't like them, they'll bite me."

"They won't bite 'ee if thee's do it right. They'll jump right in the dish, not bother wi' thee, they'm too hungry to muck about."

"Oh please don't make me feed them. Can't I run round Alf's and ask him to come and do it? He's fed them before."

"Do as you're bloody told will 'ee," Frank said, raising his voice. "Oh Christ, these soddin' ribs." Jenny thought she'd better not anger him any further and said no more. There was a sharp, bitter wind blowing so she slipped on a warm woollen cardigan when the food was ready, and took the dishes outside.

There were three cages with two ferrets in the first one, four in the second and two more in the third. Standing in front of the cages with a dish in her hand, she looked at the yellow creatures with their long snaky bodies, their beady red eyes staring back at her. They smelled the food and began rushing about, climbing up the wire doors and clambering over each other. How in the world was she to open a door with them clinging onto it? They'd fall on the ground and get away. Putting the dish on the ground, she foraged for a heavy stick with which she whacked the front of the first cage to knock them off. As soon as they fell down, she grabbed up the dish, opened the door, threw the dish in and slammed the door shut. The food slopped all over the cage and over the ferrets, but it was in.

Next was the cage of four. Whacking them down with the stick, she grabbed up the bigger dish and opened the door. One of the ferrets was too quick and hooked his claws in the door again just as she opened it. Panicking, she threw the dish into the cage, hitting a ferret on the back, which turned the dish upside down. Like quicksilver, the ferret on the door turned and made a grab at her sleeve and another followed suit. Jenny screamed, whipping her arm back with the two ferrets clinging to the woolly material by their teeth. She shook her arm wildly and both animals fell to the ground. As she jumped away from them, another ferret dropped to the ground and the three of them scattered. Slamming the door on the remaining ferret, she rushed indoors. "Nellie, the ferrets are out. What am I going to do?" she cried.

"Oh dear God," Nellie said. "How many got out?"

"They attacked me. They hung on my sleeve and were going to bite me. There's three in the garden somewhere. I don't know how to catch them, what can we do?"

"Keep your voice down, we don't want Frank to hear. We'll just have to see if we can catch them somehow."

"What's that? Have thee let they bloody ferrets out?" Frank was stomping down the stairs in his pyjamas, hair on end, looking madder than Jenny had seen him in a long time.

"They jumped at me and hung on my cardigan. I couldn't get them off," Jenny told him, shaking in her shoes.

"Thee's mean to say thee went to feed ferrets in a woolly? Thee's dafter than a loo brush. Doesn't thee know by now that ferrets be trained to attack anythin' furry or woolly? 'A course they'd jump at 'ee. Why the 'ell didn't 'ee put on thick old mack I alla's wear to feed 'em? Thee's won't be a fart's bit o' good tryin' to catch 'em. I'll 'ave to do it meself." Groaning as he stepped into his wellies and put the old mack over his pyjamas, he went out the back door, slamming it behind him.   He was gone for over an hour, searching through wet undergrowth in the chilly wind. When he came in he looked awful. "I got two 'on 'em, t'other one's God knows where. He looked at Jenny. "I'll deal wi' thee the morrow," he said, and went back to bed. Nellie took him up some hot cocoa and a hot water bottle. She said he was shivering.

Jenny heard him coughing and shouting out in pain all night. Nellie sent for the doctor in the morning, who said Frank had pleurisy. He should be in the hospital, the doctor said, but it was unwise to move him now. Nellie would have to look after him and the doctor would call again the next day. Frightened at what she had done, Jenny feared that Frank would send her away when he recovered.

Alf was asked to feed the ferrets while Frank was sick. He told Jenny not to worry, it was hardly her fault. He said to Nellie that Frank should have more sense than to ask a young kid to feed ferrets, he would have come up and done it. Nellie agreed but said what could you do, that was Frank all over.

Frank got worse, becoming delirious and not always knowing where he was. When he did know, he bellowed for Nellie to bring him his fags. If she told him that smoking was the last thing he should do in his state, he got mad. He would have crawled downstairs to get them himself, so she had to give them to him. Then he would go off into delirium again, thinking he was in the fields, throwing his burning cigarette ends anywhere as if he was outside. "Look Nell," he'd say. "See thick fox over yonder" Git me my gun quick, I'll 'ave the bugger." Nellie was having fits, scared to death that Frank would set the place on fire.

He wanted his gun again to shoot the bugger who was standing by the door watching him and waiting for him to die. When Nellie took her dressing gown off the back of the door, he stopped asking for the gun. By the end of three weeks, Nellie looked worse than Frank. He kept her up and down stairs all day, and at night she got no rest with his ranting and raving. Jenny and Verna helped all they could but Nellie got the worst of it all.

"Nellie?" Jenny said one day as Nellie flopped into the arm chair.

"When you say 'Nellie?' to me like that, I wonder what's coming next. What are you going to say now?"

"Nellie?" Jenny said again. "Do you ever wish Frank would die?"

"What a question! I'll be blowed if I know what you're going to say next sometimes. It's not right to wish anybody dead, and even if you do, you should never say it."

"I know, but it would be nicer if he wasn't here wouldn't it. I just wonder why you married anybody as nasty as Frank. I wouldn't ever marry anybody like that. P'raps he wasn't nasty when you got married, but if my husband got nasty after I married him, I'd run away from him."

"That's easier said than done," Nellie said. "First of all you have to have somewhere to run to. My life is here. If I was to run off I'd have to work to keep myself, and all I know is cleaning and sewing. That would mean having to live in someone else's house and I wouldn't like that. This is my home. And what would happen to you and Verna? Did you think of that?"

"We'd come with you, and we could all work, but I s'pose its not possible. I wanted to run away from Mrs. Stafford but there wasn't anywhere to run to. Why did you marry him, Nellie? Was he nice when he was young?"

"No, he was never nice. You do ask a lot of questions Jen, but if you really want to know I'll tell you. My family lived in the East End of London. When I was fifteen and left school, my sister, Daisy's mum, was already in service and there were two younger sisters and a brother still home. I had to go in service too because I didn't know anything else other than cleaning house. My mum looked in the papers to find me a place. There was an advert from an old lady in a wheelchair who wanted someone to do the housework, look after her and cook for her three sons. My mum made me answer the advert and I got the job. The old lady was Frank's mother, and that's how I came to be here."

"The old lady was a real old curmudgeon. She had me running all day, getting her up in the morning and helping her dress, taking her to the lav and lifting her in and out of the chair. I had to do all the house cleaning, washing, ironing and cooking for her and her three sons, all of them young men by then. Alf was the youngest, he was just thirteen, Frank nineteen and the other brother twenty. I had the shopping to do as well, all for a pittance. I got three shillings a week and my keep. My 'spare' time was my own, and you can imagine how much of that I got. The old lady was a cripple, but there was nothing wrong with her mind. None of her 'boys' did anything without her permission, and she didn't give permission for much.

"She sounds awful! Didn't you look for another job? That doesn't tell me why you married Frank though."

"I'm coming to that, Miss Impatience. I did look in the papers for another job, but when she found out she begged me not to go. She said she was going to die soon and wanted somebody she trusted with her until she went. It took her three years to keep her promise, and when she knew she really was near the end, nothing would satisfy her but that I marry Frank so that she could die knowing that somebody she trusted was here to care for her boys. Jim, the eldest was married by then. Frank was her favourite and she wanted us to be married. I didn't want to marry Frank, he was cruel and spiteful even then, just like his mother. She kept on though, and Frank usually did what his mother wanted. He liked me well enough and said we'd better do it. A damn silly reason for getting married, but I was still only eighteen and didn't have the courage to refuse. I didn't know how to stand up for myself then."

"That's awful," Jenny said, and meant it. To be trapped like that into marrying someone like Frank. "Mr. Stafford's going to get a divorce, everybody says so. Can't you get a divorce and then you could find somebody nice. You should have a nice husband who looks after you, not a pig who yells at you to make up the fire when he's sitting on top of it."

"No Jen. I'm stuck with what I've got. And its not so bad now. I used to be really frightened of him but now his shouting and cursing is like water off a duck's back to me. Its easier to do what he says than argue, although sometimes I could tip the coal scuttle over his head. But let's have no more talk of wishing him dead, don't even think it. When you wish evil on someone else, it comes back to you. Frank's too mean to die in any case."

Frank was off work for two months. When he recovered he was more bad tempered than ever. He sent Jenny's rabbit, Bucky, to Salisbury market and used the money to put towards buying another ferret to replace the lost one. Jenny was very hurt to lose her rabbit, but that punishment was better than being sent away herself.

FORTY-THREE

At school it was time to sit for the eleven plus exam. Mrs. Mergrin didn't think Jenny had pulled up enough to do very well, but every child had to take the exam after their tenth birthday whatever level they had reached. Jenny was eleven, having passed that milestone two weeks previously. Apart from Margie, there were seven pupils sitting the exam this year, including Verna and Tony, and Mrs. Mergrin said there was little hope for any of them. Pass or no, each one would be leaving the village school at the end of term. Jenny's forebodings regarding the school building had dissipated over the years until now it was just a school. It would seem strange not to be coming here again after next month, each one expecting they would be going on to the senior school further down the valley.

The little room was cleared for the exams, the infants having to crowd in with the juniors in the big room for this event, which lasted two days. When it was over, Jenny had found some parts very difficult and others not as hard as expected. Comparing notes in the playground afterwards, the children's answers had been alarmingly different. Where Jenny had thought she had done reasonably well, nobody else seemed to agree. There was no point bothering about it now, it was done and they were soon leaving. The attitude in standard ten was one of simply waiting for the holidays to start once the exam was over. Mrs. Mergrin had a hard time controlling them, especially the boys.

It was never certain when the eleven plus exam results would come through. Sometimes they came before the end of term and sometimes not until the holidays had started, and then Mrs. Mergrin had to go round taking the results to each pupil's home. It had been that way when Jimmy took the exam. This year the results came in on the last day of term and were much as expected. Mrs. Mergrin said that it was a disappointing year and she hoped that next year's eleven plus students would fare much better. Only one pupil had passed this time, and that pupil was Jenny Harding! "Stand up, Jenny," she said.

Jenny stood in a state of shock. Mrs. Mergrin was saying she had passed the eleven plus, but she couldn't have. There had to be a dreadful mistake somewhere. She, stupid daft Jenny, couldn't possibly have passed.

"Well Jenny, congratulations," Mrs. Mergrin said. "I have to admit that I am surprised, but pleasantly so, that you managed to pull something out of the hat at the eleventh hour. I wish you all the very best for the future. Class, let's hear some applause for Jenny, who has passed her eleven plus." Everybody clapped as Jenny stood, feeling her face redden with embarrassment, doubly so because she was still sure there had to be a mistake. At break, when everyone had gone outside, Jenny went to Mrs. Mergrin and asked if there were ever mistakes made in marking the exam.

Mrs. Mergrin smiled at her - a rare occurrence. "So you are as surprised as I was," she said. "No, the examinations are all well checked before any results are sent out. You really did pass Jenny. And if there had to be only one successful entrant this year, I am truly pleased it was you."

Jenny went outside, carrying with her mixed emotions. Elated that she had managed to pass after all, yet still not quite comprehending the fact. How she would like, right now, to find Aunt Edith and rub her nose in it. She had passed. She had done the impossible and had no idea how. Tony came up to her and she expected him to be pleased for her and say 'Well done'. "What d'you go and do a dumb thing like that for?" he said. "Now you'll 'ave to go to Salisbury to school and I shan't see thee. Fine girlfriend thee bist." She hadn't thought about that. She hadn't had time to think about much.

"I'll still live here," she told him. "I can see you after school and weekends and holidays. You'll still be my boyfriend won't you?"

"Oh ah," he said. "But it won't be the same though."

There was jubilation and a few tears as they said goodbye to their old school. For most it was the only school they had ever known. But not for Jenny.

Running home on winged feet, head in the clouds, Jenny burst through the front door. "Nellie, Nellie, guess what? I bet you'll never guess."

"Oh my. Looks like its pretty exciting, whatever it is. Let me see. The war ended and nobody told me."

"No. Not quite. But something like that. A different miracle. Have another go."

"Tch. I'm no good at guessing games, Jen. Why don't you tell me and put me out of my agony."

"Well here it is then. I passed the eleven plus. *And* I was the only one to pass this year. I bet you'd never have guessed that."

"Oh, how lovely. Well done our Jenny. We're going to have to do something about that. How would you like a chocolate cake on Sunday? And we'll have ham sandwiches. I've got a special tin of ham, we can have that. What d'you think?"

"Oh yes, my favourite. One of your special chocolate cakes. Thank you Nellie," Jenny said, as she gave Nellie a hug. "I was so surprised when Mrs. Mergrin said I'd passed, I nearly fell off my chair. I thought it was a mistake, but she said it wasn't. I still can't believe it really. How did I pass? I'm so stupid and never learn anything. It doesn't make sense does it."

"No it doesn't. It doesn't make a bit of sense you always saying you're stupid. When are you going to get that out of your head? If you want to know, I'm not surprised at all that you passed. Now if Verna came home and told me she had passed, I would need to sit down. Then I'd think there'd been a mistake too. No Jen, there's nothing stupid about you, except your keeping on saying you're stupid."

"Well, Mrs. Stafford always kept telling me I was. And Frank does, and Jimmy does. Nellie, p'raps we shouldn't have a special tea. I forgot about Verna. It won't be very nice for her because she didn't pass."

"Don't you worry about Verna. She won't be the least bit bothered that she didn't pass. She'll enjoy the tea as much as you, never fear. As for Mrs. Stafford and Frank, and Jimmy too, that just goes to show what they know, doesn't it. Why don't you go and meet Jimmy's bus and tell him too?"

Hopping up and down at the bus stop, waiting for Jimmy's bus, Jenny wondered what he'd say. Would he be proud of her at long last? She truly hoped so. He saw her as soon as he got off the bus. "Hello, what's up? You waiting for me for something?"

"Yes, I'm waiting for you for something," she said. "I'm waiting to tell you something actually. I'm waiting to tell you something fantastical and you're not going to believe me. I know you're not."

"Stop being daft, Jen. If you're going to be stupid, I'm walking by myself. What are you going to tell me?"

"You're not to call me daft. And you're not to call me stupid any more. Because I passed the eleven plus. Mrs. Mergrin told me today, and its not a mistake either. I did pass, and I'm the only one who did this year."

"Is that right? Did you really?" Jimmy actually smiled. "Well done, old girl. Perhaps you're getting a bit less dumb after all. Well that *is* good," he said.

They walked together to the crossroads and Jenny turned to go. "Hang on," Jimmy said. "Walk up to the Fosters with me, I've got something to show you." Wondering what he could want to show her, she waited at the Foster's gate while he went indoors. Coming to the gate, he held his hand out in a fist. "Put your hand out," he told her. She did so and he dropped some coins into her hand. "See you later," he said, and was gone. Jenny looked at the coins and counted five shillings. Five shillings! That was a lot for Jimmy to give her. She knew he only got half a crown a week from Ted Roper, so this was two weeks wages. Jimmy really was proud of her after all.

FORTY-FOUR

They had their special tea on Sunday as promised. Verna wasn't a bit put out, just as Nellie had said. Verna didn't want to go to the Grammar School in Salisbury, she said. She wanted to go up the valley with the rest of the school kids. Jenny started to think about the school she would be going to. South Wilts Grammar School for Girls. Such a posh school. Never in a million years would she have thought she would be going there. "Will Miss Hargreaves be coming to buy me a school uniform like she did for Jimmy?" she asked Nellie. Nellie said it was most likely she would. "She'll be here before long to get you all togged up for the new school," she said. All Frank had said about her passing the exam was, "Ow the 'ell d'ya manage that?"

Jenny went to tell her friend Boxer the news after tea on Sunday. As she sat on the gate and told him how smart she had been, she could have sworn he winked.

Later in the week, Jenny went to see Margie. To her delight, Margie too had passed the exam. The results had been sent straight to her house, not to the school, so Mrs. Mergrin hadn't known. Margie was going to continue to study at home and hoped one day to be good enough to take the Oxford School Certificate. Jenny didn't want to think that far ahead, passing the eleven plus was enough for now.

Miss Hargreaves came in the second week of the holidays. Jenny was excitedly waiting to see her on this visit because they were going to shop for school uniform. She was sitting on the wall waiting when Jack North came out of the garden door opposite. "Hi Jen," he said. "Pee'd your knickers lately?"

"Oh shut up, Jack. I wish you'd forget about that. There must be something else you can talk about by now."

"I'm only joking," he said. "So what's new, Jen?" She told him about her exam pass and he was pleased for her. "Tell you what," he said. "I reckon that calls for a handful of strawberries. Mother's out, so

231

we can sneak into the vegetable garden and get some. Want some strawberries?"

Jenny did. They ran round the bend and opened the door of the garden opposite his house. If his mother had been in she would have seen them, because the front windows of the house looked straight across at the garden wall. They shut the door behind them and walked past the peach trees, trained up the south wall. They had stolen a few of those in their time too. They picked more than a handful of strawberries, and Jack gave Jenny most of them. They stayed in the garden, talking and eating the strawberries for some time before Jenny suddenly remembered Miss Hargreaves. "I've got to go Jack," she said. "Miss Hargreaves is taking me to get school uniform today. I bet they're looking for me. Thanks for the strawberries," she called back to him as she dashed for the door.

Miss Hargreaves was already in the house talking to Nellie. "Sorry, were you looking for me?" Jenny asked. "I was just talking to Jack for a minute." Nellie looked at her, but didn't say anything. "That's alright, Jenny. I was just talking to Mrs. Matthews. We have plenty of time before the bus. Congratulations on passing your exam, dear. We are all very pleased."

Nellie got up. "I'll go and get some vegetables in for supper," she said, walking through the passage door. Nellie didn't look right, she hadn't smiled at all.

"Sit down, Jenny. There's something I have to say to you before we go shopping. Before I do, I want you to know that this is a Ministerial decision and not my idea at all."

Jenny sat down. Suddenly the day seemed cooler. Something was not right and she knew she wasn't going to like what was coming.

"The Ministry is pleased that you passed the exam, Jenny. You will be going to Salisbury to school now. Not to the South Wilts school though. You will be going to the portion of the Portsmouth Girls Grammar School that is located in Salisbury, just as Jimmy is at the Portsmouth Boys School." Jenny hadn't thought of that. She hadn't known there was a Portsmouth girls school in Salisbury. It was disappointing, but it was still a grammar school. She had been looking forward to going to South Wilts, but she was an evacuee and would

232

have to go to the Portsmouth school she supposed.   "The Ministry, in its wisdom, has decided that since you will be going to school in Salisbury, they want you moved into town to live. I know what you are going to say, Jenny, and I agree it doesn't make a lot of sense, especially when you are so happy here, but that is their decision and I can't change it.

Jenny sat as if turned to stone. What was Miss Hargreaves saying? No wonder Nellie had looked odd. Is this what she got for passing the exam? To be moved away once more from where she was happy? What was the use of doing anything to please anybody? They took everything away from you. She jumped up from her chair and glared at Miss Hargreaves. "No!" she said. "No it doesn't make any sense. You say they are so pleased with me that they want to take me away from where I'm happy and stick me in town. I hate the town. I never want to live in town. Why do I have to go there just because I will be going to school there? Lots of children go from here, and they didn't send Jimmy to town. Why would they do this to me? I'm not going to go. I'm not going to."

"Now Jenny. I do understand how you feel, believe me. If you think I didn't argue against it, you're wrong. But this is their decision and it is I who have to bring the bad news. All I can say is that I will find you the best home I can, one where I feel you will be happy."

"There's nowhere I'll be happy except here with Nellie, or in my own home with Jimmy and my mum. There's nowhere else. I don't want to have to live with strangers any more. If passing the exam means I have to leave, then I won't go to the grammar school. I'll go up the valley with the rest of the kids from school. They can stick their grammar school."

Working herself into a state would do no good at all, Miss Hargreaves told her. She couldn't decide now not to go to the school allocated to her, and sometimes decisions were made that seem wrong at the time, but in the end are for our own good. Sad as it was, Jenny would do better to make up her mind to co-operate and, in the long run, this would be better for them all.

Jenny didn't believe that Miss Hargreaves even believed herself in what she was saying. There was no way it would be better for her to leave here and go into town to live. If she had known this would be the result, she would have made certain she didn't pass the damned exam. Unable to believe she was really being turned out yet again, the looked-forward-to shopping expedition was nothing more than agony.

Miss Hargreaves said it would be three weeks before she came again to take Jenny to her new home. Jenny told herself she had three whole weeks to still pretend this was her home, and the move wouldn't happen. Perhaps, in that time, the stupid Ministry would change their minds and none of it would happen anyway. She spoke of it to no-one, not even Nellie. As if she understood, Nellie didn't bring the subject up either, until two days before Miss Hargreaves' expected arrival. "Its no good ignoring the fact, Jen," she said then. "We're going to have to get packing." That day they packed, keeping off the subject and turning their backs to one another as much as possible. Miss Hargreaves had bought Jenny another suitcase while they were shopping and they needed it now for all her clothes.

Jenny now owned a navy gaberdine raincoat, velour hat with blue and white hat band, a navy gymslip and three white blouses, new black shoes, new underwear and socks. Miss Hargreaves had bought her three summer dresses in a size too big since, as she said, Jenny would be twelve by the time she wore them. They were all the same, pale solid blue with white collar and cuffs. Extra clothing coupons were issued to purchase uniforms, Miss Hargreaves told Jenny in answer to her query as to where all the coupons came from. When Jenny tried on one of the summer dresses, although it was too big, Miss Hargreaves said it was a colour made for Jenny. She looked prettier in that dress than anything Miss Hargreaves had seen her in. To be called pretty brought the only smile to Jenny's lips that entire afternoon.

The packing done, Jenny walked down Boxer's field to sit by the river. Her old friend was working and not here to talk to. She didn't want to say goodbye to him anyway. She hadn't even told Jimmy she was leaving. She should go and see him, she knew, but saying goodbye to Jimmy would be more than she could bear. She realized then, just how much the village had come to be her home. Not only would she miss Nellie and Jimmy and Boxer, she would miss the village itself. That thought began to tear her apart. It was just like being wrenched from her home and family all over again. Why were they doing this to her? Intense anger at the Ministry consumed her and she wished the Germans would drop a bomb on it. It was all Hitler's fault really. He had started this war because his own country wasn't enough for him and he wanted to grab everybody else's countries. Because he was so greedy, she had no parents and no home and now was being sent away again. Would she ever understand the ways of adults who would kill thousands of people while scrapping over countries that weren't theirs in the first place?

The words of the Vera Lynn song came back to her. Where were those bluebirds? Would they ever come? Would this war ever end? One of the lines said, 'and Jimmy will go to sleep in his own little room again', just as if it had been specially written for Jimmy. But where was Jimmy's room? He didn't have one any more, neither did she. Oh God, please don't let them send me away again. Not again. Misery and anger were her companions as she waited out the last two days.

In the end, the only two people she said goodbye to were Jean and Margie.

FORTY-FIVE

1944 - 1945

Morose and silent, Jenny sat beside Miss Hargreaves on the bus to town. "The people you are going to are very nice and more than happy to give you a good home." Miss Hargreaves told her. "Their name is Emery. Mr. Emery is an accountant. He and Mrs. Emery have a son of sixteen, Ronald, who is an apprentice mechanic at the bus depot, and a daughter, Elizabeth, the same age as you. Elizabeth has passed the eleven plus also and will be starting grammar school just as you will, so you will have something in common, although she will be going to the South Wilts of course. If you make up your mind to it, Jenny, you will soon feel at home."

Wonderful, Jenny thought. A hulking son to bully her, and another precious daughter. She didn't see much of her chances there. As to soon feeling at home, she would like to see Miss Hargreaves trying to feel at home when she was being taken away from the only place she had ever felt at home. She said nothing.

"They live in River Lane, a lane that runs off Fisherton Street, one of the main streets close to the town centre." Miss Hargreaves continued. "You will soon find your way around in Salisbury because it is built in squares. If you keep turning one way, you always come back to where you started." Jenny knew her way around in Salisbury's centre, she had dragged enough heavy shopping bags around it, but she wasn't going to tell Miss Hargreaves this. She wasn't going to tell her anything.

Miss Hargreaves had telephoned ahead to order a taxi to be waiting at the bus station. As they were driving up Fisherton Street they passed a church. Miss Hargreaves pointed this out to Jenny. "That is the Congregational Church, Jenny. Behind that church is the Congregational Hall, and that's where you will be going to school.

Only the first year of the Portsmouth Grammar school is located there so everyone will be new. And they will all be girls, of course. You won't have far to go to school because here we are," she said as the taxi slowed to a halt. Jenny looked down River Lane, a narrow lane running beside one of Salisbury's five rivers, with tall houses fronting it as far as she could see. She had seen it before, but never walked along it.

They were welcomed by Mrs. Emery, a large, fat lady whose chest wheezed and rattled as she breathed. Her pale brown hair was pulled down behind her neck into a funny looking sausage, and small watery blue eyes crinkled at the edges as she smiled. She led them through a small hallway into the living room, furnished with the usual central table, chairs and rugs. It was a square, well used looking room with a fireplace, now unlit. To Jenny, the place felt damp and chilly despite it being a warm August day. The chill intensified as Mrs. Emery led them out the back, along a flagstone passage to the kitchen. This room was long and narrow, also with flagstone floor, and beyond it was something Jenny had not seen in years, a bathroom.

Jenny was introduced to Elizabeth, a girl of her own height and weight, who smiled and said a shy 'Hello'. With amber eyes that matched her hair, Jenny could see little resemblance between Elizabeth and her mother. Perhaps her father had ginger hair, she thought. Mrs. Emery chatted and wheezed as she showed them around. Jenny was to share a double bed with Elizabeth in a room on the first floor. Mrs. Emery apologized about that, but said there was no choice. There wasn't space for two beds in this room and the only other room on the floor was hers and Mr. Emery's. Ronald slept in a single room on the top floor. Jenny felt most unhappy at the thought of sharing a bed with Elizabeth, whom she didn't even know.

Elizabeth took Jenny outside to show her the garden after Miss Hargreaves had left. It was long and unkempt, showing signs of having recently been hacked down by a scythe. It didn't look as though anyone in this house cared for flowers or was interested in growing vegetables. Elizabeth suggested they walk down the lane so she could show her where her Aunt Dodie lived. As they walked she asked Jenny questions about her family. Elizabeth's voice was soft and friendly, and she seemed genuinely interested. Not ready to discuss herself at all, Jenny simply told her that her dad was a prisoner of war and her mum had disappeared. She asked Elizabeth if Aunt Dodie was her mother or her father's sister, so that they could change the subject.

"She's my dad's sister, and that's her house over there." They had walked three quarters of the way down the lane, turned through an alleyway, and walked through a couple of streets. Jenny had never been in this part of Salisbury before. It was all residential. "Do you have a boyfriend?" Elizabeth asked.

Surprised by the question, Jenny said she did. "His name's Tony, but I don't suppose I'll see him any more now. Do you have a boyfriend?"

"I play around with the boy next door sometimes and I know he likes me. He's asked me to be his girlfriend, but I don't really like boys all that much," Elizabeth said. As she finished the sentence, she smiled, looking right into Jenny's eyes in a way that made Jenny feel very uncomfortable. She didn't know why, but she felt that something about Elizabeth was a bit peculiar.

Later that afternoon Elizabeth's brother came home from work. In the region of five feet, nine or ten inches, Robert was neither fat nor thin. His hair was dark brown, as were his eyes. Jenny could see that his oval face resembled his mother's, thought the colouring differed. On being introduced to Jenny, he smiled and said 'Hello'. Startled, Jenny realized that Robert smiled exactly like his sister. There had been something odd about Mrs. Emery's smile too. Almost as if each of them was looking for something inside your head, or as if they knew something about you that you didn't know. She must be imagining things because they were all so new to her.

For some reason, Jenny had made up her mind that Mr. Emery would be a big man with sandy hair, so when he came home a little later, she had the surprise of her life. Small and slight, black hair parted in the middle and slicked down, brown eyes and a thin moustache, he looked incredibly like pictures she had seen of Hitler. Standing beside Mrs. Emery, the two reminded her of comic book pictures of Laurel and Hardy.

In bed, Jenny found it hard to sleep. She had never slept with anyone before in her life and was afraid to move around too much for fear of kicking or disturbing Elizabeth. They talked for a while, discussing the fact that both were to start school on Thursday of all days, and how they felt about going to new schools. Elizabeth fell asleep in the middle of a sentence leaving Jenny to her own thoughts. She became aware of the bedroom door opening and light filling the room but she didn't look up. She had been told that Robert would later be coming through their bedroom, the only access to the stairs to his room being through theirs. She heard the stair door bang shut behind him, but he had left their bedroom door open and light still flowed in. Thinking she had better get out and shut the door she raised herself, lifting back the bedclothes. Just then someone switched off the hall light from downstairs so she sank back into bed. Eventually she drifted into a light sleep.

Nobody made any particular fuss of Jenny or particularly ignored her. They all treated her as if she had always been there. She had to be shown where things were, but once that was done they seemed to expect her to be one of them, as if she had known them all her life. Within herself, she felt like a fish out of water. Totally alien in this place, each one of them caused her nervous disquiet, something for which she could find no particular reason. Mrs. Emery's wheezing chest did bother her, but Jenny knew that was not the whole reason for this feeling of alienation. They were, after all, completely new to her, and she had made up her mind before coming here that she would never feel at home here or anywhere else but Nellie's, so that must be the answer.

They were to go to Aunt Dodie's to tea on Wednesday. This had been a previous arrangement made specially for Elizabeth who was to start her new school the next day. Mrs. Emery said Jenny could think of it as for her too, as she also would be starting a new school. The two girls and Mrs. Emery walked round in the late afternoon, Mr. Emery and Robert to follow when they returned from work. Aunt Dodie's house was small and neat, the table laid with a white lace cloth spread with appetizing foods. Aunt Dodie herself was as neat as her house. Small like her brother, her shiny grey hair combed into a tidy bun on the nape of her neck, she turned cool blue eyes on Jenny. "So this is the evacuee, I presume. Most of your kind were settled or

returned to their own homes years ago. You must be especially
unfortunate or especially difficult to manage to be still adrift."
Resentment and hostility rose inside Jenny immediately at this remark.
Did this snooty woman think it was her fault she had no home?
Reminded of 'Lady North' and her antagonistic attitude towards her,
Jenny knew she was not going to like Aunt Dodie one bit, nor did she
want to stay in her house and eat her food. Saying nothing, she ignored
the cruel barb.

Aunt Dodie sat Jenny in the furthermost seat from herself, right
in front of the draught from the open window. It wasn't a cold day, but
in her thin dress, Jenny felt chilly from the draught. When they had
eaten corned beef, salad and bread and butter, Aunt Dodie brought a
steaming plum pie and a dish of custard in from her kitchen. Jenny
smelled the plums as soon as the pie was cut. It was one thing she
couldn't stand, plums cooked in any fashion. She loved fresh plums,
but once they were cooked she couldn't eat them. Waiting until Aunt
Dodie handed her a plate of pie, she said a polite 'no thank you'.
"What do you mean, 'no thank you'. Isn't my cooking good enough
for you?"

"Of course it is," Jenny said. "I just don't like cooked plums, so
please don't give me any. Thank you," she added.

"Don't like plums? I never heard such nonsense. Of course you
like plums. Take it and eat it all up. No-one can afford to turn up their
noses at good food in wartime. Obviously you don't know what's good
for you."

Jenny looked at Mrs. Emery for help, but none was
forthcoming. She took the plate, picking at the pastry and avoiding the
plums while Aunt Dodie badgered and criticised her for playing with
her food. By the time the meal was over and her plums still lay
untouched, Jenny was ready to run to the bus station, catch a bus to
Bishopstone and sleep in the fields rather than stay with this family.
On the way home, Mrs. Emery told her to take no notice of Aunt
Dodie. "She's a bit of a harridan and far too critical. Probably because
she's a spinster and never had a good man. If she had a good man she
probably wouldn't be so sour," she said with a wheezy laugh. "Isn't that
right, Ronnie?" she said, nudging Ronald in the side with her elbow.

Ronald grinned. "I guess so," he said. Jenny thought it a silly thing to say. She looked up at Mrs. Emery to see that both she and Ronald were looking at her with that identical secret smile again. She shuddered.

"D'you like your Aunt Dodie?" Jenny asked Elizabeth as they lay in bed that night. She felt Elizabeth turn over onto her back. "Yes. She's always been alright to me, but I think she was rotten to you today. Its probably just because your new here," she said. She felt for Jenny's hand and gave it a squeeze before turning over to sleep. Jenny lay awake, thinking of starting her new school tomorrow, of Aunt Dodie's unpleasantness and Mrs. Emery's weird remarks about Aunt Dodie. Staring into the darkness, she yearned to be back at Nellie's in her own bed. I wonder if they miss me at all. Not as badly as I miss them, I'll bet. Wondering next if Jimmy had discovered she had gone, the opening of the door and the light across her eyes made her jump. She turned her head toward the door as Ronald came into the room ... absolutely naked! He dashed along the wall, through the stair door at the other end, and his footsteps banged as he ran upstairs. Jenny shot up in bed unable to believe her eyes.

"What's the matter?" Elizabeth said sleepily. "Are those plums making you feel sick?"

"No, I'm not sick. Your brother has just run through our bedroom with no clothes on."

"Oh, is that all," Elizabeth said, laying herself down again. "Take no notice, he does that all the time. It's the only way he can get to his room."

"I know it's the only way to his room, but he shouldn't come through our room with no clothes on. How does he know if we're asleep? I don't want to look at him all naked."

Elizabeth just snickered and snuggled down. Jenny lay, more awake than ever now. This is a weird and crazy family, she thought. I'm *never* going to like it in this place, they all give me the shivers.

FORTY-FIVE

Next day she had other things to think about. Dressed for the first time in her new school uniform, she walked down the road to the church. Entering the hall at the rear, she found a similar situation to the one at the village hall at Bishopstone. This hall was bigger but the rows of desks looked the same. The small area of cement between the back of the church and the hall was all the play area there was. Girls milled about, many looking as lost as Jenny felt. Noticing one girl looking at her, she smiled. The girl came over to say hello. "My name's Joan," she said. "Do you feel as nervous as me?" Jenny said she did and they talked until the bell rang. Joan said she came from a village outside Salisbury and was evacuated with a nice family. Inside, a mistress who introduced herself as Miss Saunders, asked if anyone had friends with whom they would like to sit. Jenny and Joan caught one another's eyes and both raised their hands. As they were placed together in a double desk, Jenny thought it was nice to have found a friend so soon. It would make the newness more bearable. Now that she had passed the eleven plus, no matter how narrowly, she intended to try to concentrate and learn. She hoped it wasn't going to be too hard.

It didn't take long for Jenny to grasp the fact that she was not up to the standard of most of the others. The work was indeed hard and she had great difficulty understanding the lessons. Joan was obviously ahead of her, helping her wherever possible without getting caught for whispering. To help her catch up, she was given extra homework to do in the evenings. Her life soon became a round of constant studying. Homework took her at least two hours each evening, far more than Elizabeth's took her. Concentration was difficult at home. She and Elizabeth sat at the table, books and papers spread out, while Mr. Emery sat in his chair by the fireplace, reading the paper and listening to the wireless at the same time. More often than not, Mrs. Emery and Ronald sat at a small table playing cards or ludo. The various noises were distracting.

Every Saturday afternoon, without fail, Mr. Emery took himself to the cinema. He always went to the same cinema, the Picture House in Fisherton Street, no matter what was showing. The film changed every week, but on rare occasions a particular 'block buster' was held over for a second week. Undeterred, Mr. Emery would watch the same film again. Nothing stood in the way of his Saturday afternoon at the Picture House. As far as Jenny could remember, she had only ever been to the cinema once. On her fourth birthday her mother had taken her to see Shirley Temple in 'The Good Ship Lollipop'. The only thing she remembered from the film was the little girl's curly hair. After the show she had wanted her mother to curl her hair in the same way. Her mother had curled her hair with irons from the fire and had taken her for a walk afterwards to show off her curls. She must have looked pretty silly, she realized now. At the time she had been thrilled with her new curls, crying bitterly the next morning to find they had all gone.

Saturday afternoon was a good time for Jenny to get more homework done. Ronald worked on Saturdays, having Wednesday afternoons and Sundays as his times off. Elizabeth was outside talking to the boy next door and Jenny had the living room to herself. Mrs. Emery came into the room while she was working at her arithmetic. "How are you doing, dear," she asked. "You do have lots of homework from that school don't you. Do you think you are going to manage it all?"

"I don't know. It's hard but I want to try. I never expected to pass the eleven plus at all, but now I have I want to see if I can be as clever as my brother. I don't suppose I ever will, but at least he won't think I'm as stupid as he used to."

"That's right, dear," Mrs. Emery said, rubbing Jenny's back. "Better you learn all you can than fill your head thinking about boys. Our Elizabeth's out there talking to her boyfriend next door, but you don't want to worry about boys do you?" She caught Jenny's face between her hands, squishing it against her ample bosom. Letting go, she walked down the passage to the kitchen. Jenny shuddered again. She didn't like being squeezed. She didn't like the smell of Mrs. Emery or the sound of her wheezy chest. Why would she say something like that? Jenny didn't fill her head thinking about boys. Come to think of it, she hadn't even thought about Tony since she came here. Mrs. Emery said the strangest things. She didn't like the Emerys at all.

Worrying about her school work while trying to keep aloof from the peculiar family she had been dumped on, Jenny was sleeping poorly. Sharing the bed with Elizabeth was partially to blame for this. As the weather became colder, Elizabeth snuggled closer to Jenny, wrapping her arms and legs around her for warmth. Jenny was uncomfortable with this, shoving Elizabeth away with her elbows, but it seemed no matter how often she pushed her away, Elizabeth was always on her side in the morning, and Jenny was almost out of the bed. She was also becoming increasingly bothered at Ronald's dashing naked through their bedroom. He didn't seem to mind how cold it was, or to bother whether the girls were awake. It disturbed Jenny to think that at sixteen he must be undressing downstairs in front of his parents, and that, she was sure, was not right.

FORTY-SIX

At school she made friends with a number of girls, although Joan was her special friend. Strangely enough, maybe because they were all evacuees, none of them spoke about their families or the people with whom they were evacuated. All she knew about Joan was that she lived in the country and travelled into town by bus every day. This fact brought renewed resentment against the Ministry. There were a number of girls who travelled by bus to school, and it would have been no more trouble for Jenny to do it. She would never understand and never forgive them for sitting round a remote table and deciding to wreck her life.

She continued to struggle with school work and with her sense of alienation from the Emery family. Never feeling she could let her guard down for a moment with any one of them, she couldn't put her finger on what it was that truly bothered her. Walking the streets from home to school and back, sometimes going out with Elizabeth to walk around the back streets in the evenings, Jenny felt the loss of her village keenly. Perhaps this was what was at the back of her troubles. She had become a country girl. The roads and pavements, rows of shops and rows of houses depressed her greatly and she yearned for the fields, trees and open spaces. She seemed to be losing her own identity and was lost among these strange people who troubled her so. Mrs. Emery always wanted to be friendly, never scolded her and constantly smiled. Why then did she make Jenny's skin creep when she came close? She loved to touch Jenny, and Jenny couldn't stand it, especially when she touched her bottom, as she frequently did.

One night in November, unable to sleep at all and suffering from thirst, she got out of bed and made her way downstairs to get a drink of water. Mr. Emery was alone in the living room reading his paper as she passed through. As she reached for a cup from the dresser in the kitchen, the bathroom door opened and Ronald walked out, stark naked again, followed closely by his mother. Jenny felt herself flush scarlet as they all stood looking at one another, Ronald making no attempt to cover himself. "Oh, I ah, I just wanted a drink of water," Jenny stammered, wishing they would move away. Mrs. Emery laughed. "You should see your face, dear," she wheezed. "Don't looked so shocked, I was only washing Ronnie's back. You should have come down earlier then you could have done it for him." Ronald grinned as if it was some sort of huge joke. Jenny didn't think it funny at all. She turned and dashed back upstairs without her water. Flinging herself back into bed, she woke Elizabeth.

"What's the matter" Elizabeth asked her. "You're all cold," she said, putting her hand on Jenny's arm. "Where have you been?"

"I've been downstairs for a drink of water. Get over your own side of the bed and stay there, and stop touching me because I don't like it." She turned her back to Elizabeth and pulled the clothes over herself roughly. She'd had just about enough of this place, and if Miss Hargreaves wouldn't do anything about it when she came next time, Jenny was leaving of her own accord. She didn't care where she went, just out of here.

It was just as they were breaking for Christmas holidays that Miss Hargreaves came to see how she was settling down. Mrs. Emery had told Jenny a couple of days earlier that she was coming, and Jenny was on pins during that time, wondering what she was going to say to convince Miss Hargreaves she couldn't stay. Ever since the night she had seen Ronald and his mother coming out of the bathroom, she had been more than ever on edge. Convinced now that something was radically wrong in this household, she had tried to keep her composure so they wouldn't suspect what was in her mind. Now that Miss Hargreaves was coming finally, whatever could she say to her? What would it sound like if she said she wanted to leave because Mrs. Emery bathed her sixteen year old son? Or if she said she didn't like the way they smiled or the way Mrs. Emery touched her, or that Elizabeth always wanted to sleep on her side of the bed? It sounded ridiculous, nothing to make a fuss about. Miss Hargreaves would probably say it was no business of hers if Mrs. Emery washed her son's back. She didn't know what to say, only that she wanted to be moved, or she would leave on her own.

Miss Hargreaves came into the house, and it was the same situation as it had been at the Staffords, all over again. She asked Jenny if she was happy here, and how she was getting on at school, all in front of Mrs. Emery. Jenny could only say she was fine, no, she had no problems, yes, she liked it here. She was going to be trapped again, just as she had been then. Miss Hargreaves eventually said she had to leave and Jenny felt desperate. "Oh, Miss Hargreaves, I'll walk down as far as my school with you. There's something I want to show you, it won't take a minute."

"But it's holiday time, Jenny. The school will be closed. I'll see it another time."

"No. It doesn't matter that it's closed. You can see it anyway. I want to show you now because it might not be there next time." She was making no sense and she knew it, but she *had* to have this chance.

"All right then. We'll just take a quick look if it is that important."

Walking down the road, Jenny didn't know how to begin. She'd have to say something quickly or it would be too late, but what could she say?

"What's on your mind, Jenny. Do you really want me to see your school or is something else bothering you?"

"I don't want to stay with the Emery's any more. I don't know what to say, except I can't stay there. Please, Miss Hargreaves, don't leave me here any longer."

Miss Hargreaves stopped, looking down at her. "I can see something is troubling you, Jenny. I don't think you have any idea how difficult it is to find suitable homes for people like yourself. I was getting to my wits end by the time I found the Emerys. If you don't have a very good reason for wanting to be moved, I'm afraid the answer will have to be no. If this is just a ruse to get sent back to the Matthews, I can tell you now it won't work. Is that what it is?"

"No! No! That's not it. That's not true at all. Its just that ... its that ... I don't like the Emerys, they're weird. They are really. And I don't like it when Ronald runs through our bedroom every night with no clothes on." She was beginning to cry, more because she was so afraid that Miss Hargreaves would turn her down than anything else.

"What are you saying, Jenny? What's this about Ronald running naked through your bedroom?"

Jenny explained how Ronald undressed downstairs every night, and mentioned that she had seen him coming naked from the bathroom with his mother. Miss Hargreaves looked very concerned, glancing at her watch and looking back at Jenny. "I must think about this. I'm going to miss my train anyway. Let's find a cafe and sit down while I think."

Miss Hargreaves ordered tea and while they drank she asked Jenny to tell her again about Ronald. Jenny did, adding other things as they came to mind, feeling braver now about saying all the things that bothered her. At the end of her tale, Miss Hargreaves told her she would have to make a telephone call, but Jenny must wait here until she returned. She was gone for what seemed to be hours, at last returning to tell Jenny that she was moving her from the Emery household right away. "The only thing I have to offer right now is a hostel, Jenny, but it will be temporary. The hostel is normally for unplaceable evacuees, but you are not one of those. At the moment it's empty because they have all gone home for the Christmas holidays. We'll make your stay there as short as possible because it's not the place for you. Right now we have to get your things out of the house."

Jenny had no idea what a hostel was, and right now she didn't care. She was so relieved to be leaving. "What are we going to say to Mrs. Emery? She's going to think it very odd that you're taking me away so suddenly isn't she?"

"Don't you worry about that. I'll go in and see her first and explain things to her, then you can come in and pack your belongings." Whatever Miss Hargreaves did say to Mrs. Emery, when Jenny was called to come in and pack, all she said was how sorry they were that she was leaving them so soon. Elizabeth was in tears. She threw her arms around Jenny, saying what a shame it was she couldn't stay any longer. "I'll really miss you, Jen. I hope you'll miss me too." Jenny smiled, hoping that Elizabeth would take that as a yes. She knew she wouldn't miss Elizabeth at all, and was more than glad to be leaving.

Mrs. Emery and Elizabeth stood and waved them off as they drove away in a taxi. Jenny wondered what Miss Hargreaves could have said to them so that no-one was upset.

FORTY-SEVEN

Just as Miss Hargreaves had said, the hostel was indeed empty. The lone lady who was there to greet them showed them to a small room with one single bed where Jenny was to sleep, their footsteps echoing hollowly through the vacant halls. With her cases dumped on the floor, Jenny felt alone and afraid in the large building after Miss Hargreaves and the lady had gone. All night she lay in a tight ball in the small bed, listening to the various creaks and rumbles of an empty building. In the morning she made her way downstairs toward the sounds of someone moving about, clanging pots and dishes. She found a woman working in a large kitchen. "Hello," she said. "I'm glad to find somebody here. I thought I was the only one in the whole place."

"Well you are really," the woman said. "Why they opened this great place just for one kid beats me. I told my boss when she called me last night that I would have taken you to my place for a couple of nights, but she said your billeting officer, or whoever she is, insisted you come here. Daft if you ask me. Anyway, dear, you're here, and I'm here to see to your feeding. What would you like for breakfast?"

Jenny said a boiled egg and toast would be fine. She felt rather guilty as she sat to wait for her breakfast. This woman obviously had to come in especially for her when she should have been home for her own holiday. "I'm sorry you had to come in just to cook for me. If you show me where things are, I can cook an egg for myself or make a sandwich. You don't have to spoil your holiday for me."

"Oh, bless you love, I can't do that. If they was to find I'd left you to forage for yourself I'd get the sack. It's an inconvenience, no kidding, but it's hardly your fault. I'm going to make a pot of stew this morning that'll be enough for two or three days, then you can hot that up for yourself when you're hungry. I'll probably cop it for doing that as it is. After you've had your breakfast, I'll show you where the books and things are so you can have a read while you're here. There isn't going to be much else for you to do. 'Tis to be hoped they don't leave you here too long."

Jenny hoped so too. The place was freezing cold as she wandered around in her coat, looking in dormitories, an enormous dining hall, big study room with tables and bookshelves, the kitchen and smaller rooms. In the afternoon she took a couple of books up to her bed in the hope of getting warmer there. She dozed and read, eventually becoming bored. Putting her coat on again, she ran around the hallways and up and down the stairs for exercise, warming herself up in the process. The sound of her footsteps echoed and re echoed as if there were many others running around with her. Hungry now, she ran to the kitchen to heat up the stew. It was good. She wouldn't mind eating that for a couple of days.

After two days of lonely wandering in empty halls, reading sporadically, staring out of windows and twiddling her thumbs, Miss Hargreaves returned. She had not been very successful, she said. This was an especially bad time of year to get anyone to take an extra person. "I'm not prepared to leave you here all alone any longer," she said. "So until we can find something better, we are placing you in St. Mary's Convent. This really is just another temporary placement, Jenny, but they will look after you, and while you're there it will give us more time to find something truly suitable for you. I don't want to be put in the position of rushing round and making mistakes such as with the Emerys, so this will be the best thing for us all."

A convent! A convent for orphans and waifs. Is this what she was now? She pictured Miss Hargreaves tramping the streets, knocking on doors, telling strangers about the poor little orphan who nobody wanted. She saw her pleading with them to find room for the orphan in their homes, and she was suffused with shame. Now she was being shoved into a convent, the sort of place you read about in story books, with nuns and starving children. She had become a nuisance and an inconvenience to everyone. Just like Jimmy had always said she was.

FORTY-EIGHT

1944 -1945

Taxis were becoming a way of life all of a sudden. Jenny had always thought taxis were only for the rich, but here she was one of the world's waifs and strays, taking her fourth taxi ride in as many months. She recognized the convent at once when they pulled up outside. She had passed this place many times on her journeys back to Bishopstone, carrying the shopping. From here she could find her way back there without trouble.

In her mind, nuns wore long black dresses of soft flowing material, with white pieces of sheeting draped over their heads, like pictures of Jesus' mother Mary she had seen in books. When the convent door was opened, she got a severe shock. Standing before them was an apparition in a long, heavy brown dress, and on her head was a bright white contraption that stuck stiffly out on either side like the wings of a bird. She looked to be six feet tall and totally awesome. She stood back for them to enter, telling them to follow her to where the Mother Superior was waiting. Jenny shook with fear as she followed Miss Hargreaves along a hallway.

Mother Superior was dressed in similar fashion, but whereas the apparition had not smiled, Mother Superior did. She had obviously been waiting for them, for she used Jenny's name right away. "Hello, Jenny. It's nice to have you here," she said. Her voice, calm and gentle, allayed Jenny's first sense of panic, and her fear subsided a little. "You are very welcome to come and stay among my children," Mother Superior continued. "Despite first appearances, there is nothing to fear here. All the Sisters are very kind, and all my children are girls around your own age, so you will soon find many friends. We are of the Catholic faith and I know you are not, but don't let that alarm you."

"I'm not a Catholic," Jenny said. "I wouldn't know what to do if I have to be a Catholic."

"You won't have to be a Catholic at all, Jenny. All I am telling you is that this is a Catholic convent, but you don't have to be a Catholic to stay here. You are our guest. We have no intention of trying to turn you into a Catholic. My children all go to St. Elizabeth's School next door, but you will continue with your own school. Nothing will change. Now I will call Sister Joseph to show you to your dormitory. Enjoy your stay here, Jenny."

About eighty children lived in the convent. Jenny slept in a large dormitory where twenty beds were set in rows. Their clothes were all labelled and kept in big cupboards along the walls of the dormitory. There was no privacy anywhere. Meals were taken in a large hall, the children seated on benches at long scrubbed wooden tables. The food left much to be desired. Breakfast usually consisted of warm soggy cereals and what was described as toast. This was bread, spread with margarine and warmed in an oven until it was limp, warm and greasy, the only way to eat it being to hold your breath against the sickly smell of warm margarine. The most frequent dinner meal was toad-in-the-hole, a concoction of gristly, greasy sausages nestling in a sea of inedible,leathery batter, laced with pepper. There were no choices, either you ate the meals or went without.

Jenny found the children in the convent easy to get along with although she wanted to make no special friends here. She had not been given any hint of how long she would be staying, and her feeling of temporariness set her aside from the rest. This feeling of alienation was intensified by the fact that she was not a Catholic and that she went to a different school from everyone else. She had come during the Christmas holidays, therefore having more time to get to know the other children and to find her way around. There were a few bunches of holly and some home made decorations scattered around the walls. Christmas Day itself was celebrated with prayers and carol singing. Everyone, with the exception of Jenny, attended Mass twice on that day. Each of them had been given a small gift from the Sisters, and many received gifts from outside as well. Jenny was one of these. Nellie had made, and sent to her, a pretty blue blouse. Delighted as Jenny was that Nellie had remembered her, she was also concerned as to how the gift had been delivered. She hoped it had been sent to the Emerys and forwarded to her in some way, perhaps through the Ministry. Most of all, she hoped neither Nellie nor anyone else from the village knew where she was. She would be far too ashamed for them to know she was stuck in a convent for the unwanted.

Each Saturday morning the convent children attended early Mass at the church in the convent grounds, and on Sundays they attended services in the mornings and Sunday School in the afternoons. At these times, Jenny was left to her own devices, never forced or even invited to join the others. After Mass on Saturday, each child had a special task to perform. Jenny was included in this and her special job was to scrub the wide cement steps that curved in an arc from the dining room, down to the back door. There were twenty seven steps, and it took her almost two hours to scrub and rinse them all. If she was cold when she started, she was always hot by the time she was done.

Jenny now had well over a mile to walk to school, which meant getting off to an early start each day. When she started back after the Christmas break, she said nothing of what had happened to her to anyone, not even Joan. All the homework she had been doing was showing results and she was beginning to pull up with the rest of her class. Homework was a problem at the convent since no-one but her had any to do. At first she tried to do it in the dining room, but the other children ran around and played games in there. This was the only room they had in which to play or read or draw. Mother Superior solved the problem by allowing her to go into one of the Sisters' quiet rooms by herself in the evenings to get on with her homework.

Saturday afternoons were a treat for the children but a nightmare for Jenny. Then they were all taken into town by several of the Sisters while they bought provisions for the week. It seemed that everyone but Jenny loved walking in a crocodile to town and going round the market and shops. Not only did Jenny hate shopping, she was always terrified someone from school, or worse, from the village, might see and recognize her marching around with the convent crocodile. Made conspicuous by her school uniform, which the nuns insisted she wear, Jenny kept always to the inside of the crocodile, turning her face toward the shop windows for fear someone would recognize her.

They had barely been back to school two weeks when one morning after prayers, the headmistress made a startling announcement.

"I have some wonderful news, girls," she said. As you probably know, the bombings in Portsmouth ceased some considerable time ago. From the way things are going with the war, it would appear that the danger at home is over. That being so, it has been decided that the school be repatriated back to Portsmouth. Girls, we are going home."

Cheers, claps, whistles and stamping drowned out anything else the headmistress had to say. It was January, 1945, and they were going home. For them the war was just about over. Most of them had been away from home for well over five years, although many now went home for holidays. They would cease to be evacuees and start again to be families. Those who had families to go to. Many, of course, had lost fathers, brothers and even mothers. Few had lost everyone. When a semblance of order was at last restored, the headmistress told them they would all be leaving at the end of the week. "Time to start packing, girls."

Jenny had forgotten how many times she had packed, but this was not to be one of those times. Her friend, Joan, was jumping up and down with the rest. "Isn't it great, Jen. We're going home at last. I'll look for you on the station and we'll try to get into the same coach. Aren't you excited?"

"Yes, of course I am. I'm so excited I have to go to the loo."

It was near to impossible, she thought, to try to sound excited when you were gritting your teeth in an effort not to cry. Escaping to the toilet, she took deep breaths, forced her eyes open wide, bit her lip, ground her teeth together, doing all she could to force back the tears. How was she to get through this week, carrying on a pretence of elation, while trying not to let on that she would not be going with them? How could she possibly do it?

Somehow, she managed. Somehow, Joan caught no hint from Jenny that she was daily crumbling inside, nor that she would not be going with them. On Thursday evening, Mother Superior sent for her. "I have received a letter from the Ministry of Pensions," she told Jenny.

"They tell me the Portsmouth school is returning, as you already know. What you probably don't know is that you are to be transferred to the South Wilts Grammar School for Girls, here in Salisbury. I am sorry you will be losing your friends, Jenny, but you will still be among friends here. You have fitted in very well among us, and I feel sure you will find new friends in your new school very soon."

Funny, Jenny thought to herself. Only a few months ago she was so excited at the prospect of going to South Wilts. Now that she really was going, all she felt was immense sadness. She doubted she would make new friends quickly, or at all. By this time, the new girls had all found friends and would most likely ignore her. Besides, she didn't want any friends. All she ever did was lose them.

"Did the Ministry say anything about moving me," Jenny asked Mother Superior.

"No, my dear, not this time. But we will look after you until they do."

Surprisingly, Jenny felt relieved to hear this. Apprehensive as she had been on first entering the convent, and despite the fact that she was ashamed for anyone to know where she lived, yet she had felt relief at hearing Mother Superior say there was no word with regard to her move. She was even becoming used to seeing the strange looking Sisters flying around the convent. That was how they appeared to her. None of them ever walked slowly, they were always half walking, half running everywhere, dresses rustling and billowing behind them, and those curious stiff wings giving the impression that they really were flying.

Friday was one of the most difficult days of her life. The girls were all too excited to do any lessons, the day being taken up with packing belongings into their satchels and helping pack up school supplies, etc. into boxes. Joan hugged her as they left the school for the last time. "I'll look out for you on the station tomorrow, and you look out for me. It's bound to be horribly crowded, but I'll find you somewhere. Cheerio, Jen. 'Til tomorrow. Good old Pompy." she added, using the familiar term for Portsmouth.

Jenny asked for, and was granted, permission to leave the convent on the Saturday so that she could go to the station to wave goodbye to her friends. She had no intention of going to the station, but she wanted to see the trains go. She ran the mile and a half to a point in Fisherton Street from where she could clearly see the railway bridge. There, she stood in a shop doorway watching trains passing each way as she waited for the Specials. From where she stood, had she been able to throw a stone over the shop in which doorway she hid, she could have hit the Emery's house. It was unlikely any of them would be walking her way, but she kept a wary eye out just in case.

At last, the first of the Portsmouth Specials started chugging its way over the bridge. There was no mistaking it as the noise of cheering and shouting reached her. A sea of arms waved from every window as cheers, jeers and catcalls washed down over the street below. Passers-by stopped to look up in the direction of the hullabaloo, many of them waving back in recognition and farewell. Tears flowed unabated down Jenny's face as anguish tore at her soul. Jimmy and I should be on that train now, she thought. We should be going home too. Home to be a family again. Trying to imagine how it would be to be going home, back to parents whose faces she could no longer recall, she made no attempt to check the tears. She wondered if Joan had run up and down the station looking for her, calling her name.

Unable to bear it any longer, she turned away and began to walk back to the convent. Once she had prayed to God, 'Let there be bluebirds for Jimmy and me', and now those bluebirds should be flying for them. There weren't going to be any, were there God? Just for others, but not for us. At that point, Jenny came close to hating her mother. Did she know or care just what she had done to them? Why didn't she come back? Why, why, why?

FORTY-NINE

Starting school at South Wilts was far more traumatic than the Portsmouth school had been. This time Jenny was the only new girl. The building itself was enormous compared to any she had attended. Built in the shape of an 'E' and containing over five hundred students, it held an endless array of classrooms, various labs, art rooms, a domestic science room, huge assembly hall, dining rooms, a fancy gymnasium, geography and history rooms, tennis courts, two large paved playgrounds, an immense playing field, gardens at the front and a wide, long, stone covered driveway running its whole length. She was placed in Form 1C and given a desk at the back of the room, something for which she was grateful. Unlike the Portsmouth school, in this school each pupil had her own desk. Once again she was playing catch-up, and this time with no friend to help and encourage her, she felt completely alone.

Sick at heart at feeling alienated at school and alienated in the convent among a crowd of Catholics, Jenny began to think of converting to Catholicism. Somewhere in the back of her mind, she was sure she remembered her mother saying that the family had once been Catholic, but that Gran had changed their religion. She also thought she remembered being told that the family had come from South Africa, but was not sure if that was memory or fantasy. She would have to see Jimmy and ask if he remembered too. Jimmy had been much in her thoughts lately. If her school had returned to Portsmouth, it was likely that his had returned also. If that was so, he should have been transferred to the Bishop Wordsworth School for Boys in Salisbury. Even more prestigious than South Wilts, the Bishop Wordsworth School was highly regarded. She went to Mother Superior for permission to go to Bishopstone to visit her brother. She could ask to go on a Sunday, since she was always left to herself most of that day.

"How do you intend to get to Bishopstone?" Mother Superior asked.

"I know the way, I used to walk it all the time. It takes about two hours. Probably less because I won't be carrying anything."

Mother Superior wouldn't hear of her walking. She gave Jenny enough money for her return bus fare, and wished her a happy visit with her brother. "You know he can visit you here if he wishes," she told Jenny.

Jenny caught the bus right outside the convent. She would go first to Ted Roper's farm where Jimmy would probably be working. Walking down the familiar road, Jenny felt a lump in her throat to think that she was now merely a visitor to the village she had thought of as home. She found Jimmy driving the old tractor down the road, pulling a load of mangolds en route to the cow field. He stopped the tractor when he saw her, and she hopped up to sit on the mudguard. "Hello, Jimmy. Are you surprised to see me?"

"Yes," he said. "As a matter of fact I've been wondering how you were getting on. I heard you were living in some girls' convent, but I hardly thought I could come and see you there. I'd feel a bit daft going in among a load of girls."

Jenny was dismayed that he had heard where she was. She didn't mind him knowing, but if he knew, how many others knew she was now a reject? "As a matter of fact, you can come and see me. When I asked Mother Superior if I could come and see you she gave me money for the fare, and she said that you can come and see me if you want to. You don't have to if it makes you feel silly, but I would like it if you did. I was wondering if your school went back to Portsmouth because mine did. I go to South Wilts now. Do you go to Bishop Wordsworth?"

"I thought you might be at South Wilts," Jimmy said. "Yes, my school went back at the same time as yours. I *have* been offered a place at B.W. but I'm not going to take it."

"What? What d'you mean, you're not going to take it? Nobody offered me a place, they told me I had to go to South Wilts. I would have taken it if they had anyway, what else could I do? Why won't you take a place at a posh school like Bishop Wordsworth? You will get a chance to be anything from a school like that."

"I know that", Jimmy said. "But I've already decided that when I leave school I'm going to work for Ted. I hardly need a grammar school education to work on a farm, and that's what I want to do. So instead of going to grammar school, I'm going to the secondary school up the valley, where I can leave at fifteen and go to work at least a year earlier."

"Oh, Jimmy! I don't believe you. You've always been the one with all the brains, not me. You can't mean you're really going to work for a sloppy, useless farmer like Ted Roper all your life, and throw away the chance of a good education and a proper job. You've got to be kidding me. I don't believe you'd be that stupid."

"I don't need any preaching from you, I've been getting enough of that from everyone else. Who said anything about working for Ted Roper all my life? I just said I was going to work for him when I leave school. I want to be a farmer myself one day, and there are other farms you know. It's no good you going on about wasting education. I know all about that, but I've made up my mind and that's all there is to say about it."

Jenny could see it was useless to argue. She didn't want to leave with the feeling she had made him cross with her again. She changed the subject. "Jimmy, please don't call me stupid if I'm wrong, but I seem to remember Mum telling us once that our family had been Catholic, but Gran changed it. I think she said that we came from Africa, or p'raps it was Australia. I might have dreamed it, but I wondered if you remembered anything like that.

"Yea," Jimmy said. "She did say the family was Catholic once. She said that the Catholics wouldn't christen Mum because Gran had married a Protestant, and Gran was so mad about that she changed her religion. Mum was never a Catholic and neither were we. What d'you want to know that for?"

"Oh, nothing really. It's just that I live in a Catholic convent and it started me thinking that I sort of remembered that our family was Catholic once, that's all. We didn't come from Africa though, did we?"

"That's right too. Most of Mum's family live there - cousins and that I mean. Whoever they are, they're pretty distant relations, cousins umpteen times removed. Mum was born there, and Gran was brought up there, but I think they came to England when Mum was a baby. I really don't know much about it. We've got Danish and French in the old ancestry somewhere - Gran's parents I think. It doesn't really matter anyway. We're English and we're Protestants, so what's all this digging into family history?"

"I dunno, Jimmy. I don't know why I even started thinking we came from Africa. I thought I'd ask you just to see if I did remember it or had made it up myself." They talked idly about people in the village and things he had been doing. She told him nothing of her experiences in the Emery household. Those things were better kept to herself and, hopefully, forgotten. They reached the cow field and she clambered into the trailer, tossing off mangolds with a pitchfork as Jimmy drove round the field. When he drove back down the lane, Jenny asked him to let her off before he got to the farm. She didn't want to get herself stinky and mucky to go back on the bus, and in the Roper yard there would be no avoiding it. Saying cheerio to Jimmy, she decided to go and thank Nellie for the blue blouse.

As the Matthews' house came in sight, Jenny was unprepared for the rush of emotion that washed over her. She felt suddenly nauseous and dizzy. Sitting in the bank, she held her head in her hands until the wave receded. Glancing once more at the house, she knew she couldn't go in. She walked away, knowing they couldn't have seen her from the house. No doubt they would hear she had been in the village and Nellie would be hurt that she hadn't called in, but she couldn't do it. There was too much pain. She would go and see Margie. She thought she could handle that.

In the year she had lived with Nellie, after leaving the Staffords, Jenny had had no choice but to pass the Staffords' house on the way to school. She didn't have to pass directly by it, but she had to pass by the far end of the white bridge, from where the house could be clearly seen. Each time she had passed, she had kept her head turned away from the house, never wanting to look at it again. Today, she decided, she would stand on the bridge and look at the house. There was nothing to fear from it now. Mrs. Stafford and Celia were long gone, and she was no longer a baby. Standing on the bridge, she looked fully at the house. She stared at it in defiance. I'm not afraid of you any more, she told the house inside her head. You don't mean anything to me. But it did, and she knew the fear was still there. She tried staring at it once more, but it was not going to work. A sense of failure floated around her as she left the bridge to make her way to Margie's.

Margie answered the door to her knock, surprise and delight lighting up her face.

"Oh Jenny, come on in, how lovely to see you again. Mum! Look who's come to see us. It's Jenny," she called over her shoulder.

Jenny felt her spirits lifting. Margie always had that effect on people. Jenny couldn't remember ever seeing Margie moody or miserable.

"Well look what the wind blew in," Mrs. Roper said. "And how are you, Jenny. I hear you're living in that Catholic Convent in Salisbury. How d'you like it there?"

Jenny's heart sank again. So everyone knew where she was, it seemed. She felt herself blushing with embarrassment. "It's all right. How are your legs, Margie?"

"I'm getting a lot better thanks, Jen. I don't have to sleep on that plaster thing any more. I actually sleep in a proper bed now, and it's lovely. I still have the callipers and crutches, as you see, but I skip around pretty good now. I still can't go to school, but I'm going to keep studying so I can take the School Certificate at sixteen, same as you."

Margie's words brought Jimmy back to mind. Margie was going to study despite her handicap, and Jimmy was going to throw away his chances to work for Margie's sloppy uncle. It was so stupid. Jimmy, who had always been right, was very wrong this time.

She couldn't be sad long in the Roper house, however. Mrs. Roper made chicken sandwiches and brought in some mince pies. Oh, how good it was to eat real food again. She stayed with them until it was time to catch the bus back. On the return journey, Jenny thought over her trip. She had enjoyed seeing Jimmy and Margie, but the rest of it wasn't a great success. Going back to the village as an outsider depressed her. She wouldn't do it again. Hopefully Jimmy would come to visit her.

FIFTY

Jenny went to see Mother Superior again. She had made up her mind that she wanted to become a Catholic. In all truth, the decision had nothing to do with religion. Jenny still believed in God most of the time, but she had no particular leanings toward religion. Her real reason for wanting to change was that she was sick of being an outcast. At school, although she was probably not the only evacuee amongst the five hundred or so pupils, she knew of no others. All the girls she was beginning to know were local and had families who cared for them, putting them all on a common ground. She told no-one, of course, that she was an orphan and lived in a convent. A few knew she was an evacuee because she had been transferred from the Portsmouth school, but by no means all knew why she had joined them so late. As much as possible, she fended off any queries about her parents.

Likewise, at the convent, although she was among other orphans and unfortunates, they were all Catholic. That, and the fact that she attended a different school, singled her out once again as being different. She could not change schools; however, if she became a Catholic she could join in everything they did in the convent and at least feel part of it, and have a sense of belonging to someone or something. She told Mother Superior of her desire to be a Catholic without mentioning her true reasons. Unfortunately, Mother Superior was no fool, and understood her charges much better than any of them realized.

"No-one can become a member of the Catholic faith merely on a whim, Jenny," she said. "Of course, I am pleased that you feel you want to join us, but there is a lot to be considered before you can even think about it. The fact that, as you say, your family was once of our faith could help, or it could hinder, depending why they converted. I realize how you can feel abandoned when everyone else attends services and you are left alone, and I'm not suggesting that this is your reason for thinking of converting. But should that have anything to do with it, it is no reason for changing your religion. What I will do for you is permit you to attend one or two services so that you can begin to have some understanding of what may be involved."

Jenny thanked Mother Superior, feeling better that at least she could now attend church with the others. She had been surprised at Mother Superior's astuteness, feeling her face flush when she had hit upon Jenny's real reason. Perhaps she could go to church this very Sunday.

She now had another problem which bothered her, and which she fervently hoped no-one would find out about at school. She had head lice. The problem was rampant in the convent. Once a week the Sisters went through each child's hair with a small-toothed comb which removed the lice and tore the tiny, sticky eggs from the hairs to which they were attached. Their heads were washed in special shampoos that smelled of tar, and creams were rubbed into their hair. No matter how vigilant the Sisters were, the problem never seemed to be completely eliminated. The itching drove Jenny crazy, particularly when she wore her velour hat. She tried desperately not to scratch her head in company, but it was well nigh impossible. She would die of shame if anyone at school discovered she was lousy. Wearing her hat always increased the itching to unbearable proportions. She wished she could leave it off, but it was not permitted. Anyone seen in the town wearing uniform but no hat was reported immediately and punishment followed.

Jenny had been fortunate in not having to change her uniform when starting South Wilts. Their colours were officially dark green and white, but because of shortages caused by the war, they now permitted navy blue gymslips, skirts, gaberdines and hats, and as many pupils wore navy as did green. All she had changed was her hat band, now green and silver with the frontal badge of five wavy silver lines on a green background depicting the five rivers of Salisbury, the Avon, the Wylie, the Nadder, the Ebble and the Bourne. Something she was going to have to change before summer were her dresses. South Wilts summer dresses were small checks in either green and white or blue and white. Her pretty pale blue ones were unacceptable.

Sunday brought permission to attend her first Catholic service. Jenny was pleased to be going with the others at last, looking forward to learning something of what they did there. She came away at the end of the service utterly bewildered and feeling physically sick. Most of the service was said or sung in Latin, of which she understood nothing. Prayers were addressed to Jesus' mother, Mary, something Jenny could see no point in at all. God was the Supreme Creative Power; Jesus, His chosen Son. To pray to either one made sense. Mary was just an ordinary woman who happened to give birth to Jesus. To Jenny it seemed wrong to pray to an ordinary mortal and ignore the Great Creator. She nevertheless kept her interest in the service, it was all so colourful. Candles, statues and the colourful robes of the Priest brought life and warmth to the church. As the service got under way, someone walked up and down the aisles swinging a golden ball on a chain. Smoke poured from the ball, and when it came close to Jenny the smell, of what she later learned was incense, was so pungent it immediately made her nauseous. The church was soon permeated with the heady smell, preventing her from concentrating any further on the service. All her powers were concentrated on trying not to throw up. Her prayers were for deliverance and fresh air. After an eternity, the service was over. Once into the fresh air, she felt so giddy she had to sit down on the ground and wait until it passed.

She was told that incense often upset people at first, but that if she wanted to continue coming to service, she would soon get used to it. Judging by how sick she had felt, Jenny had serious doubts about that. She was also doubting that she really wanted to be a Catholic.

The poor food was taking its toll on the convent children, Jenny not least among them. Never robust, she became pale, thin and listless, as she had done at the Staffords. A further outbreak occurred among them, this time impetigo. Jenny was affected on her lower face, scabby sores breaking out on her chin and jaw, so unsightly that she was more than ever ashamed to be seen. It became a matter of forcing herself to go to school, so aware was she of how she looked these days. Gangly, hair limp and ratty, now with ugly sores all over her face, she was constantly grateful for her place at the back of the class. Not that anyone said anything derogatory about her. On the contrary, she was getting to know the girls in her form and being accepted by them. There were a couple who she hung around with more than others, neither of whom turned away from her scarred face. But she herself was aware of her appearance and often wanted to crawl into a hole.

She looked just about as dreadful as she could possibly look when Mother Superior again sent for her in mid March.   "Well, dear, it looks like your Ministry has finally found you a suitable home. Miss Hargreaves has written that it has taken such a long time because they have exercised great care in selecting the right place this time. Mr. and Mrs. Hogan will be coming to see you on Saturday, just to talk to you. They have no children of their own and are anxious to give a home to someone like yourself. If you are happy with them, and they with you, arrangements will be made for you to move into their home. I hope it all works out for you, Jenny. I will be happy to know you are settled in a good home."

Jenny's immediate reaction was a feeling of despondency. She had hoped the Ministry had given up begging people to take her in. Here in the convent, despite the bad food, the fact that she attended a different school and that she was not a Catholic, and even though she was ashamed for anyone to know she lived here, she was nevertheless one of a number in a similar situation. She was never referred to as 'the orphan' or 'the evacuee', nobody made excuses for her existence, nothing special was expected of her, and, above all, she was not expected to continually say thank you and be grateful for ordinary, everyday things that other children took for granted. She was accepted, impetigo sores, lice and all. Now it looked as if they wanted to uproot her and dump her in the home of strangers for the umpteenth time, and she was not going to go. She was tired to the marrow of getting to know new families, sleeping in different beds, trying to be accepted, being afraid to say or do the wrong thing and be thrown out.

She would absolutely refuse to be moved again!

FIFTY-ONE

Sister Theresa came to fetch Jenny on Saturday morning and escorted her to the conservatory where the Hogans were waiting. The man and woman rose from the couch as they entered and Jenny was aware that the woman walked towards her. She kept her eyes to the floor, refusing to look up. As Sister Theresa talked to them, Jenny walked to the corner of the room, pressing her back into it and keeping her eyes downcast. Both Hogans and Sister Theresa tried all ways to persuade, cajole and even to pull her from the corner, but she would not be budged or say a single word. Finally giving up, the Hogans left. The moment they left the room, Jenny made a dash for the dormitory where she threw herself on the bed and broke into wrenching tears. Sister Theresa found her there after seeing the Hogans off the premises.

"Oh dear, Jenny. What was all that about, and why all the tears? Mr. and Mrs. Hogan are very upset that you thought them so terrifying you wouldn't even speak to them. They were really nice people, and wanted so much to give you a good home where you could be happy."

"I don't want a good home, or any sort of home," Jenny sobbed. "I just want to stay here and be left alone. I don't want to move ever again. I like it here and I'm going to stay. Just tell them to leave me alone."

"Please don't cry like that," Sister Theresa said gently, stroking Jenny's hair as she talked. "We aren't trying to make you unhappy, dear. On the contrary. Your Ministry is concerned to find you a home and family again so that you *can* be happy. I don't think you are as content here as you pretend."

Jenny kept her face buried in the pillow. Sister Theresa just didn't understand that there was no such thing as a family or home where she could be happy. She *was* content here, and here she was going to stay.

Naturally, Mother Superior sent for her later in the day. She was still kind and understanding, but she explained to Jenny that it wasn't up to her to decide whether to stay or not, this had only ever been a temporary refuge for her and was never intended as a permanent home. For Jenny to entertain the idea of converting to Catholicism in order to remain would do no good. "No-one stays here beyond the age of twelve years, Jenny," she said. Even were we to give permission for you to stay, which we will not, you would be moved after your birthday next month. Our children go to a boarding school at twelve years of age. You could not go there since you are already a pupil at South Wilts. So you see, dear, much as we have loved having you here, it is time to go."

There was no answer to that. She would be on the move again whether she liked it or not. It was so unfair. Jimmy had been allowed to stay in the village, allowed to refuse to go to a good school, but she had no choice anywhere.

Miss Hargreaves came the following Saturday to give her further lecture on how foolish she had been to turn down such a wonderful opportunity as would have been afforded by the Hogans. They were even willing to take her on holidays abroad, but she had lost herself a good and loving home. Sick of hearing about good homes and lost opportunities, Jenny lashed back.

"I don't think I've lost anything. Nothing that I want anyway. All I've lost is the chance of being shoved onto somebody else. I don't care if they want to give a home to some poor orphan or not, it isn't going to be me. I don't want to be pushed around any more, and I don't like your 'good homes'. You said the Emerys wanted to give me a good home. I'm fed up with good homes. If I've got to move, find me another convent or something."

Miss Hargreaves softened her tone. "I do understand what you are saying, Jenny," she said. "Believe me when I say I am more than sorry for all the shifting around you have gone through. It shouldn't happen to anyone, let alone young children. But my dear, I also understand that you are becoming institutionalised, which is something that can easily happen to people who are put in homes or hospitals, or even prisons. Sending you to another convent or children's home will only make matters worse. I have found another couple who are willing to take you, but you must give it a chance this time. Please, Jenny, for your sake and mine, give this next one your best."

"How is it that Jimmy is allowed to choose where he stays, and even where he goes to school, but I am not allowed to choose anything about my own life? Does the stupid Ministry have different rules for boys and girls?"

Miss Hargreaves sighed. "It may surprise you to know that I don't make any decisions about either of you. I am merely a representative and make reports and recommendations which the Ministry either acts upon or does not. I don't agree with Jimmy giving up his education. I think he is too young to be allowed to make such a decision. It is the Ministry's opinion, however, that if, as he says, he only wants to be a farm worker, there is no point wasting a good and expensive education. I feel I have failed Jimmy. Please don't let me fail with you too."

Appealed to in this way, Jenny let down her hostility. She didn't want to get Miss Hargreaves into any trouble, but this was *her* life they were playing with. She felt she was being given the same choice as always ... none.

"Will you please see this other couple, Jenny? And will you make an effort to be sociable and give them a chance? For me?"

She gave in. She couldn't stand being appealed to. When she was being told what to do, or forced into something she didn't want, she could fight back. But an appeal to her better nature was something she couldn't resist.

FIFTY-TWO

The 'couple' turned out to be Mrs. Jones. Despite her promises, faced with another unknown person offering her another unknown home, Jenny went into her 'silent' phase once more. She just couldn't help herself. Resentment at being paraded for inspection proved too much, and she went back into her corner, eyes to the floor. Sister Theresa and Mrs. Jones did their best to persuade her to come and sit down, but once in the corner she could no more make herself move out than fly. Mrs. Jones asked Sister Theresa if she would please leave them alone for a while. With Sister Theresa gone, the room became silent. Jenny felt herself begin to tremble. She felt trapped in her corner, unable to move and almost too afraid to breathe.

"I don't think the wall will fall down if you leave it for a while. It's all right with me if you really want to stand there holding it up, but I'm sure you will feel more comfortable sitting down."

Jenny heard, but said nothing.

"Mr. Jones and I looked after two little Jewish boys at the beginning of the war, Jenny. The youngest one was only four years old, and for the first month all he would do was stand in the corner, just like you, with his thumb in his mouth. We threatened to have his name painted in the corner and put, 'This is Mickey's place,' on it. He did eventually come out of it, and he and his brother stayed with us for eighteen months until they went back home. They still write to us now. You aren't going to stick yourself in a corner for a month are you? It's most uncomfortable."

"Perhaps you would like to know something about me. My mother had thirteen children. I was number eleven, and my mother couldn't cope with so many so she gave me away when I was three years old. She gave me to my Grandmother, who I called Gee. I loved my Grandmother, but she died when I was twelve. Then I had to go and live with an Aunt who I didn't know. It wasn't easy, but sometimes you just have to give it one more try to find a little faith again."

Tears began to sting Jenny's eyes. She held her breath to fight them back. The sing-song sound of Mrs. Jones' voice was pleasant to listen to, and she was telling Jenny she understood. Perhaps she wouldn't be so bad after all.

"Mr. Jones and I are more than willing to give you a home with us. If you aren't willing to even give it a try because you like this place so much, we will understand and not try to force you. What do you say, Jenny?"

Jenny wanted to answer. She thought she would say she would give it a try, but how could she do that and save her dignity now that she had made such a fool of herself? She couldn't just 'give in'. She should make some condition.

"Have you got a horse?" she heard herself ask. It was pretty silly. She had already been told that they lived in town. Where would people in a town keep a horse?

"Have I got a horse? Well, I've got a clothes horse, but it would be a bit painful to sit on I should imagine. No. I don't have a horse, and I can't let you think you could have one if you came to us. For one thing, there would be nowhere to keep it unless you were thinking of putting it under the bed, and for another, we couldn't afford it. I'm going to leave now, Jenny. You think it over and tell the Sisters by next weekend what your decision is. If you would like to give it a try, you can come to tea with Mr. Jones and I on Saturday and look us over. Goodbye, Jenny."

She was gone. Jenny stayed where she was, feeling drawn to Mrs. Jones, yet still unwilling to venture into another unknown and strange household.

Changing her mind from day to day, sometimes from hour to hour, interfered with her school work and her sleeping. By Friday she had decided that to go to tea did not commit her to anything. She would go, then decide after she had seen the house and met Mr. Jones. After all, perhaps they had changed their minds about her by now. She took a good look at herself as she combed her hair on Saturday morning. I don't think I would want somebody who looked like this in my house. Perhaps Mrs. Jones hadn't really been able to see her properly, squeezed back in the corner as she had been. They would both see her today, impetigo sores, lank hair, the lot. Maybe the decision wouldn't be hers to make in the end.

Mother Theresa ordered a taxi to take her to No. 6 Arden Road. She gave her enough money to pay the fare and to get another taxi back. The taxi took her down town, then up Fisherton Street, past the Congregational Church, past River Lane, under the railway bridge and for another mile beyond. Then it turned down a steep hill with terraced houses on either side, stopping about a quarter way down the hill. "Here you are, Miss. Number 6." Jenny paid him, got out of the taxi and walked to the front door. She put out her hand to lift the brass knocker and the door opened. "Come on in, Jenny. I'm glad you decided to come after all."

Mrs. Jones was smaller than Jenny remembered. But how could she remember, she hadn't really looked at her at all. Now she could see that Mrs. Jones was not much taller than herself. Following Mrs. Jones down the hall, they passed a closed door on the right. Ahead of them was a flight of carpeted stairs, and another partially open door on the right. They went through here into a small, square room, the inevitable polished table in the centre, already laid for tea, and the usual fireplace in the centre of the far wall. Mr. Jones got up from his easy chair by the fire, holding out his hand as he came forward to meet her. He squeezed her hand hard.

"Hello, my girl. We're very glad you decided to give us a chance after all. Maybe, if we behave ourselves today, you may make it more than just a visit. Take your coat off and come and make yourself at home. We don't put on any side here. Mrs. Jones has made us some goodies for tea. You look as if you could do with some feeding up."

His greying hair was thinning on top and receding at the temples. Longish face and twinkling eyes, he wore his glasses on the top of his head. Jenny couldn't help noticing how large his ears were, and they stuck out a little from the side of his head. When he spoke, his voice had the same sing-song quality as Mrs. Jones' voice. Jenny wondered where they came from.

Throughout tea, they talked to her, asking questions about herself, her school and her ambitions. They told her they were both Welsh, having lived in England for twelve years. They still had relatives in Wales and if Jenny came to live with them, no doubt they would take her to visit them one day. Mr. Jones worked at the National Assistance Board as an Executive Officer. He was a civil servant, he said. The Board provided money for people who were out of work, the old age pensioners, and often to drunks and tramps, which Mr. Jones didn't approve of. Mrs. Jones didn't work, but she taught Sunday School at St. Paul's church down the road, and did lots of volunteer work. Altogether it was a pleasant visit, Jenny giving little away about herself, and listening to all they had to say. Mr. Jones went down the road to telephone for a taxi when it was time for her to leave, and both waved her off, saying they would be in touch.

Jenny wasn't sure if she wanted to go there or not, or even if they wanted her. To questions from the girls at the convent, she merely said it was 'alright'. That night she dreamed she was on the back of a wild horse which galloped so fast that she didn't dare let go, and couldn't get off.

On Wednesday afternoon, she arrived at the convent from school to find Mrs. Jones waiting for her. She said that if Jenny wanted to come and live with them, she and Mr. Jones would come and fetch her on Saturday. Jenny said yes, she would come. She felt as if someone else was answering for her, as if she wasn't really there at all. She felt herself to be in a strange sort of daze, not caring where she went or with whom.

FIFTY-THREE

1945 - 1947

Once again, Jenny was in a house with no bathroom, although this one did have electricity upstairs as well as down. Jenny's bedroom, containing a chest of drawers, a marble topped washstand with jug and basin, and a three-quarter size bed, was the middle room directly above the living room. Mr. and Mrs. Jones shared the front bedroom along the passage, the small room under the eaves at the back being left vacant. Downstairs, the 'front room' contained a mock leather sofa, two cloth covered easy chairs, a china cabinet, a small table set in the bay window, a desk, and a piano. The living room led to the kitchen, or 'middle room', a small room containing a large table under the window, a pantry and a bricked-in fireplace. An addition had been made to the house, which Mrs. Jones referred to as the 'back kitchen', but which was simply a washhouse with a deep old fashioned sink and cold tap, flagstone floor, a gas stove, small table, and a door into the adjoining lavatory. A latched back door led from the washhouse to the small garden at the back of the house. The garden was a long narrow strip, lawned at the front, a vegetable patch at the rear, and containing two apple trees and a clothes line. A narrow path divided the Jones' garden from that belonging to the adjoining house on the left, and a ten foot high fence separated it from the house to the right.

Closer to school, Jenny had now only a mile to walk instead of the three miles from the convent. She had company on the walk. Two doors down the hill from the Jones' house was a family with a daughter a few months younger than Jenny, and a son of eight. Mrs. Jones encouraged Pam to visit frequently. Her family were hard put to make ends meet, and Mrs. Jones helped out when she could, sometimes giving Pam gifts of clothing. She asked Pam to show Jenny the way to school, and they began to walk together each day. Pam and Jenny were in different forms so saw little of one another during the school day. Jenny liked Pam right away. Slightly shorter than herself with brown wavy hair and blue eyes, she was pleasant and friendly, wanting to help Jenny settle into her new home.

For Jenny, settling was not easy. Both Mr. and Mrs. Jones were doing their best to make her feel at home, trying to discover what she did and didn't like and doing all they could do to help her feel comfortable with them. Jenny wondered to herself why it was she had so little interest in them, and no desire whatsoever to feel at home. At times she wished she was back at the convent where she could feel anonymous. Other times she felt almost nothing at all. If she thought about the way she felt, it worried her a little. It seemed as if she had lost all ability to feel anything. If the Joneses wanted to keep her, that was okay; if they got fed up and threw her out, that wouldn't bother her either. She made no effort to be pleasant or to make conversation, speaking only when spoken to and offering no information about herself.

A month of this unresponsive behaviour, despite their best efforts, was apparently enough for Mrs. Jones. She told Jenny they must have a talk, taking her into the front room and closing the door. Jenny knew what was coming, readying herself for the inevitable dismissal. She sat on the edge of an easy chair, elbows tucked into her lap, hands clasped together into a fist.

"To start with, Jenny, don't sit there looking like Dracula's latest victim. I'm not going to bite your head off. It's just that you have been with us for a month now, and although that is hardly enough time for you to feel completely settled, it is time enough for you to at least show a little interest in us. You really don't seem to me to be very happy here no matter how we try. You're not a baby, Jenny, you are nearly twelve years old. Old enough to know that you are not only making life miserable for yourself, but making it hard for those around you also. That sullen look of yours and that refusal to smile are depressing. Perhaps you are hoping to be sent back to the convent. I don't know, and for the life of me I can't think what was so wonderful there. You are as skinny as a bean pole, sores all over your face, all the result of the wonderful care they took of you in that place. Now tell me, Jenny. What is on your mind? What is making you so unhappy here?

What was she expected to say? Resentful at being spoken to in this way, Jenny could hardly explain to Mrs. Jones, or anyone, why she had been content at the convent. She knew she was thin because of the rotten food there, and that she had caught sores and lice. She didn't need anyone to tell her that. She wished Mrs. Jones would get to the point without the lecture.

"Well, Jenny, what is your answer? What is it that you want?"

"I don't know." It was true, she didn't know what she wanted, other than to have her family back and go home. But that wasn't possible, she had no family and no home to go to. What did she want? The convent wouldn't take her back now that she was twelve. She truly didn't know.

"Well that's something anyway. At least you admit you don't know what you want. In that case, I will have to make up your mind for you. You may as well know I don't give in easily. Both Mr. Jones and I like you, despite all your efforts to the contrary. We want you to be happy with us, but if you say you truly don't want to stay, then I shall write to Miss Hargreaves. Somehow I don't think that is what you want. I suggest we go on trying. We want you to trust us, Jenny. It isn't easy, I know, but at least be fair to yourself by giving us all the benefit of the doubt. Having to call us Mr. Jones and Mrs. Jones hardly helps the situation. Do you think it would make it any easier if you called us Aunt and Uncle? Mr. Jones' name is Arthur so you could call him Uncle Arthur. My name is Blodwyn, a silly Welsh name. You can call me Aunty Blod. How does that sound?

It sounded ridiculous. So much so that Jenny felt her stomach tremble as she tried to smother a laugh. Blodwyn! Aunty Blod! How could she call anyone 'Aunty Blod'?

"What do you think then, Jenny? Will you feel any better if we try that?"

Jenny looked at Mrs. Jones and tried to speak. As soon as she opened her mouth an explosion of laughter burst from within. She laughed and giggled, unable to stop herself. Falling to the floor, the giggling and laughing took such hold it threatened to consume her.

Tears streaming down her face, cheeks and stomach aching, she rolled around the floor in paroxysms of laughter, wishing she could stop. Mrs. Jones had smiled when Jenny first started to laugh, now she sounded alarmed.

"I don't think anything I said was all that funny," she said. "Jenny, are you laughing or crying?"

By now, Jenny didn't know. She struggled to gasp in a lungful of air and hold it. The moment she let go the laughing started again. She was hurting all over.

"What's all the noise in here?" Mr. Jones asked, poking his head into the room.

"Oh, Arthur, I don't know what to do," Mrs. Jones said. "I suggested she call us Uncle Arthur and Aunty Blod and this is the result. Do you think I should slap her face?"

"No, no. She's just a bit hysterical. Perhaps it's a good thing in a way. Perhaps this is what she needed."

Jenny's stomach hurt badly. She was feeling foolish and wished they would help her stop. Mr. Jones pulled her from the floor by the arm. Putting his other arm around her for support, he pulled a handkerchief from his pocket and handed it to her. She took it, pressing it hard against her mouth. The laughter subsided and she walked with jelly-like legs into the living room behind Mr. Jones.

"Are you feeling better now?" he asked. Jenny nodded. Her stomach was still trembling as she fought for control.

"Mrs. Jones is right, you know. We can't have you going on calling us Mr. and Mrs. Jones. We shall never feel you belong with us that way. How about it, girl? Are you going to give us a try? Aunty Blod and Uncle Arthur?"

There it was again. Jenny's perilous hold on herself snapped, and the laughter erupted once more. Falling back into the arm chair, she rocked and shook with the uncontrollable laughter. The agony of it was tearing her apart and her face felt frozen into a permanent grimace. Mr. Jones pulled her from the chair and this time slapped her hard on the back with the flat of his hand, knocking the breath out of her. She fell to her knees where she remained on all fours, endeavouring to regain her breath. Mr. Jones lifted her to her feet again.

"I'm sorry to have to do that," he said. It's good to see you can laugh at last, but too much isn't good for you. Sit down now while I make us all a cup of tea. You must be exhausted.

Jenny flopped down into the arm chair, utterly spent. "I'll make the tea. You stay and watch her in case she starts again." Mrs. Jones said.

By the time tea was made, Jenny was asleep; not waking until Mrs. Jones shook her to come and eat. She had slept for hours. She worked her stiff neck around to ease it, realizing she was very hungry. As she ate pork chops, vegetables and gravy, the tension of the past weeks seemed to drain from her. She felt more at ease than she had in a very long time. It wasn't difficult to talk at the table and, without any forcing, she realized she was smiling.

FIFTY-FOUR

Pam showed Jenny the meadows, a series of fields to the left of the lower half of Arden Road, part of which was a football field, part swings, slides and paddling area for tots, the remainder grass, trees, bushes and pathways. A river ran through the meadows where canoes and rubber rafts could often be seen on lazy summer days. Children of all ages frequented the meadows and it was a favoured place for the youth of the neighbourhood to meet and indulge in horseplay. The river was considered too dangerous for swimming, but Jenny and Pam dangled their bare feet in it while chatting to one another. Pam introduced Jenny to some of the local children, and soon she began to feel part of this community. It wasn't long before people started to use her name as they greeted her, giving her more of a sense of belonging.

Aunty Blod took Jenny to meet the next door neighbour in the adjoining house. Miss Hoare was elderly. She had one leg shorter than the other, wearing a built-up boot to compensate for the short leg, and getting around on crutches. Aunty Blod popped in most days to see if she needed anything, and the old lady had been asking to see the new member of the family for some time. As soon as they got inside, Miss Hoare looked her over. "Why, you're only a little tot," she said. "I thought you were going to be a big girl, but you're only a puff of wind."

"No I'm not," Jenny said, defensively. "I'm almost twelve years old and as tall as most girls in my class."

"Oh, you're just a tot. That's what I shall call you ... 'Totty'. You can come to tea with me on Sunday, Totty, and we can have a nice talk."

Aunty Blod laughed when they got back indoors. "She didn't give you much chance to say no, did she? When Miss Hoare invites you to tea, it's not an invitation, it's a command. She's like that. I hope she gives you a nice tea. She has relatives in America who send her food parcels all the time. Her pantry is full of sugar, tea, coffee, chocolate, all the things that are so scarce because of rationing. She won't use it or give any of it away, she just hoards it. She's a nice old dear, and lonely, but she's also a real skinflint. I bet she makes you drink your tea without sugar."

She did. Not only did she make Jenny drink her tea without sugar, she had made trifle, making the custard without sugar also. It wasn't very pleasant, but Jenny pretended to enjoy it to please Miss Hoare. "You're a good girl, Totty," she said. "I hope you're going to come in and see me often. I get a bit lonely sometimes because all my family are in America. They all went when I was nineteen, and I was supposed to go with them. When the emigration people saw I had a displaced hip, they wouldn't let me go."

"Whyever not? What has your hip got to do with anything? You can live with a bad hip in America as well as in England can't you?"

"That's what I said. I have made my living mostly by sewing. I could have done the same there. But they said they didn't want any cripples or sick people, only people who could work and were healthy. I told them I could work, but they wouldn't listen, so my family had to go without me."

"I think that's the meanest thing I ever heard. You must have felt awful being left behind just because you had a bad hip. I don't think I like the Americans anyway. The ones in our village were always showing off and saying everything they had was better than ours. You did alright though, didn't you. Is this your house or do you rent it like Aunty Blod does hers?"

"No. This is my house, Totty. I couldn't have bought it all by myself though. My family have always sent me money to help out so that's how I had enough to buy my own house."

Jenny liked Miss Hoare, even if she was a skinflint and made everything without sugar. She could sew too. Jenny wasn't keen on sewing, so she kept it in mind that Miss Hoare could possibly help her with her school sewing projects if she got stuck.

FIFTY-FIVE

On May 8, 1945, when Jenny had barely been six weeks in her new home, a momentous announcement came over the radio. The Germans had been beaten! It was victory in Europe, or V.E. Day as it was to become known. Essentially the war was at long last over. The dreaded Hitler was dead, England and her allies had won and it was time for celebration and congratulations. The Japanese were still holding out, but it would only be a matter of time now. In any case, that part of the war was far away and didn't affect them in England.

Everywhere people went wild, tearing down the blackout blinds and burning them on great communal bonfires, switching on lights, dancing in the streets, waving banners, cheering and shouting. Strangers in the streets hugged and kissed one another, the general excitement and euphoria catching like wildfire. People in streets and localities got together to arrange neighbourhood celebrations. In and around Arden Road neighbours gathered to arrange a parade, concert and dance. As it happened, it fell on Jenny's birthday. She and Aunty Blod had birthday's close to one another, Aunty Blod's being five days before Jenny's. With so much arranging to do for the parade, both agreed that no special tea need be put on for either of them. Aunty Blod gave Jenny a dress in blue and pink stripes which complemented her fair hair and blue eyes. Nellie had remembered her also, sending a necklace of blue glass beads that toned beautifully with her new dress. Jenny was especially pleased to receive Nellie's gift, which had come to her via the convent. It meant that Nellie had forgiven her for visiting the village and not calling to see her.

It was amazing how so many people had managed to come up with costumes and fancy dress in such a short time. A lady who lived at the top of the road next to the corner shop loaned Jenny a blue and gold brocaded Chinese dress. Long and straight with slits at the sides and a mandarin collar, it fitted Jenny perfectly. On the morning of the parade she went to the lady's house where they made up her face, combed her hair on top of her head and placed a red carnation over one ear. Jenny didn't recognize herself when they were done. The parade moved up and down the streets behind a hastily put together band, crowds lining the streets throwing confetti and streamers as they passed. The parade ended up in the meadows, where games and competitions, mock football matches and general merrymaking carried on throughout the day. In the evening they all went to a local hall, adults and children alike, where a social and dance finished the day's celebrations. Aunty Blod played the piano, making a much more professional job of it than the local carrier had done at the village dances.

The parade and festivities were such a success that the organizers decided to form an association to carry on with socials and dances, raising money to help returning members of the armed forces. They called themselves the Victory Association, Uncle Arthur being voted Secretary and Aunty Blod pianist for any functions they would arrange. It was recognized that many of the returning men would not readily find jobs, and the money raised from the Association's activities would be used to help any families that found themselves in need.

The main topic of conversation everywhere was of returning husbands, fathers, sons and brothers. Even at school it was almost impossible to get away from it. For Jenny, all this talk was painful in the extreme. The war was over and the truth had to be faced. Her father would not be coming home as a repatriated prisoner. Her father was dead. She finally had to acknowledge to herself a fact she had for so long denied. Her father was dead, her mother missing. She was an evacuee, a war orphan, and what was to happen to her now? Had her mother simply abandoned them or would she come back now to claim her lost children? Was the story abut a Dutch captain true or a fantasy made up to keep Jimmy and herself ignorant of the fact that her mother too was dead? She was beginning to feel slightly more at home with Uncle Arthur and Aunty Blod, but the hope that her mother would come back and claim them was still strong.

One thing made the fact of her father's death easier to accept. Aunty Blod was an avid film fan, going to the cinema whenever she could. She was not like Mr. Emery, going for the sake of it. She went to see those films she wanted to see, not going if she thought none of films at the three cinemas worth seeing. Sometimes she would take Jenny, either on Saturday afternoons or to the early show straight after school. Jenny liked going to the pictures, but found it annoying that Aunty Blod didn't care what time she went. She was quite likely to go right in the middle of a film so that they saw the end, then had to watch a second picture, news, trailers for next week, and advertisements before seeing the beginning of the film they had already seen the end of. Jenny found that aggravating, but Aunty Blod said what did it matter so long as they eventually saw the whole 'A' film.

It was the Pathe News that made her father's death easier for Jenny to accept. It showed the most dreadful pictures of the prisoners of war being liberated from concentration camps. There were pictures of near naked skeletons picking over bits of dirty rags and grubbing in the dirt. Pictures of huge pits containing thousand of skeletal bodies thrown on top of one another. Pictures of strong American soldiers crying at the pathetic condition of their fellow man. Horror stories abounded of torture, starvation, burning alive in ovens; and the pictures they showed were enough to make any human being sick at heart and ashamed of being human. Jenny broke her heart at the horror of it all. Then she thought of how, for more than five years, she had wished her father to be a prisoner of war. Now she was grateful that he hadn't been picked up by any German ship. She was thankful he had died in the merciful ocean.

At school, Jenny lied about her 'family'. If, for instance, she tore her dress and one of the girls would ask next day what her mum had said about it, she would make up a story, saying her mum had been cross but was going to mend it for her. She never initiated discussions about her family so that she didn't have to deliberately lie, but if any of the girls asked about her mother, she didn't disabuse them. She wanted to be as normal as them, and if she wasn't she would pretend to be. The lying did bother her, so to ingratiate herself further with her schoolmates and be accepted by them, she began to be disruptive and daring. She found that the more stupid and daring she was, the more popular she became with her peers. More and more often in trouble, she was sent to the headmistress three times in as many months.

To be sent to the headmistress meant that you had committed a serious offence, the punishment for which was to receive a serious offence mark against your name, unless you had a valid reason for such behaviour. Three serious offence marks meant you faced possible expulsion. Jenny was always very nervous at being sent to Miss Marsh, the headmistress. Miss Marsh wore half glasses as Mrs. Mergrin had done. She was severe but fair, and when she looked you in the eye over those glasses, it was enough to make anyone tremble. Unfortunately for Jenny, her nervousness of late had taken the form of giggling. Whenever she was frightened or nervous, she would break into silly giggling. It would seem to onlookers that she thought the situation funny. On the contrary, she was truly nervous and angry at herself for giggling at something she didn't find funny, but unable to control it.

On her third enforced visit to Mrs. Marsh, Jenny was in a state of great anxiety. If she was going to receive a third serious offence mark and be expelled, she was in deep trouble. Miss Marsh looked at Jenny over her glasses. "What is it this time, Jenny?" she asked. "You are coming here far too frequently for my liking. What have you done this time?"

"I was caught walking on the school roof yesterday after school," Jenny confessed. "I'm sorry. I did it for a dare and I know it was silly."

"You did what? Am I to believe what I am hearing? Jenny, what is the matter with you? Do you realize what a dangerous and stupid thing that is to do, apart from being out of bounds? Am I to believe that you really, actually walked on the school roof?"

Jenny broke into a fit of giggling, wishing she could crawl under the carpet. She was making it worse by giggling, letting Miss Marsh think she thought it all very funny. She had indeed walked on the roof, and the girls who had dared her had no idea how terrified she had been. They knew nothing of her fear of heights, having given her a bunk up onto the top of a second story wall. There was concrete walkway, bordered by iron railings, outside of all the classrooms on the second story. Jenny had stood on the railings, from where the girls had pushed up under her feet so that she could pull herself up to sit astride the high wall. From there she had scrambled up the roof and walked a few yards along the crest. Being very careful not to look down, she had got off the roof by first sitting, moving carefully onto her stomach and then wiggling her way down feet first, holding on to the roof edge all the way down. The girls had helped guide her from the wall, and all thought they had been unseen. Unfortunately, one of the mistresses had still been at the school and had witnessed the stupid venture. Now she was having to explain herself to Miss Marsh and giggling about it.

"In the past few months you have come to my office firstly for being blatantly cheeky to a mistress, secondly for dropping dirty milk bottles from a toilet window to the quadrangle below, and now for walking on the roof. I have to say I am very disappointed in you, Jenny. Your academic work is not showing much improvement and you seem not to realize that your position in this school is privileged. I am really going to have to think about this." She dismissed Jenny back to her classroom, not saying whether or not she would award a third serious offence mark.

At home, in direct contrast to her former silence, Jenny became over talkative, chattering non-stop. Aunty Blod said Jenny was wearing her out with her over-enthusiasm. She seemed bothered by Jenny's sudden change of character, but Uncle Arthur said to leave the girl alone, she would probably settle down to being herself in the long run. Jenny no longer knew what 'being herself' was. If Aunty Blod told her to be quiet for a while, she would sulk, going into the front room to bang on the piano just to be annoying.

Miss Marsh wrote a letter to Aunty Blod. Jenny found out about it when she got home from school one day. The letter said that Jenny was constantly in trouble, was becoming rude and cheeky and that 'insubordination of this kind cannot be tolerated.' Aunty Blod was very upset about the letter. "I don't know what to say to you Jenny. I'm going to have to show this to Uncle Arthur when he gets home, and ask him to talk to you. You realize this letter most likely means that you are going to be expelled, don't you. I can't understand your behaviour lately. I shall go out this evening and leave Uncle Arthur to talk to you. I'm too upset myself."

FIFTY-SIX

When they were alone after supper, Uncle Arthur told her to sit at the table with him as he wished to talk to her. "Now, my girl, let's see if we can't get to the bottom of this matter," he began, his glasses pushed to the top of his head. "You will soon be breaking up for the summer holiday, and we can't have this threat of expulsion hanging over us for the next couple of months."

Jenny was frightened. She hadn't thought Miss Marsh would really expel her, but the letter looked as if she was going to do just that. She began to cry, and Uncle Arthur looked embarrassed. He got up from the table, lit his pipe and sat down again. "I don't want to make you cry, my girl," he said. "This is as unpleasant for me as it is for you. You must know that Aunty Blod and I care for you. If you are in trouble, there must be a reason and we are here to help you. Can you tell me why you are behaving so badly that Miss Marsh has felt compelled to write us a letter about it?"

Jenny couldn't. She didn't know why she had been so silly lately, nor why she had fits of sulks and rudeness. All she could do was sit silently crying.

"Come on now. You have been talking the hind leg off the donkey lately. Surely you can think of something to say now in your own defence."

"I don't know why I'm so bad. I don't know what is supposed to happen to me now that the war's over. I don't know where my mother is or if she is ever coming back for me. I haven't seen Jimmy for ages and don't know what he's doing. The Ministry of Pensions looked after me and Jimmy because we were war orphans and evacuees. Who's going to look after us now the war's over? I don't know why the teachers have been picking on me lately. I know I haven't been good, but I haven't been all that bad." Thoroughly upset now, she sobbed loudly. Uncle Arthur offered the inevitable handkerchief and sat waiting for her to compose herself, looking very thoughtful.

"I can see you have a lot on your mind, young lady," he said at length. "Some things I can answer for you, some I can't. Number one, the fact that the war is over makes no difference to your situation. Not unless your mother turns up and wants you back, that is. The Ministry will continue to keep an eye on you and your brother until you are both sixteen, so you don't need to bother about that. Aunty Blod and I want to keep you until you are an old lady, but I don't imagine we will because some day some young man will want to whisk you away and marry you. You have a home here with us for as long as you want it, so that is number two taken care of. Number three, I'm sure your teachers are not picking on you. They want you to behave, listen to your lessons and pass out with flying colours at the end of your schooling. Are you with me so far?"

Jenny nodded, not wishing to say anything.

"Good. Now then, as for where your mother is, I can't answer that. We know a little about your background, but not too much. We were told that your mother deserted you and your brother and that we are not to expect her to turn up. I can ask the Ministry to thoroughly investigate to satisfy your mind, but there can be no promise of success. Now, has anything I have said been of help to you?"

Jenny stared at the table for a long while. Finally she nodded. "Yes," she whispered. She felt better and was sorry for her bad behaviour. Uncle Arthur told her to go to bed and rest. Tomorrow would be another day and they would all start afresh.

The next morning, Aunty Blod told Jenny she must go to Miss Marsh and apologize for her behaviour and ask for another chance, promising to behave in future.

At first break, Jenny reported to the Secretary's office and was told to wait outside Miss Marsh's room. Standing in the corridor she prayed to whoever was listening not to let her giggle again this time. When she was summoned to the presence, her mouth was so dry that it was hard to speak.

"I've come to say sorry," she managed. "Please don't expel me this time. I promise to behave myself in future. I really want to have a good education and I know I've been silly." Feeling faint, she put her hands on the desk to steady herself, standing up straight again as Miss Marsh spoke.

"Whoever said I was going to expel you, Jenny? So far you have two serious offence marks against you. It takes three before a pupil is considered for expulsion and that is why I didn't give you another for your latest escapade. Even so, you have been causing a great deal of trouble, therefore I wrote to Mr. and Mrs. Jones in the hope they could talk some sense into you. I am pleased you have come to apologise and hope this means you will concentrate on your work instead of disrupting the rest of your class. Next year you will start your second year with us and I intend to watch you closely. I hope to see a big improvement in both your behaviour and your work. You may go now, and tell Mr. and Mrs. Jones that we can all look forward to seeing what you can really do when you try."

Jenny made her way to the changing room and lay on a bench. Relief that it was over made her feel weak at the knees. It had been close, she knew that. Next term she must try harder and be sure she got no serious offence marks. Uncle Arthur had been kind yesterday. He and Aunty Blod were both kind and she mustn't keep letting them down.

Uncle Arthur was kinder than she knew. Not only did he write to the Ministry as he had promised, he also wrote to Jimmy, inviting him to visit Jenny in the summer holidays. Jimmy came during the first week and Jenny was delighted to see him. She was proud to show off her big, thirteen year-old brother to Aunty Blod. Aunty Blod said she could see they were brother and sister, and even though that pleased Jenny, apart from the fact that they both had blond hair and blue eyes, Jenny didn't think she looked a bit like her brother. "Why don't you take Jimmy down the meadows where you can chatter to your hearts' content," Aunty Blod suggested. Jenny thought this a good idea so they started down the road.

"Hang on a minute. I just want to pop in to tell my friend Pam something. You can come in too if you like," Jenny said. It had occurred to her as they were passing Pam's house that she could show off her brother to Pam. Maybe Jimmy would like Pam and come in to see her sometimes. They both went inside, Jenny introducing Jimmy to Pam and her mother. They talked for a while, then carried on to the meadows. "If you think you're going to show me off to a bunch of your friends, forget it," Jimmy said. "I didn't come here to be made a showpiece.

Jimmy surprised Jenny by telling her that Ted Roper was to be married soon. Ted must be nearing forty. Another so-called confirmed bachelor amazing the village by marrying late in life. "Who on earth would want to marry sloppy Ted? Did you know he was courting anybody?" Jenny asked.

"No, I didn't know. Nor did anybody else. It's some distant cousin of his apparently. He's got her in the family way and is getting married pretty quick. I don't think his sister likes the idea too much, but perhaps he will mend his ways a bit and clean up the place before his new bride moves in. It doesn't make any difference to me. I'm still going to work for him when I leave school."

Jenny asked him how he liked going to school in the secondary school. Jimmy said it was terrible. The work was so dreary and all stuff he had done over a year before. He admitted he was bored, but still not sorry for his decision. "My teacher doesn't even remember my name," he said. "He keeps calling me Jimmy Thomas. I've given up telling him my name is Harding because he calls me Thomas again next time he speaks to me. I took rural science because I thought it would be some useful farming subject, but it turns out to be digging the school garden. Only the dozy ones who don't want to do academic subjects take rural science I found out, too late. I call it 'digging for the dim'."

"Oh, Jimmy. It's such a shame you gave up the chance of going to Bishop Wordsworth, but I know you don't want me to say that." She thought of her own folly in almost getting herself expelled in her very first year, and decided against telling him that. She also thought it best not to mention that Uncle Arthur had written to the Ministry in an effort to find their mother. Jimmy would most likely get mad. "Anything else happening in the village?" she asked.

"Oh yes," he said. "You remember the Coles who had the fire at the mill don't you? You know that Steve Cole still lives with me at the Fosters anyway. Well, young Linda Cole and Alf Matthews' stepson both went swimming in the hole you used to swim in, and both got polio. The Matthews boy is getting better and they say he won't even have any paralysis, but Linda Cole was dead in two days. Bloody shame. She was a nice kid and that family have had enough tragedy in their time. They had another son at one time who died as a baby."

Jenny well remembered the Coles. It was Linda to whom she had given her doll's pram. How terrible to think she was now dead. And how strange that Margie had caught polio from going into the river and now two more children had done the same thing. Yet in between there had been years when others had bathed in the river umpteen times and never caught polio. She wondered why.

"Oh, by the way," Jimmy said, pulling a package from his pocket. "Here's a somewhat late birthday present for you." He handed her the package and Jenny tore it open. It was a manicure set in a leather case. "Oh thanks, Jimmy. I didn't expect anything from you, It's lovely." She would have liked to give him a kiss, but you didn't do that to Jimmy. He didn't even like you to thank him.

When they got back to the house, Uncle Arthur was home. After shaking hands with Jimmy, he thanked him for coming in, then he said: "By the way, lad, we may soon have some news for you about your mother."

Jenny's heart almost stopped. Had she known Jimmy was coming that day, she would have told Uncle Arthur not to say anything, but now it was too late.

"Oh, why is that?" Jimmy asked.

Uncle Arthur explained that he had written because Jenny had been so upset regarding her lack of knowledge of her mother's whereabouts. "I'm sure you are just as anxious for some answers as she is, my boy."

Jimmy rounded on Jenny. "You just don't leave things alone do you. What do you hope to gain by this, even if you do find out where she is? Can't you get it through your thick head that she left us. She doesn't want to know us or anything about us. She's messed up your life and mine, and finding her won't do anything but make it worse. You can't ever go back in time and live those years over again as you would like them, it's too late. She doesn't care about you, Jen, so why bother to care about her? I'll tell you this much. If you do find her, don't tell me about it, I don't want to see her ever again. You've always been the same and always will be. You can't see the wood for the trees. Do what you like, but leave me out of it."

Jimmy was angry, as she had known he would be. Why did Uncle Arthur have to go blurting out what he had done? There was nothing she could do to make things better, and Jimmy left without staying to tea. Jenny was depressed that yet again she had appeared an idiot in the eyes of her brother.

Uncle Arthur apologised to Jenny for upsetting her brother. "He's a nice lad, but obviously thinks differently from you," he said. "Don't let it upset you too much. Two people can think differently on the same subject and both be right in their own way. In one way he was right, my girl. You can't re-live your life. The only way to cope is to look forward to a better tomorrow, and not look back. What's done is done. We learn from it, however hard the lesson, and use what we learn to be better people ourselves. When Jimmy comes again, we shall know what subject to avoid, won't we."

Jenny blinked back tears. She was coming to like Uncle Arthur very much. He always knew how to say the right thing at the right time. No wonder he was so highly thought of in the neighbourhood.

"Come on now, girl. How about us taking Bobby for a walk? The old girl hasn't been down to take him out today I understand. We can't have him getting lazy, he's fat enough already."

Jenny fixed Bobby's lead to his collar, and she and Uncle Arthur set out for the meadows. Bobby, a black and white mongrel, was not Aunty Blod's dog, although few people realized that fact. He belonged to the old lady who lived in the house by the corner store, where Jenny had been made up as the Chinese girl. Mrs. Perch always let Bobby out early in the mornings and it had been his habit to go around the neighbourhood visiting various people. He would bark outside chosen doors where he knew people would let him in, give him some food, then let him out again. Aunty Blod had been one of these people and gradually Bobby had spent more and more time at her house, until he eventually dropped all other calls, coming directly to her house and staying all day. He had been coming for so long now that people thought he was the Jones' dog. Mrs. Perch had no objection to Bobby staying all day provided they took him home again at night. She often came down to Aunty Blod's to ask if she might take her own dog for a walk. When she did this, after returning from the walk, she would spend the afternoon with Aunty Blod.

Aunty Blod liked the old lady, but there was a drawback to her spending the afternoon. She was deaf. Her daughter had bought her a hearing aid, but she refused to wear it, the result being that Aunty Blod had to shout everything several times over before Mrs. Perch understood. It was wearying, and after Mrs. Perch had gone home Aunty Blod often continued shouting at Jenny and Uncle Arthur. Aside from this one infirmity, Mrs. Perch at ninety-one, was remarkably fit and strong. One of her two daughters and her grandson were temporarily living with her at this time. The grandson, Matthew, was fourteen years old, blond, blue eyed and, to Jenny's mind, very handsome. She was quite smitten by his looks and the polite way he spoke. She began to volunteer frequently to take Bobby home at night, just for a chance to see and talk to Matthew. She learned from him that his mother and father were divorced, that his father was an officer in the army and that they had lived for some time in Tripoli. Matthew told her tales about how they swam in the shark infested waters of the sea there, and how the sharks would swim close inshore and had been known to take bathers who ventured too far. It all sounded dangerous and exciting to Jenny.

Bobby wasn't permitted to be lazy during the summer holidays. On days when Mrs. Perch didn't come, Jenny took him to the meadows to let him romp. One day, as she was wandering around watching Bobby, she met a young man in a brown uniform who started a conversation with her. He was obviously not English, although he spoke the language well. He told her he was a German prisoner of war, still waiting to be repatriated back to his own country. This was the first time Jenny had actually seen a German and was surprised to find him exactly like any other young man. Here was one of the hated enemy who had kept them at war for six years, the cause of so much havoc and heartache and yet, face to face, no different from any other human being. He talked to her of his family in Germany and how anxious he was to get home and see how they were managing under the occupation. As he talked, Jenny began to feel genuinely sorry for him. "You know," he said. "We are just ordinary people like you. None of us young men wanted to be forced to fight this war. We had no hatred for the English. Since I have been captured, the English have treated me well. I hope always to think of the English as friends when I am back to my own country. I hope also that you will not hate us because we are German."

"Of course not," Jenny said, meaning it. She felt no anger against this man. He had been forced to go to war by Hitler, so was as much a victim as the English were. He seemed so lonely and sad. "If I see you again, I'll talk to you. I know it wasn't your fault, any more than it was mine. I hope you go back home soon."

She told Aunty Blod about her meeting with the prisoner and was shocked at her reaction. "How *could* you go talking to one of them? They have been killing and maiming our people for six years. They killed your own father, and just look at what we have seen on the news of what they did in the concentration camps. And you go talking to that German as if he were your friend."

"He didn't kill my father. He'd only been a soldier for a year before the war ended, and for half of that time he's been a prisoner. He's just a person like us. He told me he didn't even want to fight, but he had to because he was called up."

"That's not the point," Aunty Blod said crossly. "They are all tarred with the same brush. Don't you realize how many people around here have lost fathers, sons and husbands. How do you think they are going to feel if they see you chatting away to one of those responsible for their loss? He would have killed you too if he had to, whatever he may tell you. I don't want to hear of you ever speaking to him, or any of them, again. Do you understand me?"

Arguing was going to get her nowhere. Jenny felt that if her father had been able to give his opinion, he wouldn't have wanted her to hate all Germans. She felt now that she wouldn't be able to go to the meadows any more until she was sure he had gone. She couldn't just refuse to speak to him if she saw him. It gave her a feeling of depression to think that some of the neighbours might feel as Aunty Blod did and be angry at her for talking to a German.

Uncle Arthur got an answering letter from the Ministry. They said that they had tried several times to trace Mrs. Harding, all without success. Now, with returning members of the forces and people moving around, it was impossible to do more. They hoped Jenny was settling down and would eventually forget about her mother. Someone would be coming to see her before long and if she needed anything, please let them know. Uncle Arthur looked apologetically at Jenny. "Seems like they've done all they can, girl, but don't go giving up hope now. Who knows what we might one day discover for ourselves?"

"It's all right," Jenny said. "I didn't really think they would do anything. I've asked them before. I don't think they ever have looked for my mum I don't think they want to find her or want me to find her either. Jimmy thinks they know where she is and don't want us to know. He will be glad they didn't find her anyway."

FIFTY-SEVEN

"Will you come and sleep in my house for a while, Totty?" Miss Hoare asked Jenny at one of their teas. "I've been feeling lonely in the house at night by myself since my lodger left. I had him here for five years and he left just before you came to live next door. I'm going to try to get another lodger, but perhaps you will sleep in here until then."

Jenny didn't know what to say. She liked Miss Hoare, but coming in here to sleep at night was another matter. If it was just for a couple of weeks, she wouldn't mind, she supposed. But what if it took ages for Miss Hoare to find a new lodger? Besides, Miss Hoare went to bed pretty early, sometimes as early as half past eight. Jenny had her homework to do and didn't want to be forced to bed that early. "I don't know, Miss Hoare. I wouldn't be able to come in all the time because of my homework. You don't have to feel lonely with Uncle Arthur and Aunty Blod and me next door. We come to see you a lot."

"I know, Totty. If you only came in twice a week I would feel better. I can't get upstairs you know, that's why I sleep in the front room. Mr. Kent, my lodger, used to keep his own room tidy and give a mop and dust in the other bedroom too. I just worry sometimes that if anything happened to me in the night, or if anyone broke in the upstairs windows, I couldn't get out of bed and get my boot on quick enough to get out and knock on your door. I'd make you a nice cup of tea in the mornings, though I couldn't bring it up to you."

Jenny felt mean at not wanting to sleep in Miss Hoare's house. She hadn't thought how difficult it was for her with her short leg. "Alright," she said. "If it's okay with Aunty Blod, I'll sleep in here twice a week until you find another lodger. And on Saturdays I'll come in and clean your upstairs rooms." She wasn't fussy to accept the offer of sugarless tea in the mornings, but one thing Miss Hoare had that they didn't was a bathroom. She'd had the back room under the eaves converted some years earlier. Although she couldn't use it herself because of her inability to get up the stairs, Mr. Kent had used it and she said Jenny could bath any time she wished.

Each time Jenny slept in Miss Hoare's house she found it difficult to sleep. The bed was comfortable, but she worried what she would do if Miss Hoare got sick or, worse, died in the night. She didn't know what she was expected to do if anyone broke in either. Miss Hoare looked different in the mornings with her wispy steel grey hair hanging to her shoulders. It made her look older and frailer somehow, and the hair looked dead. If a piece stuck out at the sides, it stayed that way as if it had no life of its own as Jenny's hair did. Perhaps people died gradually, their hair dying first, she thought. She began to realize that she was afraid of old people, and afraid of getting old herself one day. She had no fear of death for herself. If anyone told her she was going to die, she wouldn't be bothered about it, but the thought of being old did bother her. This was brought home to her one day when Aunty Blod sent her up to the corner shop to get the rations.

When she got to the shop, Mrs. Thomas, the owner, was serving Mrs. Day, an elderly lady who Jenny knew. They both greeted her, then Mrs. Day turned back to continue with her shopping. The packets of tea were kept on the highest shelf behind the counter, Mrs. Thomas having to stand on a little stool and stretch up to reach them. "... and I'll take a quarter of tea please," Mrs. Day was saying. Mrs. Thomas stood on the stool, reaching up her arm. "What sort do you want?" she asked. There was no answer. Mrs. Thomas turned round. "What sort of tea do you want?" she asked again. There was still no answer, then suddenly Mrs. Day keeled over, hitting Jenny as she fell. Petrified, Jenny hi-tailed it out of the shop as fast as her legs could carry her. She raced down the hill, shoved her hand through the letter box flap to yank out the key that Aunty Blod kept hanging on a string behind the door, and with trembling hands unlocked the door and rushed inside.

"Good God! You look as if you've seen a ghost. Where are the groceries?" Aunty Blod asked.

"I didn't get them," Jenny panted. "Mrs. Day just died in the shop. I was so scared, I ran."

"Oh, good heavens, no. Poor Mrs. Day. What happened?"

"I don't know. She just fell over and died." Jenny was shaking like a leaf.

"Well you didn't just leave her there, did you? What did you do? I'd better go up and see if I can help." Aunty Blod rushed out of the house, leaving Jenny shaking with shock. She returned a little later, saying Mrs. Day hadn't died at all, she had only fainted. She was cross when she learned that Jenny had rushed from the shop, leaving poor Mrs. Thomas to cope alone. "How would you like it if everyone ran away from you when you needed help?" she asked. "Mrs. Thomas is disgusted with you."

Jenny felt ashamed. "I thought she died and I didn't know what to do. It scared me and I ran away," she said, lamely.

"Even if she had died, it wasn't very nice to run off and leave Mrs. Thomas with a dead body, was it? I'm disappointed in you, Jenny."

Jenny was disappointed in herself, wondering how she would ever face Mrs. Thomas or Mrs. Day again. She also knew without doubt that she was afraid of old people. They often smelled funny and were bony. She didn't want to touch them, any more than she could bring herself to touch birds. Their bodies were all bony too. She became even more nervous of sleeping in Miss Hoare's house, making excuses whenever she could to get out of it. She hoped fervently that Miss Hoare would soon find another lodger. Perhaps she could suggest that Herbie come and stay. He was always in Miss Hoare's house.

Herbie lived a little further down the hill than Pam. He ran errands for Miss Hoare, and sometimes for Aunty Blod too. He was in his late thirties, spastic and childlike. Several times a week he called into Miss Hoare's house to see if she wanted anything. He staggered through the hallway, bashing himself against the walls, finally making it to the living room. "Mornin' Midd 'Oare. D'you wan' any choppin' doday? I can go to de chop if you like." Jenny got to know that he meant shopping, but for anything else he said she would have to look to Miss Hoare for interpretation. Herbie couldn't stand still, he wobbled and shook the whole time. Sometimes Miss Hoare asked him to go to the gas works, a few streets away, to fetch coke. Everyone used coke in the neighbourhood to eke out the coal ration. The gas works produced piles of it. It was cheap, light and burned well, but it gave no flame, nor did it give out as much heat as coal. Too much of it would coagulate and put the fire out.

When Herbie went for coke, he pushed his two wheeled wooden barrow down the hill to the first right turning, past two more streets and up the lesser slope to the gas works. With his barrow full, he dragged it behind him to the top of the street, along the slight incline of Devizes road, then had to negotiate the steep downslope of Arden road, leaning back against his barrow as the weight pushed him down the hill. It was quite usual to see him stagger past Miss Hoare's house, unable to stop the momentum, ending up in a heap at the bottom of the hill. There, usually, someone came to his rescue, helping him shovel the coke back into the barrow and push it up the hill. Once he got it along the narrow passage at the side of the house and into the coalshed, he would come into Miss Hoare's house beaming with achievement.

Herbie was one of four brothers, all similarly afflicted, who lived with an older sister. They made a precarious living by playing a barrel organ in the town. Known and liked all over town, one turned the handle of the organ as the same old spasmodic, tinny tunes assailed the ears of shoppers, and their little monkey in his red jacket danced and cavorted on top of the organ. The other three staggered around holding out caps for contributions. They had become an institution in the town, and were rapidly becoming a danger to themselves and others as they tottered and reeled along with the organ in the middle of the roads, holding up traffic and often falling down. Aunty Blod said that the police were bound to stop them one day for their own safety, but so far they had been allowed to continue. There had been eight children in the family, the first four being normal and the next four all spastic. Thinking it over, Jenny realized it would be more of a liability than a help for Miss Hoare to take Herbie as a lodger.

FIFTY-EIGHT

Jenny needed new clothes to start the new school year. Miss Hargreaves had been to see her during the holidays, remarking on how tall she was becoming, and had sent money for new uniform. She was now dressed in the correct green and white of the school.

"You're really lucky, you know," Pam said to her as they walked to school one day. "I know you're an orphan and that must be terrible. I don't know how I would feel without my family. But lots of orphans have to live in children's homes with nobody to care what happens to them, and you have Mr. and Mrs. Jones. I heard Mrs. Jones telling my mum that you were difficult at first, but now she wouldn't want to be without you. You're lucky to have found them to look after you. I really like them both."

Jenny was a bit taken aback by this. To Pam, whose parents were kindly but poor, Aunty Blod was kind and seemed better off. Jenny knew she was not that well off and had to make ends meet like everyone else. Besides, what did Pam know about how Jenny felt regarding them? She felt a little resentful at Pam pointing out her good fortune to her.

"I don't need you telling me that," she said. "When I first came, I wanted to stay at the convent and be a Catholic. Now I'm glad I didn't. Aunty Blod and Uncle Arthur are nice and it's probably the best place I could be. But I don't want you telling me I should be grateful. All my life, as long as I can remember practically, I've been told I should be grateful for everything that's done for me. You don't have to keep being grateful to your parents for feeding you or looking after you, you just take it for granted that they will. I get told all the time that I have to be grateful. Even Aunty Blod reminds me sometimes that I should be thankful for having a good home. I am thankful, but I wish I didn't have to be. I'd give anything to have my own family and my brother with me, like you have. I wouldn't care how poor we were so long as we could be together and belong."

"I never thought of it like that. Sorry, Jenny," Pam said. "I know I'm luckier than you. But you do have a smashing brother. Why don't you get him to come and see you more often? I thought he was lovely, but a bit bashful."

"I think he's smashing too," Jenny said. "But you don't know Jimmy. I can't 'get him' to do anything. He'll come if and when he wants to, which isn't very often."

Jenny did think Jimmy was becoming handsome as he grew older. When it came to 'smashing', however, there was no one she thought better looking than Matthew. She had become so friendly with him, his mother and old Mrs. Perch that she didn't need the excuse of taking Bobby home to call in for a chat. Sometimes only old Mrs. Perch was at home, then Jenny would stop and talk to her for a while, realizing what a chore it must be for Aunty Blod to have to talk to her so much. She tried to encourage the old lady to wear her hearing aid and occasionally she would put it in her ear, only to remove it shortly afterwards. She said it caused too much racket in her ear, giving her a headache. She preferred to try to lip read, saying 'yes' and 'no' in all the wrong places, or sitting smiling blankly when it was obvious she hadn't heard.

Matthew's mother had noticed Jenny's doe eyes when she looked at Matthew and was amused at this adoration of her only son. She pushed Matthew to take Jenny to the pictures, or go bike riding with her, and whilst Matthew was willing enough, Jenny felt he didn't like being pushed at her, and she herself found it embarrassing. During some of her visits to their house, Jenny began to get to know Glenda, a girl about a year younger than herself who lived next door to Mrs. Perch on Devizes Road. She wondered why she had never seen Glenda around the district anywhere. She certainly never went to the meadows with the rest of the neighbourhood youth. Glenda was shy and reticent about herself when Jenny first started talking to her, but gradually, as they got to know one another, Jenny learned that Glenda lived with her mother and two older brothers, one sixteen and one twenty. Their father had left them when Glenda was five, since when their mother had worked to keep them. Glenda never seemed to want to talk for long, always saying she had to dash back indoors because she was busy.

Eventually, Glenda invited Jenny into the house, saying they could talk longer if Jenny came in. There was no-one home but her, so it would be okay. Then Jenny found out why Glenda was never seen around. She was almost as much a slave in her own home as Jenny had been at the Staffords. She had to keep the house clean, do all the washing and ironing for the family, prepare vegetables, anything that had to be done except cooking and shopping. She attended a local secondary school and when she got home in the afternoons, and every weekend, she was chained to the housework. Jenny was devastated. She wept when she saw Glenda on her hands and knees scrubbing the flagstone scullery floor, wanting so desperately to save her from all that work and let her be a normal girl. Pulling her up gently by the arm, she put her arms around Glenda, realizing that it was the first time she had held, or been held by anyone for a very long time. As they held one another and Jenny cried, it was Glenda who tried to comfort her.

"You don't have to cry for me, Jen," she said. "I don't mind doing the work, honestly. My mum has to work so hard to keep us, though it's getting easier now that both my brothers work. My youngest brother, John, doesn't earn much because he's only an apprentice, but our Clive brings in good money now. I used to want to go out to play, but now it doesn't bother me much, except that I don't have any friends. I never tell them at school that I do the housework so they don't know why I never go out with them. They've got fed up asking me to go out at weekends or after school."

Jenny understood everything Glenda was saying, and it made her feel terrible. She didn't believe that Glenda didn't mind doing all the work. She remembered how badly she had wanted to play like other children when she had been a slave. How lucky she had been to escape. True gratitude for her good fortune flooded into her as she watched Glenda work, wishing she could help Glenda escape as she herself had done. But Glen was with her own family. Would Jenny be willing to be a slave again if it was for her own family? She thought she would. "If you'll let me be your friend, Glen, I'll come up and help you with your work whenever I can," she said.

"Oh no. My mum would kill me if I let you help clean the house. I'd love it if you'd be my friend, but I can't let you help me."

"Why not? How is your mum going to know I help you if we never tell her? I'll only come up when there's nobody here. Does your mum beat you, Glen?"

Glenda said her mother didn't beat her, but she often slapped her hard across the face. She nevertheless felt no animosity towards her mother or brothers because she was a girl and had to do housework while her brothers didn't. Her brothers were kind to her and loved her, she said. Her mother loved her too, but was tired from working. "Well I'm going to come and help you whenever I can," Jenny said. "And your mum will never know, so you won't get into trouble."

Jenny's school work began to show a little improvement. She had no illusions that she was ever going to shine at academic work, maths being a particularly sticky subject for her. She did show an aptitude for the school's main game of lacrosse however, and was told that if she continued to show promise, she had a chance of being included in the school team. It was not much to boast about, but it gave her a sense of pride that she could do something reasonably well. She continued to hedge, or downright lie, about her home situation, letting her school pals think she was living with her own family whenever the subject came up. She was grateful for the life she had now, especially since seeing what a sad life Glen had, but the ache for her own family and longing to 'belong' never left her. Her report at Christmas was a slight improvement on the summer one, and Miss Marsh wrote at the end that she was pleased to note the improvement and hoped Jenny had now sorted out her problems.

The Victory Association planned a concert for the Christmas holidays and anyone with any talent was expected to perform. Pam and Jenny rehearsed to take part in a play, and Pam was going to sing a solo. Having no singing voice herself to speak of, Jenny felt somewhat useless, wondering what she could contribute. With Aunty Blod's encouragement, she decided to write a poem about all the people who worked on the Association committee. The poem complete, she submitted it for approval, where it was accepted that she should read it at the concert.

"You see," Aunty Blod said to her. "You keep saying you have no talent, and how many people do you know who can write a poem like that?"

"That's not real talent," Jenny argued. "I can't sing like Pam. She has a lovely voice and could be famous one day. People who write little bits of poetry don't become famous. I bet I could be a dancer if I had lessons though. Do you think I could take dancing lessons?"

"Oh, Jenny, I couldn't afford to give you dancing lessons. In any case, to be a dancer you have to start lessons very young. At going on thirteen I think you've missed the boat there. You do have some funny ideas of talent. Singing songs or jumping around to music is no more talented than the ability to write. Some people who write 'bits of poetry' go on to write better things and even become authors. That's real talent. What is this sudden desire for fame anyway? Are you hoping to see your name in lights one day?"

"Don't be silly. I didn't say I wanted to be famous. I'd just like to be able to do something to make my life worthwhile that's all. What am I here for otherwise?"

"That's a nice thing to say, I must say," Aunty Blod said crossly. "If your life isn't worthwhile, then what are we all doing trying to help you? You need to have a lot more confidence in yourself, Jenny. Your life is worth as much as anyone's and you don't have to prove it. Keep on with your writing and be proud of every small achievement. I'm looking forward to hearing you read it."

Jenny still thought the poem showed little talent. She was disappointed that she was too old for dance lessons, but not surprised. She often dreamed of being a dancer, dancing to any music she heard whenever she was alone. She especially loved the melody of 'Lonely Ballerina', imagining herself dancing all alone and sad in a large empty hall, with no-one to watch her.

The concert went well. Everyone remembered the lines of the play. The comedians were good, Pam sang well and had to do an encore, and Jenny's poem was received better than she had hoped. She was nervous and her voice trembled as she read it, but she received a good ovation. Many asked for copies at the end of the show, and the committee had a copy framed to hang on the wall of the meeting room.

FIFTY-NINE

Shortly after Christmas, Matthew's mother remarried and they moved away. Jenny was more than a little sad at losing her hero, but when she thought about it further, it was probably just as well. It had become embarrassing having his mother push them together, and she would have lost him in any case sooner or later. Matthew was set on joining the army and working for a commission when he grew up. Jenny had known his mother was courting and was happy for her that she had remarried. They went to live in Kent, promising her a holiday with them either this summer or next.

Rationing was not expected to end for months, possibly years. Jenny couldn't remember what it was like to be able to buy anything you wanted without ration books. Word got round that one of the bakeries in town was starting to make its once famous small fancy cakes again. Aunty Blod remembered those cakes from pre-war times and said Jenny should go and buy some. They were only sold on Saturday mornings and first come, first served. The first time Jenny went, miles across the other side of town, she was aghast when she saw the queue. It stretched the length of two whole streets. She didn't know whether to stay or not, it being unlikely there would be any cakes left by the time her turn came. Rather than risk disappointing Aunty Blod, she joined the monstrous queue. Three hours later, ready to drop from standing and shuffling along for so long, she finally got six small cakes. There was not a great selection left, two per ration book being all that was allowed. Aunty Blod was pleased when she finally got home with her small treasures, saying that Jenny should set out earlier next time so she wouldn't have to wait so long. Unfortunately, no matter what time she left, the queue never lessened and sometimes she waited for hours in the pouring rain for the six small cakes. Delicious as they were, Jenny wondered if Aunty Blod would enjoy them so much if she had to wait so long and become so tired and dispirited to get them.

At Easter they all three went to Wales to visit the relatives. This was the regular time that Uncle Arthur and Aunty Blod went 'home'. The relatives all lived in Glamorganshire, South Wales. Aunty Blod's own Aunty Gwladys and Uncle John, together with Uncle John's brother, Davey, lived in Mountain Ash, and Uncle Arthur's sister, Margaret, lived in Cwmdare. They stayed with Margaret whenever they went, visiting other relatives from her home. It was Jenny's first ever train journey and she looked forward to it with excitement.

Her first view of South Wales was anything but exciting. They caught a bus from the station, the most uncomfortable bus ride she had ever experienced. The seats were made of slatted wood, registering every bump in the road. The view was of black rivers and even blacker hills with no grass or trees on them anywhere. Uncle Arthur explained that the 'hills' were really huge piles of coal dust that the government had promised to cover with soil one day and plant grass over. Now they were ugly, dark and forbidding. The rivers were black for the same reason, they were full of coal dust. The Welsh people, however, were as sunny as their surroundings were bleak. She was made a fuss of as soon as she entered Aunt Margaret's home.

"Oh, my curiad. Isn't she lovely," Aunt Margaret said as soon as she saw her. "You must be Jenny. You're going to have a lovely holiday my darling. You have all kinds of instant relations now, all dying to meet you. I've got pop in my cupboard and real ice cream from the dairy. I bet you don't know what real ice cream tastes like do you?" She squeezed Jenny's cheeks in her fingers and plonked a kiss on her nose.

"No, I don't think so," Jenny said. They make ice cream from semolina in the shop near us."

"Oh, well then. You wait till you taste my ice cream. You won't want to go back home with Aunty Blod after that. You can stay and be my little chicken instead." Aunt Margaret, a spinster, continued to make a fuss of Jenny throughout the holiday, even taking her tea in bed. She was kind like that to everyone. Aunty Blod said she was her favourite sister-in-law. Uncle Arthur had two sisters. The second sister, Aunt Kate, came to visit them at Aunt Margaret's. She was plump and black haired, whereas Aunt Margaret was slimmer and grey haired.

Otherwise it was easy to see that they were all brother and sisters. Aunt Kate was nice, but not as ebullient as Aunt Margaret. Aunt Kate was divorced and had one daughter, Miriam, seventeen years old and spoiled.

One of Aunty Blod's many sisters came to visit them at Aunt Margaret's also, bringing her fifteen year old son, John. Aunt Margaret said that the youngsters didn't want to sit around listening to a lot of old fogies talking, so why didn't John take Jenny to the pictures. She gave them both ticket money and bus fare and they went off together, feeling a little awkward in each other's company. John was even more shy than Jenny, hardly speaking at all. Another ride on a bone jerking bus and they arrived at the cinema. Paying for their tickets, they were shown through some tattered curtains to the auditorium. Slatted wooden seats greeted them here also. Jenny wondered if South Wales hadn't been forgotten and still existed somewhere in the dark ages. Instead of black and white, the film was brown. The voices never matched the lips of the people speaking and the film broke down so many times it was impossible to follow the story. Bored and very uncomfortable, Jenny fidgeted in her seat, relieved when it was at last over.

All smiles, Aunt Margaret asked how they had enjoyed the film when they arrived at the house. John finally found a voice. "I didn't enjoy it at all," he said. "Don't ask me to take Jenny anywhere again. All she did was fidget and complain all afternoon."

"I like that," Jenny said, affronted. "How can anyone keep still on rock hard seats, and watch a film that's all brown and breaks down all the time. I still don't know what that film was about. I don't want to go with you anywhere anyway. You can't even open your mouth to speak to a person."

The adults thought it all very funny, but John and Jenny either ignored or glowered at each other for the rest of the evening. Jenny was sure John was as glad to go home as she was to see the back of him.

They went to Mountain Ash to visit Aunt Gwladys and Uncle John. Mountain Ash lived up to it's name. It was extremely mountainous and they had a hard climb to Aunt Gwladys's house. An elderly couple, they too made a great fuss of Jenny. It was Uncle Davey that Jenny liked the best of all. Both he and his brother, John, suffered from pneumoconiosis, a lung disease common among miners. Caused by coal dust on the lung, it made John and Davey wheeze and whistle as they breathed. It must be extra hard for them to walk up and down these steep hills when they can hardly breath, Jenny thought. Uncle Davey was about sixty, his brother a couple of years older. Despite their lung problems, they were both cheerful and both had twinkling eyes. Uncle Davey was a bit of a renegade. A bachelor, Uncle Davey liked his 'bit of booze', a habit which caused his sister-in-law, Gwladys, and Aunty Blod, to disapprove of him. Uncle Davey was coming back to Salisbury to spend a few weeks with them when they went home.

While Aunty Blod and Jenny were out in Cwmdare one day, a woman Aunty Blod knew but hadn't seen for some years, stopped them in the street. After exchanging greetings, the woman looked at Jenny and asked, "And is this your daughter?"

"N ..., ahh ..., yes. Yes, this is my daughter, Jenny," Aunty Blod said. Jenny couldn't believe what she was hearing. She looked at Aunty Blod who had a half smile on her lips. They talked some more, then the woman left them.

"Why did you say I was your daughter?" Jenny asked as soon as they were out of earshot.

"Well, you are. As near as dammit is to swearing anyway, aren't you? Oh, Jenny, I know how it must feel to have people deny you, say 'no, this is an orphan I take care of,' or whatever. I used to feel that way when Aunt Gwladys introduced her own children and then explained that I was her niece. It made me feel different and left out. If you don't want me to say you are my daughter, I won't do it again."

Jenny's eyes were brimming with tears. "No. It's alright, I liked it." She hadn't realized how well Aunty Blod understood her. It was nice to have someone say she was her daughter. Even if it wasn't the truth, it was the next best thing.

She was eager to tell both Pam and Glenda about her holiday when she returned. Her first ever train ride and her first ever holiday. Her spirits were somewhat dampened when she did, however, because she discovered that neither Glen nor Pam had ever had a holiday themselves.

Having Uncle Davey to stay was fun, although he drove Aunty Blod mad with his silly practical jokes. Jenny decided he was a cross between a man and a child. Scarcely taller than herself, he insisted on calling her 'little one', getting her into all sorts of trouble by blaming her when Aunty Blod became cross at his practical joking. "Come over by yer, little one," he'd say to Jenny. "Didn't you tell this innocent man to put mustard in the apple pie your Aunty was making, when she wasn't looking?. She did, curiad, she's wicked, this little one of yours," he'd say to Aunty Blod, winking at Jenny at the same time. Aunty Blod wasn't fooled by his nonsense, but she was cross with Jenny for 'siding with him'.

Aunty Blod had a deep hatred of alcohol. She had seen too many miners ruin their health and their family's incomes by drinking heavily, and her own father had died of a combination of silicosis caused by coal dust, and liver disease from drinking. She always felt that had her father not spent so much of their meagre income on drink, her mother would not have had to give her away as a baby. Uncle Davey, however, liked to drink. Not enough to get drunk, but he liked his beer.

"Let's take that fat Bobby for a walk, little one," he said to Jenny one day. "You and me could both do with some fresh air too." As soon as they were outside he whispered to Jenny: "Take me in the direction of your nearest pub will you, curiad. I want to see if it's like the ones at home."

Fully aware that he had been here before and knew exactly what the pubs were like, Jenny wasn't taken in. "You don't want to see what the pub is like. You want to go inside. You know Aunty Blod will be mad, and I'll get into trouble too."

"No, no. I might just pop in for a quick one, just to be friendly like. I'm not a boozer, look you now. Come on, little one, be kind to a poor old man. Just you take me there and wait outside, I won't be long."

His 'quick one' took him over an hour while Jenny walked Bobby up and down waiting for him to come out. He had told her not to go home without him and she was tempted to do just that. He eventually emerged smiling broadly, the pupils of his eyes tiny pinpoints. "We'd better go for a bit of a walk now to blow the fumes away, curiad," he said. "Don't you go telling your Aunty Blod now will you. She doesn't understand that a man needs a drop of beer now and then to keep him going."

"I won't have to tell her, Uncle Davey. She'll know where you've been." Aunty Blod wasn't stupid. She smelled his breath as soon as they got in the door, despite the walk to 'blow the fumes away.' He hotly denied her accusation of drinking, trying to get Jenny to say they had just been walking. Jenny didn't want to tell on him, but it was silly to lie about it, you could smell his breath across the room.

Uncle Davey stayed with them a whole month, and Aunty Blod was heartily glad when he went home.

SIXTY

Jenny had kept her promise to Glenda, going to her house to help out whenever she could. As summer holidays came around, she went more often to Glenda's house, gradually getting to know the family. Although neither she nor Glenda let them know Jenny helped with the housework, it became accepted that she was Glenda's friend and she was permitted to visit. Jenny couldn't take to Mrs. MacKenzie, Glenda's mother, no matter how much Glenda defended her. A hard-faced woman, who Jenny never saw smile, she was strict and quick to criticize. Glen's two brothers were entirely different, the younger one, John, slim, polite, serious, and so shy that he rarely spoke unless spoken to first. Clive, at twenty-one, was husky, outgoing, and pleasant. He looked straight into Jenny's eyes when he spoke, his own eyes always seeming to be laughing. Both boys were dark haired and handsome, Glenda fair and pretty. Jenny thought that either Mrs. MacKenzie had been much more attractive when young, or Mr. MacKenzie had been a handsome man.

Jenny was never able to visit Glenda without a feeling of sadness. No matter how much Glenda said that she didn't mind doing the housework to help her mother, Jenny couldn't really believe her. She was constantly reminded of her own feelings when chained to drudgery at the Staffords. It was a time she wanted to forget. Being reminded of it in this way made her want so badly to be able to free her friend, and allow herself to forget a period in her life that she wished to bury. Since there was no way to free Glenda, all she could do was help her. Before long, however, Jenny found that she wasn't going to the MacKenzie's house only to see Glen, she was being emotionally drawn to Clive. It was stupid, of course, she realized. There was no way a twenty-one year old man was going to even look at a thirteen year old schoolgirl who wore gymslips, but she could do nothing about the strong attraction she felt for him.

Beside Clive, Matthew had been a mere boy, her affection for him nothing to compare with what she felt now for Clive. She found herself thinking about him at home, at school, at night in her bed. Becoming a frequent visitor to the MacKenzie house, she seemed to melt inside each time she looked at Clive. If he spoke to her, which he often did, her heart swelled in her chest until she thought it would burst. Her emotions played havoc with her in ways she couldn't understand or barely cope with. There were sensitive spots behind her knees, she discovered. When Clive was close to her, these spots tingled and her legs turned to jelly. In a moment of confidence, she admitted to Glen that she was in love with Clive, swearing her to secrecy. Glen thought it funny that Jenny loved her brother, promising not to tell.

Glenda broke her promise. She said later that she thought she was doing Jenny a favour by telling Clive. She thought it might make Clive interested in Jenny, but it didn't work that way. The next time Jenny went to the house, having no idea that Glenda had revealed her secret, Clive asked her to go for a walk with him. Shocked, she wondered if this meant that he *was* interested in her after all, agreeing to the walk with hammering heart.

Walking to the meadows beside him, he asked her how she was doing at school and what she wanted to be when she left. Hearing him talk this way, she became confused. He obviously saw her just as a schoolgirl, so why was he taking her for a walk? She felt suddenly very silly, and at the same time panicky. He was a man, and she didn't know what was expected of her. Perhaps this wasn't such a good idea after all. Worshipping him in secret was one thing, going to the meadows with a man so much more knowledgeable and experienced than herself was very different.

As they walked the pathways of the meadows, he stopped, took her shoulders gently, and turned her towards him. "Jenny," he said. "I don't want you to take what I am going to say as any sort of insult to yourself, nor do I want you to be angry with Glen. Glen told me that you were in love with me, and I think we should talk about it."

Jenny had never felt so stupid in her life. Hot with embarrassment and anger at Glenda, she could only stand and say nothing.

"Don't look like that please, Jen," he said. "I feel honoured and flattered that you think of me in that way. Glen really didn't tell me anything I hadn't already guessed. You're a really lovely girl, but you're only thirteen and I'm twenty-one. Believe me, Jen, if you were a few years older, I would be very interested in you, and I'm not just saying that. But as it is, I can't promise you I'll wait for you to grow up. I won't insult you by saying all you feel is puppy love, but people's feelings change as they grow. In a year or so you'll probably wonder what you ever saw in me, because you will have grown and changed. Can you understand me, Jen? I'd like to think you'd grow up and still love me, but I don't believe you will."

Jenny hung her head in mortification. Having her heart laid bare in this way, kind and gentle though he was, devastated her feelings and her pride.

"Listen, Jen" he said. "I'm not giving you any sort of line here simply to save your feelings. I honestly am flattered, and I honestly do think I could care a lot for you if you were older. But I'm just a builder's labourer and you're going to do much better than that for yourself one of these days. I have a girl friend too. Glen doesn't know that I'm seeing her again, or she would have told you, I know. Emma was my sweetheart once but we broke up. I've only just started seeing her again. She's a nice girl. You'd like her and she'd like you. To tell you the truth, if you were older, I'd be in a real quandary right now. Jenny, look at me. I truly care for you, and there will always be a place in my heart for you. You have given me your first love, and I appreciate that."

Jenny tried to avoid looking at him, so he couldn't see the tears in her eyes. She understood what he was saying, and her love took a different direction. She wished he was her brother or her father, and knew she would always keep a special place in her heart for him too. If he was only a builder's labourer, he was in the wrong job.

"Will you promise me that this will make no difference to your friendship with Glen, and that you won't feel embarrassed when you see me, Jen? I'd hate to think you'd avoid me after this. Please stay my friend as well as Glen's. Come on, smile now, and let's promise we'll always be friends."

Jenny's heart lifted. If he didn't have a girlfriend, and she herself was older, he would want her as his sweetheart. She looked up at him and smiled. "Yes, I'll still be friends with Glen. I like her a lot. Thank's for being understanding because I do feel an idiot."

"Then don't," he said. "I think you're anything but an idiot. I think you're a lovely girl, like I said before." Putting a finger gently beneath her chin, he tilted her head. "Will you let me kiss you?" he asked. Jenny nodded, and he pressed his lips very gently to hers, giving her a beautiful, tender kiss. "Come on, let me take you home," he said, taking her hand. "This will be something just between you and me for always."

Jenny knew that she would never forget him, or the beautiful things he had said to her. Strangely enough, she felt no jealousy towards his girlfriend, Emma. On the contrary, she felt an odd sort of gratitude. The gamut of confused feelings she had gone through whilst Clive was talking to her made her realize she was not at all ready to think of boys and romance. She didn't think she would feel embarrassed at seeing Clive again. He had kissed her as if he really felt for her, and that had saved her wounded pride.

SIXTY-ONE

Glenda had no free time to spend with Jenny, but Pam did. Both of them helped do jobs in the house such as dish washing and vacuuming, and Jenny still did Miss Hoare's upstairs for her, but they both had plenty of free time. Jenny slept less often in Miss Hoare's house now, although Miss Hoare still hadn't found a new lodger. During the summer holidays, Pam, who loved babies, always wanted to find someone who had a baby, and ask to push it out in its pram. Jenny went along with it for a while, but found babies boring. She preferred animals, particulary horses and dogs, so while Pam pushed babies around, Jenny offered to take neighbours' dogs for walks. This satisfied her need for animals for a while. Until she found a horse.

The horse belonged to a disreputable looking man by the name of Gerry Jarvis. Every bit as scruffy and grubby as himself, the horse was used to pull an old cart in which Gerry collected pig swill. He kept pigs on the allotments behind the meadows, where he had a large boiler inside a ramshackle old shed. Into this boiler he poured the edible refuse he collected, boiled it, then mixed it with bran to feed the pigs. Jenny struck up a friendship with Gerry just so that she could talk to the horse. Maybe Gerry would let her give the poor thing a grooming, or even ride him sometimes, she thought. First of all, she just talked to Gerry, offering to help him mix the swill. "This stuff really stinks when its boiling," she said as they worked. "Do you know how much people complain about the smell when you're doing this?"

"People alla's 'ave to complain about summat," he said. "A little bit o' stink and muck don't 'urt. Muck means money. 'Aven't you 'eard that 'afore?"

"Yes I have. But it's hardly a little bit of stink. It gets so bad that people have to shut their windows to keep it out."

"Don't you pay no mind to they folk. Most of 'em's just jealous of a guy gettin' on and making a bit 'o money. I get's quite a bit with these pigs, 'an I feeds 'em for next to nothin' by collectin' stuff nobody wants."

A thought occurred to Jenny just then. She never got pocket money, and there were times she needed money of her own. Pam earned herself a bit of money by baby sitting, but that had never appealed to Jenny. "Gerry," she said. "Would you let me help you collect the swill and pay me a couple of shillings a week?"

"Oh, I don't know about that. I've never thought of takin' on anybody to 'elp 'cos I don't really need it. I s'pose it wouldn't 'urt though. Okay, if you comes along on Tuesdays and Thursdays in the evenin', an' on Saturday afternoon after four o'clock, so long as you're a good 'elp, I'll give 'ee 'alf a crown a week."

Jenny was delighted. "I'll brush Digger for you too if you like. He looks as if he could do with it."

It wasn't very nice work, handling half rotten vegetable peelings, but it was something she would rather do than sit with squalling babies like Pam did. Gerry produced a filthy, moth-eaten brush for her to brush the Digger. "'E don't need brushin' at all," he said, in answer to her complaints that the brush was almost useless. "'E needs that dirt an' grease in 'im to keep 'im warm in the winter."

Jenny agreed he needed something. When his harness was removed, he was a pathetic sight, thin and bowed of back. She couldn't ask to ride him, the poor creature would probably collapse. She had missed Boxer badly ever since she had left the village, often thinking of him with an ache in her heart. Most likely he had forgotten her by now, and this poor creature, Digger, was never going to take his place. Digger was docile and obedient, but he had no life in him. Jenny pointed out his poor condition to Gerry, asking what he gave the horse to eat.

"I gives 'im plenty 'o grub, but 'e don't eat too much. 'E's seventeen years old 'an don't ave all 'is teeth. That's ow 'e comes to be so thin. I don't work 'im very 'ard. If 'e was to stop work, 'e'd most likely kick the bucket."

Aunty Blod knew that Jenny fussed the horse and brushed him sometimes, being none too pleased when Jenny came home greasy and smelly. "I wish you wouldn't hang around that smelly horse," she said. "I don't know why you are so crazy about horses, they scare the life out of me. You watch it doesn't kick you."

"That poor thing couldn't kick a flea, he hasn't got the energy. I wish I could have him so I could feed him up and let him rest. He wouldn't be a bad horse if he was looked after properly, even if he is old."

"You and your bleeding heart," Aunty Blod said. "It's a pity you can't find something more worthwhile, and less expensive, to worry over. Feeding horses doesn't cost peanuts you know."

Jenny helped Gerry collect pig swill for three weeks before Aunty Blod discovered what she was doing. When she did, she was angry. "I know you've been hanging around that man's horse, and that's bad enough," she said. "Now I find that you have been riding round the streets on that cart with him, picking up pig swill. That has got to stop, Jenny. Gerry Jarvis has a bad reputation, and people are talking about you hanging around with him."

"I'm not hanging around with him. I only go with him because he gives me half a crown a week. Where am I going to get money for birthday and Christmas presents if you stop me? I don't want to go baby sitting like Pam."

"I don't know about that. I'm sure you can find something else if you try. All I do know is that I am responsible for you, and Gerry Jarvis is not to be trusted. You're to keep right away from him from now on."

It was no use arguing. When Aunty Blod decided you couldn't do something, you couldn't. Just like she had been over the German, she wouldn't hear any different opinion.

As it was, Miss Hargreaves came for a visit shortly after Jenny had been stopped from seeing Gerry Jarvis. Aunty Blod told her about Jenny's pig swill collecting, and Jenny explained that she was only doing it to earn money. Miss Hargreaves said that the matter of pocket money was one of the topics she had come to discuss, more new uniform for the growing Jenny being another. She agreed to include two shillings a week in Aunty Blod's monthly cheque as pocket money for Jenny.

Jenny's love and need for animals got her into more trouble when she started back to school. There were always lots of dogs roving around the meadows. Jenny patted and encouraged them, often throwing sticks and playing with any dogs she found. They were as attracted to her as she to them, resulting in their following her whenever they saw her. Jenny went home at lunchtime, playing with the dogs on her way there and back. Dogs started following her home, waiting around while she had lunch, then following her back to school. She managed to get rid of them at first by taking them to the meadows and shooing them away. They soon got wise to this, however, thinking it a game, and came racing back to follow her again. Even if she got to school without them, before long they would turn up, roving around the school until they sniffed her out, and sitting outside the classroom door. There was no getting away from the fact of who had encouraged them there, they jumped all over her as soon as she left the room. This time, Miss Marsh sent for Jenny.

"Why is it, that in a school of over five hundred pupils, whenever the name Jenny Harding is mentioned, I can put a face to it immediately?" Miss Marsh began. "This business of the dogs is no light matter. All these animals running around the school are causing serious problems. Apart from the fact that someone could be bitten, they are unhygienic. You should have enough sense to know that a herd of dogs cannot be left to run wild all over the school. Go out right now and gather them up. Then take them back to wherever you found them, and report back to me to hear what I have to say further."

"Yes, Miss Marsh. I'm sorry."

There was no problem getting them to follow her out of the school. What to do with them once she got them to the meadows was the question. She tried throwing sticks to get them to go in the opposite direction, but they returned with the sticks, thinking it a great game. She stamped her foot and shooed at them for ages, even having to smack some across the nose before they became bored and wandered off. She was angry with herself as she made her way to Miss Marsh's room for the second time. Why had she got into trouble again for something so stupid?

"If there is no further recurrence of this silliness, I will do no more about it," Miss Marsh said. "You have shown some small improvement and it would be a pity to spoil things now over something so senseless. If you are that fond of animals, perhaps you should think of doing something with them when you leave school. In the meantime, curb your enthusiasm, and learn to think before you act."

Sweating with relief, Jenny left the office. She still got into minor scrapes, and her work had not improved enough to lift her from the 'C' stream. She was erratic, she knew. Sometimes she buckled down and worked hard, other times preferring to mess around and waste time. She was drawn to the more disruptive elements in the class, especially Margaret Verdon. Margaret had the ability to throw her voice, so that it sounded as if it was coming from someone other than herself. She sat at the front of the class, sometimes lifting the top of her desk, pretending to look for a book, and make some remark that sounded as though it came from the back of the room. The remarks that Margaret made were always so witty that the class erupted in laughter. Unfortunately, Jenny sat at the back, often being accused of saying things she never had. Everyone, including Jenny, knew who the culprit was, but no-one was going to tell.

Innocent though she was concerning the things Margaret did, she was not always innocent of other disruptions, being quite willing to be distracted by any foolery. Thinking over what Miss Marsh had said, Jenny thought she might like to be a vet when she left school. That would mean going to University, which in turn would mean getting far better marks than she was doing at present. There was always next year to start pulling up, of course. One day, perhaps, she would begin to understand maths and physics. Both were a total fog to her right now.

SIXTY-TWO

It seemed to Jenny that the older she got, the more intensely she missed having a family of her own. Much as she loved Uncle Arthur and Aunty Blod, neither they, nor anyone, could give her the sense of belonging she so desperately sought. She was becoming very jealous of the girls at school who spoke of their mums and dads, carefully guarding her secret that she had neither, worrying in case any of them should discover the truth. She had also been wondering for some time just what had happened to her father. She told Uncle Arthur one evening when they were alone that she had never known exactly what had happened to her dad. She had only known what Mary had told her years ago, never being sure that Mary had told her correctly.

Concerned as always, Uncle Arthur said he would write to the Admiralty on her behalf and see what he could discover. Jenny genuinely loved Uncle Arthur. He was always willing to listen and try to help if he could. It was no wonder everyone liked him so. He was always busy. Apart from his normal work, he was secretary of the Victory Association, which still carried on its dances and socials, secretary of the Workers' Education Association, or W.E.A. as he called it, and helped with the Blind Club also. The W.E.A. was a voluntary Association which helped in re-educating people, particularly returned members of the forces, so that they could obtain better jobs. Uncle Arthur helped anyone who asked. Whether it was sorting out their taxes, or helping to work out budgets for them, he would do his best.

Aunty Blod was kind and helpful too. When it came to her mother though, Jenny found Aunty Blod unwilling to discuss the matter. If Jenny ever mentioned that she wanted to find her mother, or at least know what had happened to her, Aunty Blod would either change the subject or not answer. Jenny got the distinct feeling that Aunty Blod was jealous or resentful of her mother. It was as if she didn't think Jenny should want or need her own mother when she had

Aunty Blod herself as substitute. If this was truly how she felt, Jenny was flattered and pleased that Aunty Blod wanted to be so important in her life, but it made it very hard to talk about anything that deeply troubled her. Jenny was beginning to work out a plan of her own that she hoped would give her some answers, but it required co-operation from Aunty Blod and Uncle Arthur. Uncle Arthur would probably not be a problem, but Aunty Blod was a different matter. Jenny was willing to wait.

It was six weeks before Uncle Arthur showed her a letter he had just received from the Admiralty. "Well, my girl, here's your answer," he said. "I hope this puts your mind at rest concerning your dad. I'm sure it's no more or less than what you expected." He handed her the letter, and Jenny read:

'Herbert James Harding, deceased. - Royal Navy

In reply to your letter of the 25th January, I have to inform you that the above-named Electrical Artificer, first class, was regrettably reporting missing, presumed killed, on the 8th April, 1940 while serving on H.M. Destroyer 'Glowworm', which was sunk that day off Norway by the German Warship 'Admiral Hipper'.

Mr. Harding's name is commemorated on the Portsmouth Naval Memorial, panel 43, column 1, sited on Southsea Common.'

Jenny was quiet as her emotions see-sawed. Seeing her father's name in print like that made it all so impersonal. She visualized her father being blown into a raging sea and drowning, and she hoped it had been a swift death. "I hope this 'presumed killed' is right and that he wasn't picked up to be a prisoner in a concentration camp," she said, feeling terrible guilt at her once innocent wish that he was a prisoner. "It would be so awful if he was."

"Don't torture yourself thinking things like that," Uncle Arthur said. "It's against all odds that he was picked up. Just let your mind rest now that you have it in black and white."

Dad's name was on a memorial. One day she would go and see it.

Jimmy called to see her on one of his very rare visits, early in March. He had to come to town, he said, and thought he would take a chance that she would be at home. He had turned fifteen two months ago, and would be leaving school at Easter.

"Are you just going to leave and start next day, working full time for Ted Roper?" Jenny asked.

"No such luck," he said. "The Ministry, in it's wisdom has decided that I have to have some training in agriculture. As if I haven't had enough training in how to milk cows and plough a field as it is. Anyway, they are sending me to Devon, to some farm to 'train' to be a farm labourer. Learning 'farming methods', as they put it. Bloody daft, isn't it. If they want to waste their money sending me to learn something I already know, that's up to them."

Other than the fact that Tom Roper had married, and that his new wife gave birth to a baby girl a month later, nothing earth shattering had happened in the village, he said. The Matthews had adopted Verna at last, so that problem wouldn't arise again.

Jenny was glad that Verna was now adopted and wouldn't have to make dreadful decisions like that ever again. "Do you ever see Boxer and Kitty? I'd like to know how they are, especially Boxer."

"Those two nags?" Jimmy said. "They were made into dog meat ages ago."

"Oh no! Not Boxer! I can't believe it!" Jenny cried, appalled at the way Jimmy had so casually wrecked her entire world. "I'd like to make the Norths into dog meat. Who did that to them?"

Jimmy laughed. "I thought that would get you going," he said. "No, they didn't do any such thing. The Norths do have two brand new tractors, though, and the horses have been retired. Jack North told me his Gran wouldn't let them go to the glue factory, so they've been sent to Somerset somewhere, to pasture. That's the truth, I swear."

"You pig! You just said that to upset me." Jenny punched her brother in the chest. "I'm glad they sent them to pasture. Now Boxer can eat his way happily through the rest of his life." Sad though she was to think she would never see Boxer again, it was good to think of him wandering his fields happily, with friends of his own kind around him. He deserved that at least.

"Your sister and her horses," Aunty Blod said to Jimmy. "She should have been born in America, where the cowboys ride all day. I swear that's all she's interested in. As long as she can stink of horse, she's happy."

Jenny had been wondering off and on throughout the visit, whether or not to tell Jimmy about the letter from the Admiralty. She couldn't see any reason for him to be angry about it, but with Jimmy you could never tell. It seemed mean to keep it to herself, though. He would probably like to know that Dad's name was on a memorial. In the end she decided to take the risk, slipping upstairs to fetch the letter from the bedroom.

"I thought you might like to see this, Jimmy," she said. "I never did see the paper you had about Dad, and I wanted to see something for myself. Uncle Arthur wrote to the Admiralty for me, and this is what they sent."

Jimmy read the letter in silence. He got up from his chair, excusing himself by saying he wanted to go to the toilet. "I have to go now," he said when he came back. "Thanks for showing me the letter. It's nice to know there's a memorial." He hurried to the door, calling out 'Goodbye' as he went.

Jenny ran after him. "Jimmy, wait a minute. I want to ask you something," she called.

He stopped, turning around. "I've got to get going, Jen. I don't want to miss my bus."

"I know that," she said. "I just wanted to be sure you weren't cross about the letter. I find it so hard to understand you sometimes. You either get angry with me, or think everything I do is wrong or silly. I'm afraid to mention Dad or Mum because you make me feel so bad if I do."

"Then why do you keep doing it? I wouldn't think you'd need to ask why I don't like talking about it. I loved my Dad, and ...," He turned away. Jenny knew there were tears in his eyes, she felt her own eyes prickling in response. "Just leave it, will you?" Jimmy said.

She knew she should leave it, but she persisted. "I would leave it, Jimmy, if only you would tell me why you always get so mad when I mention Mum. I don't have anyone but you, and you don't have anyone but me. You're the only one I can talk to about Dad or Mum who knows them. Nobody else remembers anything about us as a family except you and me. If I can't talk to you about them, who can I talk to? I want to remember us all as a family, and I still wish we could be together."

"There you go," he said. "I've told you before that you can't go backwards, and we never will be a family again. As for 'Mum', as you call her, she's no mother of mine. She's a bitch. If you're determined to find her, or find out what happened to her, like I said before, leave me out of it. All women are bitches, and she's the worst of the lot. You'll be a woman yourself soon, so watch out you don't turn into a bitch as well."

Stunned, Jenny watched him stalk off up the hill. He must really believe that story about the Dutch captain. He wasn't prepared to give Mum any valid reason for leaving them. He hated her. How often did it end this way when she saw Jimmy? More often than not it ended in a quarrel, or with her feeling upset because she could never get close to her brother. Did he really hate all women because of what Mum had done? She shivered. What sort of life would he have if he blamed all women for the misery his mother had brought him?

When she came to think of it, Jimmy hadn't much reason for caring for women. None of them in his life, since Mum, had given him any reason to care. He was never close to Nellie, believing that she was as much to blame for his dismissal as Frank. He certainly wasn't close to Mrs. Foster, and he had never let Jenny herself come near him. Did she hate her mother too? Did she believe those tales? More than ever determined to find her mother, or at the very least, find out what had happened to her, Jenny thought of her plan again. If she found Mum, and it turned out not to be her fault at all, then she would tell Jimmy and it could help him understand. If the stories were true, of course, she would never let him know what she discovered. He didn't feel the same way as her, that to have a family and belong somewhere, to someone, was more important than anything else in the world.

SIXTY-THREE

It was close to her fourteenth birthday before she found a way to bring her plan to Uncle Arthur and Aunty Blod's notice. Now that she had some money of her own, she decide to find something really nice for Aunty Blod's birthday. Aunty Blod loved Bobby, the dog, so she sneaked him out one day and took him to have his photograph taken professionally. When that was done, she bought a lovely silver frame to set it in. It did look beautiful, she was sure Aunty Blod would like it.

Aunty Blod was delighted. She said it was one of the nicest presents she had ever received, setting it in a place of honour on the sideboard. The following evening, Aunty Blod mentioned it again, saying how Mrs. Perch had admired it so, when she was down that afternoon. "It will be your own birthday in four days," Aunty Blod said. "Is there anything special you would like, or would you prefer a surprise? Don't say a horse, because the answer to that is, 'No'."

This was the opportunity to say what she really wanted. If they refused, it would be a long time before she could do it by herself, and then it could be too late. It might already be too late. How to say it when she was sure Aunty Blod would be upset?

"If you aren't sure what you want, I'll get what I think," Aunty Blod said.

"No. I do want something special. I really do."

Aunty Blod waited, expectantly. Uncle Arthur looked up from his paper. "Don't keep us in suspense, my girl. If there's something you want, out with it. Unless, of course, it is a horse."

"No, it's not a horse, although I would love one. I know that's impossible. It's something else."

"Fire away, then. We'll soon tell you if it's on the cards or not," Uncle Arthur said.

"More than anything in the world, I want to be taken back to Portsmouth, so that I can try to find my grandmother."

A pregnant silence followed her request. She looked from Aunty Blod to Uncle Arthur. Blank faces told her nothing. They thought it strange. They were going to refuse.

"Why should you want to find your grandmother, of all things?" Aunty Blod asked. "I thought you told me once you hadn't liked her." Her voice sounded strained and unreal.

"Because I think she may know where my mother is. And if she doesn't, she might at least be able to tell me what happened to her."

"So we're back to that, are we? Well, I don't know what to say," Aunty Blod said.

"Well now, let's be practical here," Uncle Arthur said. "In the first place, you don't even know if your grandmother is still alive. Secondly, and more to the point, you don't know where she lives. Even supposing we *could* find her, she may not know any more than you do concerning your mother's whereabouts. You do realize too, don't you, that Portsmouth took a dreadful shellacking during the war, and you may not recognize anything at all?"

"I know, and I've thought about that," Jenny said. "I do remember that my gran lived somewhere in the North End, and I remember that we lived on Kirty Road. If we find that first, there might be someone still there who remembers my gran, and knows where she lives. We lived on the outskirts of Portsmouth, not near the docks, so perhaps that didn't get bombed too much. I know that Gran could be dead."

"It's a tall order," Uncle Arthur said. "It could take days, perhaps weeks, to find her. Then only to find she has died, like you say. You'll have your answer before your birthday, my girl. That's all we can say just now."

In her bedroom that evening, Jenny heard Aunty Blod and Uncle Arthur discussing her strange request. Aunty Blod was against it, as Jenny had suspected she would be. "She'll find her grandmother, then her mother, then she'll want to leave us, Arthur. Doesn't matter what we've done for her, her own mother is bound to come first."

"Not necessarily," Uncle Arthur said. "More than likely it will prove to be a wild goose chase. If not, it probably won't turn out the way she dreams it will. Has it occurred to you that if we don't let her do this, she may resent us for it for the rest of her life, and leave us at her first opportunity? She may well still choose to stay with us, if a choice results from this. I have a feeling she is going to end up more hurt than she knows, but we should let her try."

The following day, Uncle Arthur told Jenny that they had decided she could have her wish. "We'll go on Sunday," he said. "One day won't give us much time to locate someone who has been lost trace of for five years, but we'll give it a go if that's what you want. Aunty Blod won't be coming, it will be just you and me, my girl. How does that sound? If you want to change your mind, speak now, or tomorrow I'll buy the tickets for the early train."

"I don't want to change my mind," Jenny said. "Thank you for saying you'll take me. I wish Aunty Blod wouldn't be upset about it. I love her, but this is important to me. Her own mother gave her away, so you'd think she could understand how I feel."

"She understands. She has her own reasons for not feeling too happy about it, but she'll come round eventually. So, Portsmouth it's to be then?"

Jenny tried not to raise her hopes too high for the next couple of days. Aunty Blod was quiet and reserved, not mentioning the subject at all. It saddened Jenny, making her feel guilty at hurting Aunty Blod, and she wished it could be otherwise. She was really going on a search for her mother at long last. It could be a disaster, as Uncle Arthur had said. It could result in nothing at all. But she was going.

SIXTY-FOUR

Unable to sleep on Saturday night, Jenny was up at four in the morning, wandering around dressed and ready by the time Uncle Arthur came downstairs at five. "The train doesn't go until six-thirty," he laughed. "We'll get a good breakfast in us before we leave."

She cooked breakfast while Uncle Arthur washed and shaved. When at last they were ready to go, she felt she was dancing on pins. They both called 'Cheerio' up the stairs to Aunty Blod. There was no answer.

Settled on the train, Uncle Arthur said that he had never been to Portsmouth and knew next to nothing about the place. When they got there, it would be up to her few snatches of hazy memory to get them through.

"I went to Solent Road School," Jenny said. If we get a bus to Solent Road, I think I might recognize the top of the lane that went down to Kirty Road."

"Then you must have a good memory. I hope you're right," he said.

At Portsmouth station they asked their way to the bus depot. Jenny was dismayed at the size of the town when they found the depot at the centre. She recognized nothing. Wherever she looked there was still war damage. Half walls, boarded up windows, and rubble everywhere. Uncle Arthur could see her confusion. "You weren't quite prepared for all this, were you? Well, don't give up yet, girl, we'll see what we can find."

They found a bus with 'Solent Road' on the front, and climbed aboard. The bus started away, and the conductor came for the fares. "Where to?" he asked Uncle Arthur.

"Solent Road, please."

"Yes, sir, I'm sure. This bus is going all the way along Solent Road. What stop d'you want?"

Uncle Arthur and Jenny looked at one another. "How long is Solent Road?" Uncle Arthur asked the conductor.

"Several miles, sir. I've got other passengers to take care of. I'll come back when you've made up your mind where you're going."

"No," Jenny said. "We want Solent Road School."

"That's two and threepence please." The conductor punched two tickets, handing them to Uncle Arthur.

"That was a bit of good sense," Uncle Arthur said. "Keep that brain ticking, my girl. I feel we're going to need it."

As the bus sped along, Jenny strained her eyes through the window, hoping to recognize something, growing more despondent by the minute. "Look, there it is. We've got to get off," she cried suddenly, pushing at Uncle Arthur.

The bell dinged. "Solent Road School," the conductor called out.

"Well, what caused all that excitement? I must say, I'm agreeably surprised. What did you see to cause such sudden alacrity?"

"Over there," Jenny pointed. "That's the top of the lane. And the school is over this road and up that hill."

"Alright. So if this is the place, tell me what we're going to find down this lane."

"There are trees on the left, and further down is a left turn into my old road. It's a cul-de-sac, and we lived at the curve. The other house on the curve was the Loader's. At the end of this lane is a farm. I can remember something else now. Right here where we're standing, I once saw a person who was half a man and half a woman. He must have been dressed for a party or something, but I didn't know that then. On one side he had a man's suit on and short black hair. On the other side he had long fair hair and a dress. I was scared to death."

"Amazing," Uncle Arthur said. "How is it you remember all this so clearly?"

"I don't know. I can even remember being in my pram and my mother pushing me along the street. I had soft toys in my pram and I threw one out. My mum picked it up and I threw it out again. She told me to stop or she would leave the toy in the street. I understood what she said, but I threw it out again, and she did leave it. I cried and

330

wished I hadn't done it. But d'you know what? If she had picked it up, I knew I would throw it out again."

"That really is something," Uncle Arthur said. "You should develop that memory, it could come in very useful in years to come."

Everything was as Jenny had described. As they stood at the end of the cul-de-sac looking down it, memory came flooding back, and her knees felt weak. It was all she could do to keep moving in the direction of the house she had left so long ago, to go, as she had thought, to school. They reached the gate and stood staring at the front door. A plaque had been nailed to the door which read 'N.S.P.C.C. - National Society for the Prevention of Cruelty to Children.'

"Upon my Sam," breathed Uncle Arthur. "Are you sure this is your house?"

Jenny could hardly speak. The irony was not lost on her. "Yes," she whispered. "Let's not stay here." She wondered if the shed her father had built still stood at the back. She didn't want to look.

"Let's go next door to see if the people know what happened to the Loaders," Uncle Arthur suggested. "That's what you said their name was, isn't it?"

The door was opened by an elderly lady Jenny didn't recognize. "Excuse us for bothering you," Uncle Arthur said. "We're looking for a Mr. and Mrs. Loader who once lived here. Would you have any idea where they could be found?"

"I'm Mrs. Loader," the lady said. "What can I do for you?"

"Mrs. Loader?" Jenny queried. "I'm Jenny Harding who used to live next door. I didn't recognize you. Do you remember me?"

Mrs. Loader looked stunned. "Little Jenny? Of course I remember you. I remember you all. My dear, come in and let me look at you. You've grown so much since I last saw you, I would never have recognized you."

Mr. Loader was sitting smoking his pipe. Every bit as astonished as his wife, the elderly couple were obviously emotionally affected by her visit. They talked about her family, and how sorry they were at the loss of her dad. "Such a dear, sweet man," Mrs. Loader said. "When he and little Jimmy walked down this road, we used to say they were like two peas in a pod. So alike. And how is your dear brother?

We loved you both. Oh dear, it's so sad. This war has a lot to answer for."

Neither of them had any idea where Jenny's mother had gone after the house was sold. They had heard nothing from her since that time. "But your grandmother is still alive, as I expect you know. She comes over occasionally to visit with us, although she hasn't been for some time."

When Uncle Arthur explained that they didn't have grandmother's address, Mrs. Loader wrote it down for them, insisting they have something to eat before leaving. "Your Gran will be so pleased to see you, dear," she told Jenny.

On the bus heading to North End, Uncle Arthur tapped the back of Jenny's hand. "How are you doing, old girl? Is it getting a bit too much?"

"No. I'm fine," Jenny said. She realized she had become quiet. She wasn't feeling fine in truth. She was feeling as if she wasn't really here. It was as if she was in a dream, one that had happened before, so long ago. She couldn't tell whether she was four years old, or fourteen. Talking with the Loaders about her parents had taken her so far back. Sadness, and a sense of great loss, were the only emotions she recognized right now. She wasn't even sure any more if she really did want to find Gran.

She recognized the house the moment they were in view of it. A young woman answered their knock. No, she said. Mrs. Beech didn't live here any more. She and her husband rented it from the old lady, who lived with friends in the next street. Following directions, Uncle Arthur found the house and rapped the door knocker. This time the door was opened by a woman in military uniform. Mrs. Beech was in, she said. Please to wait while she fetched her.

Grandmother came into view from the darkened passageway. She was older than Jenny remembered, but Gran without a doubt. She turned her sharp-eyed look on Jenny and Uncle Arthur, then back to Jenny. "Oh!" she said. Seeming to check herself, she looked at them both again. "Who are you?" she asked.

"Don't you know me, Grandma. I'm Jenny."

"Jenny? Jenny? How can you be Jenny? Come inside and let me look at you."

They followed her down the hall to a large, airy room. Grandmother looked closely at Jenny. "Yes, I see who you are," she said. "What are you doing here, and who is this gentleman?"

Uncle Arthur introduced himself, and Gran told them to sit down, watching them suspiciously. Jenny wanted to blurt out all sorts of questions, but Uncle Arthur cautioned her with a look. He explained to Gran that Jenny had wanted to come and see her as a special birthday treat, and that seemed to please her. She relaxed a little. "I'm glad to see you after so long, Jenny. You've grown so, I would have passed you in the street without knowing you. How is Jimmy? He must be quite big now."

"Jimmy's alright, I suppose," Jenny said. "We were parted from each other years ago. If you've really been wondering about us, why didn't you write after Granddad died like you promised?"

She knew at once she had said the wrong thing. Gran's expression changed instantly.

"So many things happened that I hadn't time to write to you, I had to wind up your grandfather's business, then go to work myself. I'm still working at my age. Then there were all the problems with your mother. What could I do with two small children?"

Gran had been first to mention Mum. Jenny could barely contain her excitement. "What problems did you have with Mum? Where did she go? Where is she?"

"What problems? I had no problems with your mother. Don't ask me where she is, I don't know. She didn't tell me her business, and it's none of yours." Gran was obviously agitated now, but Jenny was angry. Ignoring Uncle Arthur's frowns, she retaliated.

"Yes it is my business. If it isn't my business why my mother left me and my brother, whose is it? I have a right to know where she is. We could have died with no-one to take care of us, and I almost did. I do have a right to know."

"No, you don't." Now Gran was angry too. "If I have no right to know what happened to my own daughter, you don't either. The only thing I know for sure is that she went on the boats to Dunkirk and never came back. She must have been killed, but I never could find out."

Uncle Arthur changed the subject, asking what work Gran did, and about Granddad's business. Jenny realized he was being diplomatic. That was all very well, but why was Gran so mad? She knew more than she was saying, of that Jenny felt certain. She didn't think the story about Dunkirk was right at all. Gran had made that up.

Gran was telling Uncle Arthur that she worked in the bus depot, helping maintain the buses. "That's a very unusual occupation for a woman, especially one of your age," Uncle Arthur said.

"Unusual or not, that's what I do. Women had many strange occupations during the war, and lots of us are still doing them. You may lead sheltered lives down there in the country, but here we knew what war was. It's going to be a long time yet before things are straightened up, if they ever are."

The afternoon passed with no further reference to Jenny's mother. When it was time to catch their bus back, Gran said she would walk with them to the bus stop. A woman was waiting there who recognized Gran and spoke to her. They talked for a few moments, then Gran turned to Jenny.

"By the way," Gran said to the woman. "This is my granddaughter, Jenny."

From far off, Jenny was aware of the woman saying 'Hello' to her, and of her own reply. Everything geared down to slow motion and voices grew fainter and fainter. What had Gran said? "This is my granddaughter, Jenny."

At last! At last! Someone had said, "This is my," - and meant it! No excusing her, no referring to her as 'the' anything. Simply - "This is my granddaughter, Jenny."

Suddenly she was crying like a baby. Years of belonging nowhere and to no-one washed out of her in a flood. She had come full circle and was a real person again.

"Whatever is the matter with her," Gran asked Uncle Arthur, alarm and consternation showing on her face.

"Don't worry, she'll be alright," he said. "It's been quite a day for her, she's tired out. Putting an arm around Jenny's shoulders, he gave her a firm squeeze. "Alright, old girl? Won't be long now and then you can rest and relax. That mind of yours needs time to sort itself out, I know. You've done well, my girl. I'm proud of you."

Leaning back against the seat in the train, Jenny's thoughts ran this way and that. Odd how her memory had been so good with places, yet so poor with faces. She had recognized neither the Loaders, nor her own grandmother at first. Gran had been even more cantankerous than she remembered her to be. But Gran had given her the best gift anyone could possibly give her, one Jenny had thought she would never possess, and grouchy Gran had no idea just what she had given her. She was no closer to finding her mother, having discovered no more about her than she already knew.

"Gran lied. She knew more than she told us about my mother," she said to Uncle Arthur.

"I know that, girl," Uncle Arthur said. "But it was going to do no good to try pumping her, she had no intention of telling us any more."

Jenny closed her eyes, emitting a deep sigh.

"Now what's going on in that head of yours?" Uncle Arthur asked, patting her knee.

"Oh, I don't know. I wish I was thirty years old, married, and knew just who I was and where I was going."

Uncle Arthur turned in his seat. "Don't ever wish your life away like that, my girl. Life is short enough, as you will soon discover. Some day you'll find out all you wish to know. Until then, be thankful that you're alive, and enjoy each day as it comes. There's always tomorrow, girl .... and tomorrow is another day."

ISBN 155212471-1

9 781552 124710